DEADLY SIN

DEADLY SIN

A Chief Inspector Bliss Novel

James Hawkins

A Castle Street Mystery

THE DUNDURN GROUP
TORONTO

Editor: Barry Jowett
Copy-editor: Andrea Waters
Design: Alison Carr
Printer: Transcontinental

Library and Archives Canada Cataloguing in Publication

Hawkins, D. James (Derek James), 1947-
    Deadly sin : a Chief Inspector Bliss mystery / James Hawkins.

ISBN-13: 978-1-55002-644-3
ISBN-10: 1-55002-644-5

    I. Title.

PS8565.A848D42 2007   C813'.6   C2006-904608-5

1   2   3   4   5   10   09   08   07   06

 Conseil des Arts du Canada   Canada Council for the Arts   Canadä   ONTARIO ARTS COUNCIL CONSEIL DES ARTS DE L'ONTARIO

We acknowledge the support of the **Canada Council for the Arts** and the **Ontario Arts Council** for our publishing program. We also acknowledge the financial support of the **Government of Canada** through the **Book Publishing Industry Development Program** and **The Association for the Export of Canadian Books**, and the **Government of Ontario** through the **Ontario Book Publishers Tax Credit** program and the **Ontario Media Development Corporation**.

Care has been taken to trace the ownership of copyright material used in this book. The author and the publisher welcome any information enabling them to rectify any references or credits in subsequent editions.

                                     J. Kirk Howard, President

Printed and bound in Canada
www.dundurn.com

Dundurn Press	Gazelle Book Services Limited	Dundurn Press
3 Church Street, Suite 500	White Cross Mills	2250 Military Road
Toronto, Ontario, Canada	High Town, Lancaster, England	Tonawanda, NY
M5E 1M2	LA1 4XS	U.S.A. 14150

This book is dedicated to my first granddaughter
Charlie Eloise Hawkins
who began her journey on the labyrinth of life on
August 21, 2006

With very special thanks to my dear wife, Sheila, and
to Eileen Wilson for their unstinting support and
encouragement

A classical left-handed seven-circuit Cretan labyrinth — mythical home of the Minotaur.

Enter here ↑

Note that the labyrinth is not a maze. Trace a finger around the pathway and you will discover that, like life itself, every journey begins and ends at the same point. You can decide to take that journey quickly or slowly, thoughtfully or carelessly, morally or immorally. However, once your jouney has begun you have no choice but to follow it through to the end.

chapter one

"Lights ... cameras ... action ..." mutters a joker in the darkness.

"All right. That's enough. Let's be serious," commands a "voice from on high" in the dimly lit surveillance room, forcing Chief Inspector David Bliss and his team to focus on the dozen video monitors in front of them.

The snooty tone of Hugh Grant's voice double stutters to life from a couple of loudspeakers. "There's a ... um ... a light drizzle falling in London this lunchtime as the royal cavalcade ..."

The humidified air in the soundproof room on the tenth floor of New Scotland Yard stills at the sound of the voice, but a stifled fart followed by a mumbled "Sorry" threatens the solemnity. David Bliss cranes around, searching for a red face in the darkened room, but he's jerked back to the screens by the stentorian-voiced commander.

"Situation report, Chief Inspector."

"Guinevere and Lancelot have left Point Alpha and are now approaching Point Beta," sings out Bliss as he watches the Queen's Rolls-Royce passing under the Admiralty Arch at the end of the Mall, and then he mutters to the officer sitting to his right, "Gawd knows who picks these stupid code names."

The "voice" hears. "I did, Chief Inspector," it booms from the back of the room. "Any objections?"

"No, sir. Sorry, sir," apologizes Bliss without turning, and then he switches to a new set of surveillance cameras to follow the royal procession along the Strand through central London.

The crowds are sparse close to the palace, mainly accidental witnesses drawn to the spectacle of the monarch's passage by the phalanx of police motorcyclists and the sudden lack of traffic. But a quick check of the Queen's destination shows Bliss a different picture. Placard-waving demonstrators bulge steel barricades; eggs and tomatoes spatter against riot shields — damaging nothing but the egos of battle-hardened officers who would rather have a barrage of rocks as an excuse to break ranks and split heads.

"The ... um ... recent inter-religious disturbances in Birmingham and Bradford have heightened the controversy over this visit ..." continues the radio commentary in the background as Bliss focuses on the crowd, searching for familiar "rent-a-mob" figures — anarchists, anti-royalists, anti-establishments, anti-everythings — who can be surgically taken out by undercover men already on the ground.

Unit commanders report in relief as the motorcade passes on to the next sector without incident, while Bliss concentrates on the increasingly aggressive mob. A time check — seven minutes to destination Point Omega — and the occasional brick begins soaring over the heads of the crowd.

"A press statement from the palace," carries on the ex-Etonian in his best BBC, "confirms that Her Majesty is determined to proceed with this visit in an effort to promulgate harmony between the Christian and Muslim communities."

"Harmony. Hah!" scoffs Sergeant Bill Williams on Bliss's left.

"Keep your comments for your mates in the bar, Williams," spits the commander, leading Bliss to mutter, "This is worse than school" in support of his wingman.

Six minutes twenty seconds, and it's Bliss's call. "Her Highness will not be amused if we have to pull the plug," the divisional commander — Chief Superintendent "Foxy" Fox — proclaimed at the briefing half an hour earlier, leaving Bliss to question aloud if the head of the royal household would prefer to take half a brick in the eye for her country.

A faceless figure wearing the denim uniform of a welder creeps into a shaded corner of one of Chief Inspector Bliss's surveillance monitors and gingerly puts down a large canvas tool bag. The obvious bulk of the man's body armour and the darkly tinted face mask should ring alarms in the Metropolitan Police's surveillance centre, especially as his perch is high above the royal route in a partially constructed office tower, but Bliss misses the image as he swipes perspiration from his forehead and concentrates on the agitated mob.

"It is perhaps the first time in history that the titular head of the Church of England has officially attended Friday prayers, albeit only as an observer," the BBC voice continues, filling airtime with unnecessary chatter while the heavily protected motorcade makes its way along the Strand towards the gold-encrusted minarets of an East End London mosque. But Bliss tunes out the affected voice as he spots a potential problem some distance away from the monumental edifice.

The commentator also has a monitor. "It seems that a large group of demonstrators has broken police lines ..."

"Well, Chief Inspector. What're you gonna do?" demands the commander, sending Bliss scrabbling through a thick manual of orders searching for an alternative route to the mosque's back door.

"Too late, Bliss," shouts the commander, ramping up the pressure. "Diversions have jammed all alternates. The city is at a standstill."

"Bugger," mutters Bliss, but his problems are just about to multiply and he has yet to spot the interloper in the construction site.

"Unauthorized aircraft entering restricted airspace," calls Sergeant Williams as the junior officer monitors a feed from Air Traffic Control.

Bliss takes his eyes off the surging crowd to deal with the airborne threat, and seconds later a couple of Air Force jets are screaming to his aid.

But the phoney workman continues unnoticed by the surveillance team as he sheaths his brown-skinned hands in white latex gloves before unzipping his tool bag. Then he stops and carefully checks the skyline. Six rooftop snipers wearing police baseball caps scour the busy streets below for terrorists, but who looks for a workman on a building site?

In skilled hands, the rifle that emerges from the tool bag, a modified Springfield M25, can take down a five-hundred-pound stag at half a mile. The man has skilled hands, but he isn't planning on filling his freezer with venison today.

The squadron of police motorcyclists in the vanguard of the royal convoy is being squeezed to a halt by the time Bliss returns to the situation on the ground. Lady Guinevere's Rolls-Royce is still a mile from the mosque, and he zooms in for a closer look at the surging mob: are they religious fundamentalists determined to stop the perceived heresy or just pumped-up pedestrians hoping to snap a royal close-up on their videophones?

"Well, Bliss," demands the commander. "Do you want to send in special forces?"

"Special forces," muses Bliss, knowing that, on his word, a bunch of testosterone-hyped hit men in full riot gear will storm out of the shadows and smash heads.

"Yes ... or ... no," harangues the commander in Bliss's ear, but Bliss is peering intently into the swelling crowd, searching for kids and smiles. The radio commentator isn't helping. "Opinion polls suggest that there are as many Muslims hostile to this visit as there are Christians," he is saying, but Bliss finds only flag- and camera-waving friendlies, and he is happy to see the crowd melt back to the sidewalk as the cavalcade approaches.

"No special forces, sir."

"Good call, Chief Inspector," says the commander once the royal car has passed, although the praise falls flat as a mob of sign-wielding protesters a mile down the road at the mosque batter a hole in the cordon and rush the steps.

The sniper's visor is up. He levels the rifle to his shoulder.

Bliss is watching the handful of cross-waving protesters as they give a dozen uniformed men the runaround in front of the invited guests. He could bring in the heavies, but he vacillates. If the Queen gets wind from the press that a bunch of harmless loonies have been clobbered by the riot squad, he'll be clearing out his desk at the Yard by the end of the week.

The lineup of grey-robed mullahs, imams, and Islamic officials on the mosque's steps are in the sniper's sights, and he smiles as he moves along the rank, drawing a bead on each face in turn. "Pop!" he mouths, then moves on. "Pop! ... Pop! ... Pop!" Twenty seconds, ten shots, and any semblance of religious harmony will be back to where it was during the Crusades.

Commander Fox has other targets in his sights, and he makes a stab at the demonstrators on Bliss's screen who are now kneeling in prayer. "Oh, for chrissakes. Are you going to do anything?"

Bliss reaches for a microphone, takes a breath, and takes control. "Slow the procession; send in a surgical squad, fast — no gas, no stun guns, no dogs. The world is watching. All units — one-minute delay."

"One minute?" queries the commander disbelievingly.

Bliss crosses his fingers. One minute can be absorbed — a clipped speech, a few hurried handshakes with some of the minions, one less prayer. But more than a minute and he'll have to consider revising schedules.

"The police are moving in to clear the demonstrators …" the BBC is reporting, and Bliss watches, praying that no one gets happy-handed with any of the sacrificial Bible punchers, knowing that nothing will make the news editors or the bishops happier than an armour-plated cop beating the crap out of a sandal-wearing Jesus look-alike to clear the way for the Queen to pay homage to Mohammed.

"Thank God for that," mutters Bliss a minute later as the last of the zealots are carried away — still chanting, still praying.

The Queen's car rolls gracefully to a stop at the foot of the mosque's marble steps, and a footman slips forward to open the door. The sniper switches aim. The BBC switches to a fashion guru whose tone is closer to disgust than disdain as she takes in the unfashionable sight. "Her Majesty appears to be wearing some form of Muslim burkha," she says as the hooded Queen steps from the car into the sniper's view. Then all of Bliss's surveillance screens simultaneously fade to black.

"Power cut," yells Sergeant Williams, but Bliss has other ideas.

"Line sabotage," he says. "We're on generator backup. Someone must've cut the feed —"

"Well!" screeches the commander. "Don't just sit there. Do something, Chief Inspector."

"Yes, sir," replies Bliss, as he frantically stabs buttons. But the screens stay blank.

"And now Her Majesty is waving to the crowd ..." continues the BBC reporter, although his voice is almost drowned by whistles and boos.

"Alpha Charlie two-zero," shouts Bliss into a microphone, desperately trying the Queen's bodyguard. "Get Guinevere back in the car. Get her back in the car."

"Now Prince Philip has joined Her Majesty as they are welcomed by Shi'ite Imam Al-Shamman," the reporter carries on. "But it appears that many of the specially invited onlookers aren't happy with the Queen's wardrobe ..."

"Now what're you gonna do, Bliss?" nags the commander, and Bliss unsuccessfully tries the bodyguard again.

The sniper's aim is unwavering as he follows the Queen up the steps.

"The royal guests are slowly making their way towards the reception party on this historic occasion ..."

Bliss has an idea, punches a button, and springs to life a picture from a police helicopter hovering over the scene. "Direct radio feed — no wires," he says proudly as he scans the scene from overhead, then he freezes in horror.

"All units. All units!" he yells into the microphone as the sniper on his screen tenses to squeeze the trigger. "Red alert! Red alert! Red alert!"

"Sit down, Chief Inspector," says the assistant commissioner sternly as Bliss is ushered into the inner sanctum of New Scotland Yard an hour later. The door shuts with a firm *clunk* behind him.

"You know Commander Fox," the A.C. continues, pointing to his second-in-command as Bliss takes the strategically placed chair in the centre of the room, although the senior officer makes it clear that he has no intention of introducing the two men who are eyeing the newcomer from the comfort of a black leather settee.

Secret Service — royalty protection, thinks Bliss, glancing at the clean-shaven pinstripe pair who are lounging, jacketless, with the smugness of Mafia capos at a lynching.

The air is heavy despite the brilliant sunshine of the August day. Bliss sits and waits, guessing that anything he says now will only tighten the noose. The assistant commissioner puts on reading glasses to scan a sheet from the single slim file on his desk. The senior officer has already read it twice and knows the conclusion. But this is politics; the stakes are high, careers are on the line, pensions are at risk. Commander Fox sits alongside the A.C. with a poker stare waiting for orders, readying to pull on the rope with the others.

Why bother with this nonsense? Bliss questions inwardly, knowing his resignation has been in his pocket for several years. *Stuff you*, he thinks with an eye on the assistant commissioner. *I can play your stupid game — and win. Twenty-eight years on the streets for Queen and country and you think you're going to rip me apart just to please those poncy schoolkids on the settee. Look at them; softer than baby's shit. They wouldn't last five minutes in Brixton on a Saturday night.*

"Well, Chief Inspector," says the A.C., putting down his glasses with deliberation. "It seems that, overall, your performance was very satisfactory." Then he waves to encompass the room and laughs. "You just saved us all from King Charles and Queen bloody Camilla."

"A satisfactory performance," fumes David Bliss as he walks home along the Thames embankment amid the jostle of a million similarly stressed escapees.

A mirrored image of London Eye, the giant millennium Ferris wheel, catches his attention as it slowly revolves in the river as if driven by the relentlessly flowing water, and he slips out of the miserable stream of homebound workers to watch.

"Old Father Thames keeps rolling along ..." he hums under his breath, trying to put his woes in perspective, but the torpid river's apparent immortality drags him down with the realization that it will still be coursing through England's ancient capital long after him. "I'm fifty tomorrow," he muses gloomily, realizing that he is on the cusp of a downhill run with no hope of a trophy at the end. But is he halfway? He knows his chances of reaching a century: one in twenty-six, discounting nuclear holocaust and other global catastrophes. Four out of a hundred — better numbers than the lottery, but not the sort of odds to bet your life on.

"Repent. The end is nigh," sings out an aging sandwich man as Bliss passes, but it's a song he has been singing for more than thirty years. His voice is hoarse, and his credibility is as tattered as the raincoat and the heavy billboards that weigh him down.

"Give us some change for a cuppa, guv'nor," pleads the mendicant, slipping from under his boards and sidling up to Bliss. "It's bleedin' boilin' out 'ere."

"You need a cold drink ..." starts Bliss, sees the light starting to form in the old beggar's eyes and pauses. "Maybe you should get shot of that old coat."

"Not bloomin' likely," he snarls, baring a mouthful of nightmarish teeth. "I wouldn't have nuvving to wear fer winter."

Bliss feels for a coin and jokes. "Don't worry, mate. If you're right, it'll be a damn sight hotter for most of us by then."

"It ain't funny, guv'nor. Look at all the bleedin' 'urricanes an' erfquakes. Mark my words, the end is near."

"But when — today?"

The perpetually disappointed doomsayer squints at the clear blue sky as if checking for a portent — a flock of ravens; a lightning bolt; the hand of God. Finding nothing more apocalyptic than a jumbo jet spewing pollution en route to Heathrow he turns back to Bliss and whispers, "Nah. Not today, guv'nor. We're aw'right today. Next week p'raps."

"I'll be waiting," mocks Bliss sternly as he hands over a pound coin, but as he rejoins the homebound flood of office labourers he sinks lower, thinking, *What if he is right? What if I have only one more week?* Mid-life crisis, he tries telling himself, but is it mid-life?

In the August heat the Friday rush hour of weary workers is as torpid as the river. Global warming is on everyone's lips as the mercury bumps off the scale for the third week in a row, and most are heading for the coast and the cool waters of the North Sea or the Channel.

"Heat Wave Takes Elderly Toll," shouts the headline in the *Evening Chronicle*, but Bliss delves deeper to discover that it's editorial hype. "Health officials estimate that as many as a thousand may die ..." continues the article, leaving him wondering how many of them will be happy not to have to struggle through another winter.

A counter-flow of foreign tourists bucks the tide as homebound workers stream into the stifling stations and subways, but most of the visitors have come prepared, wearing saris, djellabas, and kaftans; many of them are thankful for the relative chill of the sweltering English weather.

Bliss balks as he is swept towards Embankment tube station. The persistent threat of a fanatic's bomb and the thought of being stuffed into a smelly sweatbox for half an hour turns him off, and he heads for Waterloo Bridge. *The walk will do me good*, he persuades himself, not needing to check his midriff, and as he crosses the river his mind is still on his age. Fifty years of relentless gravity may be having a negative effect on his gut, hair, and eyelids, but by craning back his head and straightening his spine he still has no difficulty seeing over the heads of the throng.

Which of them have the genes, the fortitude, and the luck to beat the odds and get a birthday card from the

Queen, he wonders, picking out faces with a detective's eye
— white, red, brown, and black; Caucasian, Afro-
Caribbean, and Asian; sallow, ashen, and flushed; flabby,
drawn, and downtrodden; pretty, ugly, and plain. Who are
they? What are their hopes, dreams, and ambitions? Which
of them could be talking to God, listening to God, or
scheming to play God? And which God? Whose God?

He stops mid-bridge and searches for a moment's sol-
ace amidst the constant rumble of buses and taxis as he
leans over the stone parapet to gaze into the languid water.
His presence makes an eddy in the stream of silent pedestrians as they eye him watchfully, even fearfully. Couples, families, and troupes of tourists may pause to marvel at the historic riverside views without causing a stir, but not a lone
man in a business suit peering introspectively at the river.

Where are we going? he wants to know, questioning
both his own future and that of humanity, and time takes a
very long breath as his eyes lose their focus in the slowly
swirling sludge.

"Are you all right, sir?" queries a suspicious voice eventually, and it takes Bliss a few moments to bring himself back.

"Brain fart," he explains, turning slowly to the uniformed constable with an embarrassed laugh. "I was trying
to look into the future."

"Really," says the young officer guardedly, and Bliss
immediately catches on to the constable's look of cynicism.
He quickly pulls out his warrant card, explaining, "I'm
D.C.I. Bliss from the Yard," as if his status guarantees
immunity from suicidal tendencies. But his identity puts a
new complexion on the officer's baby face, and the young
man stutters, "S-s-sorry, sir ..." Then he attempts to deflect
the blame with a vague sweep of his hand. "O-o-only, some
people were worried ..."

"No problem, son," says Bliss, recalling similarly
embarrassing moments in his early years, but as he carries
on across the bridge he can't help laughing about the

young officer. He's probably still a teenager — maybe twenty; his mother sits at home fearing a terrorist attack while he spends most days as a city guide and photographer's model praying for one. *I was probably like that*, reflects Bliss, and he pictures a tall, keen, athletic young man who, in his own mind, hasn't changed a great deal. Most of his hair is still holding on, although the colour's fading. "You can get stuff for that," his adult daughter, Samantha, frequently reminds him. But what then — dentures, spectacles, and Viagra? And after that — incontinence pads, colostomy bags, and a constant diet of minced meat, rice pudding, and Vera Lynn?

"You're only fifty, for chrissakes," he tries telling himself as he walks along the riverside path but he realizes that, like the Thames, he is a lot nearer the wide open ocean than most of his colleagues.

It is low tide. The receding water has bared mud banks spattered with supermarket buggies and rusted bicycle frames, and a lone gull quietly worries at a bag of garbage. The guidebooks may trumpet the sighting of an occasional salmon, but the river still lacks the splendour of the Danube or the romance of the Seine, although Bliss knows well that the celebrated French river is no cleaner. Maybe Parisians see garbage differently, he surmises — like art nouveau — adding to the charm rather than detracting.

But just how much bluer is the Danube or sweeter the Seine? he asks himself as he gazes into the brackish water, then he picks up his feet, reminding himself that someone in France is waiting for a phone call.

"It's bloody hot here," Bliss complains to his French fiancée once he's poured himself an icy lager, but Daisy LeBlanc is steps from the Mediterranean and shrugs it off.

"Did you have zhe good day?"

"Not really. I nearly killed the Queen."

"I zhink zhat is good, *non*?" laughs Daisy. "Like Marie-Antoinette — zhe guillotine. Perhaps zhere are many ozher zhings you can learn from zhe French, *non*?"

"No," he says, laughing. "But maybe zhe French can learn how to say 'the.' Anyway, it was only an exercise. Just testing communications and testing me."

"Did you pass?"

"Did I pass?" he echoes, unsure of the answer. Was he supposed to pass? "The real thing is next Friday," he says without answering. "I've got a week to study the manual."

"Too slow; too little; too late. You're gonna have to do better, much better," Commander Fox bitched at the debriefing once the Secret Service squad left. "You're rusty, Bliss, that's your trouble. You've had a year off and you've gone soft."

"I was writing a book," he protested, but Fox didn't let up.

"Wake up, man. You're supposed to be a policeman, not a bloody author."

I solved the mystery of the Man in the Iron Mask, he wanted to complain, but he knew it wouldn't get him anywhere. Originality and creativity are not widely applauded in the police.

"Judges can be funny about policemen with overactive imaginations, Chief Inspector," the commander admonished. "Stick to your job. Stick to irrefutable facts."

But what facts are truly irrefutable? Bliss wondered and reflected on the times he witnessed the meltdown of a cast-iron case because a dozen dozy jurymen were befuddled by the mendacious shenanigans of a defence lawyer.

"You put her at risk. You took your eye off the ball. You'd better pray there's no sniper next week," Commander Fox concluded.

A sniper! Bliss is still fuming inwardly. Why would anyone gun down a little grey-haired old lady without a penny in her purse?

"Are you all right, Daavid?" asks Daisy, sensing a vacuum, and Bliss straightens his thoughts.

"Sorry, dear. I was just wondering why someone would want to kill the Queen. It's not as though she has any real power. They'd just be aggravating an ancient theocratic wound."

"What is zhis zheocratic zhing?" asks Daisy confusedly.

"Don't worry." Bliss laughs. "I'm flying over next Friday after the Queen's visit, and I'm going to spend the whole weekend working on your tongue."

"Oh, Daavid …"

"Fifty years old and still a bloody teenager," sniggers Bliss to himself as he puts down the phone. It buzzes almost immediately. *She's remembered my birthday*, he thinks with a bounce, but he is quickly deflated. "Daphne?" he queries, recognizing the aging voice.

"I need a little help, David," says Daphne Lovelace, calling from her home in Westchester, Hampshire.

"Help is what you usually give others, Daphne," replies Bliss, having no difficulty recalling the times the eccentric spinster saved his bacon despite her advancing years.

Daphne Lovelace, O.B.E., a woman with a hat for every occasion and an adventure for every dinner party, is a lot closer to beating the longevity odds than she is willing to admit — unless it suits her. It suits her now.

"It's an utter disgrace, David," she spits. "Someone of my age shouldn't have to put up with it."

"Your age?" queries Bliss, though it is rhetorical and he knows it, so he skips, asking, "What shouldn't you have to put up with?"

"Listen," she says and waves the phone in the air.

The thumping bass of rap music, the revving of motorbikes, the barking of dogs, and a foul-mouthed woman screeching abuse coalesce into a cacophony that makes Bliss duck.

"Daphne," he shouts. "Is that your Gilbert and Sullivan society or are you having a rave?"

"It's the new neighbours," she protests angrily, then carries on carping about the family that has moved in next door: wall-shaking music, air-rending exhausts, loud people with even louder motorbikes who entertain a constant stream of unsavoury characters at unsavoury times, and two muscular terriers who throw themselves at the fence every time she ventures into her back garden.

"They've smashed my windows, peed on my gladiolis, and even pulled up the carrots I was growing specially for the horticultural fair," she complains, although it's not the worst. The worst is the disappearance of her cat, Missie Rouge, and she is close to tears as she says, "They probably ate the poor thing."

"You're exaggerating," says Bliss. "Anyway, I thought it was an elderly couple next door. I met them."

"Phil and Maggie," she agrees with a loud sniff. "They died."

"Not the heat —" starts Bliss, but Daphne cuts him off.

"Oh no. They were ever so old," she says, as if aging is an affliction from which she is immune. "Maggie went first. She was in one of those church-run seniors' homes, Auschwitz-by-the-sea, and Phil just pined."

"It happens," suggests Bliss, ignoring the jibe, though Daphne can't understand how her new neighbours got the house.

"Phil and Maggie had no family — none worth speaking of. I'd do their shopping and get their prescriptions. And I cooked for Phil …"

I guess you were expecting a handout, thinks Bliss uncharitably as Daphne continues with her list of good-neighbourliness. But he finds it surprising that she didn't anticipate the existence of a relative in the woodwork. "Actually, I'm really busy," he says, cutting her off eventually, and he suggests she take her complaint to Superintendent Donaldson at Westchester police station.

"Ted retired last month," complains Daphne, as if he did it deliberately. "There's a schoolgirl running the place now, and she good-as-much told me to buy earplugs."

Donaldson's replacement was clearly unaware of Daphne's record and status. Not only was the elderly spinster the station's charlady for more years than anyone could remember, she probably solved more crimes than many of the less inspired detectives. The number of criminals convicted in the five years since Daphne handed in the keys to Westchester police station's tea cupboard has decreased annually, though no one at the weekly C.I.D. meeting would dream of attributing the decline to her absence. However, no one would deny that whenever she slowly lowered her polished copper pot onto the detective inspector's desk, scratched her forehead, and mused, "That's funny — my milkman (or baker or butcher) was telling me about …" anyone with any sense would put down their tea and pick up a pen.

"I told little Miss Marple straight. I said, 'I was cleaning the constables' toilets here before you pooped your first nappy.'"

"I bet that went down well," mutters Bliss, but Daphne fails to see why diplomacy should trump the truth.

"Call themselves detectives," she rants. "Most of them couldn't spot a turd in a toilet, and as for …" but Bliss tunes out her diatribe, knowing he'd probably agree and guessing that much the same would have been said of him and his peers in his early years.

"If I had neighbours like that in olden times I could have bribed a witch to put a hex on their virgins and poison their goat," Daphne is concluding when Bliss comes back, and he laughs it off.

"Now don't go getting yourself in trouble. I've bailed you out often enough."

"Bailed me out, Chief Inspector! I seem to remember —"

"All right, Daphne," says Bliss, needing no reminder of the times the shoe was on the other foot. "Only you'll have to join the queue. I've already got one little old lady on my plate this week."

"Old!" snorts Daphne indignantly, as expected, though she calms once he's revealed the identity of his other charge.

"I suppose I'll have to yield to royalty," she says as she puts down the phone and refills the teapot. "Keemun," she muses as she pours, knowing it is the Queen's favourite, and then she has an idea.

"Your Majesty," she writes, after she has dug a mono-grammed Sheaffer fountain pen and a bottle of India ink from her bureau.

"Subversion: the art of demoralizing the enemy by per-sistently undermining their morale," writes Daphne in a notebook, once she has leant on the Queen for support, then she pours another tea, sits back, and closes her eyes in an effort to blot out the neighbours' noise.

Images from another lifetime take shape, images undimmed by more than six decades: corrugated iron huts draped with camouflage netting in the woodland behind a solid Victorian mansion; the air heavy with the stench of latrines, cigarettes, and cheap floor polish; a hundred keen and excited women in drab fatigues being groomed for death — young women, most barely in their twenties, who a year earlier would have been giddily choosing dresses for engagement parties and coming-out balls.

"Dishearten, demoralize, and discourage by destroy-ing, disrupting, and denying," ran the mnemonic of the psychological warfare officer as Daphne and her classmates were prepared to take on the Nazis in occupied France, and Daphne recalls it with a clarity that proves conclusively to her that she's not coming down with Alzheimer's, but twenty minutes later she puts the kettle on again. It's not that she's entirely bereft of ideas for ousting the enemy on her doorstep; she simply has no way to get her hands on the necessary explosives, detonators, or strychnine. "I'll have to be subtle," she tries telling herself, but in her mind she sees a plume of smoke rising from the rubble, while sombre-faced undertaker's men carry charred bodies to a black van and someone dumps the limp carcasses of two pit bulls into a hastily dug grave.

"That'll teach you for eating my poor little pussy cat," she sniffles, but the mirage evaporates instantly as the dogs spy her peering out of her kitchen window and launch themselves against the wire fence.

"Shut up! Please shut up!" she says as she clamps her hands over her ears, but the pulsing thunder of a bass drum beats into her.

"Shut up! Shut up!" she yells as she escapes the kitchen with the teapot, but the noise tracks her through the hallway into the living room.

"Shut up! Shut up!" she screeches as she stands, rigid, in the centre of the room, then she lets go, drops the pot, and slumps onto the settee where she buries her head under a pillow and bursts into tears.

chapter two

Four unopened birthday cards lie on David Bliss's hall floor on Saturday morning, but none bear a French stamp. *Daisy's forgotten*, he tells himself, but resists the temptation to phone in case he is proved right. "She'll probably call later," he muses as he drags himself to the kitchen for a coffee.

Samantha, his married daughter, called just as he was getting into bed. "Sorry, Dad, we thought you'd be going to visit Daisy in France," she explained, after apologizing for the fact that she and Peter, her chief inspector husband, had made alternate plans for the weekend.

"Oh, don't worry, Sam. I'm far too busy to bother with birthdays at my age," Bliss protested with a brave lilt, "and I've got a lot of work to do on the Queen's visit." But sleep evaded him. "Hot and sticky," the late-night forecaster had predicted, and Bliss's mind wandered the hallways of his life, peeking into rooms — some distant, full of warmth and smiling families, balloons, cakes, and candles; others, more recent, empty and cold — as he sought a comfortable spot on the perspiration-soaked sheet.

"Fifty years," he muses as he pulls a face in a grimy mirror and sees a bleak day ahead. At least nothing fell off or fell out during the night, he wryly tells himself, although cracks are beginning to appear. The crinkles may be laughter lines — nonetheless they are lines, and the morning stubble has a definite greyness.

The phone buzzes. "At last," he sighs, but it is Samantha with another apology.

"Don't worry about me," he repeats valiantly, "I've got masses to do."

The fridge calls, but one glance reminds him that he hasn't found time to shop. *What am I doing?* he questions. *It's my birthday. I'll treat myself.*

Daphne Lovelace, in contrast, has shopped. Since the pandemonic invasion next door she has become a frequent loiterer at Patel's corner store, and her larder would be more at home in Mumbai than Westchester. But it's Saturday morning and, unless she beards the beasts and ventures into the wilderness that until recently was her vegetable garden, she is hopeful that peace will reign until the neighbours surface around lunchtime.

It is barely nine-thirty when the spell is broken as Mavis Longbottom bangs on Daphne's back door and wakes the dogs.

"How on earth do you put up with it?" asks Mavis as she pushes her way into the kitchen and slams the door in the face of the snarling pit bulls. "It's like the Hounds o' the bloomin' Baskervilles."

"It's worse," says Daphne with her hands over her ears.

"Can't you do something?"

"Maybe," replies Daphne, but her projected stratagem has stuck at blasting a broadside of Tchaikovsky or Strauss from her stereo and incinerating a pan of vindaloo day and night. However, in her more rational moments, she realizes that if it comes to open warfare she has a limited arsenal. "I phoned the noise-abatement people at the council," she complains as she drags her friend away from the window and picks up the pot to pour a second cup. "But they're useless. They couldn't hear a farter at a funeral. 'Just listen to those damned dogs,' I said, holding the phone out, and little miss lug-ears said, 'I 'spect they just want to play.' 'Play,' I said, 'Rip me to shreds is more like it. Just like my poor little pussy.'"

"They didn't?" Mavis questions in alarm, but Daphne shrugs.

"She never disappeared before that lot came."

The screech of a woman's voice yelling "Shuddup" momentarily quells the baying animals, and Daphne mutters, "Thank God for that" only seconds before the rumpus begins anew.

"I can't think with all this noise," snaps Daphne, slamming down the teapot.

"You need a labyrinth," suggests Mavis.

"I'm confused enough without getting stuck in a bloomin' maze."

"No, not a maze. Labyrinths are pathways that lead you to a new understanding. At least, that's what they're supposed to do."

"I don't understand —"

"Precisely. That's because you've never walked one," insists Mavis, then she grabs Daphne's arm. "Come on. I'll show you. There's a famous medieval one at the cathedral."

"Wait a minute," says Daphne, breaking free. "I'm not dressed — not for a cathedral. And I'm certainly not going there without a proper hat."

Daphne's chosen hat, a cardinal calotte with a single silk rose, which she created especially for Princess Diana's memorial, hasn't seen daylight for nearly a decade.

"Black would probably be more suitable," she glumly admits to Mavis as they slide out the front door and head for the bus stop, "but I've had my fill of funerals of late."

Hardly a week in recent years has passed without a familiar name cropping up in the obituary column of the *Westchester Gazette*. Most, like neighbours Phil and Maggie Morgan, slipped into eternity with just a few lines, while some demanded a column inch or even two. A few even hit the headlines, though none as spectacularly as Minnie Dennon, Daphne's closest friend, who rode out of town and off the planet on the front of a hundred-mile-an-hour express train after she was defrauded of her life's savings.

"It must be terrible being old," suggests Mavis with a sympathetic glance in Daphne's direction. "Losing all your friends like that."

"At least I haven't lost my eyesight and my teeth," retorts Daphne, well aware that Mavis would never find her dentures without her glasses.

"Here's the bus," says Mavis, feigning deafness, but as she reaches out to steady her friend, Daphne snatches her arm away.

"I can manage, thank you."

Only five years separate the two women, but in many ways they are from different worlds, and it is only lately that Mavis has climbed Daphne's social ladder as others have fallen off the top. Mavis was still playing hopscotch at the outbreak of the Second World War when eighteen-year-old Ophelia Lovelace changed her name to Daphne and catapulted herself into adulthood by signing up to be parachuted into France to aid the resistance. The closest Mavis ever got to France was the perfume counter at Boot's the Chemist and a French Tickler she once bought "just for a giggle" on a girls' day out in Brighton.

When Daphne was entrenched behind enemy lines the day after D-Day, Mavis was entrenched in the bar of the White Swan with a young Canadian corporal who had missed his boat. And, when the war ended, Daphne turned her smile to the east and used it to open chinks in the Iron Curtain for fleeing dissidents, while Mavis primarily used her smile to prise open various husbands' wallets — some, though not all, her own.

"It's a classical left-handed seven-circuit labyrinth," enthuses the cathedral's lofty sexton, with the raciness of a commentator describing the Derby course at Epsom, but Daphne sees only an unkempt spiralled path of cracked flagstones and screws her face in confusion.

"What's it supposed to do?"

"It!" snaps the sexton, as if she has just called Jesus a Jew. "It!" Then he softens reverently. "Madam, the labyrinth is an ancient and sacred design given to us by the Lord himself."

"Oh —"

"And," he carries on, with a warning finger, "you would be wise never to underestimate its power."

Daphne gives a critical eye to the circular pattern of stepping stones laid into the scraggy, scorched grass, but her face betrays her skepticism.

"The labyrinth will help you find answers, find your centre," explains the tall man solicitously as he reaches down to take Daphne's hand and lead her around the looping path under Mavis's watchful eye. "Just clear your mind ..."

Daphne abruptly halts and jerks her hand free. "I think I can find my own way, thank you very much," she says, and the sexton backs off.

"Have faith in your prayers and all will be revealed," he calls confidently as he walks away, clearly ignorant of the fact that the only prayer Daphne has in mind is for divine guidance in the manufacture of dynamite and the making of rat poison.

The tightly knitted pathway takes Daphne in circles, and after fifteen minutes she reaches the centre but is no nearer a solution. However, the tranquility of the cathedral's sanctified grounds has mollified her, and, as she unwinds, she has an idea.

"I shall invite them for Sunday tea," she tells Mavis with a note of triumph as they walk back to the bus stop. "Homemade scones and a Victoria sponge. Then I'll lay it on thick about my insomnia and stress-related arthritis."

"Arthritis?" says Mavis disbelievingly.

"I could have," retorts Daphne. "For all they know I could have a pacemaker and a spastic colon. Lots of people do at my age."

"But you don't."

"That's not the point. I will if I have to put up with their racket much longer."

The morning drags for Bliss as he tries to concentrate on preparations for the royal visit with one eye on the telephone. *Every pot boils eventually*, he tries telling himself as his mind constantly drifts to the Provençal port of St-Juan-sur-Mer and Daisy. *Maybe it's her mother again.*

Daisy's mother has no objection to her middle-aged daughter's relationship that she can articulate in Bliss's presence, but that doesn't stop her griping about the British betrayal at Dunkirk behind his back. "*Les cochons anglais* — the pigs left our men on the beaches and ran off like *les poules mouillées* — like wet chickens," she complains whenever she has the chance, and she is always quick to add the question of hygiene in Britain, where, she has heard, bidets are rarer than in the Bastille.

However, it is the recent death of her nonagenarian mother that has hobbled her daughter, Daisy, to her side.

"I suppose I could manage on my own if I had to," she has mournfully acknowledged a thousand times, though never without questioning aloud why Daisy couldn't find a nice Frenchman.

"*Les hommes!*" Daisy's mother snivelled after the funeral. "Men — they are all the same. They steal your heart then run off and leave you to cry alone to the grave." But the plaint wasn't for her mother, whose husband was marched away at the end of a Nazi bayonet and tortured to death in the dungeons of the infamous Chateau Roger. It was for herself, abandoned with a young daughter over forty years ago. And now that her mother is gone she mourns the fact that *un sale étranger* has turned her daughter's head towards *la perfide Albion* — the perfidious Albion.

The suggestion that Britain is faithless is not shared by Bliss as he studies the risk assessment for the Queen's visit and sees that it is off the charts. Crusading Christians of all stripes are invoking damnation on the House of Windsor, while in Tehran and Mecca, where the spectre of a woman entering a mosque during prayers could cause mass conniptions, fatwas are being drawn up against anyone involved.

However, the meticulously prepared manuals attempt to cover every potential risk: bomb squads with panting dogs sniffing into sewers and garbage bins; marksmen staking out rooftops; traffic teams towing abandoned cars and keeping the streets moving; an army of constables manning barricades; mounted officers grooming their steeds for battle; public order squads encased in riot gear readying their shields and rubber bullets; marine units patrolling the river in inflatables; and the airborne unit patrolling the skies in choppers. Two thousand three hundred and six officers, assuming they all show up, and Bliss has the job of synchronizing them all to protect one woman — a year's preparation for a thirty-minute visit. But this isn't any visit. This isn't Her Majesty cutting a ribbon or kissing a baby.

This is impossible, Bliss tells himself as he follows the route with his finger and speculates on the number of buildings that could conceal a terrorist — a fanatic bent on martyrdom with an anti-tank mortar capable of immolating the armour-plated Rolls and its occupants in Allah's name before a marksman could draw a bead. And what if the evangelical doomsayers are right? What if God in His wrath sends a bolt of lightning to cremate the heretics?

It is 2:00 p.m., and the buzzing of Daphne's telephone barely breaks through the thunderous music threatening to shatter her glassware.

"You'll have to speak up. I can't hear myself think," the elderly woman shouts, forcing Samantha Bliss to repeat, "You haven't forgotten, have you, Daphne?"

"Forgotten …" she starts vaguely, then she wakes up. "Oh, it's you, Samantha. No. Of course not."

Bliss gets the next call. "I thought you were going away, Sam," he says testily.

"We are. I just wanted to make sure you were all right."

All right? Bliss questions to himself then runs a quick check: physically fit-ish; mentally stable; financially sound; emotionally …?

"I still haven't heard from Daisy."

"Oh, Dad. Did you call her?"

"'Leave a message' was all I got. She's at the beach I expect. I don't blame her. If it wasn't for this royal visit that's where I'd be."

"I'm sure she'll remember," says Samantha as she hangs up.

The number of Muslim officers scheduled for duty occupies Bliss for much of the afternoon. "Screen everyone," will be the order of the day, but who will screen the screeners? What if one of the helmeted firearms specialists is a sleeper just biding his time, then *bang* as he spins from the crowd and blasts the Queen?

"Daisy — finally," muses Bliss, without bothering to check the call display when the phone buzzes at 5:00 p.m., and he's tempted to let his answerphone take revenge.

"Hello," he says coldly at the third buzz, but it takes a few seconds to get his mind to switch gears at the sound of a man's voice.

"How are you getting on with the manuals, David?" demands Commander Fox gruffly.

"Updating, improving, plugging loopholes," answers Bliss unenthusiastically, well aware that trying to stop a fanatical terrorist with martyrdom on his mind is as difficult as stopping a gambling addict on a winning streak. "I do have one major concern regarding —"

"Not on the phone, David," warns Fox. "Meet me at seven — no, make that six-thirty — in my office. Let's see where we stand."

It's Saturday and it's my fiftieth bloody birthday, he wants to shout, but lets it go — anything beats midsummer reruns and Chinese takeout.

The heat drives Bliss off the tube at Charing Cross, but the flowing river has a cooling effect as he retraces his steps to the Yard along the wide Thames embankment. It's relatively quiet — even the tourists are flagging — but the impending royal visit has forced the extremists out of the shadows, and Bliss is repeatedly accosted by evangelists of all colours pressing pamphlets on him.

"The rapture is upon us ..." begins one leaflet, and before he can screw it into a ball and bin it, an earnest sixteen-year-old disciple is on his arm, pleading, "Please, sir. You must have faith and repent now or you'll be left behind."

"Left behind where?" queries Bliss, and he stops while the wide-eyed young girl warns of the impending eschatological moment when God will take all his believers to heaven while leaving all the skeptics to suffer the hellish nightmare of life on earth.

"You go and enjoy yourself, dear," laughs Bliss as he walks away. "I've got more chance of being taken out by an alcoholic Santa on a powered lawnmower than being whisked off to heaven on a fiery chariot."

"But, sir ..." she is still begging as another leaflet is thrust at him.

"Only through Jehovah can you find true salvation," yells the girl's competition, so Bliss shoves his hands into his pockets and picks up his pace.

"Chief Inspector," calls the duty desk clerk, stalling Bliss as he heads for the elevator. "Message for you."

"7:00 p.m. La Côte d'Or on Park Avenue — Fox," reads the note, and Bliss would ignore it and go home to bed if it weren't for the possibility of wrangling a steak out of his senior officer's platinum expense account.

"How old are you?" he asks the young clerk, but doesn't wait for a reply. "Do yourself a favour, mate," he says as he walks to the door. "Don't wait till you get old to enjoy yourself."

A cruising cab screeches to a halt. "What a way to spend your birthday," he grumbles. "Lugging a bloody briefcase all round London on a Saturday night."

"Where to, guv'nor?"

"La Côte d'Or," he says and sees an uncertain look on the cabby's face. "Park Avenue," he adds, before he catches on and takes a look at himself — golfing shirt, walking shorts, and a pair of rope-soled sandals; so much for the steak.

The gatekeeper at La Côte d'Or has a pencil-thin greased moustache and slicked-back hair. He wishes he could speak French but contents himself with a heavy accent as he gazes through Bliss, saying, "*Bonsoir*, Monsieur. Have you zhe reservation?"

Bliss is tempted to produce his warrant card and muscle his way in, but he hasn't the energy. "I'm meeting a friend — Mr. Fox."

"Perhaps he is expecting you, *oui*?"

Bliss rolls his eyes, telling himself, *This is crazy. It can wait till Monday.*

"Have you zhe tie and zhe jacket, sir?" continues Greasy as he focuses into the space above Bliss's head.

"Does it look as though …" Bliss starts, then mellows. "Never mind. Please tell Mr. Fox that I'll see him on Monday morning as scheduled."

"Just one moment, sir," says Greasy, dropping the accent, then he snaps his fingers at a skinny youth who is trying unsuccessfully to fill the pants of his predecessor. "John will find something suitable for you if you'd care to follow him."

"These look brand new," muses Bliss a few minutes later as he takes the linen jacket and slacks from the boy, and then he spots the designer's label and gives a low whistle. "No wonder you charge so much for dinner," he quips as he slips on the coat and knots an Armani tie.

"Shoes, sir," says John, handing Bliss a pair of hand-made Italian slip-ons without questioning his size.

"You're good," replies Bliss as he steps comfortably into them.

"Commander Fox has taken zhe private dining room zhis evening," explains Greasy, leading Bliss past some of London's hottest celebrities who are basking in the cool of a monumental ice carving of the Trevi fountain centred in the main room.

"He would," mutters Bliss, and mentally ups his order from Tournedos Rossini to Lobster Newburg, although he knows he'll be lucky if he gets a nibble at the olive bowl.

Candlelight glitters off diamonds and quartz alike, and as Bliss sweeps the glitzy restaurant he is unable to pick out the real from the fake. A few faces have a certain familiarity; movies or television, he assumes, though he rarely watches either and is at a loss for names.

Greasy stops, hands on double doors, and turns to give Bliss a quick final inspection before pulling.

"*Bon anniversaire, monsieur,*" he says as he swings open the doors, and Bliss stands mute for a second before bursting into laughter.

"You bastards," he says through the laughter as fiancée Daisy, daughter Samantha and her husband, Peter, Daphne Lovelace, and a host of colleagues stand with raised glasses, singing "Happy Birthday."

"Hope you like your birthday present, Dad," says Samantha as she hugs her father.

"Present?" he asks.

"The suit."

"I bought you the tie," chirrups Daphne as Daisy gives him a kiss that brings a cheer and a round of applause from the room.

"And I bought zhe shoes in Italy especially for you. You like, *non?*"

"I like, no," he parodies, but the biggest surprise of the evening comes after the cake and the port, when Samantha proposes a toast to her father then casually turns to him, adding, "A really great dad who is soon to become a grandfather."

The congratulatory cheer is immediately superseded by ageist quips, and one wag slips out to borrow the restaurant's wheelchair. "This is for you, granddad," he yells as he pushes it into the room. Half a dozen strong hands grab Bliss and drop him into the chair, and while he is still struggling to find the right pigeonhole in his brain for the information, he is shot out of the door and boisterously raced around the restaurant under the noses of the glitterati. Greasy's upper lip quivers as he steps in to stop the fracas, and his French takes a dive as he mutters, "F'kin idiots."

"Zhat is good news, *non*?" says Daisy on Bliss's return.

"Yes. That is good news, no," he agrees ambiguously, with a feeling that he is on the verge of another huge step on the road to eternity.

Daisy's visit is short-lived. "I have to go back to France tomorrow for my mozher," she explains as they are driven home by Samantha after the birthday dinner, but Bliss has his own surprise.

"Never mind. I'm taking the week off after the Queen's visit on Friday. We could go to Venice."

Daisy turns up her nose. "Venice — in August?"

"Corsica then," he suggests, then snuggles close. "Anywhere, as long as I'm with you."

"It is zhe festival of fireworks in Cannes on Saturday," she reminds him excitedly, and he happily makes it a date.

By midweek the heat has sparked a rash of mini riots as short-tempered drinkers spill out of bars and find nothing to dampen their spirits. Lexicographers perspire as they try to keep pace with the superlatives of exuberant meteorologists. "We're experiencing a superthermic episode," enthuse TV weathermen, as yet unable to invent a simple antonym for "ice age," and the words *deforestation*, *desertification*, and *de-glacierization* crop up daily.

The ill-tempered rhetoric over the impending visit is exacerbated by the relentless hot spell, and Bliss is taking heat from some of his colleagues.

"It's all right for some," sneers one chief inspector at Wednesday morning's site visit, as he sees himself frying by the roadside for hours on Friday while Bliss sits in air-conditioned comfort. "Some pinky-assed people get a year off the job to live in France and write a poxin' book while the rest of us sweat our bollocks off."

"So?" Bliss questions.

"Well, where is it then?" Lester Clarke demands angrily. But it's not the book that is bugging him. It is the fact that Bliss has been parachuted into the driver's seat ahead of him.

"I thought writing it was hard enough," admits Bliss. "But apparently it's almost impossible to get published."

"Waste of bloody time if you ask me," snorts Clarke as he storms off, and Bliss is beginning to wonder if his colleague doesn't have a point.

"Prime targets," says Commander Fox, directing his clutch of senior officers to the relevant page as they stand on the spot where the Queen will be presented to the imams and mullahs. "Toilets — and not necessarily a bomb. What if someone snuck a mini surveillance camera into a loo? A bootleg video of the royal backside hitting the seat and the sound of a royal tinkle would be priceless."

Across the road from the mosque, a team of eight workers tart up the façade of the public library. The days of whitewashing coal heaps and erecting hoardings around public toilets and other unseemly sights to spare the Queen's sensibilities may be over, but savvy councillors still know that the best way to get potholes fixed and a new coat on a public building is to host a royal walkabout.

"I bet she thinks that fresh air smells like wet paint," cracks Bliss under his breath as he watches a couple of painters atop a cherry picker artistically decorating a lamp standard that no one will ever see from the ground without binoculars.

"I don't want too many uniforms lining the streets," carries on Fox, knowing that the easiest way to get a poke in the eye from the palace is to be visibly heavy-handed. "Her Majesty expressed concern at the cost ..." a rebuke to the commissioner, copied to the Home Secretary, will begin, and he'll be writing apologies for a month. "Hide them round the back; stuff them into buses; take off their uniforms and try to make them look human."

A pickup truck laden with paving stones and sand pulls onto the pavement and two workers begin unloading tools as Fox goes through the manual: parade times; radio call signs; plainclothes officers' identification badges; code names; refreshment facilities; prisoner handling; use of deadly force protocols ... the list appears endless, and Bliss tunes out, knowing the details by heart.

The sound of a pickaxe punctuates Fox's orders and draws Bliss to the curbside where the Queen is due to dismount from the royal car.

"Aw'right then, guv'nor," says one of the workmen as Bliss takes an interest in the truck's contents.

"What are you doing?" asks Bliss.

"Ain't you 'eard, guv? The bleedin' Queen's comin' Friday. Can't 'ave her Ladyship trippin' over, can we?"

"No," agrees Bliss, "we can't." But he watches worriedly for a few minutes as he realizes how easy it would be for the men to slip a remotely activated mine under the stones that they are realigning.

By Wednesday afternoon desperation has drawn Daphne Lovelace back to the labyrinth, a wide-peaked red hat plonked fiercely over her forehead. Sunday tea was a disaster: they came, they ate, they went, Misty and Rob

Jenkins and the little Jenkinses — three teenage thugs, in Daphne's eyes, with tattoos and metal rings in every painful place and iPods that were never off. "The dogs?" they said. "Just puppies." The stereo? "Ignore it." Late-night revelries? "Boys will be boys." Motorbikes? "A Yammy and a Kawasaki," said Rob Jenkins as if Daphne should be impressed. "And I'm savin' up for a Harley," piped up one of the lesser Jenkinses, and at that point Daphne decided she might as well keep the second Victoria sponge for herself.

The spectre of a long-haired woman drifts out of nowhere as Daphne circles the labyrinth with her eyes down, seeking inspiration, or at least some peace and quiet.

"Oh dear. I can feel your pain," says the woman as she slowly passes on an adjacent path.

"Aren't we supposed to keep silent?" whispers Daphne a touch harshly from under her hat.

"I could hear you from over there," insists the woman, bringing Daphne to a confused halt, protesting, "I haven't said anything."

"Not you — your soul. Crying out; searching for answers; seeking salvation before you journey into the next world."

Daphne steps back and lifts her hat to take a close look at the spindly, barefoot, and obviously bra-less middle-aged woman, thinking, *A peony in her hair and a guitar and she could have walked straight here from Woodstock.*

"Let me help you, Daphne," the woman continues as she takes the older woman's hand and peers into her eyes.

"How do you know my name?" shoots back Daphne, forgetting that she signed the visitors' book at the entrance.

"The Lord is all-seeing. He has sent me."

"That's good of him," she says as she looks around praying for help from a less ethereal source. Then the woman hands her a business card and echoes the information.

"Angel Robinson, spiritual guide and psychic," she says, adding, "Give me a call when you're ready," as she drifts away.

"I should get her to contact Maggie and Phil," muses Daphne half-seriously. "Perhaps she can find out what I did to upset them."

"I expect nothing — I repeat, nothing — to mar today's proceedings, Chief Inspector," Fox warned Friday morning before leaving to conduct operations at the scene, and as noon approaches, Bliss makes a final check to ensure that everyone is in place.

"It's in the lap of the gods now," he says to Sergeant Williams as the pageant begins and he hears the BBC welcoming listeners to "this monumental occasion" while reminding them that it was only recently that the Queen was described as the enemy of Islam by some of the more radical imams.

The procession is flawless. The cameras work. There are no stray aircraft, no rooftop snipers, and few rubber-neckers along the route.

"So far so good," Bliss sighs as the motorcade makes it through the centre of London unhindered, and by the time he checks back with the BBC they have wheeled in an expert to dissect the body theocratic.

"This is a difficult time for the Crown," admits the sage. "Not only are we seeing a growing rift between Christianity and Islam as well as outbreaks of ethnic violence between Hindus and Sikhs, but there are splits within the Anglican Church itself over the ordination of women, same-sex unions, and voluntary euthanasia. In addition, there is a rise in anti-Semitism, continuing sex scandals in the Catholic Church, not to mention the growing movement of radical evangelism."

"That just about says it all," says Bliss as he switches his focus to the front of the mosque, where Commander

Fox awaits the royal car. Behind Fox, the reception party are beginning to find their places at the top of the marble staircase, while the discordant wailing of a muezzin calls to the faithful and unfaithful alike.

The crowds are smaller and quieter than he anticipated, driven underground by the midday sun, and a few hardliners are easily marked and hustled away. A number of placards suggesting that either Jesus or Mohammed should perform physiologically impossible sexual feats have been "accidentally" knocked from protesters' hands by plainclothes gorillas and trodden into the ground KGB-style, and as the motorcycle outriders reach the destination, Commander Fox's voice comes over Bliss's radio: "Everything's in order here, Chief Inspector."

Bliss checks the clock, and the royal car glides to a stop as the second hand touches the top.

"Bang on time," says Williams.

"Guinevere and Lancelot arrived safely at Point Omega," sings Bliss into his microphone, and hundreds of men and women lower their shields and tear gas guns to light up cigarettes or dash to port-a-loos, but the rooftop marksmen are still on high alert. The walk from the heavily armoured car up the steps to the mosque — lined either side by a throng of hand-picked flag-wavers — is the only time that the royal personages are actually exposed, and Bliss flicks constantly from camera to camera, making sure to check in with the eye in the sky. Marksmen on rooftops, each with an identification tab clearly visible, scan their allotted areas through scopes. The radio chatters constantly as they check in: "All clear … All clear … All clear …"

"Don't get complacent. Don't let your guard down," mumbles Bliss on the edge of his seat as the imams and mullahs wait, still smiling at their coup — even if they are risking their necks and have driven away some of their more fervent congregants.

The Bishop of London, wearing a colourful frock, and a handful of cassocked lesser clerics are also in attendance, Bibles in hand, ready to undo any theological damage that the Islamists may do, even though the royals will take no part in the proceedings and will simply walk in the front door and then be shunted into a back room with the women and girls. But the Christians stand well apart from the followers of Mohammed and mistrustfully eye the dignitaries in their drab grey galabiyyas and dishdashas.

"Her Majesty is wearing an ivory ..." begins the commentator, and Bliss fades him out in momentary panic as he realizes that he never ordered anyone to specifically check the repaved area under the Queen's feet. Seconds stretch to eternity as Bliss waits for a blast, and then he takes a breath as she is escorted to the steps by Commander Fox.

"Prince Philip is resplendent in his field marshall's ceremonial uniform," says the BBC reporter, seemingly as surprised as everyone else as the Duke of Edinburgh alights from the royal limousine.

"I thought this was supposed to be informal ..." mumbles Bliss as he frantically flicks through the orders of the day.

"Maybe he's losing his marbles," suggests Sergeant Williams with little concern.

Bliss has found the page, stabs at the words *civilian dress*, and fumes, "His bloody aide-de-camp should've picked up on this."

"You know how stubborn the old bugger can be," responds Williams. "He's making a statement. What does it matter?"

"Because, Sergeant, protocol is protocol," explains Bliss fiercely. "Not every Arab goes around singing 'Rule Britannia' and wants to be reminded that our army's been crapping on their doorstep since the Middle Ages."

"Nothing we can do about it now," shrugs Williams as the Duke returns Commander Fox's salute before following his wife up the steps towards the reception party.

"Hurry up ... hurry up," encourages Bliss in a tense whisper. This was the only bit he objected to during the initial briefings. "Why not have the official greetings inside — out of danger?" he asked. But the Queen's equerry was adamant.

"Everyone must see the respect accorded by each side. You must appreciate, Chief Inspector, that this visit has great historical significance."

Historically significant or not, a touch of comedy is creeping in a few steps behind the Queen, where Prince Philip appears to have gotten into a fight with his ceremonial sword.

"What's his bloody lordship up to?" sniggers Williams in Bliss's ear as Prince Philip struggles with his scabbard.

"No idea, Sergeant," says Bliss. "First he shows up dressed like a —"

"Do you know," cuts in Williams. "He once saw the Nigerian president in his Muslim robes and said, 'God, man. You look ready for bed!'"

"Really."

All eyes and cameras switch to the aging Duke of Edinburgh as the protection officer steps in and takes hold of Philip's sword arm.

Williams smirks, saying, "Unhand me, you varlet," in a Shakespearean tone as Philip angrily waves off his guardian and, with a sharp tug, draws his sword.

"What the hell is he doing now?" mutters Bliss.

The midday sun flashes off the brilliantly burnished weapon, and the imams shrink back in unison as Philip lunges towards the lineup. The Queen finally catches on and spins with a confused look.

"What on earth are you doing?" she mouths and takes a step towards her husband as he raises the sword. "Philip!"

"Oh my God," breathes Bliss as the sword begins its descent, then the Queen's protection officer takes a flying leap. The blade slashes downward as the aging woman falls under the weight of her bodyguard, but the tip slices into a bony calf.

"Jeezus," spits Williams as the Duke's man grabs the weapon and the Queen tumbles backwards down the marble steps in the embrace of her saviour.

Commander Fox is on the radio in a flash. "Get an ambulance, Chief Inspector."

"Yes, sir."

"And a bottle of Aspirins."

"For the Queen?" queries Bliss.

"No, you fool. For me."

chapter three

Deny, deny, deny. Everyone from the Prime Minister down is singing from the same page.

The Prince Philip, Duke of Edinburgh, KG, KT, OM, and a Scrabble bag of other official abbreviations, did not attempt to run his wife through with his ceremonial sword. He simply stumbled while trying to free his scabbard.

"Free it from what?" is the question on everyone's lips. It wasn't as though he could have gotten it caught in his fly. But the only other possibility is that he made a deliberate thrust at the Queen, and that is an option no one is prepared to consider — other than Internet bloggers, tabloid journalists, the foreign press, and a very large chunk of the populace who viewed it live on the BBC.

"You do realize that attempting to harm the monarch is high treason," the assistant commissioner says to Bliss at a hurriedly arranged debrief while they wait for other senior officers to be rounded up. "I've got a feeling it still carries the death penalty."

Don't blame me, thinks Bliss, suggesting, "Maybe he's going a little senile, sir. Apparently his mother went completely dotty in her old age."

"Wake up, man," spits the A.C. "He's been round the bloody twist for years. Remember when he asked that blind woman if she knew where he could get an eating dog for an anorexic 'cos he wanted one for Princess Diana."

Bliss doesn't bite. "How is the Queen, sir?" he asks coolly as Commander Fox and several of the field officers arrive from the scene of the skirmish.

"Not amused," laughs Fox on his way in. "One stab wound, some bumps, some scrapes, and a very sore bum. She'd probably have carried on, but the medics aren't taking chances — they're going to keep her in for a few days' observation."

"And the Duke?"

"Heatstroke can be a terrible thing, especially in the elderly, Chief Inspector," says Fox, putting on a deadpan face as he pulls up a chair and starts building an alibi for Prince Philip. "Surely you've been reading the papers. There's been all kinds of weird goings-on."

So that's the official tack, thinks Bliss, as the A.C. nods approvingly. "Heatstroke, Commander. Yes. That would explain it nicely. His Highness, realizing he was about to faint, pulled out his sword and stumbled as he was overcome."

"Why did he pull out his sword, sir?" digs Bliss, then wishes he hadn't as Fox takes his head off.

"Don't be a fool, man. If we don't come up with a cast-iron defence some lefty pinko on the front bench is going to demand a trial. And where would that leave us?"

"Right," says Bliss, resisting the temptation to say, *With a very strong case of attempted murder, assault occasioning grievous bodily harm, and, possibly, high treason.*

"Now," carries on the A.C. as the door finally closes behind the smokers and the eternally tardy. "I've ordered sandwiches and cold drinks to be sent in. Take off your ties, get your minds in gear, and don't make any plans for this weekend."

Bliss checks his watch.

"Going somewhere, Chief Inspector?" demands the A.C. in a tone that tells Bliss that his five o'clock flight to Nice will be leaving with at least one empty seat.

"No, sir."

"Damn right you're not. If we get this wrong the Queen won't be the only one with a sore arse for the next month."

"Right, sir," says Bliss, and he sits back as a couple dozen senior officers play footsie with the facts. The weather takes most of the heat, followed by a handful of civilians — Prince Philip's equerry, his aide-de-camp, and his wardrobe mistress — who all should have made sure he was wearing appropriate clothing. The Met's own men, the royalty protection officers, and the Queen's detective could be in the firing line for not alerting anyone to Philip's breach of etiquette, but Bliss's peers are working on that as he tunes them out.

Why didn't his own P.O. stop him? Why the slow reaction from the Queen's P.O.? Why didn't anyone see it coming? These are the questions the cadre of white-shirted officers are readying to deflect as Bliss closes his eyes and finds himself in Cannes with his arm around Daisy.

It is late afternoon on the Côte d'Azur. A million urban northerners clog the Mediterranean shores, seeking respite from the oppressive heat, as Bliss dreams of strolling with his fiancée under the shady palms and oleanders of Cannes' beachside gardens and of watching the evening's fireworks display from the Promenade de la Croisette. The promenade, the wide seafront boulevard that follows the gentle sweep of the bay, is lined with the world's glitziest hotels and is so familiar to Bliss that he can picture every one of the opulent façades facing the golden beaches and multi-hued blue waters.

Daisy's hometown, and Cannes' dowdy neighbour, St-Juan-sur-Mer, was Bliss's domicile for a year while he laboriously wrote the manuscript that now sits, unread, on several publishers' slush piles. So he knows the Croisette's restaurants, the bars and glaceries that can stretch a visitor's plastic to the limit in a single bite. He has felt the deeply cushioned comfort of the Carlton and the Miramar, and he is well aware of the ritzy, air-conditioned clubs and casinos filled with Middle Eastern men who have thrown off their white robes in favour of silk suits as they play away from home in a Mecca of immorality, where easy women, hard drinks, and gaming chips come and go with a flick of a finger.

"Chief Inspector!" calls Commander Fox from outside, but Bliss has left the bustle of the waterfront in Cannes and is blithely floating across the serene cerulean bay to the infamous island of St. Marguerite, one-time home of the Man in the Iron Mask — the subject of his historical novel.

"Mr. Bliss!"

The ancient stone fortress that incarcerated the masked prisoner in isolation for eleven years guards the island from atop its rocky outcrop and looms above Bliss as his mind spins him back to the seventeenth century.

"Dave! Dave!" whispers the man on his right, but Bliss is walking the dusty parade ground where Louis XIV's feared Legionnaires once marched, towards the impenetrable cell block where the famous inmate was housed. Then he takes a sharp elbow in the ribs.

"Sorry, sir. It must be the heat," he says, giving his head a shake.

"The Home Secretary wants a report on his desk yesterday," says Fox above the guffaws of Bliss's colleagues. "You claim to be a writer — so write."

"I do fiction, sir."

"Precisely. And it'd better sound bloody convincing."

Blame is still being shunted around the table as Bliss takes a pen out of his briefcase, and he can't help smiling at the fact that officers who have collectively spent over five hundred years trying to nail violent offenders are now twisting their brains to let one off the hook.

The weather is still the most favourable suspect, but a close second is the suggestion that Prince Philip simply stumbled and fell after pulling out his sword to give it to his equerry, feeling it inappropriate to enter a mosque armed.

"Well, which do you want?" asks Bliss with his pen poised, and he can't help thinking it might be amusing to simply stroll out to the press corps who are baying at the gate and say, "Okay. The gig's up. The old fool caught us on the hop."

"Heatstroke," decides Commander Fox firmly, but the assistant commissioner sees a mine in the road.

"Hang on a minute, Roger. What if he suddenly pops his head out of the palace and says, 'I did it — the miserable old bat was getting on my nerves'?"

A superintendent from the Public Order Unit wonders aloud how the Queen will parse the incident in her annual Christmas address, and as the laughter subsides, a mimic pinches the bridge of his nose and takes on the Queen, saying, "In August of this year, my husband tried to put the wind up me …"

It is nearly seven o'clock by the time the meeting breaks up. Heatstroke wins the day, and Bliss's circumspectly worded report wins general approbation, although, as he walks home in the evening sunshine, he can't help but reflect that the penalty for attempting to pervert the course of justice is life imprisonment.

Daphne Lovelace is on the phone the moment he walks in the door.

"I thought you were going to see Daisy."

"So did I," he replies sourly, but his sex life is on neither his nor Daphne's agenda.

"I saw it on television," she carries on, without need of elucidation. "I couldn't believe my eyes."

"Heatstroke ..." starts Bliss, but Daphne has more faith in her eyes than that.

"David, I may be getting on a bit —"

"It was just a slip of the sword," he cuts in quickly. "Anyway, what possible reason could he have?"

"Henry VIII made a habit of it."

"True. But Philip's not exactly short of male heirs. Anyway, Henry didn't get his own hands bloody. He had enough sense to use the official executioner."

"I could do with one of those," snorts Daphne, although, under questioning, she admits that all is quiet on the western front. "I think they're away for the weekend," she adds, before returning to the errant Prince Philip. "They did say it was the heat on the news."

"Then that must be right," says Bliss, and a few minutes later he gets the same information from Daisy.

"I'm really sorry," he says after explaining the situation. She understands, she claims, but since the death of her grandmother the distance between them has grown. Spring was scented by millions of Provençal orange blossoms for the couple as he put the final touches to his historical novel, but now the tender fruits are withering in the summer's relentless sun.

"Just a few days — maybe a week," he says with his fingers crossed.

"But you will miss all zhe fireworks."

"I know," he replies.

"Perhaps zhen I should come back ..." starts Daisy, but she trails off as her mother calls. "I am sorry, Daavid," she says, "but I zhink she needs zhe toilette."

Bliss feels her slipping. "I'll call in the morning. I love

you." he says hurriedly, but she has gone. "Damn. Damn. Damn," he is still swearing as the phone buzzes again.

"Fox," barks the commander. "My office at eight tomorrow morning."

Bliss senses that someone has turned up the heat, and he drops the phone to switch on the television. The airwaves are buzzing with the news and repeatedly show the attack from every angle, but no one, it seems, is buying heatstroke. Pundits are pointing out the obvious: that, unless someone at the palace forgot the electricity bill, Their Royal Highnesses live in a perfumed world more closely controlled than an upscale tobacconist's humidor.

"Inherited insanity" is the word on the air, and there is no scarcity of regal examples to call upon. Mary Queen of Scots and Charles VI of France, both distant relatives of Philip, get a mention, as do many of his more recent kin, including his mother, several Georges — especially the second, who died when he fell off the royal loo at Kensington Palace, and the third, who was nutty enough to be certified — Prince John, various cousins, and even Edward VIII, who, it is suggested, must have been totally round the twist to ditch the crown for a doubly divorced Yankee gold digger.

Syphilis, porphyria, and alcohol take much of the blame for the procession of royals with psychoses, although inbreeding is certainly not excluded. Heatstroke is not even on the list, and the official line is stretched still thinner when a retired chauffeur augments his pension with tales of driving the couple around in an icebox, fiercely insisting to a reporter, "The Duke would never get in the car unless it were bloomin' freezin'."

By midnight, Bliss is struggling to sleep, while political commentators and royal watchers are being dragged off the beaches in Bali and out of bars in Melbourne to keep the discussion going. There is even suggestion that the

Lord Chancellor could return from his holiday home in the Seychelles. However, whilst his role in deposing a mentally incapacitated monarch is enshrined in law, there is apparently nothing on the books to deal with the lunacy of a monarch's spouse, beyond the commoners' Mental Health Act.

As the night wears on, the television editors run out of sensible ideas and turn to the ramblings of the Internet, where conspiracy theorists have nicknamed Prince Philip "Osama bin Windsor."

"The Duke of Edinburgh has been electronically implanted and is being remotely controlled by Islamic fundamentalists," claims one of loonier sites, retaliating for an earlier suggestion that Christian fundamentalists were responsible for the earthquakes and tsunamis that annihilated Muslim communities in Asia. (The Christians were quick to hit back, irrationally bolstering the Muslims' egos by accusing them of prayerfully invoking devastating droughts, hurricanes, and tornadoes in America.)

"Prince Philip — Victim of Heat?" queries the *Guardian* on Saturday's front page as Bliss blearily checks out the headlines on his way to the Yard, though less charitable rags lead more enigmatically, loudly asking, "DID HE?" or, more paradoxically, "DUBBED by the DUKE!"

Bottom-feeding paparazzi should be having lobster lunches today, but so many staffers snapped the royal visit that newsrooms are knee-deep in cuttings, and despite a flurry of passionate pleas from the Home Office and the palace, most editors have opted to show a puzzled woman cowering under her husband's sword.

Feminist organizations and abused women's groups are vitriolic in condemnation of Prince Philip, and more than one call for his immediate arrest.

"What happened to the government's zero-tolerance policy on spousal abuse?" demands a political correspondent in the *Times*.

Big Ben's clock is winding itself up to strike eight as Bliss arrives at New Scotland Yard. A few hardy pressmen have camped out on the footpath in the hope of scooping a quote from a dozy copper, but Bliss is sharp enough to keep his head down as he makes for a rear door.

"Peter Roberts, the assistant commissioner, is chairing the meeting," says Commander Roger Fox chattily as he leads Bliss to the almost deserted top floor, then he stops with his hand on a door and puts on a straight face. "Official Secrets Act, Dave," he says, and waits momentarily for the threat to sink in before opening the door.

"Ah. Chief Inspector. Good of you to come," starts Roberts, rising from the head of the table with a smarmy smile, and numerous sympathetic eyes turn silently on Bliss, leaving him wondering if he has been involuntarily volunteered for something nasty.

"Pleasure, sir," says Bliss guardedly as he scrutinizes the half-drunk coffees, the croissant crumbs, butter wrappers, orange peel, and apple cores, and the rolled sleeves and furrowed brows of six men and two women.

A moment's awkward silence is broken by the assistant commissioner as he quickly encompasses the room with a sweep of his hand. "Paulson, royal protection; Commander Fox — you already know; Mr. Michaels — Home Office; Mr. Simpson ..." Roberts hesitates, then changes tune. "Coffee, Chief Inspector?"

Bliss pours himself a cup as he scans the room and comes up with several familiar faces. The pinstriped pair who were not introduced at their previous meeting are still not being introduced, but they've lost their business suits and are looking more sheepish than smug.

"The Home Secretary is appointing an independent security expert, Chief Inspector," announces Roberts unenthusiastically as he pulls Bliss into the conversation. "But, pending his evaluation of the situation, your job is to protect the Queen."

"From her husband?"

"Chief Inspector," says Commander Fox, stepping in. "As difficult as this may seem, we have to divorce the two."

"That won't go down well with the Archbishop ..." starts Bliss, deliberately misconstruing, and Fox bites back.

"Be serious, Chief Inspector; divorce the woman from the Crown. Ignore the fact that she's just a grey-haired old biddy with a plum in her mouth. You are charged with defending the Queen from a very serious threat."

"That's impossible, sir," says Bliss as he sits, realizing that he's being handed a live grenade "He'd only need a table knife. We'd have to chop the blades off all his swords and blunt his razors. What if he smothers her with a feather pillow in the middle of the night? What am I supposed to do — take a sleeping bag and kip on the floor between them?"

"Chief Inspector," admonishes Roberts with an embarrassed eye on the pinstriped duo. "The palace is fully co-operating. Mr. Paulson and Mr. Simpson will make sure that he doesn't have access to weapons. Anyway, they've slept in separate rooms for years. Your job is to come up with strategies to ensure her safety in public."

"I still don't get it," complains Bliss. "This sounds like a job for a trick-cyclist with a straitjacket, especially if he's likely to try again."

One of the pinstripers comes to life, and Bliss hears an American Midwest accent. *They look like a couple of evangelical Bible-thumpers,* he thinks as he evaluates the shiny-shoed, short-haired, smooth-shaven college boys, and the one on the left pulls himself forward in his chair and focuses on Bliss. "Chief Inspector. I am authorized to advise you that the President is very concerned about the security of the royal family."

"And you are ..." starts Bliss, guessing CIA rather than Mormon, but Fox slaps him down.

"You don't need to know that, Chief Inspector."

Lefty holds up a hand. "No. Fair question, Commander," he says, though doesn't answer as he paints on a sickly smile and replies, "We are merely observers and advisors, Chief Inspector."

"Isn't that what you called your people in Vietnam?" snipes Bliss, and he is pleased to see several faces redden.

"Yes, Chief Inspector," snarls Lefty's running mate, rising heatedly. "And if we'd gotten support from certain other countries we would —"

"Gentlemen," steps in the assistant commissioner as he waves the man back to his chair. "Can we please deal with the issue at hand."

Lefty's partner is puce with rage and gets christened "Pimple" by Bliss, but he climbs down a few notches once he's paused for breath. "Chief Inspector," he says, as if he's dealing with an obdurate minion, "this is FYI only, but I can inform you that the President had good reason to suspect an attack on the Queen was imminent. He's concerned, as we all are, about the effect this could have on the security of the nation."

"Which president? What nation?" Bliss questions with deliberate obtuseness, and he is pleased to see Pimple's cheeks flush back up.

"The United States has a vested interest in global security, Chief Inspector," preaches Lefty, adding, "And the President has tasked us to take whatever steps necessary to guarantee freedom from terrorism wherever it may occur."

The idea of the CIA labelling the Duke of Edinburgh as a terrorist stings, but Bliss is still smarting from a previous encounter with America's Big Brother, so he forces a smile, saying, "Well that's jolly nice of your president," and then he mentally prepares for war.

Daphne Lovelace is also on the warpath. Her dreams of a quiet weekend were dashed when her neighbours roared home at the head of a motorcycle mob at 2:00 a.m. They were still partying when she was finally driven onto the streets around six. Missie Rouge has been astray for more than a week now, and, despite her protestations that the cat was snacked on by the pit bulls, she still combs the neighbourhood daily for several hours, morning and night, with a scraggy photo in hand.

"Have you seen my kitty?" She repeatedly questions neighbours and their children, but many of the strangers look upon her warily. Not long ago she could have named every resident and most of their offspring, but now she is a foreigner — not by nationality; by age. She is a lone passenger on a runaway bus after everyone else has bailed. Most of her long-time neighbours and friends got off at the cemetery, while a few still wait patiently in hospices and nursing homes for a passing hearse.

Daphne knows that one day soon there will be a bend in the road that's just too sharp, a wall too high, a ravine too deep, and sometimes, when she looks at all the empty seats surrounding her, she wishes that it would be today.

"I'm looking for my cat," she explains to the young couple who bought Hilda Marshall's place after the spry octogenarian fell off a camel at Moulton-Didsley's annual Cabbage Fair, but the young man shrugs her off as he herds a pack of fractious children into their minivan.

"She's called Missie Rouge."

"Sorry, luv," says the mother as she struggles to strap down a squirming, sleep-deprived four-year-old. "Try the RSPCA."

"She's ever so pretty," carries on Daphne determinedly with the photo in hand. "Sort of a reddish colour."

"'S'cuse me," says the woman, pushing past to grab a fleeing five-year-old.

"I've got a picture," she calls to the woman's back, then she gives up. "Thanks," she mutters as she meanders off down the street, wondering if she'll get lucky; wondering if today will be the day the wheels come off her bus.

The future is also uppermost in Bliss's mind as he ambles home alongside the ageless Thames and pictures himself as a grandfather. It's a happy picture: flying kites, riding bikes, hiking, camping, sailing, and swimming. Nothing like the memories of his own grandfather, he tries telling himself, with the image of a greying, wizened old man asleep in the chair in mind — then he makes the mistake of tallying the years.

"He was only just fifty," he mutters downheartedly, so he switches focus to his ex-wife and her husband, George, and wonders how they are coping with the news. *At least I won't be the one having sex with a grandmother*, he laughs to himself, although his mirth is short-lived with the realization that he won't be having sex with anyone at all if he doesn't do something about Daisy.

"I wonder what she'll be doing today?" he says as he stares into the murky river seeking Mediterranean blue, and then the sun comes out.

"Taxi!" he yells excitedly as he dodges the Embankment's speedy traffic, and seconds later he is on his way to France.

Why not? he asks himself repeatedly as he speeds homeward for a change of clothes. *The Queen is in hospital for the weekend, the Duke has been sent to a doghouse somewhere deep in the country beyond the telephoto lenses of the press, and I can cobble together a protection plan just as easily on a beach in Provençe. All I need is a return ticket for the first flight next week.*

"We'll get our act together at ten on Monday, Dave," Commander Fox instructed as the morning's meeting broke up. "We've got an appointment with the Home Office's man at eleven. Let's show him who the security experts are, shall we?"

The price of the last-minute seat to Nice leaves Bliss half-expecting champagne, but he's not entirely disappointed when all he gets is Evian water. A bottle of Bollinger with his name on it waits for him in an ice bucket at the Carlton Hotel in Cannes, and a table for two will be laid on the beach as soon as the sun has dropped into the Mediterranean. And, if Daisy's mother is able to pull herself together and put aside her fears, he and Daisy will take a second bottle of champagne to a room with a sea view and lie naked in each others' arms as fireworks burst triumphantly across the indigo sky.

chapter four

"We're just passing Paris on our starboard side," the crackly-voiced captain explains above the persistent background buzz on the intercom, leaving Bliss crossing his fingers over the rest of the plane's equipment as he looks down on the City of Lights.

"Hey, Mum, I wanna see the Eiffel Tower," sings out the squirmy six-year-old on Bliss's left, and a child's boney elbow digs into his groin as he follows the snake of the Seine across the urban landscape.

"Sorry, sir ... just excited," explains the young mother as she yanks her infant back into his seat, but this is third time, starting with the Channel and the White Cliffs of Dover. "It's his first trip," she carries on as she straps him firmly down. "You know what they're like ..."

Bliss grumbles "Kids" in agreement, but he sees the young boy's face crumple, and the start of a tear, and is momentarily spun into the future, where he quickly adds flying and patience to his grandfatherly responsibilities.

"Here — you have the window," he says with a smile, already unbuckling. But he pauses long enough to peer down at the French capital in time to make out the monstrous Notre Dame cathedral on the Île de la Cité.

It is a scorching afternoon, and Daphne, under the shade of a broad-rimmed sombrero, also has her sights on a French cathedral, Norman to be precise, built on the marshlands of Westchester in the late eleventh century by the ruddy-faced King William II — William Rufus — when Normandy and England were united against the rest of France.

"There has to be more to this than meets the eye," Daphne mutters in puzzlement as she weaves her way around and around the cathedral's medieval labyrinth seeking some kind of revelation. "It just doesn't make any bloomin' sense."

But life itself no longer makes much sense, and as she plants herself in the centre of the labyrinth and peers up at the cathedral's crucifix-topped spire, she is more certain than ever that she has been deceived. Despite her age, she still vividly recalls a time of childhood innocence when loving thy neighbour, turning the other cheek, and being nice to your snotty little brother would ensure a life of peace and happiness; a time filled with the syrupy mantras of rosy-faced Sunday school teachers and rosy-nosed village parsons who cherry-picked the Bible and dusted the carefully chosen fruit with their own particular sugary glaze. But as a twenty-year-old at the outbreak of war in 1939, the frosting was cracking and turning sickly as she watched newsreels of straight-faced chaplains blessing the deadly munitions while petitioning the Almighty to annihilate the enemy in His name.

I suppose it's a waste of time asking you to vaporize the Jenkinses, she thinks angrily as she stares skyward.

You'd rather take nice quiet people like Phil and Maggie, and Minnie and —

"Hello. Are you still looking?"

Daphne snaps herself back to earth and spins to find Angel Robinson on her shoulder.

"You won't find the answers you seek here, Daphne," continues the flowery woman with a psychic's conviction. "But I could lead the way for you."

The certainty of Angel's tone, and the strength of her gaze, root Daphne to the labyrinth's core, while one invisible hand brushes the hairs on the nape of her neck and another squeezes her chest.

"I ... I ... really should ... um ... should get going," stammers the uneasy woman as she tries to unglue her feet.

"You're not alone," continues Ms. Robinson with a soothing hand on Daphne's forearm. "You're surrounded by kind spirits."

"I'm sorry, but I really must go — lots to do," jabbers Daphne, breaking the gaze. "I don't mean to be rude, but I do have to get some food for my cat."

"Really?" the other woman questions with a raised eyebrow, and Daphne turns pink as she looks for a quick exit. But she is in the centre of a web, and the only way out is the narrow winding path that brought her in.

"Excuse me," says Daphne, fiercely pulling her sombrero over her eyes, but Angel's face says that she isn't moving.

"What are you afraid of, Daphne?"

"Afraid of something?" she says, and is equally torn between life and death as she looks for a way to escape. But it took her a long time to wind her way into the labyrinth, and Angel blocks her only means of retreat.

"We all have to die, Daphne," carries on Angel, reading the old woman's mind — every old woman's mind. "It's just a transition to the next world — a better world. It's like taking the bus to Bournemouth."

"I never liked Bournemouth much," snorts Daphne, lifting her hat and standing her ground. "Full of snobby old fogeys and toffee-nosed twits. So, if that's what heaven's like, I'd rather pass, thank you very much."

"I'm not talking about heaven —" starts Angel, but Daphne has heard enough, and she clamps down her hat and barges forward.

"Sorry. Must go."

"I'd really like to be your friend," claims Angel as she is swept aside.

"I've got lots of friends, thanks," calls Daphne over her shoulder, and in desperation she short-circuits the labyrinth by crashing through the invisible barriers segregating each loop of the path, while moaning, "Fat lot of good this bloomin' thing is. I'd get more answers from a phone book."

But Angel's parting words bite as Daphne takes the bus into the town centre and fails to recognize any of the thirty or so other passengers.

"I do have lots of friends," she angrily insists to herself, although it is unfortunate that both the cemetery and the crematorium lie on the same route. And she sinks further when she passes the seniors' nursing home where her neighbour, Maggie Morgan, died.

"I've still got Mavis," she tries consolingly, but inwardly she admits that since the younger woman discovered the sexual side of the Internet she has become completely undependable.

"You should give it a try," Mavis enthused when Daphne complained of being dumped from a Paul McCartney concert in favour of Gerald Swain, a wig-wearing geriatric who called himself Buzz online and claimed to be a retired rock star living in Clapham under an assumed name. "You can meet some really interesting fellas."

"I don't —" Daphne started, but Mavis was on a roll.

"You really should make more of an effort to keep up with modern technology, Daphne," she insisted, determinedly shaking the older woman by the shoulders and peering intently into her eyes. "It ages you terribly if you don't."

"Modern technology," Daphne echoed thoughtfully, as if seriously contemplating the notion of dragging herself out of the Dark Ages, but then she scratched her temple and put on a bemused look. "That's funny, Mavis," she said, "and I may be entirely wrong, but didn't they invent the telephone so that people wouldn't have to waste endless time typing letters and waiting for a reply?"

"Well, I suppose —"

"And didn't they reckon that computers would do everything by the turn of the century so no one would ever have to work?"

"Yes — all right. You made your point."

Trina Button is someone else who is still wedded to the phone, although in Trina's case, "welded" would be more appropriate. Trina is perhaps Daphne's most reliable, but also unlikeliest, friend. The zippy Vancouver homecare nurse with streaky blonde hair and a fire-breathing dragon tattooed on her bum is, in so many ways, worlds away from the aging Westchester spinster. She is in her early forties, with a long-suffering husband, two teenagers, and a guinea pig, and she is so attached to her cellphone that she anxiously awaits the day she can have one implanted.

"C'mon, Daphne, pick up," she is muttering into her hands-free microphone as she scoots across the Lions Gate Bridge into the centre of Vancouver. It is barely seven o'clock on the Pacific coast of Canada. Saturday. Schools aren't in, offices are closed, and the city's roads are almost deserted. A native bear, cougar, or elk could safely cross today, but it's many decades since anything larger than a racoon or an escaped domestic goat has dared Vancouver's traffic. Survivors long ago retreated from the smoggy jungle of concrete and glass to the surrounding mountains, followed by many of the tourists, while others have sought solitude on one of the numerous forested islands that dot the coast.

Trina's Volkswagen Jetta is on autopilot as she gives up on her English friend, balances a pad on her knee, takes a swig of coffee and a bite of muffin, and phones her dispatch office.

"I lost old Mr. Darnley yesterday," she admits as she asks for a new assignment.

"I'm not surprised," says Margaret.

"I was," bitches Trina. "First visit — ten minutes. I just pulled down his underpants and stuck him on the loo and *plop* he was gone. He didn't even touch the stewed banana I did for his lunch."

"Stewed banana?" queries the dispatcher.

"With bacon," stresses Trina, sensing her culinary arts are being challenged.

"Oh, well. At least you didn't get personally involved this time," says Margaret cheerily, recalling occasions when Trina's heart burned at the iniquities of life and she turfed her own children out of bed in favour of some broken-down geriatric. But Trina's patients are often nearing the end of the road. It is an unspoken rule amongst the dispatchers. Not because of Trina's great nursing skills or exemplary compassion, but because, at that stage of their life, the medical professionals have already inflicted the bulk of the damage. "Sorry, Trina," adds Margaret after checking the schedule. "Everyone's been taken care of today."

"Her Majesty, Queen Elizabeth II, will remain in the care of …" the BBC newscaster is saying as Bliss watches the satellite television on the back of the aisle seat in front of him, but the picture dies as the captain announces their imminent arrival in Nice.

The Mediterranean's Bay of Angels, in the shadow of the snow-capped Maritime Alps, is flecked with sails of every size and hue as the plane swoops low to land. Close to shore, the sweeping bay is an artist's palette of turquoise, aquamarine, and sapphire, but as the water deepens towards the horizon, the colours slowly meld into a vibrant azure that fuses perfectly with the sky. It is David Bliss's favourite sight in the entire world, which today is being enjoyed by a Machiavellian six-year-old who is well on his way to a career as a con man.

"Look at that, Mum ... Look at that, Mum ..." he shouts excitedly time and again as he thumps against the window, while all Bliss can do is turn his watch one hour ahead and wait for the bump as the sea gives way to asphalt.

Daisy will be so surprised, he tells himself with a grin as he walks from the terminal to a line of cabs and then is hit by the aromas of the Niçoise August. The fragrances of jasmine, orange blossom, and hibiscus, so reminiscent of Mediterranean springtime, have been zapped by the heat and replaced by the stink of car exhausts and the stench of sewers in the city's languid summer air.

"St-Juan-sur-Mer," he calls to the driver as he leaps in and slams the door against the putrid fumes, then he tries to back out as he spots the cigarette in the driver's hand.

"Monsieur?" yells the driver with his foot already on the floor, and Bliss coughs accusingly.

"Le cigarette."

"*Bof!*" spits the driver with a shrug and winds down his window as he drives off.

Bliss sits back in resignation as the hot, smoky stench blasts into his face. Tonight will be different. Tonight he will bask in the moonlight on the Carlton Hotel's private beach in Cannes. He will breathe the ozone-fresh Mediterranean air, scented only by Daisy and her bouquet of roses, and together they will dine on foie gras, oysters fin clair with a dash of Tabasco and a squirt of local lemon juice, and

Côtelettes à la Provençale. They will sip mimosas made with Bollinger champagne and swim in a pink rhapsody of seductive words set to the gentle swish of wavelets on the golden sand. And afterwards — there will be fireworks.

While a smiling Bliss heads for St-Juan-sur-Mer with little more than his birthday suit and a pair of swimming trunks in a carry-on bag, Daphne Lovelace rounds the corner from Sheep Street with a nice cup of tea and a slice of Victoria sponge on her mind. Then her heart sinks and her inner voice yells, "Run." Half a dozen motorbikes are her-ringboned against the curb outside her neighbour's house, and a tattooed mob litters the sidewalk. She has options: she could take to the roadway; she could have tea at the Mitre or with Mavis; she could even walk around the block and cut through the copse to approach from the other end of her street.

"I'm buggered if I will," she mutters determinedly, and for the second time in a day she sets her sombrero to "attack."

"Hello, Daph, me old duck," shouts Bob Jenkins as he dangles his legs from the windowsill of what was once the Morgans' front parlour. "How'r'ya doin?"

Daphne cringes and fights the temptation to tell him to get down, that Phil and Maggie will be furious. "Nice motorbikes," she says, swallowing hard and painting on a smile as she keeps walking, but she is carefully measuring her pace, choosing her moment. One "accidental" nudge and the whole lot will topple like dominoes.

"Fancy a spin?" laughs Jenkins, stubbing out his ciga-rette and slipping off the windowsill in her direction.

There was a time in her youth when a high-speed chase on a Norton or an Indian would have seemed as tame as the parish church's annual bicycle picnic: twenty-five giggly teenagers on wide-tired Raleighs, girls riding behind the boys to avoid unseemly sniggers and smutty comments. No skirts short enough to show knees, no make-up, no visible bra straps, and definitely no trousers — all, according to the vicar at the consecration service, "As the Lord God has ordained in the Bible." Girls' underpants were also a matter of interest, but not to the vicar. Mrs. Cloverdale, the organist, was responsible for knickers, discreetly warning of God's disapproval of anything fancy, frilly, flimsy, or likely to cause unnecessary excitement during the ride. On the other hand, some of the boys' underpants were, it was strongly rumoured, of very great interest to the vicar.

"Don't take any notice of 'im," says Misty Jenkins as she emerges from the house with a case of beer. "He's pullin' yer leg."

"No I ain't —" starts her husband, but she stops him with a scowl and turns to Daphne.

"We're off to the beach in Bournemuff for a bit of a rave, luv. Give ya a bit of peace for a few hours. Though we had to leave the dogs out — they'd rip the friggin' place to shreds without us — just yell at 'em if they get on yer nerves."

"I'll probably shoot them," snarls Daphne under her breath, but Jenkins reads her lips and his face instantly darkens.

"Touch my dogs an' I'll beat the fuckin' —"

"Rob!" screeches Misty. "Leave the old biddy alone. She ain't worth it."

"Well —"

"I said leave it." And then she turns to Daphne with half a smile. "Sorry, luv. He can be a bit touchy at times."

David Bliss is also experiencing touchiness at Daisy's home in St-Juan-sur-Mer.

"Ah, Madame LeBlanc, *bonjour*," he trills, with a supermarket bouquet and an exaggerated bow. But his fiancée's mother recoils and tries to shut the door.

"Madame," he calls confusedly, but the door is still closing.

"Madame," he repeats, and sticks out a foot. The door stops, but Geneviève Leblanc uses it as a shield while she eyes him as if deciding between the Grim Reaper or a door-to-door Bible puncher.

"Daisy wasn't expecting me," Bliss carries on chattily in French as he thrusts the flowers forward, hoping to warm the woman.

"*C'est évidente, monsieur,*" she replies, shrugging off the flowers.

"*Monsieur?*" queries Bliss. What is this "monsieur"? "It is David — remember?" he says while trying to hold her gaze.

"Daavid?" she questions vaguely with a heavy accent, and he is appalled at the apparent deterioration of the woman in the few months since her mother's death. Not only has she forgotten his name, she doesn't know where Daisy is, when she will be back, or whom she is with.

"I could try her friends," suggests Bliss with a disarming smile, but Geneviève is still hiding and merely shrugs when it comes to names, addresses, and telephone numbers.

"I'll just come in and wait then …" he starts and makes a move, but she stands firm and he backs down. "She's probably shopping — Cannes, I expect," he prattles on, still smiling, thinking, *It'll give me time to get a room at the Carlton and pick up a bouquet of roses.* "I'll come back at seven. Tell Daisy I'm taking her somewhere really special tonight."

Geneviève Leblanc's silence tells a story, but Bliss isn't listening as the door slowly closes and the lock clinks into place.

The spare front door key to Phil and Maggie Morgan's old home has been calling Daphne ever since the Jenkins tribe blasted off to the beach.

"They would've changed the locks," she assures herself for the *n*th time as she is drawn back to her hallway by the dull brass key hanging on the mahogany umbrella stand.

"For emergencies," Phil said as he handed it to her nearly twenty years ago, when he and Maggie, in their early sixties, made their last serious effort to explore the world. But the travel agent's "Romantic Getaway Weekend of a Lifetime" turned into three days of hell in a frigid back street mausoleum at the end of November in Clacton-on-Sea, from which they never really recovered.

"This is an emergency," Daphne finally convinces herself as she takes down the key and plops on the deerstalker hat that she bought, half-seriously, to mark the founding of an international investigation agency with Trina Button following a misadventure in the foothills of Washington's Cascade Mountains. Then she puts on a sad mien and apes to the umbrella stand's mirror. "It's quite possible that Missie Rouge, my poor little pussy, snuck in to visit Phil, not realizing that he has died, and has become trapped."

She isn't convinced, so she tries it again with a tattered black beret, a smudge of mascara under each eye, and the hint of a tear. "Better," she decides, but there is still something missing. And then she seizes on Missie Rouge's rhinestone-studded collar — Christmas, Easter, and the Queen's official birthday only — and rushes to the kitchen to open her last can of Kat-O-Meat.

"N-n-nice … doggies," she stutters two minutes later as she cowers in her own back garden while the dogs trampoline off the wire fence in front of her. "Here you are then," she shouts, tossing the fish-caked collar over the top. The collar is shredded in seconds, scattering jewels and hardware across the garden. Then the pit bulls start on each other for the scraps.

"I wish I'd chucked in a handful of razor blades now," she mutters as she heads to the Jenkinses' front door, then, as she fishes the key from her pinafore pocket, she puts a crack into her voice as she polishes her defence. "See for yourself — my little kitty's collar is all over the garden. She must be here somewhere."

With the hotel booked, champagne on ice, and roses bought, Bliss has an hour to kill. *She has to be here somewhere*, he constantly reminds himself as he sneaks around the swanky shops of the Rue d'Antibes in Cannes, hoping to leap out of the shadows to surprise her. But ten look-alikes have him running in circles, so he takes to a sidewalk café, orders Evian water, and hopes that the tide will eventually turn in his direction.

There is no way Daphne's key will fit — but it does, and the blood pulsing through her temples makes her pause for a deep breath.

"It definitely isn't going to turn," she bets herself, but her hands shake and her knees wobble when it does.

Now what?

"There's no harm in just looking around; see what they've done to the place," she tells herself, her thoughts full of nostalgia as nearly four decades flash through her mind, and the door slowly opens on a smiling middle-aged couple with Micky, their docile golden Labrador, at their feet.

"Let me show you around," Maggie said as she invited her new neighbour to view her agglomeration of furnishings — lovingly polished family treasures, much like Daphne's own, that would give a Southeby's evaluator the giggles; knick-knacks and bric-a-brac that wouldn't raise an eyebrow at the weekly auction in the basement of the Corn Exchange; familiar old masters "painted" on cheap cardboard; and a collection of porcelain figurines. "Wedgwood, Meisson, and Royal Doulton," Maggie declaimed, circumnavigating the room with her pointing finger, adding smugly, "They're very valuable."

But the *Antiques Road Show* snitched on her eventually.

"Could I have a little sugar, please," Daphne asked innocuously on one rare occasion when she was invited into the front parlour for tea, but she had mischief on her mind and a magnifying glass in her purse.

"I thought you were sweet enough already," quipped Maggie on her way to the kitchen.

"Oh, no. Not really," replied Daphne with a Martha Stewart smile, and she had one of the porcelain dogs upside down in a flash.

"It is real you know," insisted Maggie fiercely as she quickly popped her head back into the parlour.

"Oh! You startled me," said Daphne, but she recovered quickly. "I can see that," she said, pointing to the inscribed "Staffordshire" on the base, while knowing very well that, according to the TV expert, it had been stamped by a Chinese knock-off merchant in the early nineteen-hundreds.

Maggie Morgan's carpeted front parlour was not unlike Missy Rouge's bejewelled collar: generally reserved for glittering occasions like Christmas, weddings, Easter, and special events, but never humdrum anniversaries like birthdays. A funeral might qualify, but only if the vicar was in attendance, and then only under Maggie's strict supervision. Slippers, no pipes or cigars, nothing messy — cucumber and salmon sandwiches at a pinch, but never flaky mince pies or anything with jam or cream.

"I simply can't abide messy eaters," Maggie would loftily proclaim, and everyone would sheepishly edge forward on their seats and take a firm grip on their false teeth, while she paraded around like a schoolmarm with a little silver-plated dustpan and brush behind her back.

"I wonder what happened to all her china," Daphne is musing aloud as she finally sidles into the front hallway, then she stops in horror at a scene reminiscent of Basra or Baghdad after a visit from a stroppy bunch of U.S. Marines.

"Oh my God," she breathes and feels her blood draining at the junkyard jumble of scrapped motorbikes and dog-eaten furniture — Maggie's furniture and Maggie's prized figurines with dismembered ears, arms, and legs — set up like a fairground shooting gallery by a catapult-crazy fifteen-year-old. The kitchen, dining room, and parlour look much the same, with grease-spattered floors and walls, ripped curtains, and trashed furniture. Only the eye-popping plasma television and ear-rending stereo system rise above the chaos.

Daphne has suffered war at close quarters — parachuting into Normandy in advance of D-Day and fighting her way through enemy lines to Paris. She retched at the sight of Frenchmen's houses razed to rubble, their women and children, along with their precious belongings, pulverized into a sickening, fly-ridden morass of twisted bodies. She cried at the hurriedly dug graves of compatriots and foes, and she hid in shame for the role she played. But that was in a lifetime she left behind, until now, when the devastation inside her old friend's house shocks her back to the horrors of war, and she snaps.

"Let's see how you like it," she hollers and picks up a crowbar.

Daphne Lovelace, the aging war veteran, is deafened by her fury, and the sound of a key turning in the front door doesn't register as she blindly takes revenge on behalf of a dying generation whose sacrifices no longer engender respect.

The sun is sinking into the Mediterranean, along with Bliss's dreams, as he paces outside Daisy's front door. And then his cellphone rings.

Daisy, he thinks, but it's an English number that he doesn't recognize.

"Westchester Police Station, Anne McGregor," says the superintendent. "I'm sorry to bother you on the weekend, Chief Inspector, but we are trying to trace the next of kin of a Miss Ophelia Lovelace of 27 ..."

"Ophelia?" he says vaguely as the voice continues, then his brain kicks in. What did Daphne say about *Hamlet*'s Ophelia when he first knew her? "Who would want to be named after a silly nincompoop who committed suicide because she thought her man didn't love her?"

"Are you still there, Chief Inspector?" queries Ms. McGregor.

"Oh, dear. I was expecting something like this," says Bliss, his voice sinking. "What was it — heart attack, stroke?"

"No. Nothing like that."

"Accident?"

"No. She's all right. It's just that she's in custody and we need a family member to take care of her because of her age and mental state."

"They've got the wrong man, David," yells Daphne in the background as she makes a grab for the phone. "I told you this lot couldn't find a turd in a toilet."

"In custody?"

"Be quiet, Ms. Lovelace," says McGregor, gently pushing Daphne away, but the commando inside the elderly woman escapes and she leaps forward with a kung-fu yelp and chops the phone from the officer's hand.

"Shit!" shouts McGregor as the handset hits her office floor, but as she stoops to retrieve it Daphne sends her flying with a hard shove.

"Daphne ... Is that you?" Bliss is querying as the superintendent drags herself across the floor on her knees towards the phone, but Daphne beats her to it, scrabbles under the desk, and curls herself around it.

"Get out of there," orders McGregor as she grabs a leg and pulls.

"They're beating me up, David. Call the press," yells Daphne into the phone as she tries to kick off her attacker. "Police brutality."

"Give me the phone," demands McGregor, but Daphne is on a roll.

"Hundred-year-old woman attacked by a —"

"Daphne, you're not a hundred ..." Bliss is saying as the superintendent manages to get a grip on the handset.

"Give it to me," she orders as she tussles over the instrument, but her hand is in front of Daphne's face and the old soldier still has a good set of teeth.

"Bitch!" screeches the superintendent as she whips her hand away. "I'll bloody do you for that."

"She's threatening me now, David. Police intimidation."

"What on earth's going on?" tries Bliss, but Anne McGregor has had enough. Pulling herself upright she tries to re-establish dignity.

"All right, Ms. Lovelace. One last time," she says. "Give me the bloody phone."

"She's swearing at me now, David. Call the police. I want to lay charges."

"Daphne —" starts Bliss, but Anne McGregor has finally snapped and she rips the phone line out of the socket.

"Oh," complains Daphne testily as she slides from under the desk. "That wasn't very sporting of you."

chapter five

It is 9:15 p.m. in Cannes, and the palm-fringed promenade is already teeming. David Bliss sits apart from the bustle, on the Carlton Hotel's grandiose terrace bar, and considers dragging a complete stranger from the crowd with the promise of a no-strings feast. *I've bloody paid enough for it*, he tells himself, *someone might as well eat it. But who?*

It takes him only a few minutes to scan the nightly parade of buff-bodied, pinch-bummed young men, pinch-faced old dames, and near-naked nymphets to realize that he is in the middle of a minefield. Adding up the potential cost, he concludes that it will be much cheaper to swallow the price of the meal. In any case, Daisy will come, he convinces himself. But he's left so many messages on her answering machine that he's drained his cellphone and he'll be out of reach once he leaves the hotel.

He tried Daisy's door a dozen times between seven and nine, and at first the faint shadow of her mother fell across the curtains. But following his second visit, the tight steel shutters came down and the ghostly figure evaporated.

He stretched his reservation at the Carlton's beachside restaurant until time ran out. "Zhe final sitting is nine-thirty and zhere are no refunds," the maître d'hotel haughtily insisted when he booked and paid. "Zhis evening is special for zhe fireworks only."

"Please follow me, Monsieur," says the portly head waiter as Bliss finally gives in. The penguin-like man in his tailed morning coat waddles across the beach, weaving his way through candlelit tables of picnickers who are slumming it on Beluga caviar, truffled trifles, and lobsters while they swig Cristal champagne at five hundred a bottle.

"Five hundred what?" any ordinary person might ask, but not the Carlton's lofty guests, most of whom will shrug off five hundred as easily as five thousand or even five million.

Bliss's table for two, as requested, is at the water's edge, with an unobstructed view of the island of Ste. Marguerite and, when the time comes, a grandstand seat at the waterborne fireworks display. But now, as he sits alone staring at his bouquet of roses, he has an army of diners looking through him as they studiously survey the armada of mega-yachts manoeuvring into position for the show. Size matters in this bastion of the mega-rich. Reputations rise and fall by the metre.

"He's only got a pokey thirty-metre job," the owner of a fifty-metre cruiser will sneer. Then a hundred-and-fifty-metre leviathan carrying a chopper and a mini-sub steams majestically into the bay and they all squirm.

Bliss has neither a yacht nor yacht envy. But he does envy the other diners — fashionable newlyweds, elegant mature couples, and flashy short-term cheaters — who can, at least, reach across the table and find reassurance in the kiss of skin on skin. As he sits alone on the very fringe of the sand, he feels like King Canute urging the tide to turn in his favour. "C'mon, Daisy. Where are you?"

The lobster and oysters may be superb, but fish, chips, and mushy peas in newspaper might be more comforting, and as he eats he feels the pitying stares of the other guests and almost expects someone to sidle up and say, "Hello, granddad. All on your own, are ya?"

"It's not what you think," he wants to say. "She's just a bit late, that's all." But as ten o'clock approaches and the three gargantuan barges anchored in the bay prepare to launch their exuberant cargo high into the sky, he slips out of his front-row seat and slogs his way up the soft sand beach to the exit.

"*Bienvenue mesdames et messieurs ...*" the commentator is calling enthusiastically as she welcomes visitors to the Cannes international fireworks festival, but Bliss keeps his eyes on the ground and makes for the hotel lobby with Daisy's bouquet of roses in hand.

"Messages?" he asks hopefully, not bothering with French, but the concierge shakes his head.

"*Pardon, monsieur. Mais non.*"

"I'll be in my room," he says as he heads for the elevator.

Daphne Lovelace should be in the cell block, but the Custody Officer hadn't the heart — "She is eighty-five for gawd's sake." So he has put her in the medical room, complete with a comfortable examination couch and an unmonitored telephone marked, "Strictly For Doctor's Use Only."

David Bliss is first on her list, followed by his daughter, Samantha. Neither answers, so she tries Trina Button in Canada. It may be midnight in Westchester, but in far-off Vancouver the slanting rays of the sun glint golden on the windows of waterfront condominiums and turn the distant snow-capped peaks into a glittering coronet.

"I tried calling you," yells Trina as she zips in and out of the afternoon traffic in her Jetta, but Daphne shushes her then puts her in the picture.

"Great — good for you. That'll teach 'em," cries Trina, but she's only been listening to the best bits. Her mind is on her mother, a woman of similar age to Daphne who acts at least twenty years older. "I'm thinking of putting her into a home," she explains as her mother sits alongside with a pair of headphones clamped to her ears and a sublime expression on her face. "She keeps stealing things, and she doesn't know what she's doing or saying half the time," carries on Trina. Then she lifts one of the headphones and yells, "It's Daphne," above the din of the Smash.

Winifred Goodenow's face clouds instantly, but rapture returns with the headphone. She is deaf to the conversation but would argue vociferously if she knew what her daughter was saying. In her own mind she is coherent, veracious, and very fit. "I'm in training for the El Camino trail," she tells everyone she meets, but she's spent a lifetime on pointed stilettos and can hardly hobble to the end of the street.

"Gotta go," babbles Trina as she slams her foot to the floor to beat a light. "I'm taking mum to the chiropodist, then I'm going to yoga. I'll call you."

"All right," whispers Daphne. "Just don't make a fuss and don't come rushing over. But I might need you to bail me out later on."

"Roger wilco," trills Trina, still unaware of her friend's plight. "Just give me a shout. Trina Button, international investigator, to the rescue."

However, Daphne shouldn't need help. "Lock the old cow in solitary for a few hours to teach her a lesson," Anne McGregor instructed as she left for the day, "then give her bail."

But it's only half a dozen years since Daphne swept the halls, cleaned the toilets, and made the tea, and she still has friends.

"Hello, Daph. How'r'ya doin'?" inquires one officer after another as they pop by to show concern. And, each time, Daphne puts on a brave smile that fades as soon as the door closes.

And then Sergeant Martin Paulson, the Custody Officer, returns with the news that she is free to leave.

"No thanks," says Daphne, turning her head against the wall and burying her face in the pillow.

"I'm not asking you, Ms. Lovelace," says Paulson, putting on his policeman's voice. "I'm telling you. I'm granting you bail in your own recognizance ..." Then he pauses. "What do you mean, no thanks?"

"I don't want to go home," starts Daphne, and she sniffles loudly into the pillow as she holds back the tears. "I never want to go home again. I have nothing to go home for.... All I had was Missie Rouge. I just want somewhere quiet where I can die in peace. A cell will do fine."

Paulson laughs. "As much as I'd like to accommodate you, I can't. We're full up. Anyway, our cells are only for real villains and persistent offenders."

"Okay," says Daphne, rising in apparent resignation, then abruptly turning, picking up a heavy glass jug, and throwing it through the window. "There," she says defiantly as Paulson stares in disbelief at the shattered glass. "Can you keep me in now?"

The stupefied officer hesitates, but Daphne already has her hand on a stainless steel bedpan and her eye on another window.

"I'll charge you with criminal damage," he cautions with a warning finger.

"Naturally," says Daphne with glee as she brings back her arm.

"What are you — crazy?" he asks, catching hold of the bedpan.

A crazy old lady, muses Daphne thoughtfully to herself. *Maybe that's exactly what I should be*. "All right," she concedes as she slowly relinquishes her hold on the bedpan. "I'll take bail."

"Heat-related disturbances spread across the country for the third weekend in a row ..." the breakfast-time television presenter is saying as Anne McGregor fries bacon for herself and her husband, Richard, in the pseudo-rustic kitchen of their swankily spruced-up thatched hovel in Moulton-Didsley.

"Not again," groans Anne, as global warming is blamed for riots in Glasgow and Birmingham and outbreaks of violence nationwide. "But thank God it's not religion this time."

Torched cars, firebombed public buildings, and attacks on innocent bystanders all get reported. "While, around the world," continues the presenter, taking a wider view to dissipate blame, "super-hurricanes and super-typhoons are in danger of spiralling off the Saffir-Simpson scale, tornadoes are repeatedly topping F5, and storm-driven tsunamis lash low-lying coasts."

"I bet that was the problem with the old crumbly who took a fancy to your finger last night," laughs Richard, pouring himself a coffee and picking up the *Guardian*.

"For gawd's sake don't suggest that," says Anne. "I can just see the crafty old crone now — standing in the dock, saying, 'It were the heat, M'lord ...'"

The buzz of the phone stops her. It is Ted Donaldson, the man whose expansive backside warmed her chair for fifteen years. "Lunch at the Mitre?" he inquires.

"Sure, why not," she says, and doesn't bother to ask the occasion.

"The silly old bat thinks she can pull strings to get off," says McGregor as she puts down the phone and aggressively flips the bacon.

"Well, I bet that'll work for old Phil," says Richard, pointing to the headline: "Archbishop to Counsel Prince." Then he mocks the Duke as he whines, "I do have friends in very high places you know."

Daphne isn't pulling strings. She is being rousted off a wooden bench in the railway station's deserted waiting room by a uniformed ticket inspector. She has been there since six o'clock, following several hours aimlessly wandering the dark streets calling out for Missie Rouge and a stop for a tea and a pee in a transport café off the main London road from which she called Ted Donaldson.

"C'mon, luv. This place ain't for sleepin'," says the uniformed man as he holds open the door. "You need a ticket to be in here."

I could always take the Paradise Express like Minnie, Daphne tells herself dreamily, but she considered that several times during the night as she stood on the platform while speeding trains whistled past. "At least it would be quick," she soliloquized, but images of her friend's body splattered across the cab of a hundred-mile-an-hour locomotive kept her back from the edge.

"What's the time?" she inquires wearily as she puts on her shoes and plops her moth-eaten beret over her dishevelled mop, but the inspector isn't listening.

"Where's your stuff?" he demands, scouting around the room for a supermarket buggy or an old pram.

"Stuff?" she muses. "What stuff? I don't have any stuff."

"Stuff," he repeats. "C'mon, luv. Don't piss me about. Just take all your bloody junk with you or I'll call the fuzz."

"It doesn't matter anymore," she says as she shuffles out. "Nothing matters anymore."

It is Sunday morning. Early worshippers seeking Communion scurry past the labyrinth on their way to the cathedral as Daphne seeks spiritual guidance in its looping pathway. "I'm definitely missing something," she tells herself as she winds around and around, and she would telephone

Angel but she's left the woman's card at home and is fearful of returning in case the Jenkinses are waiting for her.

"I knew you were up to somethin' you old bat," Rob Jenkins spat nastily into her face as he roughly disarmed her the previous afternoon, adding viciously, "I'm gonna fuckin' screw you for this." However, he sweetened his tone for the young constable who raced to the scene, siren screaming, at the report of a lunatic going berserk with a crowbar.

"Misty, my wife, worried she'd left the iron on," he claimed as their reason for returning. But Daphne, still boiling, was in full flight as she was led to the police car while the street looked on. "Ask her where her bloomin' ironing board is," she ranted. "I bet she's never ironed a bloody shirt in her life. Look at the place. She wouldn't know an iron from the hole in her bum."

The question of Misty Jenkins's domestic prowess was never tested. Daphne Lovelace, O.B.E., had been nabbed red-handed, and for all the constable cared, the Jenkinses could have curtailed their daytrip to Bournemouth for a game of tiddlywinks or a full-blown sex orgy.

"I knew you'd be here," a voice says softly in Daphne's ear, and she spins to find Angel. "I heard you calling. I knew you needed help."

"Really," says Daphne sarcastically. "If you know that much, how come you never tell me what I'm supposed to get from this damn thing."

"Answers —" she starts, but Daphne cuts her off.

"All I get is sore bloomin' feet. Anyway, you said I wouldn't find answers here."

"Okay. So what happened the first time?"

"Well, I invited the Jenkinses for tea, but that was a disaster. All they did was brag about being a ruddy nuisance."

"But you gave conciliation a try, so it wasn't a complete waste of time. And what happened the next time?"

"I met you. And I met you again the next time."

"I remember," laughs Angel. "You rammed your hat down over your eyes and nearly mowed me down. Did you learn anything?"

A lightbulb goes off in Daphne's mind, and she brightens. "Yes. I did. When the Jenkins crowd blocked my way home and I was ready to turn around, I thought, *I'm buggered if I will*, and I did the same thing I did to you."

"So, you learnt that it was up to you to fight your way through," insists Angel, but Daphne isn't convinced. She's been fighting most of her life — fighting for independence, fighting for her life, fighting the Nazis and the Communists, and, since she teamed up with Trina Button as part of a crazy crusading duo, fighting drug smugglers from Vancouver and the CIA in Washington State.

"I don't know about that —" starts Daphne, but Angel is in teaching mode.

"You already have all the answers deep inside, Daphne," she lectures, undeterred, as she takes Daphne's hand and lays it across the elderly woman's breast. "A labyrinth is a metaphor for life itself. You enter in ignorance, then, in its twists and turns, you learn what you need to know. The path takes you in all directions — north, south, east, and west — but it always leads you to the centre ... your centre ... your core, where you find tranquility and equilibrium. Then, as you weave back out, you pick up solutions along the way and emerge rejuvenated and ready to begin life anew. All the labyrinth can do is lead you on your path of self-awareness and enable you to find the right direction."

"It still sounds like mumbo-jumbo," scoffs Daphne, but Angel gives her hand a supportive squeeze, saying, "You'll find your way, Daphne. Just have faith."

Bliss is lost as he loiters outside the bar L'Escale, on the quayside of the ancient fishing port of St-Juan-sur-Mer, waiting to get a coffee. He has run out of leads and ideas in his search for his fiancée. The shutters were still down and the doorbell rang hollowly when he made an early-morning call, so he pushed a note through the letterbox and left the roses on the step.

It is Sunday morning in Provence, the fourteenth-century heart of popish power. Most of the locals are on their knees, while many of the heathen northern tourists are still on their backs, cursing the quality of the wine rather than the quantity. Angeline, the bar's normally bouncy waitress, had a late night as Saturday's new arrivals tested their legs against the local plonk, and she looks out blearily as she opens the blinds. Then she wakes up.

"Ah, Monsieur Bliss," she gushes, rushing out to throw her arms around him. "Zhe famous detective who writes zhe novel." Then she stops to look around. "But where is Daisy?"

"I don't know," he admits, pointing to his fiancée's shuttered real estate agency a few doors away. "I wondered if you've seen her."

"On Friday, *oui*. She was excited about zhe weekend. She was going away …" Angeline pauses and deflates. "Oh," she says, turning red under her Mediterranean tan. "Maybe I will get you zhe coffee, *non*."

"Yes … no … maybe … " he vacillates, then leans on her to let him use the bar's phone to call his daughter.

"We went waterskiing yesterday," Samantha bubbles as she picks up, but Bliss is unenthusiastic.

"Be careful," he warns. "Just remember you're carrying the future of the Bliss dynasty."

"Okay, granddad —" she starts, but he cuts her off.

"Daisy hasn't phoned has she?"

"Daphne was trying to get hold of you last night. She left messages, but I haven't been able —"

"Daphne …" he murmurs, cutting quickly in as a memory comes back. "Damn. I'd forgotten all about her. Apparently she got collared for something — shoplifting, probably, that's the favourite with little old ladies. Give her a call if you've got a minute; she probably needs a lawyer."

"Okay."

"But you haven't heard anything from Daisy?"

She pauses, digesting the request. "Is everything all right, Dad? I thought you were spending the weekend together."

He briefly explains, adding, "She's not here and her mother is buggering me about, pretending to be deaf and stupid."

Samantha tries to cheer him. "That's the trouble with eccentric old grannies."

"I just hope that doesn't apply to grandfathers as well," he says as he puts down the phone.

Ted Donaldson has one eccentric old lady on his mind as he bumps into Superintendent McGregor at the front desk of the Mitre, although Daphne Lovelace would bristle at being termed a grandmother.

"I can't talk business, Ted," warns Anne before he can get in a hello. "I know what you've got on your mind, but I can handle it. I'm a big girl now."

"I noticed that," says Donaldson, with a cheeky leer that is supposed to soften her as they walk towards the dining room. "But I still remember the day you joined."

"You should," laughs the young senior officer. "You recruited me."

"And I remember the tears running down your cheeks when I told you that you'd have to leave your mum and go off to training school."

Anne McGregor turns sheepish and stops. "That's not fair, Ted. It was a long time ago."

"True," he agrees as he pulls out a chair and picks up a menu. "But now you're a tough cookie. You've done well, and I'm proud of you. But beating up on a defence-less old lady …"

"All right. You win," says McGregor, slapping down her menu in resignation. "But this is going to cost you big if you expect me to listen."

"Extortion," he laughs, then swipes a hand across the menu. "Anything you like, Anne, although I'm going for the roast beef and Yorkshire pud buffet myself."

"In this heat!" exclaims his guest as she dabs her forehead with her napkin. "I don't know how you do it."

"Practice," he says, patting his rotund midriff, and a few minutes later his plate overflows as he lays out Daphne's case.

"She reckons she tried complaining about these people but nothing was done."

"It doesn't give her the right to break in …"

"Anne," he holds up a forkful of roast potato. "I'm not here to defend what she did — she's quite capable of doing that herself — but I think you should look at it from a PR perspective. There's a back story here that can explode into a national debate — octogenarian wartime hero, Order of the British Empire for services rendered, takes on neighbours from hell when police refuse to help."

"I didn't refuse —" starts McGregor, but Donaldson stops her with an asparagus spear.

"Moot point, Anne. If this catches fire in the media she could be headlining the six o'clock news as she leads a pack of elderly vigilantes on Downing Street. Anyway, from what I gather, the place was such a tip you'll have a hard time proving what she broke."

"How d'you know …?" she starts, but then raises a quizzical eyebrow. "What about the television and stereo?"

"Okay," he concedes, adding pointedly, "But I shouldn't bother asking them for copies of the receipts."

"And what about the sick bay window at the nick?"

"Accident. I distinctly remember cracking it with my elbow just before I retired. I'll happily pay for it."

Anne McGregor puts on a "pull-the-other-one" face, but Donaldson is unabashed.

"Christ — she worked for us for thirty years," he says, stabbing a Yorkshire pudding for emphasis.

"She was the station's cleaning lady," spits McGregor.

"And so will you be if you persist with this case," retorts Donaldson as he rises for another shot at the buffet. "Do yourself a favour, Anne. Get hold of Social Services first thing tomorrow and get someone to say that she's going a bit batty. Then quietly drop the charges."

"And what if the Jenkinses kick up?"

"Start demanding receipts — proof of purchase — cheque stubs. Get someone in traffic to do a full workout on their bikes the next time they hit the road; have a word with the council and Inland Revenue about their unpaid taxes."

"What unpaid taxes?"

"Precisely, Anne. We don't know, do we."

Around and around shuffles Daphne, eyes on the cracked flagstone path, as she plots a course of redemption. Messages have been pouring in all afternoon, but not from her phone. Bliss, Samantha, Trina, and Ted Donaldson have all tried that, but an answering machine is another modern convenience that Daphne has scorned. The words she has been hearing are purely metaphysical — spiritual communications from a world beyond the grave — the tortured souls of Phil and Maggie Morgan: begging, encouraging, and pleading with her not to let the Jenkinses get away with the desecration of their corporeal abode.

The morning's communicants returning for evensong stop in disbelief at the bereted old lady who, despite the heat, is still shambling around the labyrinth while fiercely muttering to herself.

"Is she all right?" several question, but the cathedral's bells are insistent and they scurry inside to pray for their salvation, leaving Daphne to work out her own.

By Monday morning, thirty unanswered messages clog Bliss's home answerphone, but he doesn't bother to check before leaving his hotel. He tried to change his flight to Sunday to give himself more time to prepare for his meeting with the man from the Home Office, but it's a midsummer weekend and the airline's representative had barely repressed laughter in her voice as she told him that he was lucky to get it in the first place.

At least the time difference is on my side, he tells himself in the cab as he heads for the airport and his 10:00 a.m. appointment with Fox. The phone calls — a dozen each from Daisy and Trina, and the rest from his daughter, Samantha, acting on behalf of the other two — will have to wait.

The Côte d'Azur drops quickly behind as the jet reaches high in order to crest the Alps as it heads north. Bliss is unmolested as he watches the Mediterranean disappear, although ninety minutes later he would happily switch to the aisle as lightning slashes through the black clouds above London and he finds himself heading for Luton.

"Bugger," he mutters under his breath as the announcement is made, and a quick check of his watch tells him that he's in trouble.

The tropical downpour may have flooded London's streets and settled the dust, but the oppressive humidity has done nothing to lift the Monday morning blues, and Fox flies off the handle when Bliss phones from Luton.

"Oh, for Christ's sake, Dave. Now I'll have to make up some porky pies to cover your ass."

"Sorry, sir —" starts Bliss, but Fox cuts in.

"Stay there; I'll drive up and get you. But you'd

better have some bloody good ideas for our man at the Home Office."

"Oh shit," groans Bliss as he puts down the phone. Then he pulls out a pad and sketches a beady-eyed bureaucrat with Coke-bottle glasses and ink-stained fingers as he tries to come up with ways to keep the wayward Philip from killing his wife.

A tranquilizer gun, a syringe full of anaesthetic, CS gas, velvet-lined handcuffs, and a straitjacket all make it to his list before he scrubs them out. "This is impossible," he tells himself under his breath as his mind goes back to his meeting with the assistant commissioner and the two Americans.

"The President had good reason to suspect an attack on the Queen was imminent," one of snappily dressed foreigners claimed, and Bliss plays with the notion as he gathers a handful of dailies off the newsagent's stand and tries to piece together a consensus.

The heat wave is still taking the brunt of the blame, as it was supposed to do, but several of the trashier tabloids are backing the conspiracy theorists, even if they have peppered their columns with words such as *speculative*, *unproven*, and *wacky*.

"The Duke: Electronically Implanted?" runs one headline, although the editor has been wise enough not to blame any particular faction. Internet bloggers and loony American televangelists, on the other hand, have no such qualms and are universally pointing their fingers towards the Middle East.

So, questions Bliss to himself as he waits for Fox, *I wonder what Lefty and Pimple actually know*.

"What's the CIA's involvement?" he asks as soon as he gets in the car, daring Fox to come up with a denial.

"They tipped us off, though God knows how they figured out something might happen."

"I'd call it an educated guess, only I wouldn't want to give them that much credit."

"Now, now, Dave. Be nice about our cousins," says Fox, but Bliss can't help wondering aloud about the bloggers' assertions.

"What if someone has implanted Prince Philip with some kind of chip?" he asks rhetorically as Fox concentrates on a busy roundabout. "What's their motive? The Queen hasn't got any political power. She hasn't even got a lot of money anymore. J. K. Rowling's got more than her, and she's an author."

"Aren't you writing a book?" asks Fox.

"It's finished."

"Wow. Good for you. So now you'll make a fortune."

"Yeah. Right," chuckles Bliss. "Do you know how difficult it is to get published?"

"Well, you could always use this case to write another one."

"Possibly," says Bliss with little interest.

"Obviously you couldn't write about our royal family, though. You'd have to fictionalize the whole thing and call it Camelot or something."

"Why?"

"Because they'd sue the pants off you if you didn't."

The rain stops as suddenly as it began, and the sun turns up the heat as they approach the city centre.

"It's gonna be another scorcher," croons Fox, but Bliss has his mind on the Home Office appointee.

"Some clueless bureaucrat, I suppose," he moans as they drive down Whitehall.

"You know him," says Fox. "That's why he asked for you to be assigned."

"I don't know anyone at the H.O.," protests Bliss bluntly. "It's out of my league."

"Edwards, Michael Edwards," says Fox with a mischievous smirk, and Bliss feels his face draining.

"Not —"

"That's the one," steps in Fox. "Ex–Chief Superintendent of the Yard," leaving Bliss simultaneously slack-mouthed and steaming.

"I don't bloody believe it," he seethes, recalling the tyrannous reign of the senior commander whose career skidded to a halt when he was caught taking backhanders from a suspected murderer and driving under the influence. "I thought we'd seen the last of that bastard."

"Language, Dave," warns Fox insouciantly. "Our Mr. Edwards is flavour of the month at the big house."

"How the hell did they fiddle that?"

"C'mon, Dave. Don't be naïve. That was his reward for going quietly."

"But he was supposed to plead to drunk driving."

"He did. But you know how it works. They wheeled him in front of a smiley magistrate one misty dawn while the press and everyone else were still in their pits, and the Beak says, 'How d'ye fancy a conditional discharge?' 'Suits me,' says Edwards, and next minute — he's walking. I'm surprised they didn't give him a couple of quid from the poor box to pay for his bus fare home."

"Bugger," spits Bliss. "But how the hell did he get into the Home Office?"

"He probably put someone's bollocks in a vice and started turning," says Fox, knowing first-hand of Edwards' proclivity for blackmailing his way into or out of any situation.

"Knowing Edwards, it was the Home Secretary himself," mutters Bliss angrily as they get out of the car.

chapter six

Tony Oswald is tall, beefy, and midnight black. He could easily have been recruited as a "heavy" for the mob — almost any mob — but his mother rarely let him onto the streets alone after dark.

"I could bloody kill my mum," he often swore at the youth club, Boy's Brigade, and amateur dramatics, though he wouldn't say that now as he parks his Peugeot, plucks his briefcase off the back seat, and strolls up the street to Daphne's house.

Jon-Jo, the most junior member of the Jenkins gang, sits astride his father's Yamaha with a sneer and a cigarette as props, and waylays Tony on his way to Daphne's front door.

"Hey, bro. Whassup?"

Oswald stops, gives the youngster a brilliant smile, and breaks into stage Yorkshire. "By gum, lad. Tha'art bin watching them ald 'merican fillums. Thy needs t'pull thy socks up."

"Wha?" says Jon-Jo with a furrowed brow and a full glottal stop.

"Now't," chuckles Tony as he walks on.

Daphne is watching — peering through a tight crack in the parlour curtains. She slipped home after dark on Sunday evening, cutting through the copse at the end of the cul-de-sac, and collapsed onto the settee too exhausted to make it to her bedroom. Apart from a couple of fitful hours while awaiting bail, and a couple more on a solid railway station bench, she has not slept for two days — one of which she spent walking the labyrinth.

Her phone rang Sunday night until she finally pulled the plug, but she can't switch off the front doorbell.

"Ms. Lovelace," Tony Oswald calls loudly after the third ring and a couple of hard knocks.

Daphne steps back from the window, her heartbeat thumping in her ears, and quietly picks up the brass-handled poker from the fireplace.

"Ms. Lovelace," he tries again in polished Oxbridge. "It's Tony Oswald from Social Services. I wonder if I might have a few minutes of your time."

"Social Services," Daphne echoes under her breath, but she's seen the agony-filled images of smashed-faced septuagenarians crying into television news cameras — once proud veterans beaten into shamefacedly admitting the loss of their life savings, their confidence, and their independence. "He said he were from Council or summink," they whimpered, adding tearfully, "He even had a briefcase," as if no self-respecting con merchant would ever stoop so low.

"Ms. Lovelace," Oswald tries again and is about to give up when a thin voice stops him.

"How do I know?" sings out Daphne from the hallway.

"Here," he says, trying to push his identity card through the letterbox, but the metal flap is stuck: plastered shut with masking tape. "Superintendent McGregor asked me to look in on you," he carries on. "She was worried."

Daphne bends. "You'll have to wait," she yells. "I'm not dressed." Then she races upstairs and pulls on some clothes.

Daphne's mahogany umbrella stand never aspired to be a Sheraton or Chippendale, but it has dutifully done everything asked of it for more than eighty years. At the height of the Blitz, in 1941, it stood guard against the might of the Luftwaffe; solidly blocking Daphne's parents' front door against bombs, shells, and shrapnel. None ever came. But each night, as her father manhandled the heavy piece into position, he would confidently announce, "It'll take more than Jerry and his flying circus to get past this bugger."

The umbrella stand has gained weight in direct proportion to Daphne's age, and by the time she has pulled it away from the door she is breathless.

"Won't be a mo," she wheezes, pulling herself upright on the doorknob, then she has another attack of nerves and grabs a silver-handled walking stick that Mavis presented to her on her eightieth.

"I won't be needing that bloomin' thing for yonks," Daphne snorted as she dropped it into the stand, and it has been there ever since.

"All right," she says, primping herself up, and she pulls back the latch and flings open the door.

"Ms. Love…" starts Oswald, then his huge nigrescent eyeballs pop. On the outside of her pink winceyette pyjamas, Daphne is wearing a pair of tiger-striped knickers and a lacy bra embroidered with tiny red hearts.

"Come in," she chirrups. "I was just going to make some tea — Keemun. It's the Queen's favourite, you know."

"Right …"

The kitchen is hot and dark — the curtains are firmly clamped in the middle with clothes pegs. A couple of wooden chairs have been piled onto an oak sideboard, complete with crockery and a withered geranium, and the assemblage has been forced against the back door.

"Can't be too careful," whispers Daphne, sensing Oswald's concern. "They could get in anywhere, you know." Then she carefully removes a cork from the tap in order to fill the kettle.

"Right …" says Oswald as he slowly takes in the rest of the room. The fireplace chimney is stuffed with an old blanket, the light switches and ventilator have been taped over, and the upended kitchen table is jammed against the pantry door.

"It'll only take a few minutes," says Daphne as she lights the gas under the kettle. Then she gives a nod in her neighbours' direction and snorts, "As long as they don't blow it out again."

"Right …" says Oswald again, then he pulls a couple of kitchen stools up to the sideboard and invites her to sit.

"I'd like to talk about what happened Saturday if that's all right with you," he starts as he takes out a notepad and pen, then he reels off the list of her transgressions. "Burglary, possession of an offensive weapon, criminal damage, and assault on Superintendent McGregor."

"Offensive weapon?"

"The crowbar."

"That was their own fault. Who keeps a crowbar on the dining table?"

"But you smashed their television and slashed their speakers with it. That's criminal damage."

Daphne boils. "Damage!" she screeches. "Damage! Did you see the way they've wrecked Phil and Maggie's place?"

"I understand it's their place now," says Tony with a consoling hand on her forearm. "They can do what they want —"

"It's not theirs," she fumes, snatching away her arm and getting up to fill the teapot.

"What *are* we going to do with you, Daphne?" Tony asks, shaking his head. Then Daphne brightens with an idea.

"Maybe it's time I went into an old people's home,"

she suggests as she sits down with the pot, and she has in mind the Church of England seniors' residence where Maggie Morgan died. "That place on Grove Road would do. St. Martin's, I think."

"St. Michael's," corrects Tony, and then he looks deep into her eyes and softens his tone sympathetically. "I do understand how difficult this must be for you, Daphne," he says, as if making it plain that whilst there are many different ways to get into a seniors' home, there is generally only one way out. "But it's probably wise, and it's good that you have faith in God."

"Doesn't everyone when the time comes?" asks Daphne with an innocent mien as she pours clear hot water from her teapot. "Sugar?" she questions, offering Oswald a silver saltcellar.

"Umm," he hums. "Do you have any milk?"

"It's already in," says Daphne shirtily. "You always put the milk in first. Everyone knows that." Then she picks up her cup of hot water and sips it with a rapturous expression. "Oh. Now that's what I call a good cuppa."

"Surprised, Chief Inspector?" says Michael Edwards with a grin as he holds out a hand to Bliss.

Disgusted would be another way of putting it, but so would appalled, shocked, and angered. "G'morning, sir," Bliss replies coldly, head down as he makes a play of opening his briefcase. "Sorry I'm late."

"I didn't expect any different," mutters Edwards as he props his weight against a leather-topped office desk and throws down a file marked "Top Secret."

Keep cool, Bliss cautions himself. Pretend the conniving little creep is just another civil servant.

"So. Let's roll up our sleeves and see what the wizards of the Yard have conjured up," carries on Edwards mordaciously. "Let's put all our cards on the table."

Bliss doesn't have any cards and he knows it, so he bluffs: "Increased observation; separation whenever possible; get the Queen to wear body armour —"

"Yes, yes, yes," cuts in Edwards, then he wanders the room for a minute, throwing out his own suggestions: "Beef up the Queen's protection team; arm selected palace staff; put something in Philip's drinks …" He pauses and goes to sit at the desk, but stops himself. It's a form of Pavlovian reaction — his pain receptors recalling the time Bliss angrily overturned a heavy wooden desk on him and broke his wrist. So he firmly plonks his backside on top of the desk, leans menacingly over his erstwhile attacker, and hectors, "That's all very well, Chief Inspector, but a five-year-old playing cops and robbers could have told me that. I was expecting something better. C'mon, man, stop piddling about and give me some bright ideas. Something I can take to the Home Secretary."

Beyond invoking Sharia law and lopping off the aging prince's right hand, Bliss doesn't have more to offer. But he isn't in the Home Secretary's sights. Michael Edwards, a man who could have doubled for the Fuehrer had he grown a moustache and learned to paint, is in the hot seat — he's the so-called security expert. After thirty years of bulldozing his way through the corridors and typing pools of Scotland Yard, where officers and secretaries alike would whisper to newcomers, "Cover your backside, protect your crotch, and never, ever bend over," he'll be the one who gets screwed if anything happens to the Queen.

"Sorry, sir," says Bliss. "But I'm only the punkah-wallah. I thought you were supposed to be the guru."

Edwards "Harrumphs" his derision, then pointedly sits at the desk as if offering Bliss a rematch. "Well, let me tell you what I've got …" he starts smugly as he begins to open the folder, then he stops, taps the "Top Secret" designation, and warns, "If this leaks, I'll know exactly where to look. *Capisce?*"

"*Si*," says Bliss and watches as Edwards ceremoniously puts on his glasses, pompously buffs his fingertips on the palms of his hands, and then cautiously extracts a single sheet as if he expects it to explode.

"Hmm," Edwards hums as he carefully scans the document, then he looks up, questioning. "What do you know about MK-Ultra, Chief Inspector?"

Bliss lets an expression of deep thought blank his face, while wondering if now is a good time to tell Edwards that he has left his fly open and his shirt tail is poking out.

"It sounds like a hemorrhoid cream or a spermicidal condom to me," he says eventually, leaving Edwards to find out about his fly for himself, and then he sees the vexed expression on his former commander's face and pushes further. "I'll go for the hemorrhoid cream myself. There's nothing worse than a pain in the backside."

Edwards gets the message, but he has Bliss on his hook so he would rather let him squirm.

"I could've guessed that you wouldn't know," he says as he returns the paper and closes the file without explanation, then he changes tack. "I've asked for a meeting with His Highness's psychiatrist. You might wish to attend."

"He has a psychiatrist?" says Bliss in surprise.

"So would you if you had a family like his," sneers Edwards. "Kings, queens, jacks, and a bunch of bloody jokers. Anyway, I'll pass on your suggestions to the Home Secretary, and in the meantime, we expect you to do your best."

"My best? How?"

"Well, I understand you're authorized to use force if necessary."

"Yes. But what if he gets hold of a gun?"

"Then you'd have to shoot him, wouldn't you," says Edwards, straight-faced.

"At least I'd go out of the Force with a bang," laughs Bliss.

"You'd go down in f'kin history, mate. The cop who plugged His Royal Pain-in-the-backside. Immortal, that's what you'd be. But isn't that what you're after?"

"No, it's not," spits Bliss, miffed at the suggestion, while inwardly wondering if he could get away with murdering the man in front of him on the grounds of temporary insanity or extreme provocation.

"Then why'd you write a poxin' book?"

Now I get it, thinks Bliss as he is escorted by a tight-lipped security guard to the street. *No wonder Edwards asked for me. They want a fall guy. If Phil flips again and actually harms her, they'll all point at me and say, "Ask him. He was supposed to protect her."*

"Your visitor's pass, sir," demands the guard, with his hand out at the door, and Bliss sinks under the weight of the hot, humid air as he hands over the pass and walks off towards Scotland Yard.

The robotized voice on Bliss's answerphone seems to have run out of patience as she intones, "You have … thirty-seven … new messages. To listen, press …"

Daphne, Trina, Samantha, Donaldson — he skips, one after another, until a familiar voice stops him.

"Daavid. Where are you? Angeline said zhat you were here?"

The next six calls begin similarly, and he cuts the recording and phones.

"Daisy …" he starts, pronouncing it *en français*, like "Dizee," and she jumps in.

"Daavid. What happened? I look everywhere for you. Angeline, she said …"

"I was in Cannes," he says. "It was supposed to be a surprise. But your mother said she didn't know where you were."

Now Daisy is surprised. "You saw my mozher?" she questions confusedly.

"*Oui*," he says, then leaves her an opening. The silence deafens him after a few seconds. The crushing pain of disappointment he felt Saturday night at the Carlton is nothing compared to his anguish as he waits for the lies.

He doesn't have to wait long. "I went to Corsica for zhe weekend wiz my cousin," she explains. "Didn't my mozher tell you?"

Play it cool. Tread carefully. "Your cousin?" he counters.

"He works on zhe ferry …"

"So, why didn't your mother know?"

Again the silence — longer this time. *Maybe she's waiting for me*, he thinks. *Maybe she's put the phone down.*

"Daisy," he calls.

"*Oui*. I am here," she says, but she still doesn't have an answer.

"I asked you —"

"Daavid. I know," she says with tears in her voice. "But zhis is very hard for me. I cannot … I cannot …"

"Well, call me when you can," he snaps and drops the phone.

That was unnecessary, he tries telling himself, and reaches for the handset. Then he pulls back, thinking, *Cousin — that's a good one. He's probably some garlic-breath'd, Gitanes-smoking, pot-bellied plonker with a puny little Renault.*

Daphne Lovelace is at home, packing — just one small suitcase, as per Tony's instructions.

"Christ, that was quick," says Anne McGregor as she meets Tony Oswald at her office door.

"She wanted to go to St. Mike's," says Tony as he shakes the superintendent's hand. "They usually have vacancies, and this heat has certainly made a big difference. Anyway, not everyone wants to spend their last few days repenting before they get the sky-shuttle."

"Hah! That's rich," spits McGregor, still peeved. "I let her off for burglary and assault and she wangles a free pass to the Almighty."

"Well, it's not particularly free," he stresses, suggestively rubbing a thumb and forefinger together. "That's the main reason why they usually have spaces. That, and the fact that most of them are halfway out the back door before they get in the front."

"Well, that's that then," says Anne McGregor resignedly as she pulls Daphne's charge sheet from her in-tray and writes, "No further action — Divine retribution," in the box marked "Outcome and disposal."

"So, did you have to twist her arm?" she inquires as she drops the charge sheet in the out tray.

"No," he laughs. "Far from it. I usually take them in kicking and screaming, but she's got no family or friends — none close, anyway — so I think she's happy to go."

David Bliss is one person Daphne would call a friend, but he has been so wrapped up with Edwards and his messed-up weekend that he still hasn't tried to contact her.

He is in his office, on his computer, checking his emails every ten minutes, waiting for Daisy to pop up with a good excuse while hoping she doesn't. Lies are his life. He has spent a career face to face with transgressors, victims, and witnesses and has often been bamboozled by all three. But he can't get away from the screen and the hope that she just might come up with a plausible story, and he doodles around until he follows links that take him down a worm-hole in cyberspace, where he finds himself in a world as mind-boggling as Middle Earth.

Pastor Paul Robinson is there, on digital TV — bouffant hair, rubbery lips, tombstone teeth, and an Aston Martin in the parking lot — proselytizing against the evils of Islam and preaching that the Duke of Edinburgh has been possessed by the Devil at the behest of Allah to punish the Queen for daring to defile a holy site.

"What a load of rubbish," Bliss mutters, then digs deeper, reading the maniacal ramblings of otherwise intelligent men; scholars of all stripes, vehemently and sincerely debating such ethereal matters as the precise location of heaven, the cubic capacity of the Ark and the exact number of animals Noah crammed aboard, and whether or not Allah really does have an unlimited supply of virgins at his disposal to dole out to martyrs — seventy-two to a bed — and what happens to them once they're deflowered.

The phone buzzes. *Daisy*, he thinks, grabbing it quickly, but it's his daughter, Samantha.

"I still haven't been able to get back to Daphne."

"Neither have I," he lies, and immediately feels a pang of guilt. "I'll try again in a minute."

"What about Daisy?" she asks, and he wishes she hadn't.

"My own fault," he says, guessing she'll catch on from the tone of his voice.

"Oh, Dad."

"I should just quit my job and pack my bags for France …" he begins, then quickly changes tune. "Have you seen this Pastor Paul idiot on satellite?"

"Careful, Dad. He's got a bigger following than Céline Dion."

"He's also got more hair. But I just don't get it."

"It's called free speech, Dad," says Samantha, ever the defence lawyer.

"No, it's not what he says that bugs me," explains Bliss. "It's that people believe it. That they believe all this 'love thy neighbour' stuff, then go round slitting each other's throats."

"They can believe what they want."

"Not when it hurts other people," he insists. "Anyway, doesn't it strike you as odd that it's always the ones who pray the hardest who get clobbered the worst?"

"That's just God's way of testing them," she says, playing Devil's advocate.

A buzz cuts into the line. "Got another call," he says, and quickly switches.

"Daavid," whimpers a voice hoarse from crying. "I have to talk wiz you."

"Go on, then."

"No ..." she sniffs wetly. "I cannot talk on zhe telephone. Can you come back?"

"You're kidding ..."

"Please, Daavid."

Now what? "I'll call you back," he says. "I have to think, and I've got someone on the other line."

"Promise."

"Yes. *Oui — je promesse.*"

That's the problem with long-distance dating, he reminds himself as he pauses before cutting back to Samantha. *What is she trying to tell me?* "It was just a fling; I was lonely; you let me down; you promised me a romantic break and I waited for you; he meant nothing to me; I want you." It's all about trust, he tells her in his mind. *How can I trust you now? The first time I let you down, you rush off with your "cousin" for a dirty weekend in Corsica.*

"Dad?" says Samantha.

"Sorry, love. Where was I?"

"You were profaning the Almighty."

"Who, Paul Robinson?

"No — well, yes. I suppose you could include him, but I meant the other one."

"Oh, Him," emphasizes Bliss, then returns to his rant. "What gets me is that they all claim that they're right, that God is on their side, and that they're the only ones who'll go to heaven."

"Maybe —" tries Samantha, but Bliss steamrolls her.

"And the worst thing is that they've spent two thousand years killing anyone who disagreed with them." Then he launches into a lengthy list of religiously inspired programs that were designed to wipe out the Muslims, Cathars, Catholics, Huguenots, Quakers, and Jews, before concluding, with a sardonic laugh, "If they don't stop killing each other soon there won't be room in heaven for the rest of us."

"But ..." is all that Samantha has time to say when a messenger rushes into Bliss's office without knocking.

"Commander-Fox-wants-you-now-sir," gushes the boy in a single breath, and he is gone before Bliss can quiz him.

"Gotta go," he calls to Samantha as he drops the phone, and a minute later he is in the control room watching the monitors as hundreds of officers descend on the scene of a traffic accident at Hyde Park Corner.

"It's the Queen's Rolls," explains Fox, stabbing a screen, and the air is alive as controllers call in units to cordon streets, set up barricades, and escort ambulances. "She was on her way home from hospital."

"That's all I need ..." Bliss is sighing as a telephone operator hands him a phone and makes it worse.

"Mr. Edwards at the Home Office for you, sir."

"This better not be what it looks like," spits Edwards into Bliss's ear.

"Bugger," mouths Bliss, then clamps a hand over the mouthpiece while he turns to Fox.

"Where's the Duke, sir?"

"Balmoral — shooting grouse or something. The season's just started, apparently."

"Thank goodness ... Shooting?"

Ten minutes later Bliss is back on the phone with Samantha.

"False alarm. One of the paparazzi broadsided her limo on his motorbike."

"Let's face it, Dad," says Samantha. "If he bumped her off it's not as though the House of Windsor would fall — it would just get a facelift."

"Not a particularly attractive one, though," adds Bliss, before explaining that he phoned Ted Donaldson in Westchester and discovered that Daphne had been arrested.

"What on earth for?"

"Being slightly loony as far as I can tell. I think she's finally lost her marbles," he says, then gives a blow-by-blow account of her savage attack on the Jenkinses' television set and Superintendent McGregor's index finger. "It was quite a bite, apparently," he says as Samantha steps in, seizing an opportunity to headline.

"I'll happily defend her. I could make mincemeat of —"

"Calm down. They're not prosecuting," says Bliss. "Ted came to her rescue. But she is going into an old people's home."

"Oh no," sighs Samantha, knowing the connotation. "But she was as fit as a fiddle the last time I saw her."

"In body, yes …"

"Alzheimer's?" questions Samantha, but Bliss doesn't know.

"She must be pushing ninety — she's eighty-five at least."

Trina Button's mother is also in her mid-eighties, but Winifred Goodenow is fit in neither body nor mind. However, that is not her assessment as she shuffles along the side of a busy Vancouver highway in the fluffy pumpkin bedroom slippers she stole from the bargain bin at Wal-Mart after last year's Thanksgiving.

Tornadoes whisked up by flying trucks and buses threaten to whip her into the ditch, but she struggles on with her sights firmly set on the distant mountains.

"I'm practising for the El Camino," she yells to concerned motorists as she mistakes the forested mountains of British Columbia for the stark peaks of the Pyrenees, while her daughter is at Vancouver's central police station tying knots in the duty officer's brain as he attempts to fill out a missing person report.

"Colour of hair?"

"Brown," replies Trina with absolute conviction.

"Good."

Then Trina vacillates. "Well — brownish. More like the colour of banana cake if you accidentally leave it in the oven for four hours — know what I mean?"

"Not really, ma'am."

"Okay. Imagine a Starbucks latte — the regular one, not the double-shot, dark roast, French vanilla."

"Right …"

"Now add a couple of extra teaspoons of cream — real, not that synthetic stuff." She leans in conspiratorially. "Java-Bean puts that stuff in their coffees. It tastes like …"

"Wait, wait, wait," sighs Constable Merchant, screwing up the form and pulling out a fresh one. "I can't write all that."

"Well, is this really necessary?" inquires Trina. "Can't you just tell your people to look for her? I mean, how many loopy old ladies with fluffy pumpkins on their feet do you have on the loose at any one time?"

"I'm sorry, but it's essential, Mrs. Button," explains the officer officiously. "I can't put out a bulletin until I've got all the information."

Trina swings her arms high above her head and takes a deep breath as she calms herself with the tadasana yoga pose, saying, "I understand perfectly." Then she slowly exhales. "You are just doing your job, officer."

"Precisely, ma'am. So if I was to put that your mother's hair was on the slightly creamier side of a cappuccino, would that be right?"

Trina slowly relaxes her arms and brings her hands together in front of her in the namaste pose. "Yes. That's absolutely correct, officer."

"Great. Now we're getting somewhere," says Merchant with a wan smile as he starts to write. But Trina drops her arms and grabs his pen in alarm.

"That's not her colour now, of course. She's just sort of battle-axe grey now. That was the colour when she had colour."

Merchant loses it. "For goodness' sake, woman," he shouts. "According to you your mother is a banana-shaped, peach-skinned, coffee-headed …"

"What's going on?" demands the duty sergeant, Dave Brougham, as he barrels out of his office.

"Sergeant Brougham," yells Trina, spotting a familiar face. Then she rushes across the room and grabs him by the lapels, shouting. "You've gotta find her. She'll get run over. You've gotta find her."

"Don't tell me your bloody guinea pig's escaped again," snarls Brougham as he peels her off. "I'm fed up with you — always complaining …"

"Guinea pig?" echoes Trina thoughtfully, then lightning strikes. In her panic over her mother's disappearance she has forgotten to lock the creature into its cage. "Oh my God. Yes," she shrieks and rushes back to the duty officer, yelling, "Quick. Get out another form."

Brougham is right behind her, and he grabs her harshly, shouting, "Shuddup. I've warned you before about wasting police time. Now get out before I have you arrested."

"But Serg—"

"Get out."

"But Serg—" It's the duty officer now.

"And you can shuddup too," Brougham shouts over his shoulder as he hustles the squirming woman towards the front door. Then she drops from his grasp and curls into a ball on the floor.

The front door opens, and Inspector Mike Phillips of the RCMP marches in then stops dead.

"Trina?" he says, recognizing the bundle at his feet as a woman he has known for several years. "What on earth are you doing?"

"The balasana pose," she explains. "It's yoga."

"Why?"

"Well, I had to give up kick-boxing cuz I kept kicking myself in the head and giving myself concussions."

chapter seven

"Let us offer a prayer to our patron saint," intones Samuel Fitzgerald in a sacerdotal whine as Daphne Lovelace shuffles into the common room wearing her favourite Sunday hat and expecting sloppy porridge and a plastic mug of stale tea.

"St. Michael the Archangel. Defend us in the day of battle," Fitzgerald passionately implores, raising his eyes reverently to the brown stain on the ceiling where a blocked upstairs toilet has overflowed. "Be our safeguard against the wickedness and snares of the Devil ..."

Daphne stops and searches for a seat. Four empty high-backed upholstered chairs have been arranged to one side of the altar (a collapsible picnic table covered with a disposable mauve tablecloth from Marks and Spencer's "Trendy" collection, supporting a silver-plate candelabra and a brassy crucifix with a wobbly base). But as Daphne heads for one of the vacant seats,

Fitzgerald's wife, Hilda, blocks her path, whispering, "Go to the back, Daphne."

"This week we have said farewell and Godspeed to four of our dear, dear friends," continues Fitzgerald, with a crack in his voice that belies his brutish appearance as he gestures to the empty chairs. Then he walks behind them, meaningfully laying his fight-gnarled hands over the back of each in turn as he ascribes to the furniture the identity of its recently departed occupant.

"Petunia Rickworth of this parish, aged eighty-two; Nathaniel Wentworth of Mouton-Didsley, aged seventy-nine; Martha …"

Daphne tunes out the Sunday preacher, who on the other six days is the gardener and general factotum, while she looks around the room at the shells of seventeen women and four men, slumped in their seats like inadequately propped scarecrows, and wonders which of them will be next.

"And Pricilla Grantley, " Fitzgerald carries on, as Daphne attempts to elbow herself between two women seemingly asleep on a settee.

"Bugger off," swears one of the women with one eye open as she spreads herself.

"Those of you who wish to may come forward for a blessing," invites Fitzgerald, and a few struggle out of their seats and shuffle forward so that the gardener-cum-plumber can lay his enormous soil-stained hands on their heads, but at the back of the room, Daphne crumples into a flood of noisy tears.

"I don't like it here. I wanna go home," she snuffles loudly, and Hilda Fitzgerald comes running.

"What is it, dear?"

"There's nowhere to sit and I wanna go home," cries Daphne as she stands, slump-shouldered, with tears dripping onto the floor.

"Have you taken your tablets this morning?"

"Yes," sniffles Daphne. "But I don't want to stay."

"C'mon, then. Let's get you back to your room," says Hilda, offering a Kleenex and a guiding hand, and Daphne meekly follows.

It has been nearly a week since Daphne packed her suitcase and said a tearful goodbye to the only home she has known for more than forty years, but she still gags on the stench of stale urine and boiled cabbage as she drags her feet back to the room she shares with the bodily remains of Emily Mountjoy.

Hilda Fitzgerald, a fifty-five-year-old care assistant who doubles as the residence's cook, guides her aging charge firmly along vinyl-floored corridors, passing other residents who are now just shadows of the people they once were — creatures of the twilight, both haunted and haunting — as they shuffle silently like phantoms caught halfway between day and night, waiting for the light to go out and the reaper's scythe to strike.

"We like to think of ourselves as heaven's waiting room," Patrick Davenport, the home's supervisor, explained pompously as he greeted Daphne at the front door on the previous Monday, like St. Peter with his arms wide in welcome.

"I see," said Daphne, stepping into a dismal entrance hall with furniture as old as the inmates, and in similar condition.

"It's a great comfort to know that all of our guests will soon be sitting beside the Almighty," Davenport continued as he led Daphne past the common room where a dozen pairs of eyes looked hopefully her way. Was she a visitor? A long-lost relative? A saviour coming to take them to a better place?

It might be a comfort for you, thought Daphne as she peered at the expectant faces and wondered who they were before time took its toll. *But how do they feel about it?* Then she looked inwardly and wondered who she had been.

"This way," said Davenport, guiding her into his piously austere office as her mind flashed through more than eighty years of snapshots, questioning which, if any, were real: the golden-haired schoolgirl; the clumsy ballerina; the lover; the traveller; the wartime parachutist; the saboteur; the artist's model; the secret agent; another lover, and yet another; the police station's tea lady; the aging adventurer; and the lonely spinster.

"You can keep a few personal things," Davenport explained as he rummaged through her suitcase with the eye of a customs officer, while she scanned his framed collection of sacred quotes: "One book" — (his tone said "The Bible") — "basic toiletries, family photos, and some pocket change." Then he looked up. "We'll take care of all your jewellery, money, and other valuables."

"Isn't that what they told the Jews?" mumbled Daphne acidly under her breath, and Davenport caught it.

"What did you say?"

"I said, 'What a lovely June.'"

"It's August," snapped Davenport viciously, then he softened. "I'm sure you will be very comfortable here, Miss Lovelace. Or may I call you Daphne?"

David Bliss also received a rebuke on Monday and has been fending off his ex-boss ever since.

"It was just a minor prang," he said, shrugging off the accident involving the Queen's car, but Michael Edwards steamed at his lack of concern.

"How do you know that? Got proof, have you? Got sworn statements from everyone involved? Grilled the clown who pranged her, have you?"

"No, but —"

"Don't 'but' me, Chief Inspector. The Home Secretary is demanding a proper investigation, not some flim-flam f'kin ..."

Edwards ran out of expletives, and Bliss realized that it wasn't the Home Secretary demanding a full-scale inquiry. It was Edwards, protecting his own backside. *He'll be blamed if Philip gives her so much as a sore throat*, Bliss thought with a degree of satisfaction as he promised to look into the matter.

"Now," says Hilda Fitzgerald, leading Daphne back to her bed, "I'll get Amelia to bring up your breakfast. We did tell you that we always hold Sunday morning service in the common room. I 'spect you forgot."

"I did," sniffles Daphne.

"It's all right. Just dry your eyes and try not to upset Emily. And don't forget, we have prayer meetings twice a day and Bible classes Thursdays at seven. It's all on the notice board."

Emily Mountjoy, a sunken-cheeked, wispy-haired skeleton, sits motionless in an armchair with her unseeing eyes glued remorselessly to the roof of the City Library, where she was the senior staff member for more than thirty years. She is, however, totally incognizant of the world and of Daphne's desolation. She is beyond distress. Nothing that Daphne does, or says, will upset her. Her mind died long ago, and her body is finally catching up. However, in some ways, Emily is more advantaged than many of the other residents who are still fully sentient, watching in horror as their bodies head to the grave before they do.

Daphne tried communicating with Emily throughout the week but has drawn a blank.

On Tuesday, Daphne's first full day at the home, she picked a family portrait of a couple and their three young children off Emily's bedside table, asking, "Is this you?"

Emily didn't answer; didn't take her eyes off the library. But Daphne sank a little deeper when she returned to her own bed and looked at the bare table beside her.

Where were her pictures of a smiling husband and a clutch of rascal-faced schoolchildren?

"So. You were never married then," said Patrick Davenport later Tuesday morning when he escorted a paunch-bellied parson to Daphne's room.

"Married?" Daphne questioned, with a look on her face that said she was trying hard to recall.

"This is the Reverend Rowlands of St. Stephen's-in-the-Vale," Davenport continued, already knowing the answer, and he carried on talking while the red-faced vicar was in the background having a coughing fit as he tried to recover his breath after climbing the stairs. "He takes the service here on the fourth Sunday of the month, except when it falls on Christmas or Easter."

"Or one of the other special days," chimed in Rowlands, once he had loudly blown his nose. Then he looked at Daphne and said, "We've met before, haven't we?"

Daphne wrinkled her brow. "Have we?"

"Yes. Weren't you making inquiries about the Creston family awhile ago?"

"Was I?"

"Miss Lovelace is having a few problems with her memory, aren't you, dear?" said Davenport.

"Am I?" replied Daphne, looking quizzical.

"The reverend will visit your family or friends if you'd like him to."

"Will he?" inquired Daphne, but when it came to giving names she balked.

"Is there anyone at all whom we should contact?" queried Rollie Rowlands as he gently clasped her hands. "Any friends or relatives. Who's looking after everything for you at home?"

"Home," repeated Daphne, as if the memory of her neat suburban house was already fading. Then she shook her head. "No one, I don't think."

David Bliss is one person who could be looking after Daphne's affairs. She has taken care of him often enough in the past. But he was in Scotland on Tuesday, having a clandestine meeting with the Duke of Edinburgh's protection officer.

"The old boy has no idea what the problem is," the seconded Metropolitan inspector told him over a beer and pork pie in the corner of a pub on the outskirts of Aberdeen. "He doesn't remember getting dressed that morning. Doesn't have a clue about the sword incident. It's like it never happened."

"Why didn't anyone stop him putting on his uniform?" asked Bliss.

"He's not a kid," shot back the inspector. "And by the time anyone spotted him it was too late."

"Good mornin', Miss Lovelace," calls a perky voice as a bright-eyed youngster bustles into Daphne's room with a breakfast tray. "I poached you an egg 'specially," adds Amelia Brimble, and Daphne's face lights up.

"Thank you, my dear."

Amelia pulls a sympathetic face. "Mrs. Fitzgerald said the service was a bit much for you this morning."

"Was it?"

"And she says I gotta make sure you take your pills."

"I already did …" starts Daphne, then she pauses with a thought and squirrels a five-pound note from the inside of one of her slippers. "Amelia, dear," she whispers, "this is for you for being so nice to me."

"I'm not supposed …"

"Don't worry. I won't tell a soul. Only I haven't got any children to leave it to, so you might as well have it."

"If you're sure."

"Oh. I am, dear," she replies as she runs a gentle finger down the girl's cheek. "You're a lovely girl. If I had a daughter I'd want her to be just like you. How old are you?"

"Sixteen and a half next month."

"Well. One of these days you'll make some nice young man a wonderful wife."

"Oh, Miss Lovelace …you are a one," giggles the young girl as she pockets the cash.

The question of Daphne's lack of progeny also arose on Wednesday when Doctor Williamson visited.

"You can have your own doctor if you really want," Patrick Davenport made clear when he signed her in. "Only Doctor Williamson is here most days, so it's easier."

"She's in good shape physically," Geoffrey Williamson reported following his examination. "But her mental condition is worrying. She doesn't even remember if she has any children."

"The doctor wants you to take these for your memory," Hilda Fitzgerald told Daphne later as she handed over the first of many tablets, but Daphne looked confused, insisting, "There's nothing wrong with my bloomin' memory."

Wednesday was also the day Tony Oswald, the social worker, tracked down Mavis Longbottom.

"I had no idea," she cried, without admitting that since she started experimenting with Internet dating she has hardly seen her old friend. "But she did seem very confused a couple of weeks ago."

"Really?"

"Yes. The neighbour's dogs were getting to her, so I took her to the labyrinth at the cathedral hoping she might sort herself out."

Daphne is still walking the labyrinth. She has been walking the labyrinth all week, although not the one at the cathedral.

"You're free to leave the grounds at any time," Davenport pointed out when she first arrived, but he quickly stomped on the idea. "Though not without a good reason and not without permission."

"Auschwitz," she silently muttered under her breath, but each day she has paced out the loops and whorls of a labyrinth on the parched lawn at St. Michael's.

"That's all she does most of the time," Amelia explained to Tony Oswald when he wondered how Daphne was settling in. "Round and round she goes." The young attendant chuckled. "Hour after blinkin' hour. Nattering away ten to the dozen. Like a little clockwork mouse."

Mavis Longbottom has called each day since she heard the news on Wednesday, saying, "I feel so bad. I really should visit." But Davenport persuaded her otherwise. "Not until she's properly settled in," he advised. "It would just upset her even more."

However, Mavis found Samantha Bliss's phone number in her address book — Daphne had once given it to her as someone to contact in case of emergency — and she gave the young lawyer a call.

"I'll let Dad know," Samantha quickly said. "Only he's in Scotland at the moment."

Bliss was in Edinburgh on Wednesday with Michael Edwards, meeting Prince Philip's psychiatrist. Edwards chose the restaurant — the Wichery, just outside the castle's gates. "Home Office perks, old boy," he explained with a grin and a wink when Bliss whistled at the prices.

"Amnesia of the whole day — blotted it all out," Professor Peter Morteson informed them over the lobster-topped seafood platters, and Edwards questioned whether or not Prince Philip might have deliberately wiped his mind.

"It's possible, Michael," said Morteson, making it clear by his tone that he would need to do much more research before committing himself. "There's plenty of anecdotal evidence that people can black out horrendous memories — selective amnesia."

"But getting dressed wouldn't have been traumatic," suggested Bliss. "Why wouldn't he remember putting on his uniform? And why did he put on his uniform in the first place?"

The psychiatrist shrugged. He only asked questions. He didn't have answers.

Tony Oswald visited Daphne on Thursday. "Just to see how you're doing," he said, but she eyed him as a complete stranger, wrapped her housecoat tightly around her bosom, and steeled herself to run.

"Her mental capacity seems to be deteriorating quite rapidly," the social worker pointed out at the patient evaluation meeting afterwards, although Paul Davenport had an answer.

"We don't know how long this has been going on, Tony. Most people cope if there's no one to notice when they cook dinner at three in the morning or put their pants on back to front."

"True," Oswald replied, then Amelia chipped in.

"She seems quite upset about her cat."

"We don't allow pets ..." jumped in Davenport, but Oswald laughed.

"It's all right. She doesn't have a cat." Then he explained how Daphne had rambled to the arresting officer about the cat's collar, adding, "But I had a good look around and couldn't find anything. And the neighbours said they'd never seen a cat."

"I'll talk to her about it," said Davenport. "It was probably a childhood pet. It's amazing how the early memories seem to stick when everything else goes."

Samantha Bliss is someone else worried about the failing memories of the aged.

"You're fuckin' useless, Dad," she complained bitterly Thursday evening when Bliss admitted that he had forgotten to telephone St. Michael's to check on Daphne.

"Language!" he retorted, then protested that between the Queen and Daisy he already had his hands full.

"What's happening with Daisy?" Samantha wanted to know, but Bliss was evasive.

"We'll probably sort something out," he replied, without admitting that Daisy was still being cagey on the phone and insisting that she would only talk face to face.

"Daavid. Zhis is very difficult for me," she'd whimpered when he called back as promised on Monday evening, and he sympathized. After all, she'd stood by him when he was driven off the rails by the reignition of an old flame — a woman of such beauty that he even changed his novel, and the course of history, in an effort to win back her love. But when his scheme backfired and he was badly burnt, Daisy was there to salve his wounds.

"I'll come as soon as I can," he'd told her, but was mindful of the stern warning he'd received following his late arrival in London that morning. "Don't you dare leave the country again without permission," Commander Fox had barked, and he made it clear that any future absences would be treated as a serious disciplinary matter.

Winifred Goodenow, Trina Button's mother in Vancouver, is also under notice.

"If you run off just once more ..." Trina angrily warned when Inspector Mike Phillips brought Winifred home on Monday evening minus her slippers, but the elderly woman's only concern was her footwear.

"I want my pumpkins ... I want my pumpkins ..."

she moaned constantly until Trina bought her another pair on Friday.

Friday was the day that David Bliss's daughter visited Daphne and found the old soldier steadfastly slow-marching the invisible labyrinth on the lawn at St. Michael's.

"Round and round she goes," explained young Amelia Brimble to Samantha as they watched from the sidelines. "Nattering away to herself like a little clockwork mouse."

"Daphne was quite shitty with me," Samantha told her father, calling him from her cellphone. "I said I'd look after her affairs pro bono — as a friend. But she got quite snotty and said she already had a lawyer, thank you very much."

"Judging by what she did to get nicked, I'm not surprised," said Bliss, and he promised to visit on Sunday afternoon — Edwards permitting.

Sunday lunchtime comes early at St. Michael's.

"We give the most of the staff the afternoon off," Patrick Davenport explained to Daphne on her first day, and now, as twelve o'clock approaches at the end of her first week, Daphne shuffles back along the sterile corridors to the common room where meals are taken by residents fit enough to leave their beds.

The altar and the tableau of death have been stored away for another seven days, and Daphne spots an opening alongside a wheelchair-bound resident she befriended yesterday.

"Worn those feet out yet?" laughs the man as Daphne sits, and she gives him a smile of recognition.

"John Bartlesham," he introduced himself after watching Daphne's two-hour stint on Saturday, then he joked, "You're not Scotch, are ya?"

"No," replied Daphne frostily. "Why?"

Bartlesham laughed. "The way you were goin' round and round with yer head down I thought you were a Scotchwoman who'd lost a penny."

John is still very much alive, but he is trapped in a body broken by his years as a demolition contractor.

"Eighty-two years and a few months, that's me," he told Daphne proudly from his wheelchair as they sat together under the shade of a knobbly oak of similar age. "Three-quarters of a million hours, give or take a few thousand," he detailed, having had plenty of time for calculations. "Seven hundred and fifty thousand hours of living and learning, eating and drinking, blowing stuff up and ripping it down. Now my turn's come."

But unlike the buildings he has demolished over the years, John is going neither easily nor with a bang. He is weathering slowly like a farmyard's massive old barn — built to withstand a century of storms — whose cornerstones are slowly buckling under the weight.

"Mince and mash," says Hilda Fitzgerald as she slaps plates onto the table in front of the two seniors.

"That makes a nice change," sneers Bartlesham, then he takes out his dentures for inspection before cheekily asking, "Any chance of watery rice pudding for dessert?"

Daphne eats in silence as her mind traces and retraces the labyrinth while she seeks answers. Then Amelia Brimble appears in the doorway and sings out, "You've got a visitor, Miss Lovelace," as if the elderly woman has won the lottery.

"Really?" says Daphne with little enthusiasm, but she has only completed the first week of a life sentence and has yet to grasp the fact that getting a visitor is winning the lottery.

chapter eight

"Chief Inspector ...?" queries Daphne, pulling up short as she shuffles into the visitors' room.

"It's David," corrects Bliss with a warm smile as he puts down a bag of grapes and advances with his arms out. "How many times have I told you? You're not on duty anymore."

"Oh. Yes ... silly of me," she replies, but she dithers and shies away as he tries to enfold her. "I keep forgetting things," she admits as her face flushes.

"Don't worry," says Bliss, guiding her to a cracked leather armchair. "It happens to us all. Anyway, thank goodness you remembered I was a chief inspector."

"So I did," says Daphne, brightening, and then she sinks. "But they say I forget most things."

The visit lasts an hour but is over after three minutes: the weather; the food; Prince Philip; the Queen ... all as good as can be expected. Then they start again: the food; the heat; the Queen; Prince Philip ...

Bliss searches for an exit. "Would you like to take a walk?"

"No, thank you."

"I could take you out for a little drive," he suggests bouncily as he starts to rise, but Daphne shakes her head.

"They don't like us going out. Worried we might not come back, I expect."

"Probably a liability issue," acknowledges Bliss as he sits down again. "Is there anything you need?"

Daphne's face says she has something on her mind, but the thought and the expression vaporize after a few seconds. "No. I can manage, David. You just look after the Queen."

"See? You remembered my name."

"Did I?"

"Yes."

"It must be the tablets," she says, then starts at the beginning again. "It's jolly warm today, isn't it?"

Samantha is breathless as she picks up at the first buzz. "Dad," she blurts, "I just climbed a mountain — my first one."

"What?"

"I just had this incredible urge to climb, so we drove to Wales."

"What?"

"Don't keep saying 'what' like that."

"Sorry, Sam. It's just that most pregnant women want anchovies or a Humphrey Bogart movie."

"I know," she says. "Bizarre, isn't it."

Absolutely terrifying, thinks Bliss, but manages to stop himself from castigating her. He doesn't want to encourage her to do it again. "I thought I'd let you know that I've visited Daphne."

"How is she?"

"Confused," says Bliss, and realizes that he is also

talking about himself. "One minute her memory seemed okay and the next it was fuzzy."

"Meaning?"

"I don't know. I couldn't figure her out. I'm wondering if she just got cheesed off always being on her own."

"Like you?"

"I'm not," he protests, but she laughs over him.

"Parachuting next week."

"Don't you dare," he shoots back, but she's still laughing as she flicks the off button.

The idea of aging on his own nags Bliss as he drives through Westchester to check on Daphne's house. The shuffling inmates of St. Michael's may be only one generation ahead of him, but as he waited in the entrance lobby for a staff member to take him to the visitors' room, the white-haired Lilliputians who eyed him suspiciously could have been aliens.

Twenty years — thirty at best, he warns himself as he turns into Daphne's road, and then he jams on his brakes at the sight of a mob. Ten skinheaded teenagers, led by all three of Rob Jenkins's sons, swashbuckle their way down the road towards him and force mothers to grab youngsters off the street. Then a small pebble pings off Bliss's roof.

Bliss winds down his window. "All right, lads," he calls as he flashes his police ID to the leaders. "What's going on?"

"What d'ya want, granddad?" challenges the eldest Jenkins.

"Police," says Bliss, nodding to his card as he opens his door.

"We ain't done nuvving," spits Jon-Jo.

"Someone just threw a stone —" Bliss starts, but derisive laughter and four-letter words drown him out.

Ten to one. He's had worse odds in his twenty-eight years in the Force and fought his way out of them, but he can feel the heat as they swarm in. Just one spark and he will be in the midst of an inferno, so he backs down.

"Just watch it, that's all," he says as he slides back into his seat.

"Up yours, granny," sneers a jug-eared lout, and his car takes a beating as they thump and kick their way past.

A young mother reappears, questioning, "Are you all right, sir?" as the hooligans turn the corner.

"Shaken," admits Bliss, as he dials 999. "Do you know who they are?"

The woman's face says yes, but she quickly backs off. "I ain't gonna get involved. I got young kiddies."

"I'm police," says Bliss, offering his card, but it back-fires as she lashes out and storms away, yelling over her shoulder, "Then you oughta be locking that damn lot up instead of little old ladies."

Daphne Lovelace, he guesses, and a few minutes later he is standing, slack-mouthed, in the remnants of his elderly friend's front garden, together with the uniformed constable who arrested her.

"She would slash her wrists ..." Bliss says, shaking his head in dismay at the hacked-down shrubs, trampled perennials, heaps of garbage, and graffiti-sprayed walls.

"I bet I know who did this," muses the constable, Roger Ingliss, with an eye on the Jenkins household, as they approach Daphne's front door.

Bliss's hand goes to his nose. "What the hell ..."

"Shit," says the constable pointing to the excrement smeared over the doorstep and crammed through the letterbox.

It is nearly midnight by the time Bliss arrives home, and he rips off his clothes inside the front door and heads for the bath without checking for missed calls.

"Sporadic gunfire was reported across a number of

cities this evening," the nighttime newscaster is trumpeting as Bliss finally slumps in front of the television in his dressing gown, then his phone buzzes.

It is Daisy. "I've been calling ..." she sobs, and he explains that he put his cellphone in his car while he climbed through a smashed window into Daphne's house, then forgot it as he spent the rest of the evening cleaning up and making good.

"Daavid, I want to see you," she insists, and with Prince Philip tucked safely away on the Scottish moors for another week, he makes a vow. "Next Friday. I promise."

"Please, Daavid. I love you."

"Much of tonight's violence appears religiously based," the reporter continues as Bliss's mind spins. "Mosques, temples, and churches have been fire-bombed — several destroyed ..."

"Daavid?"

I love you, too, is the response he is looking for, but with the memory of a lonely weekend in Cannes still gnawing at him the best he can do is, "We'll talk on Friday."

"Put everything on hold. The balloon's gone up," says Commander Fox as Bliss walks into a wall of activity Monday morning: men and women rushing around with folders; canteen staff laying out coffee cups in the conference room; technical staff setting up monitors and computers; secretaries polishing their nails.

"The rioting?" questions Bliss, but Fox shakes his head sombrely.

"No. The f'kin palace has rescheduled — Friday after next."

"Oh, for goodness' sake," moans Bliss as the conference room fills with unit commanders and support staff. "That's all I need."

"Have you got problems at home?" queries Fox with a knowing lilt, but Bliss shrugs it off as a stone-faced assistant commissioner shuffles papers with his head down, preparing to announce the bad news officially.

Thirty-two officers and staff but no sign of Edwards or the CIA, Bliss tallies quickly as the assistant commissioner clears his throat to bring the meeting to order.

"Whose bloody bright idea was that?" demands a special ops superintendent above the rumble of disbelief, and the assistant commissioner sternly jumps on him.

"Her Majesty the Queen, officer. She thinks it the best way to bring an end to the riots, but maybe you've got a better plan."

"Oh, no, sir," he says, deflating, then questions, "And what about Prince Philip, sir?"

"She can't go without him, can she," strikes back the A.C. "It would look as though she's keeping him in the Bloody Tower."

"It's a bit like dragging a four-year-old party pooper back to say sorry to the red-eyed birthday girl," suggests Bliss. "I just hope he doesn't try it again."

"It's your job to stop him, Chief Inspector," says the A.C., and then he passes the floor to Commander Fox, who offers an olive branch to the assembly by pointing out that nothing needs to be changed from the original plan, other than names of officers on leave or off duty through sickness.

"Another meeting Wednesday," concludes Fox, "and we'll have it sewn up."

The rumble of dissent returns as officers begin to leave the room, but Fox grabs Bliss's arm. "Michael Edwards is on his way over from the Home Office with the Duke's trick-cyclist."

"Just what I need to start the week off," mutters Bliss *sotto voce*, but Fox lets it go.

"The event shouldn't cause us any problems," begins Fox, explaining that Prince Philip's clumsy antics may actually have taken some sting out of the rescheduled visit. Al-Jezeerah and the other Arab stations have repeatedly run clips for the amusement of their audiences, and every comedian and cartoonist in the world has lampooned the royals. "The whole thing has become one huge joke," Fox is saying as Michael Edwards and Professor Morteson arrive to review the video of the original incident and to strategize.

"I suppose they could travel separately this time," suggests Edwards as they watch the motorcade approaching the mosque, and then the videographer narrates as the Queen alights from the car.

"Commander Fox salutes and spins to escort her up the steps to the waiting dignitaries," he says as the cameras follow the Queen up the steps. "Prince Philip, in his military uniform, catches up —"

"Wait a minute," says Bliss, reaching over to hit the pause button. "Why did it take him so long?"

"'Cos he had to get out the other side of the car and walk round," says Fox.

"Do we have a recording of that?" Bliss calls to the videographer, and the man begins checking his logs.

"Forget it. Let's get on," says Edwards irritably. "It doesn't matter how he got there. He got there."

"Right, sir," says the technician and he starts the show again.

"Here Prince Philip is following Her Majesty up the steps —"

"Cut, cut, cut," interrupts Bliss with something on his mind, but Edwards steps in and grabs the remote.

"Just watch the f'kin film, Chief Inspector. Christ, you sound like Cecil B. DeMille."

"Who was that, sir?" asks Bliss, feigning ignorance.

"Before your time. Now just shut up and watch."

The Queen is shaking hands with the first of the grey-robed dignitaries when the shot widens to include the

Duke as he unleashes his sword. Now Edwards hits the pause button.

"So. What do we see?"

"He looks angry," says Bliss. "See the way he threw off his protection officer."

"Professor?"

"Frustrated more than angered, I would say, Michael. It looks to me as though he somehow got entangled with his scabbard and momentarily lost his composure."

"Any response, Chief Inspector?"

The whitewash continues, thinks Bliss as he wonders what to have for his dinner. "No, sir. Fine with me." But, as the meeting breaks up, he sidles up to the videographer, asking, "Can you make me a copy?"

"Here," he says, "take this one. It's all on memory cards. I can make as many copies as I want."

"I'd still like to see if we've got him getting out of the car."

"I'll let you know."

"I'm going to be in Washington for a few days," Edwards loudly brags as he picks up his briefcase. "The Home Secretary thought I should sit down with the top brass at the Pentagon. See what they've got to offer."

"Absolutely, sir. Good thinking," says Bliss with undisguised sarcasm, knowing exactly whose idea it would have been to pick the taxpayers' pockets for a first-class junket to America.

Edwards scowls, but he balks at taking on Bliss in the presence of Professor Morteson.

By the time Bliss has returned to his office to take another look at the video, Daphne is back, circling her imaginary labyrinth in the noonday sun, muttering, "Here kitty-kitty-kitty … Here kitty-kitty-kitty …" fifty times a minute.

Amelia chuckles as she stands in the shade of the oak by the side of John Bartlesham's wheelchair. "She's just like a little clockwork mouse."

A distinguished voice says, "Amelia. Is that Miss Lovelace out there?"

"Oh. Hello, Mr. Jameson, sir," says the girl, turning to the stately figure behind her. "Yeah," she says, laughing, "that's my Daffy."

Robert Jameson of Jameson and Fidditch, Legal Services, distinguishes himself by his ability to withstand all weathers in a three-piece worsted suit, complete with a starched pocket handkerchief, a white rose boutonniere, and, in summer, a Panama hat.

"Miss Lovelace," he says, doffing his hat as he walks onto the field and stands in her path, but she swerves around him and picks up her labyrinth without missing a step.

"Here kitty-kitty-kitty … Here kitty-kitty-kitty …" she continues, with her eyes on the ground, as Jameson stands and wipes perspiration from his brow and hat band.

"You won't stop her, Mr. Jameson," laughs Amelia from the boundary. "Not till her spring runs down."

"Miss Lovelace," Jameson tries again solicitously, as Daphne's circuit brings her close, but this time he falls in step. "I wonder if I might have a few words with you about your will."

"Here kitty-kitty-kitty …" she starts anew, then stops, gives Jameson a fierce look, and starts again. "Here kitty-kitty-kitty …"

"You might as well come in an' 'ave a cuppa tea, Mr. Jameson," calls Amelia. "She won't stop till she's done."

Daphne is done ten minutes later and, as she sips her warm tea in the supervisor's office, she explains that she has no family as far as she can recall.

"Of course, I may have forgotten," she adds with a far-away look. "They say I forget things."

"What about children, Miss Lovelace? I think you'd remember them."

"I lost the only one I ever had," she says, without explaining that the baby she has in mind wasn't hers. It was the child a critically wounded Frenchwoman entrusted to her in the heat of battle, and it became one of Hitler's victims.

"All right then," says Jameson, as he stems a flood of perspiration from his brow with his sopping handkerchief, and she focuses intently on his blue eyes as he explains in considerable detail the legal difficulties that her beneficiaries might encounter should she die intestate.

"So, I'm sure you understand how important it is," Jameson concludes with a flourish, and Daphne slowly puts down her plastic mug, wipes her lips with a napkin, and sits back as if she is finished.

"Miss Lovelace?" queries Jameson, leaning expectantly into her after a prolonged pause.

"Yes?" she says.

"Did you understand everything?"

Daphne's face slowly metamorphoses from wide-eyed interest to scrunch-faced concentration, and Jameson sighs in disbelief when she eventually scratches her head and says, "Would you like to try again?"

Doctor Williamson pokes his head into the office five minutes later, just as Daphne finally seems to be grasping the benefits of tidying herself up before she trots off to the cemetery in the back of a black Bentley.

"Won't be a minute, Geoffrey," calls Jameson, then he turns back to Daphne and changes tune. "Maybe I can make it easier for you," he offers helpfully. "Maybe you should give someone power of attorney over your affairs. Then you wouldn't need to worry about a thing."

The doctor is examining Emily Mountjoy in her room by the time Daphne has given Jameson tacit approval to draw up necessary papers, and she is blocked at the door by Hilda Fitzgerald.

"Emily's not at all well," says Hilda. "Maybe you should take a little walk while we sort her out and take her to the sickroom."

"She seemed all right earlier," protests Daphne, but Hilda's face isn't promising. "It's her heart," she confides with a grimace of distaste, depicting Emily's heart in the same vein as the Antichrist, leaving Daphne no choice but to return to her labyrinth.

By mid-afternoon the videographer has dug deep into the digitized mind of his computer and uncovered the images Bliss requested. But after ten viewings of Prince Philip leaving the royal limousine and walking to the mosque's steps, Bliss still has questions and seeks a second opinion.

"Can you spare a minute?" he asks, phoning his son-in-law, D.C.I. Peter Bryan, and a few minutes later they sit together in front of Bliss's computer screen.

"He gets out of the car on the offside, straightens himself up, brushes off his collar, and walks around the back," narrates Bliss. "Now watch carefully," he carries on, stabbing the screen with a finger. "He reaches the pavement and stops. Now look at his face."

"He looks as though he's crapping his pants," says Bryan; Prince Philip stands rooted to the spot while his face puckers in strain.

"Indelicately put, but absolutely true, Peter," says Bliss, adding, "Then he pulls himself together and heads for the steps to the reception party."

"Gas," suggests Bryan as Bliss stops the disc and repositions Philip onto the pavement. "The old boy didn't want to desecrate the mosque with a raspberry and be damned in Hell for eternity, so he just stopped to give his head a squeeze and clear himself out before he went up the steps."

"There goes my chance of heaven," laughs Bliss, recalling his days as a young choirboy, but Peter Bryan isn't so sure.

"I bet you could get in on appeal."

"Really?"

"Yeah. Let's face it, they're all the same. They all want you on their team. It's the emperor's new clothes syndrome. And what else have they got to offer apart from absolution for sins, bingo, and a shot at heaven?"

"Some very nice music," suggests Bliss, but his son-in-law is on a soapbox.

"They're like travel agents plugging package holidays at a tourism fair," claims Peter Bryan, as he mimics a Bible-barker. "'We've got the best deals on heaven,' yells a guy wearing a bishop's mitre. 'Constant sunshine; lots of old friends; great for family reunions; strawberries and champagne; harp and lyre orchestras.' Then an evangelist in a Stetson waves you over. 'Don't listen to that lot of old fuddy-duddies, Dave. We'll give you all that, plus — and you are just gonna throw your hands in the air and burst into tears when you hear this — you will get to sing in the choir.' 'Really?' you say. 'Oh, yeah. Hallelujah! Praise the Lord. Everyone gets to sing in the choir in our heaven.' 'That's very tempting,' you're saying, when this guy in a white robe drives up in a Mercedes. 'You come with me, mister,' he says in a dodgy accent. 'We go for very short ride and then I take you to special place with seventy-two virgins — all very nice girls — just for you.' 'Well … I don't know,' you say. 'I'm not sure I feel comfortable getting into a car with a suspicious-looking package on the floor and an Mk 47 on the back seat.' 'Forget heaven and all that nonsense,' calls out a guy in a turban at the next booth. 'We offer a full return package. Come with us and in no time at all you'll be back. And, who knows, you might be a maharajah next time.' 'Are you serious?' you say, then this chap with a beanie…"

"All right," laughs Bliss, "you've made your point. So I guess my grandchild won't be christened then."

"Ah. Now that would be a very dangerous assumption for any man, Dave. Especially one married to your daughter."

"Sad news," says Davenport, waking Daphne with an early-morning cup of tea and a consolatory milk chocolate digestive on Tuesday morning. "Our dear friend Emily passed over during the night."

"Oh my goodness. I had no idea," says Daphne, but it's not until Amelia bustles in with clean bedding that she gets some answers.

"You're getting a new roommate today, Daffy," says Amelia, ripping off Emily's sheets, as if the change is something for Daphne to relish.

"It's Daphne, my dear, not Daffy. I'm not a duck."

"'Course you're not," agrees Amelia, then she laughs lightly. "I bet you were quite a lady in your day."

"My day," muses Daphne sadly, realizing that, like Emily Mountjoy, her day is nearing its end. "What happened to Emily?"

"You do ask a lot of questions, Daffy."

"That's because I forget everything."

"Well, I couldn't say for sure. You'd have to ask Mr. Davenport."

"I think he told me, but I must've forgot," she replies offhandedly. "I don't want to bother him again, he's such a nice man."

Amelia scrunches her face in mock pain.

"Isn't he very nice?" whispers Daphne, but Amelia knows the signatory of her wage cheques and keeps her own counsel. However, the ferocity with which she shakes the duvet into its cover is answer enough.

"Does he live here, in the home?" probes Daphne once the dust has settled.

"No," snorts Amelia. "He's got a blisterin' great mansion on King's Road. I have to go up and clean sometimes when his maid's on holidays."

"He has a maid?" queries Daphne, surprise lifting her voice.

"An' a cook, an' a gardener," confides Amelia as she clears Emily's bedside table of its meagre contents, then she wistfully stares at the family photograph.

"Was her family with her when she died?" asks Daphne.

Amelia frowns in puzzlement, then catches on. "Oh. This ain't Emily's family. Emily didn't have no family ... not a soul."

"So who ...?" Daphne nods to the photograph.

"Oh. That were Mrs. Johns. She had your bed before you. She used to talk to Emily a lot. So when she passed on I thought Emily might like it — to remind her." Then she proffers it like a prize. "Would you like it, now?"

"Thank you," says Daphne, looking as though she might treasure it forever, then she ferrets into her slipper for another five-pound note and asks Amelia to buy her some Tums for her indigestion.

"Mrs. Fitzgerald has some —"

"No. I tried the ones she has — they don't work," cuts in Daphne with a smile. "I always have Tums, but don't tell anyone. They're only indigestion tablets, but I don't want to upset Mr. Davenport."

"Okay, Daffy."

"And keep the change, dear."

The undertaker's black van is paying its second visit of the week. It picked up two passengers from St. Michael's on Monday, and Emily Mountjoy has company on the road to the funeral parlour today.

"It's this bloomin' heat," moans Hilda Fitzgerald when she finds Daphne to tell her that Mr. Jameson has returned with some papers for her to sign. "Four gone and it's only Tuesday."

"Oh, you poor thing," sighs Daphne, patting the cook's hand as if she has suffered a personal tragedy. And Hilda smiles her gratitude before explaining that Robert Jameson, the lawyer, asked her and Patrick Davenport to witness the papers granting him power of attorney over Daphne's estate. "If that's all right with you," she adds as she escorts Daphne to the office.

"Sign here ... here ... and ... here," says Jameson, proffering his gold-plated Schaeffer Executive to Daphne, once he has expressed the honour he feels at being chosen to represent her.

Daphne takes the pen and weighs it carefully. "This is right, isn't it?" she asks of those around her.

"Yes. Of course," says Davenport. "Mr. Jameson has power of attorney for several of our guests, and everyone has been very satisfied with his services."

"Very well ..." she starts, then pauses with a thought. "But what if my memory comes back?"

"You can rescind at any time," soothes Jameson as he dabs his brow. "You needn't worry."

"Yes. Don't worry, dear," chimes in Hilda in the background.

"Right," says Daphne as the tension dissipates from her face. "I've made up my mind."

"Good," says Jameson, then his face drops as she hands him back the pen saying, "I think I should get a friend to look at it first. If that's all right with you."

"What about the Reverend Rowlands?" suggests Davenport, stepping in quickly. "He told me that he's known you for quite some time."

"Has he?"

"Shall we ask him?"

"Round and round," says Amelia, watching Daphne from the kitchen window as lunchtime approaches. But Daphne has only one eye on the ground. With the other she is watching the ambulant residents shuffling slowly towards the common room, and she is carefully timing her footsteps as she circumnavigates the lawn.

Nine minutes and twenty-seven seconds, she calculates, for a single circuit that carries her around one quadrant of her imaginary labyrinth, but her scheme only needs one — the one that keeps her out of sight of the common room windows.

"Lunch, Daffy," calls Amelia from the kitchen door, and Daphne pauses to reply, "Another ten minutes, Amelia."

"It's mince. I'll keep it warm," yells the girl as she ducks back in to start serving.

Two minutes, Daphne gives herself as she begins walking again, but this time she is checking the car park. Most of the staff spots are empty. Amelia's bicycle is propped against the "Visitors" sign, but there are no cars. And she saw Patrick Davenport and Robert Jameson leave together in the lawyer's flashy yellow Lotus, en route to a Rotary Club lunch at the Mitre.

"One minute," she says, and peers at the kitchen window. "Good," she breathes to herself, knowing that Hilda, Amelia, and the rest of the staff are delivering meals and helping residents to eat. Just one more check — Hilda's husband, the part-time preacher and gardener.

Samuel Fitzgerald has a shed filled with mowers, cutters, clippers, and all manner of gardening supplies to one side of the lawn, and with a slight deviation, Daphne sneaks a look through the window.

The gardener, with a Bible open on his lap, is laid back in an old Windsor chair with his feet up on a wheelbarrow and his eyes firmly closed.

"D-Day," says Daphne triumphantly, and instead of looping back at the end of her labyrinth, she keeps walking — straight past the old oak tree and onto the gravel driveway. The wrought iron entrance gates are wide open, and she picks up the pace as she makes for them. Once she clears the gates all she need do is take a sharp right through a beech thicket and she will emerge at the bus stop on the High Street. From there — the world.

Fifteen yards to the gate and Daphne's feet are going as fast as her heart. She risks a quick look over her shoulder — all clear. Another twenty-five paces and she will have put the scent of stale urine behind her forever.

Ten paces and she can smell the fresh air. She takes a deep breath and sighs in satisfaction. Just five more paces to the gate — ten feet — and the air around her explodes in a cacophony of sound and lights.

She freezes momentarily and considers running, but footsteps are already pounding down the driveway behind.

"Miss Lovelace. Miss Lovelace," calls Samuel Fitzgerald as he catches up to her and gently leads her back towards the home. "You can't go out that way, dear. You've set off the alarms."

chapter nine

The soft summery air of the Pacific tears at Winifred Goodenow's lime green headscarf as she stands on the prow of a car ferry and watches the jagged mountains and lush forests of British Columbia's offshore islands rush towards her in the early-morning sunshine.

A multicoloured flotilla of pleasure craft dot the surrounding sea as the giant ferry from Vancouver cuts a deep furrow across the blue ocean; ahead, close to a rocky islet alive with squabbling seals and cormorants with their wings hanging out to dry, the resident school of orcas breach to blow.

"Whales. Just off the port bow," sings out the First Officer on the ship's P.A., and a hundred passengers in shorts and T-shirts stream out of the lounges and restaurants to watch.

Amid the excitement, no one notices Winifred's bloodied bare feet, and neither the taxi driver she waved down in

Vancouver nor the ferry's ticket seller at the port cared about her oddball appearance — after all, she paid.

"She's wearing an orange linen tablecloth with bunches of petunias and a red wine stain ... Bordeaux, I think." Winifred's daughter, Trina, anxiously gushes, as she contorts the brain of yet another Vancouver City policeman. "No," she adds, staying his hand. "It was an Okanagan Cabernet Sauvignon —"

"Madam," cuts in the officer. "It doesn't matter."

"Oh, it does. You've no idea how difficult Bordeaux can be to get out. I've tried all sorts of —"

"Madam. I don't care what kind of wine it was," he shouts. "What do you mean when you say your mother's only wearing a tablecloth?"

"Well, not just a tablecloth," says Trina, and the officer's face relaxes a notch. "She's also wearing a lime green tea towel and a couple of dishcloths. Though I'm not sure what she's done with the dishcloths."

"Oh, no! Not you again," spits Sergeant Dave Brougham, walking in off the street to start duty, and Trina immediately lunges forward into the virabhadrasana yoga pose.

"What on earth are you doing now?" inquires Brougham, as she roots herself to the spot on one leg and thrusts her arms out in front of her as if readying to dive.

"Preparing for battle," says Trina determinedly. "Mother's gone again. We have to find her."

This is Winifred's fourth escape in just over two weeks, and each time Trina has taken greater precautions, even locking away her mother's clothes and shoes each evening. But somehow, during the night, the determined woman levered her way out of the basement window after rifling the dining room linen closet.

With the brightly coloured tablecloth wrapped around her, sari-like, and the tea towel scarf covering her head, Winifred blends with the throng of gaily dressed holidaymakers as she leaves the ferry and jostles for a place on a sightseers' bus.

"Ticket holders only," yells the driver amid the crush, but Winifred pulls her tea towel over her face to slip under his radar and is tucked tightly into a corner when they set off to explore the island.

"Don't waste your time, Constable," orders Dave Brougham as he slides behind the inquiry counter and gives Trina a look of undisguised contempt. "Get hold of Inspector Phillips over at the RCMP. He found her twice last week." Then he snorts derisively. "Hah! Typical of the Mounties — they don't always get their man, but they can always find a woman when they want one."

"What about Daphne Lovelace?" queries Trina. "She's bound to know where Mum is."

"Now we're getting somewhere sensible," says Brougham as he takes off his jacket and grabs a pen. But Daphne's number strikes him as odd, and as he picks up the phone, he questions why a woman in England would know where to look.

"Because Mum and her are the exactly same age and have the same birth sign," says Trina, as if it should have been obvious.

Daphne couldn't answer her phone if Brougham called. She is confined to her room, and she too has had her clothes and shoes confiscated, although she dug in her heels, asserting angrily, "You said I could leave if I wanted to."

"Only with permission, Miss Lovelace," Davenport said firmly, adding, "I've asked Doctor Williamson to give you something to calm you down."

"I'm quite calm, thank you. I just want to leave," she shot back, hauling herself off the bed, but Hilda Fitzgerald hauled her back on.

"Now stop being silly. You'll upset Miss Montgomery," the matronly domestic assistant said as she firmly locked the squirming woman down. But one look at her new roommate told Daphne that she had another Emily Mountjoy as company — a skeleton with a pair of dead eyes staring sightlessly into a grim future — so she snapped back, "And what will you do if I don't?"

"God will punish you …" began Patrick Davenport, then he questioned with a skeptical eye, "You haven't been taking your tablets, have you?"

"I have."

"Don't lie," he warned. "You know that lying is a sin." And he rummaged through the drawer in Daphne's bedside table until he found a half-eaten packet of Tums. With triumph written on his face he demanded, "All right. So where are the tablets we gave you? What did you do with them?"

"I don't know what you mean," bluffed Daphne, knowing that Amelia, who had the job of watching to make sure she swallowed her daily dose of tranquilizers, never noticed her palm them in exchange for a couple of Tums.

Doctor Williamson's arrival saved her. "I hear you've been a naughty girl," he said as he shot a sedative into her arm a few minutes later, and within seconds she was asleep.

Winifred Goodenow's unauthorized daytrip to Vancouver Island comes to an abrupt end when her plan and her makeshift sari simultaneously unravel as she painfully totters towards the ferry in the afternoon's warm sunshine.

"No ticket, no ferry," lectures the collector loftily from his booth when she mumbles that she has lost her return ticket, then he looks down at her and shrieks, "Oh my dear Lord!"

The sun may still be shining on the west coast of Canada, but it is well after midnight in Westchester as Daphne surfaces dozily from the drug. It takes more than ten minutes for her to shake herself awake, but her body is still heavy and her head light as she single-mindedly drags herself downstairs to the payphone in the entrance foyer.

The two night attendants have finished their rounds — thirty-seven patients and one cadaver, none of whom, they hope, will give them any more trouble — and they have turned down the lights and are both flat out on settees in the common room.

Daphne creeps past in the dimness and has gently picked the phone off its cradle before realizing that she has no coins. "Reverse the charges," her mind tells her, but it doesn't give her instructions.

"Hello ... hello," she whispers when a woman asks her to insert a coin, but the sound of her own voice makes her jump, and she drops the phone and scuttles to a dark corner.

"C'mon. Pull yourself together. You can do it," she tells herself as her mind spins, but she's woken one of the orderlies.

"Who's there?" calls the woman as a tinny voice joins in.

"Please hang up and try your call again ... Please hang up ...."

"Who is it?" demands the orderly, hastily straightening her hair and her bosom as she emerges from the common room.

Daphne cringes into the doorway of Patrick Davenport's office and feels it give behind her.

"Who's there?" continues the orderly, and then she spots the phone. With a puzzled look she replaces the receiver, shrugs, and heads back to sleep.

Inside the office, Daphne lays on the floor fighting for breath. *You're too old for this*, she tells herself. *You can't do it. Go back to bed.* But she has the labyrinth in her head now, and the voice of Angel Robinson encouraging, "So, you learnt that it was up to you to fight your way through." So she hauls herself up to Davenport's desk and grabs his phone.

The only light is from a security lamp outside the window, and the numbers swim on the page of her address book. Four wrong numbers in succession — all irate at being disturbed in the early hours — but she gets Bliss on the fifth.

"David," she whispers, but his sleepy mind warns him it could still be a dream.

"Hello — who is this?" he asks as he tries to surface. "Daisy, is that you?"

She tries again. "It's Daphne …" she says, and although the words start off sensibly in her mind they're tangled by the time they reach her mouth.

"I don't know what you're saying," Bliss interjects irritably as Daphne rambles about religious zealots, labyrinths, angels, and forced injections. But he is still half asleep himself.

"Oh, go to bed, Daphne, I'll come and visit next weekend," he says eventually and puts down the phone. Five minutes later, now wide awake with concern, he angrily mutters, "You're a bloody nuisance at times," checks his call display, and phones back.

"Now it's engaged," he snorts, and drags himself to the kitchen to put on the kettle.

Daphne is still on the phone, calling for international assistance.

"Mum. Is that you?" says Trina Button breathlessly as she grabs the phone, and for a few moments Daphne's garbled rant has her convinced. The truth unravels slowly as the Englishness of the accent comes through, but Daphne is sinking fast. Exertion and the residual effects of the soporific weigh her down, and she leaves Trina hanging as she struggles back to her bedroom.

The room rotates giddily around Daphne as she slumps onto the bed, while, in another part of the old mansion, Hilda Fitzgerald is being rousted from her upstairs quarters to speak to David Bliss.

"Sorry to bother you, Hilda," says one of the night staff. "But there's a man on the phone about Miss Lovelace, and I don't know what to tell him."

By the time Hilda reaches the office she has her mind in gear and she puts Bliss in the picture: "... not taking her medication ... caused a little trouble ... started wandering — not uncommon in cases like hers ... Doctor's given her a sedative ... she's very confused."

"She certainly seemed strange the other day," agrees Bliss. "Not at all sparky — not able to hold a conversation."

"That's not unusual," Hilda assures him. "A lot of our guests repeat themselves over and over, as if they're stuck in a loop. It's a type of obsessive behaviour. Just like Miss Lovelace's obsession with walking in circles. That's what happens when areas of the brain deteriorate."

"Oh, dear. Poor Daphne."

"It's very sad," agrees Hilda. "But don't worry. We'll do our very best for her."

"Thank you," says Bliss, dropping back onto his bed. "I shall sleep easier now." But his phone is buzzing by the time his head hits the pillow.

It's Trina Button, panicking. "David. You must do something. Daphne's being kept prisoner by a religious cult."

"No she's not. She's in an old people's home," replies Bliss, but Trina isn't listening.

"They've drugged her —"

"A sedative."

"— stolen her shoes —"

"To stop her running."

"— brainwashed her —"

"What?"

"With religion. Aren't you listening? It's a cult."

Bliss stops her eventually. "I've just got off the phone with them," he explains. "They're very nice people. They're very concerned about her and they're doing their best."

But "nice people" is not an image that equates with reality as Hilda Fitzgerald crashes into Daphne's room and stands over her, shouting, "Don't you dare get out of bed in the night again. And don't you dare use the office phone for personal calls. Do I make myself clear?"

"If you're so worried about her, then come over and see for yourself," suggests Bliss, irritably. "I've got a job to do and an important meeting in the morning."

"I can't," croaks Trina as tears start to flow. "My mother's missing again. She's been gone all day. And the police are useless."

"Well, I'm not sure about that," says Bliss defensively, but Trina is.

"This lot in Vancouver couldn't find the hole in a donut," she snivels, and Bliss softens.

"I'll visit Daphne again as soon as I can. But she's perfectly safe where she is."

Safety is on Daphne's mind as well as she cowers under the bedclothes, whimpering, "I want to go home. I don't like it here."

"Shuddup, you stupid old bag," yells Hilda, and then she rips back the sheet and slaps the crying woman viciously across her face. "Shuddup, shuddup, shuddup," she screeches as she slaps, and then she drags Daphne from the bed and forces her to her knees. "Now you'd better start praying, lady, 'cos you need all the help you can get."

"Ungodly Warfare," proclaims Wednesday's *Daily Mirror,* headlining a report on the continuing violent clashes across the country. And while the weather takes some of the heat, there is no question that ethnicity and religion are playing the largest role.

Smiling gangs of skinheads, with swastika tattoos and pierced lips, wrap themselves in Union flags and sport crucifixes on gold chains as they adopt thuggish poses for the paper's centre spread.

"Christian Warriors???" questions the caption, but the photos leave no doubt that, in some minds, nationalism, Nazism, and a solid conviction that Christianity was founded by the British can be fused into a tritheistic doctrine that justifies heavy-booted advocates seeking out anyone worthy of a kicking.

"And the Queen, God bless her cotton socks," snorts Commander Fox, tossing the newspaper onto the table in disgust at the Wednesday morning planning meeting, "believes that her rescheduled visit to the mosque will help calm the situation." But Lefty and Pimple, the American president's henchmen, don't look convinced either. The glum-faced CIA operatives are not officially present, as the minutes will clearly show, but they sit in plain view and make notes as Fox runs his eye around the room and takes a mental roll call of his senior officers and staff.

"Right," he says, apparently satisfied with attendance. "Michael Edwards, the Home Secretary's security advisor, has asked me to stress his boss's determination to put an end to this nonsense, but, to be frank, I'm worried that this visit might make it worse."

Judging by the faces of the Americans, the President takes a similar view, and several members of the British Parliament have risked the ire of the Prime Minister and the palace by going public with their criticisms.

"My guess is that her people are censoring what she sees," suggests Fox as he carries on. "She probably believes it was the heat and that it's likely to cool off a bit in the next week or so."

David Bliss yawns and slumps in his chair as the meeting gets underway. He won't be in the hot seat this time; someone else will be staring at the surveillance screens while he is purportedly preventing Prince Philip from becoming a recidivist. But he is still devoid of any realistic strategies, and, as he drifts off, he reminds himself that he's not expected to do anything; he's just the fall guy.

It's been more than a week since the attack, and for most of that time the Queen has been at one end of the country with Philip at the other. And if the palace schedulers do their job, it will stay that way until the day of reckoning — the day that he will again walk up the steps to the mosque, in a complete reversal of Muslim custom, one regulation pace behind his wife. Supermarket tabloid editors may be upset by the arrangement, but the owners of hotels, pubs, and restaurants surrounding Balmoral Castle are booking cruises and refurbished kitchens on the backs of an army of camera-wielding paparazzi who daily scour the fortress's walls in the hope of catching Philip with his pants down.

However, the Duke of Edinburgh's reclusion within the Scottish stone bastion is in itself the subject of caustic amusement. "Prince Doing Porridge in Scotland!" laughs the caption under a computer-generated image of the Duke wearing stripes and a ball and chain in today's *Times*.

Daphne Lovelace also feels the weight of chains as she sits, staring fixedly out of her bedroom window at the lawn where her feet have traced a labyrinth during the past nine days. She hasn't moved since Hilda Fitzgerald and Patrick Davenport visited with her breakfast and stuck the papers granting Robert Jameson power of attorney over her affairs under her nose.

"Sign," said Davenport, grabbing Daphne's hand and fitting a pen between her fingers.

"I don't —" was as far as she got.

"Do you want another one?" warned Hilda with her hand at the ready, and Daphne signed.

Amelia hustles in with mid-morning mugs of tea for Daphne and her new companion. "Ooh. You haven't touched your breakfast ..." she is saying when she grinds to a stop. "Oh my God!" she cries. "Whatever happened to your face, Daffy?" And she quickly puts down the mugs and crouches at Daphne's feet. "Did you bump yourself in the night?"

"Sleepwalking," Daphne claims in a monotone without taking her eyes off the lawn.

"Is that what happened yesterday when you was goin' round and round?" Amelia burbles on. "Did you just sorta wander off like you wuz asleep?"

"Something like that," Daphne replies, then she turns to the young girl and asks, "How did I set off the alarms?"

Amelia has a nervous glance over Daphne's shoulder before confiding, "I ain't s'posed to tell anyone, but they put thingies in your clothes."

"Thingies?"

"Yeah, little tiny electronic thingies. Here, I'll show you," she says, standing to open Daphne's wardrobe door. "Oh. Where's all your clothes, Daffy?"

Trina Button's mother could also use some clothes, but since her return from Vancouver Island in the back of Sergeant Brougham's police cruiser, Winifred has hobbled around her daughter's house in a luminous pink housecoat.

"You won't get very far in that," Trina told her as she exchanged it for her tablecloth, but after a day on the run Winifred's feet are in such a state that it will be some time before she makes another bid to escape.

An invitation to dinner from Peter Bryan to "celebrate our first successful ultrasound" offers Bliss a respite from an evening of phone-gazing as he wrestles over his future with

Daisy and promises him a juicy steak, although he can't get his mind off Daphne.

"I told her I'd visit this weekend," he tells Samantha in the kitchen, once the baby stuff is dealt with and he has recounted his early-morning phone conversations with the folks at St. Michael's. "But I've promised Daisy for Friday, and I'm supposed to be taking care of the Queen."

"So many women, so little time," laughs his son-in-law from the dining room as he opens a bottle of claret.

"None for me, Peter," calls Samantha, meaningfully patting her midriff.

"That's the trouble. I've got lots of time," says Bliss as he follows his nose to the Bordeaux. "Edwards is in Washington — God knows why — and I'm sitting around like a bridesmaid at a funeral."

"A what?" asks Bryan.

Bliss rolls his eyes. "I'm at the wrong church," he says, then explains. "I should be in France, but Fox slapped a moratorium on all leave until after the visit. So here I am, with bugger all to do as long as the warring Windsors are kept apart."

"So what are you going to do about Daisy?" calls Samantha from the kitchen.

"I'll just sneak a poet's day on Friday and slip back Sunday evening. Fox will never know. And Daphne will have to wait a week. It's not as though she's going anywhere in a hurry."

"A what day?" queries Bryan.

"Oh, come on Peter, wake up," he says, then spells, "P-O-E-T-S: piss off early tomorrow's Saturday."

"Just don't get caught," says Samantha as she sashays in with the main course, but Bliss takes a sideways look at his plate and pulls a face.

"Organic spinach salad with goat feta, green olives, and hummus," she details, adding, "We have to think of the baby now, Dad."

The meal could have been worse, thinks Bliss, over the fresh fruit salad *sans* cream, but he makes a mental note to have a fat-lover's lunch in the canteen beforehand the next time he is invited.

"You could always write another book if you're bored," suggests Samantha as she collects the dessert plates. "You've already written about the Man in the Iron Mask."

"Fat lot of good that's done me," he complains. "I haven't heard a dicky from any of the publishers." However, his bulky manuscript has not been shoved to the bottom of every publisher's slush pile. One publisher, at least, is using it as a prop for the window of his dingy garret in a laneway off Leicester Square.

"But what if you solved a whole series of historical mysteries?" Samantha carries on enthusiastically. "Wouldn't that get you noticed?"

"Such as?"

"I don't know. There must be dozens ... what about the Bermuda Triangle, the *Mary Celeste*, or the lost Ark?"

"Be sensible," he protests. "I don't know anything about them."

But she is not deterred. "You didn't know anything about the Man in the Iron Mask till you found his island."

"That's true —" he is saying, when she cuts him off with a triumphant yelp.

"I know — Jack the Ripper."

"Why?"

"Firstly, it was in the same area as the mosque: Whitechapel."

"That's just a coincidence."

"Of course it is. But wasn't it one of Philip's relatives who was supposed to have done it?"

"Was it?" asks Bliss with a glimmer of interest.

"Yes," jumps in Peter Bryan. "It was the Duke of Clarence."

"All right," says Bliss with little intent. "I'll think about it."

With nothing important on his desk, David Bliss takes a detour to work on Thursday morning. However, he isn't seeking clues about the notorious Victorian-era murders of a string of prostitutes as he walks the streets of Whitechapel in East London. He is back at the mosque, and he is not alone. Since the Queen's ill-fated visit the richly ornamented building, with its gold-plated dome, has become a morbid curiosity on the tourist maps and now ranks with the Dealey Plaza book depository in Dallas and the pavement outside John Lennon's apartment in midtown Manhattan.

"I bet you can still see some of her blood," a ghoulish ten-year-old tells his mother excitedly as he drags her up the steps, but he is quickly disappointed.

"Never mind," says the woman. "We'll go to the Tower, where they chopped off loads of queens' heads."

"Brilliant, Mum!"

But amongst the knot of sensation seekers are crucifix wearers, staring with a mixture of wonder and hostility at the opulent new building, questioning why their ancient churches continue to crumble while mosques, synagogues, and Hindu temples seemingly spring up daily across the country.

"They reckon there's five million quids' worth of gold on the roof alone," sneers one in a combination of jealousy and awe, while another queries aloud, "Do you think they'll put a plaque on the mosque saying 'Queen Elizabeth fell here'?"

Will anyone ever put a plaque on my wall saying "David Bliss was here," Bliss wonders as he stares at the enormous building and questions what legacy he might leave. A handful of lifers will still be doing time, he guesses, then rebukes himself. *What do you expect — immortality? You tried that. You spent years turning up the truth about Louis XIV's nefarious machinations, and another year writing a novel, and where did it get you?* But he actually has Daphne in mind as he ponders the insignificance of a human life: years of struggling, learning, and working; triumphs and failures; heartaches and tears; laughter, joy, and love. Then your heart or brain fails, or you take a wrong turn and walk into a mugger's knife or a hit man's gun, and it's all gone. Perhaps a few snippets remain, Bliss tells himself, running over the personal items in Daphne's house: photographs and letters; certificates and awards; a painting or two; and a few pieces of embroidery.

"Not much to show for eighty-five years," he mourns aloud as he realizes that, by the time the wreaths have been taken off Daphne's grave and dumped on the compost heap, almost everything else will have vanished.

At least you will have a grandchild to carry your genes into the future, he is telling himself as he wakes up to the fact that he is standing on the exact spot where Prince Philip froze to the pavement. *Maybe he saw something, maybe he spotted some kind of danger that made him freak,* Bliss thinks as he spins around looking at the various buildings surrounding him. Then he glances down at the paving slab he's standing on. "Got it," he breathes and rushes into the road to flag a passing cab. "Scotland Yard," he calls to the driver as he leaps in, and his tone says *and step on it.*

"Do we have general coverage of the front of the new Whitechapel mosque?" Bliss gushes as he races into the surveillance unit's office and grabs the videographer.

"Yeah — all mosques and Muslim centres since 9/11, sir. We have them all covered."

"Great," says Bliss thinking quickly. "The day before ... no ... two days before the Queen's visit, on the Wednesday. I want everything you've got. Any angle; any quality. My office ASAP."

"Peter," Bliss says with a call to his son-in-law an hour later. "I could use a second pair of eyes."

The surveillance footage is black and white and washed out with bright sunlight. "Best I can do," said the videographer when Bliss complained. "These cameras are good, but we're not the bloomin' BBC."

"Watch," Bliss instructs his son-in-law, once he has isolated a segment. "That's me walking down the steps of the mosque to talk to two blokes who turned up with a truckload of concrete slabs."

The camera is positioned directly across the street, on the front of the public library, but the men's pickup truck blocks a full view as the overall-wearing workers unload pickaxes and shovels and begin work.

"And there's us talking," continues Bliss as he points to a gauzy image of his head and upper torso as he converses with the men. "They reckoned they were relaying the paving slabs so the Queen wouldn't trip," says Bliss, while the silent conversation continues on the screen. "But they looked smooth enough to me."

Bliss's figure drifts back up the steps to Commander Fox's briefing as the two men continue digging up paving stones.

"I can't see properly," complains Bryan. "I can't see their faces at all."

"One was stocky and darkish with a goatee and glasses and the other was about my height with blue eyes and bad teeth," says Bliss. "But just watch what happens. You can see enough."

The polished head of a pickaxe catches the sun as it is drawn back to smash a slab, then a replacement stone is lifted off the back of the truck as Bliss, Fox, and the rest of the officers walk down the steps behind the men and drift out of camera range.

"Now watch carefully," says Bliss after a few minutes, as the taller man puts down his shovel to light a cigarette.

His cupped hands shield the flame of a match, but they also cover his face as he slowly pivots three hundred and sixty degrees and even cranes around the cab of the truck. "I reckon he's making sure the coast is clear."

"It's possible," interjects Bryan as the workman flicks away the matchstick and opens the cab door. With a final furtive look over his shoulder he ferrets underneath the seat and comes out carrying something wrapped in a blanket.

Bliss pauses the tape. "What is it?"

Bryan gives him a quizzical look. "I dunno. An elephant?"

"Don't be silly, Peter. It's square — like a box or something."

"Well, how the hell should I know what it is? I'm not a bloody X-ray machine."

"I know, I know," mutters Bliss. "I've watched it fifty times and I can't figure it out. But look what happens next."

As the picture restarts the man disappears behind the pickup to the spot where they were digging, and seconds later he throws the empty blanket into the back of the truck. Within two minutes all of the tools and the broken slabs have followed the blanket, and the men jump into the cab and take off.

"Absolutely nothing," says Bliss, freezing the frame and pointing to the pavement. "Not a trace."

The two men peer intently at the screen for ten seconds, then they look at each other, and five frantic minutes later, with shovels and a pickaxe from the equipment store and a half a dozen hazard cones from the traffic department, they race to the scene in an unmarked car.

chapter ten

"Miss Lovelace is not receiving visitors today," insists Patrick Davenport when Mavis Longbottom finally decides on direct action and turns up on St. Michael's doorstep.

"Look, I've been calling for weeks," Mavis exaggerates, digging in. "I need to talk to her about her house and stuff. When can I see her?"

Davenport drops his eyes to the power of attorney's papers on his desk and quickly flips them over, questioning, "You're not a close relative or anything, are you?"

"No. She doesn't have any relatives, not as far as I know. That's why I want to make sure she's all right."

The manager paints on a reassuring smile. "She's fine," he claims. "She's just having a little difficulty adjusting. Now, why don't you leave us your number?"

Mavis has no choice, but, as she cuts across the lawn on her way out, she hesitates with the feeling that she is being watched and a shiver runs up her spine.

Daphne Lovelace, her old friend, is the person watching. Sitting alongside Esmeralda Montgomery with her eyes focused fiercely on the imaginary centre of the lawn's labyrinth and wanting to cry out, "Mavis. I'm up here." But she is bound and gagged — not by ropes or chains, but by the presence of Hilda Fitzgerald and the Reverend Rollie Rowlands.

"The poor old soul's had a bit of a fall," explains Hilda, as if her victim has damaged hearing as well as a bloodshot eye, then she flits around, primping up Daphne's hair and straightening her dressing gown, while the vicar stoops in front of Daphne, pulls what he hopes is a sympathetic grin, and coos, "Oh, you poor thing. Whatever happened?"

The tentacles of a deep bruise spread across Daphne's face in the shape of a podgy-fingered hand, and her left eye is partially closed by the swelling, but she stays silent, focusing intently on Mavis, her friend, as she disappears through the residence's gateway.

"She must've fallen out of bed in the middle of the night," sneaks in the home's enforcer before Daphne can respond. But she needn't worry. Daphne has no intention of burdening Rowlands with the truth.

"Would you like Hilda and me to say a little prayer for you?" Rowlands prattles on as he sits on his heels at Daphne's feet. Then he takes her hands and peers into her eyes. Daphne's contemptuous stare fails to ward him off, and he begins without awaiting a reply. "Our Heavenly Father. We thank Thee for saving our dear sister Daphne from serious injury when she fell —"

"For God's sake leave me alone," shrieks Daphne with so much venom that Esmeralda jumps in her seat.

"Oh, dear," says Rowlands, falling backwards, but Hilda Fitzgerald is quick to grab both him and the opportunity to make her case.

"It's her mind, the poor old thing," says the woman, dragging the fallen vicar to his feet before tapping her temple suggestively. "She's like this all the time — doesn't know what she's saying or doing anymore."

The heavy concrete paving slabs at the foot of the mosque's steps have the two chief inspectors sweating, until a yellow patch of levelling sand, the size of a snooker table, lays exposed.

"It's just flippin' sand," moans Bliss as he prods at the footings with his pick.

"Maybe it was just a tool in the blanket," suggests Bryan, but that makes no sense to his father-in-law.

"These things aren't ceramic bathroom tiles, Peter," he complains, kicking the displaced blocks. "They weigh a bloody ton."

"Could it have been a spirit level?"

"No. It was square and boxy. And what happened to it afterwards?"

"Beats me," says Bryan. Then he stops and watches as pedestrians walk past without missing a step and sightseers hop over the disarranged stones to get to the mosque. "Amazing, isn't it?" he carries on. "Two blokes in suits drive up in a civvy car and start hacking up the pavement and no one takes a blind bit of notice."

"True —" starts Bliss, when the wailing of a police siren cuts him off.

"What's going on here, then?" questions a uniformed sergeant stepping out of the car.

"Who snitched?" asks Bliss, with his ID in hand, and the sergeant gives a nod to the mosque.

"They did," he says. "They called 999 and said they'd evacuated out the back 'cos you were planting a bomb."

"We were hoping to dig one up," mutters Bliss, without explaining. "Tell them not to worry — no bombs today — and we'll put it all back. But for chrissakes don't tell them who we are."

"Were you really expecting a bomb, Dave?" asks Bryan as they manoeuvre the heavy stones back into place.

"I don't know what I was expecting ..." starts Bliss, but he has a very suspicious eye on the grey-robed clerics who have gathered at the top of the steps to stare, then he says, "C'mon. I've got another idea."

"Can you talk or has the cat got your tongue?" Daphne questions Esmeralda once her tormentors have left, but the other woman's unflinching stare doesn't give her an answer.

"Humph. They've got you have they — the God's squad," Daphne rambles on. "That's what I call them — God's squad. All high and mighty like butter wouldn't melt in their mouths, but they're a bunch of bloomin' hypocrites. Knocking old ladies around ..."

A glimmer of life appears in Esmeralda's eyes, and Daphne catches it. "Is that what happened to you?" she asks softly, but the look in the woman's eyes turns to fear. "You can tell me," pleads Daphne, laying a comforting hand over Esmeralda's. "I'm not one of them. I don't believe in all that religious stuff. All they ever do is try to kill each other."

Esmeralda slowly surfaces, but she comes out on the wrong side for Daphne. "God will punish you in Hell for eternity for saying such wicked, wicked things," she admonishes with the malevolent pleasure of a pulpit pedant, as the fear in her eyes turns to pity.

"Is that what they told you?" shoots back Daphne, but she's too late, Esmeralda has gone back inside.

"Hello, Daffy," calls Amelia as she flounces in with a lunch tray. "Mrs. Fitzgerald has sent you a little treat 'cos you've been poorly."

Daphne's face brightens with a sardonic smile. The old carrot and stick routine, she laughs to herself as she turns to the young girl.

"Well, that's very nice of her, Amelia my dear. What is it?"

"A lovely bit of poached haddock with a creamy sauce."

David Bliss also has lunch in sight as he queues in the staff canteen.

"Are you trying to upset our Muslim friends?" queries Commander Fox with a grin as he sidles up with his tray.

"No," protests Bliss, before explaining the workmen's suspicious behaviour. "Although I find it funny that they didn't complain when the other blokes dug up the pavement."

"Maybe that was because me, you, and half the Met. Police was standing on their front doorstep at the time."

"Good point, sir."

"So. What did you find?"

"Nothing," says Bliss as he takes a double portion of steak pie.

"I don't suppose you thought of simply asking the workmen what they were doing before you upset our bearded brethren."

"If only I could," says Bliss, doubling up on mashed potatoes, and then he explains that he has checked with the Public Works Department and all the contractors authorized to repair the city's road and none have any record.

"That's very interesting," admits Fox, and then he nods to Bliss's loaded plate. "What's up — lady of the house on strike?"

"Sort of," shrugs Bliss as they search for a vacant table, but he is still focused on the pickup truck outside the mosque, explaining that he couldn't see the licence plates because of the camera angle.

"What about other cameras?"

"No luck so far," admits Bliss. "But there's dozens of possibilities." Then he reels off a list. "Red light and speed cameras. A couple of nearby banks and a warehouse have got security. Then there's the congestion fee cameras and some intersections with traffic management cameras."

"Phew!" exclaims Fox as he puts down his tray. "That would be quite a job."

"Especially as I haven't got any of the numbers ..." starts Bliss, then he drops his plate on the table and jumps up.

"What is it?"

"You know what Newton reckoned, guv," he says as he readies to run. "What goes down must come up."

"What about your lunch?" hollers Fox, but Bliss is already halfway back to the surveillance unit.

"Ooh, Daffy. You haven't eaten your lunch again," scolds Amelia as if she is dealing with her six-year-old sister. "An' Mrs. Fitzgerald did it specially."

"Please don't tell her," says Daphne, pulling the girl into a conspiracy. "She'll be so upset after all the trouble, but I just didn't fancy it."

"I don't rightly know ..." starts Amelia, but Daphne slides a twenty-pound note into her hand and whispers, "I'm very partial to the pork pies at Marks and Spencer's."

"Well ..."

"You could take your young man to the pictures with the change."

The force's videographer has his head in a pedophile's porno collection as Bliss rushes in.

"This jerk needs his bollocks chopped," says the technician without looking up, but Bliss is in a hurry, demanding all the coverage from the Whitechapel camera for the days following the ill-fated visit.

"At least a week," says Bliss.

"You'll have to give me some time," says the man as he

stops a terrified ten-year-old moments before she is raped. "I've got to have this ready for court tomorrow."

"It's urgent ..." starts Bliss, but the videographer is already hitting "play."

"And so is this. Just leave me a note of what you want and I'll give you a call as soon as I can."

A message awaits Bliss as he returns to his office, and he screws up his face at the sound of the voice. "Bliss, it's Edwards. I'm back from Washington. Call me."

"So, what's the current situation?" snaps the Home Secretary's man as soon as he answers.

"I've run across something very interesting," Bliss tells him, then fills in the details.

The phone goes quiet for a few seconds as Edwards digests the information, then he comes back a different person. "I wouldn't worry about it if I were you, Dave."

"What?"

"Well. As you say yourself, there was nothing there."

"Yeah. But there obviously was —"

"Dave ... Chief Inspector. Hang on a minute. You know one of the reasons you and I never got on when we were on the job together ... you never did what you were f'kin told. You were always prancing off on your own f'kin hobby horse and leaving everyone else to clean up the shit."

"Sir —"

"Canada, America, the south of f'kin France —"

"But —"

"No. No more 'buts.' Just listen for a f'kin change, Chief Inspector. If I say leave it, I mean leave it. Unless you want the Home Secretary himself to get on the blower and chew yer f'kin ear off."

That went well, Bliss tells himself as he slams down the phone.

"You look as though someone just pinched your sandwiches," laughs Peter Bryan as he strolls in.

"Edwards," spits Bliss, nodding to the phone just as it buzzes, and he is right again.

"Dave ... Sorry ... P'raps I was a bit hasty," splutters the ex–chief superintendent. "I'll come over and see what you've got."

Bliss shakes his head in wonderment as he puts down the phone.

"What is it, Dave?"

"Have a look out the window, Peter. See if there's a herd of flying pigs, will you," he chuckles before explaining.

The unease felt by Mavis Longbottom as she left St. Michael's has been gnawing at her all day. If Minnie Dennon or any of Daphne's other long-time friends were still alive, she would go back mob-handed and demand admittance. But without them, she needs an excuse — one that Davenport can't frivolously dismiss — and as she takes the bus to Daphne's house with the emergency key in her purse, she is hoping to find one in the mail: an unpaid bill, a cheque that needs a signature, a pension payment, or something similar.

Anxiety over of the Jenkins family and their pit bulls has kept Mavis at bay since Daphne's incarceration, and she steels herself as she walks up the opposite side of the street and crosses at the last minute.

The desecrated garden has recovered a little thanks to Bliss's work, but the faded remains of swastikas and four-letter words still mar the walls as she approaches the front door.

"Oh, no," she is sighing aloud, with the key in the lock, when a woman's voice spins her.

"Are you Miss Lovelace ... Ophelia Lovelace?"

If there is a familiarity in the voice it doesn't register with Mavis as she takes in the visitor, an athletically tall woman in her late sixties.

"No," she replies, with a quizzical lift, wondering who would call Daphne by her first name, and the woman hovers with a degree of tentativeness before asking, "Does she live here?"

Mavis holds back while she tries to place the woman. Stylishly dressed — en route from a wedding or a christening perhaps — with a floppy-brimmed straw hat. Obviously not a friend; someone official because of the name — a name Daphne hasn't used since her teenage years — but she isn't offering a business card ... a Jehovah's witness?

"Well?" questions the woman eventually.

"Sorry ... I could give her a message," suggests Mavis, reluctant to admit that the house is vacant, but a sudden bout of nervousness turns the woman pink and has her backing away, mumbling, "Don't worry, I'll come back another time."

"Can I tell who wanted her?" calls Mavis, as the woman hits the street and almost breaks into a run, and she watches for a few seconds before shrugging. "Weird," she says and turns to put the key in the lock.

The stench knocks Mavis back as the front door opens. Bliss did his best — picking up the excrement and garbage, scrubbing the carpets, breaking the seals on the doors and other apertures, and fixing the broken window. But the incessant heat and a new round of vandalism have undone some of his handiwork. A dead rat and a fly-infested bag of feces lie on the doormat, surrounded by a pile of flyers and bills. Several houseplants have succumbed to the heat, and the stink of rotting food comes from the kitchen's refrigerator.

Death surrounds Mavis as she stands in the hall amidst a swarm of flies, and she crumples in tears at the knowledge that, without its exuberant and energetic mistress, the house is just a smelly abandoned building.

The gentle rap of knuckles on wood is as startling as a voice from the grave, and Mavis momentarily shrinks in fear before wiping her eyes and straightening herself with the thought that the strange woman has returned.

"Hello —" she starts as she opens the door, then she shrinks back, slack mouthed, at the sight of Tony Oswald. "Oh!"

"I was just passing and thought I'd check on the house for Miss Lovelace," says Oswald, introducing himself with his card, and Mavis bursts into tears again.

It only takes half an hour for them to clean away the mess, but nothing will shift the smell from the broken fridge.

"I'd better get someone to come and take it away," says Oswald holding his nose, leaving Mavis to question how Daphne will manage without it.

"Mavis," he begins, with a soft hand and a sympathetic look, but she doesn't wait for the rest.

"She's not coming back is she?"

Oswald shakes his head in dismay. "I'm sorry," he says. "But they don't do return tickets to places like St. Michael's."

"I know," agrees Mavis softly. "I guess I've known since she went in, I just didn't want to admit it."

"We never do," he sighs. "There's no great rush, but she's going have to decide what to do with the house. Has she mentioned it to you?"

Oswald's eyes screw in critical surprise when Mavis explains that she hasn't visited Daphne. She spots the look and is quick to deflect the accusation on to Patrick Davenport.

"I'm sure he has his reasons," says Oswald as he rises to leave. "Why don't we go together tomorrow morning. I'll call and make an appointment."

The speed at which Michael Edwards arrives to view the video, as well as the degree of interest shown by his ex-boss, surprises Bliss as he runs and reruns the grainy clip of the two workmen and their pickup.

"Stop ... rewind ... slow ... back again," sings out Edwards, time after time, as he presses his face against the monitor.

"It must be a tool or something," he pronounces confidently as he finally pulls away, but Bliss won't bend and loudly counts the tools as they come off and are thrown back on the truck as he reruns the clip again.

"One wheelbarrow, two pickaxes, two shovels, one trowel, and a long metal bar that they were using to line up the slabs. And that's it."

Edwards shrugs off the evidence. "I still reckon it's a tool or something."

"I don't think it could be," persists Bliss, and he makes a point of stopping the recording to show that nothing was left behind. "What happened to it?"

But Bliss is pushing the wrong man, and Edwards pushes back.

"So. Did you get their names?"

"No, sir."

"What about the licence plate number?"

"I didn't notice —"

"You were suspicious enough to speak to them," breaks in Edwards pointedly. "But you didn't take the number?"

"That's valid, sir," admits Bliss. "But they seemed genuine."

"Let's get this straight, Chief Inspector. Just for the record. You interviewed the two men and were satisfied that they were bona fide workmen."

"Well, at the time —"

"No. Were you satisfied? 'Cos if you weren't I'm sure Commander Fox would want to know why you were derelict in your duty in not recording the number on the back of the fucking truck — get me?"

"Yes, sir."

"So. You were satisfied. Yes?"

Bliss's answer is in the form of a hostile stare that

invites Edwards to perform an impossible act of self-abasement.

"Good, Chief Inspector. Glad we agree," says Edwards in ignorance of Bliss's thoughts. "So, let's just concentrate on protecting Her Majesty from now on and forget about any silly misjudgements you may have made in the past."

London's architects turned their backs on the sluggish slate grey Thames for centuries and used it as a sewer, but today, as David Bliss strolls along the flower-bedecked embankment on his way home, he stops to watch the timeless waters and wonder how many bags of quick drying cement it might take to permanently sink Edwards.

His cell phone snaps his daydream. It is Daisy reminding him that he hasn't called in several days.

"I'm sorry," he says, although whether he was punishing her or pushing so that she would bounce back, he doesn't know. "But I'll definitely get a flight tomorrow evening."

"Daavid …"

A moment's hesitancy warns him to expect the worst and it comes.

"Not zhis weekend please. I cannot explain, but …"

"All right," he says curtly. "I've got plenty to do anyway."

"But, Daavid —"

He is not listening. He doesn't want to hear "cousin" or any other excuse. If she stops now before the lie it will be easier to forgive her — if he chooses to.

"Daisy," he cuts in calmly. "It's okay. I really do have a lot to do, and I promised a little old lady that I would visit her. So, you have a good weekend and I'll call next week."

Utter relief cracks Daisy's voice as she whimpers, "Zhank you, Daavid. I love you."

Now what? he questions as she waits, but the words come out ahead of him. "I love you too."

With one pack of Marks and Spencer's pork pies eaten and another secreted behind the drawer in Esmeralda's bedside table while her roommate was visiting the toilet, Daphne is in survival and escape mode.

Life, such as it is in St. Michael's, is going on around her as the undertaker's van comes and goes, Amelia Brimble bustles in and out cheerily calling, "Hi Daffy," while Esmeralda Montgomery's gleeful eyes watch expectantly for Satan's lightning strike. But Daphne Lovelace, O.B.E., is in another place altogether.

"Eat and you might be drugged or poisoned. Don't eat and you will starve. The choice is yours. The end result's the same," says the voice in Daphne's mind as she stares at the tuna sandwich on her untouched tea tray. But it's not her voice. It's a voice from another life in another world — a world that Hilda Fitzgerald and Esmeralda Montgomery could never imagine.

In Daphne's mind it is Paris in the summer of 1946, and it has been two years since the cobbled streets crunched under the weight of German jackboots. She's a young woman on the run — not from the Nazis but from England and her home, from the need to face her family and herself with blood on her hands. She has been on the run ever since D-Day, when she saw death at close quarters and knew that she'd had a hand in it.

"Daffy, dear," Amelia tries. "I've brought some scrambled egg for your supper 'cos you didn't eat tea." But Daphne barely surfaces as she waves the plate away.

"Just don't tell Mrs. Fitzgerald," she whispers, before returning to the sepia-edged movie in her mind.

"You must start escaping the moment you are captured," instructs the voice, but now she has an image to go with it. He is tall, six feet or more, with the face of a choirboy, the charm of a charlatan, the cunning of a

Shakespearean fool, and the fearlessness of a musketeer. She loved him. But everyone loved him — he was that kind of man.

"Never assume that anyone is going to attempt a rescue mission," Michael Kent says as he lectures her in the art of espionage. "Never hope that your captors are simply going to let you go. It's the same as being in a shipwreck — if you wait to be rescued, you will be too weak to save yourself when help doesn't arrive."

"Amelia," calls Daphne, reaching out to the girl as she returns for Esmeralda's tray.

"Yes, Daffy."

"I need some more money, dear," she whispers as she slides her bank card from her purse.

"Oh. I couldn't, I'm not allowed …"

But Daphne holds an ace as she forces the card into Amelia's young hand. "We wouldn't want Mrs. Fitzgerald to know about the Tums and the pork pies or what happened to her lovely fish, would we?"

"Do I make myself clear?" continues Kent once Amelia has pocketed the card and memorized Daphne's PIN number. "There will be no rescue. We can't afford to lose you, but we won't risk losing others to get you back."

But Kent isn't talking about snatching Daphne from the grip of a few fanatical Waffen SS officers who are still holding out in the mountains and forests of Bavaria in the belief that Hitler will be resurrected from the grave. A new and even deadlier enemy is rising.

"From Stettin in the Baltic to Trieste in the Adriatic an iron curtain has descended across the continent," said Winston Churchill in March of 1946, and by that autumn, with a smattering of Russian and a couple of dodgy passports, Daphne Lovelace and a handful of others were being readied to pierce holes and drag Soviet dissidents to the west. But, hidden by the curtain, Stalin's ferocious lapdogs waited like the multi-headed hydra.

"Never put up a fight if the Reds catch you," warns Kent in Daphne's mind. "The stronger you fight the harder they fight back, and never forget that when the thumbscrews come out even your best friend will change the colour of his shirt. Give as much as you can afford to give. Don't antagonize. They will be looking for any excuse to kill you."

"Miss Lovelace," calls a voice from outside, and Daphne snaps herself back to the present as Hilda Fitzgerald roughly shakes her. "Time for your nighty-night pills."

Daphne winces as the woman hands her the powerful tranquilizers then stands over her like a schoolmarm. But Daphne has no Tums now, and Hilda isn't a pushover like Amelia.

"I'm waiting," snorts the dragon while Daphne reaches for a glass of water and makes a play of swallowing. Then she orders, "Open wide," before turning tail and hitting off the lights. "There — that wasn't so bad, was it?"

Not bad at all, thinks Daphne as she retrieves the tablets from underneath her bottom dentures before rinsing out the residue.

"Stay alert to stay alive," Kent is telling her in her mind as she closes her eyes and looks for a way out. "Successful escape is timing," his voice continues. "There are always opportunities as long as you still have the strength," he says, before adding ominously, "Miss one chance or mess one up and you might never get another."

But she escaped. Her innocently pretty face and disarming smile opened chinks in the curtain on more than one occasion.

"Of course, you have certain advantages if you are caught," Kent made clear with a leer, and she was willing, very willing, to rehearse escape tactics with him. Although, he was very quick to warn, "Don't assume that because you let a guard sleep with you that he won't kill you."

"And the disadvantages?" she queried.

Kent shrugged. "He'll sleep with you whether you let him not."

Daphne's face has weathered well. However, eighty-five years of sun and storms have opened a few crevices and taken off the sheen, and Hilda Fitzgerald's livid handprint hasn't helped. But Daphne has no plans to use her looks to evade captivity and incarceration now. Once she escapes she has no intention of being caught, and as she lies back in bed in the moonlight, she traces a rudimentary left-handed labyrinth on the ceiling and meditates her way out of it in preparation for the real attempt.

It is the left-handedness of the pattern that is crucial. Her first abortive attempt, intended only to test defences, had taken a right-hand turn away from the front of the building — the core — in order to reach the gate. To the left lies a seemingly impenetrable line of six-foot fences bordering the gardens of half a dozen Victorian villas. It is the path that Daphne knows she must take, despite the obstacles, but before she starts the journey she has one more task to perform at the core, and she sets her internal alarm clock for 2:30 a.m. and prays that Davenport hasn't started locking his office since her previous incursion.

chapter eleven

A creaky floorboard awaits every footstep as Daphne gingerly creeps from her room in the moonlight. This time her mind is sharp. Dr. Williamson hasn't paid a visit with his hypodermic since her brush with Hilda Fitzgerald's hand, and, one way or another, she has ducked the daily regimen of drugs that was intended to keep her docile.

Saturnine scenes of heroic religious battles filled with limbless bodies spurting blood are barely visible in the blue lunar glow as Daphne descends the stairs. But whether the gloomy sacred paintings lauding crucifixion, immolation, and sacrifice are meant to be uplifting to the elderly residents or drive them to suicide, Daphne can't decide.

"I have fought a good fight. I have finished my course. I have kept the faith — Timothy 7," says a caption under the image of a seventeenth-century horseman waving a bloody sword as he rides to heaven, and beside it is a parchment with a quote from the Book of Revelations: "Behold, I come as a thief in the night …"

It has been a particularly busy night for the staff working the graveyard shift. The reaper has struck twice, and his victims, together with their belongings, bed linen, and clothes, had to be gathered, bagged, and tagged to await collection in the morning.

"I'm bloody glad to see the back of her," utters one of the middle-aged female attendants as she finally slumps into an armchair with a Cornish pasty and can of Coke at 3:00 a.m., but Iris, her co-worker, had a soft spot for the other deceased resident.

"I'll miss old Charlie," she reminisces with a smile. "Mind you, you had to watch the old bugger. He could be a bit happy-handed at times. I remember when …"

Patrick Davenport's office lies off the entrance hall, just beyond the wide-open doors of the common room where the attendants are dissecting the newly departed. Daphne freezes against the wall and melts into the shadows as she seeks a way to pass unnoticed. She's been here before, though not for over fifty years: dodging itchy-fingered border guards with a petrified Belarusian scientist or top-ranking Russian turncoat in tow. And, while neither of the care attendants may have Kalashnikov's, in the aging adventuress's mind the stakes are just as high and the penalty for failure the same.

"Create a diversion," the voice in her head whispers, and a minute later the alarm monitor on Iris's belt goes off. "Damn," says the caregiver. "It's old mother Laver in nine. I bet she's having another bloody panic attack."

Daphne slinks out of the shadows as soon as the two assistants have hustled past, and by the time they have woken the confused woman in Room 9 and reset the alarm button, she has tiptoed into Davenport's office and squeezed under his knee-hole desk.

"I got your money," whispers Amelia as she nervously slips in before breakfast and slides it into Daphne's purse. "But I shouldn't do it again. Mr. Davenport wouldn't like it."

"This is for your trouble," says Daphne with a knowing smile as she takes out one of the crisp twenty-pound notes and drops it into the girl's pocket. "But I would like you to get me a few more bits and pieces."

"I don't —"

Two fifty-pounds notes follow, together with a scrap of paper. "I've made a little list."

"What are you doing here, Amelia?" grunts Hilda Fitzgerald sharply as she barges in, red-faced, unannounced.

"She's a lovely girl," says Daphne as she gives the teenager's hand a conspiratorial squeeze. "She always pops in to say good morning."

But Amelia colours up and bumbles around, brushing imaginary crumbs off the bed, spluttering, "Yeah …umm … G'mornin' Daffy … umm."

"Well, you can leave now," Fitzgerald carries on, with a menacing eye on Daphne. "I'll deal with Miss Lovelace this morning."

"Yes, Mrs. Fitz—"

"And take Mrs. Montgomery with you. Give her a bath or something."

"Oh, it's not her bath day today —"

"I said give her a bloody bath, girl. Are you deaf or just plain daft?"

"Now," spits Fitzgerald to Daphne as she slams the door behind the fleeing girl and her patient. "You and me are going to have a little chat."

Peter Bryan has a confused look as he wanders into David Bliss's office mid-morning.

"I'm having trouble with that pickup truck, Dave," he says as he scans the notes in his hand. "I checked the

Council again — they definitely didn't authorize or order it to be done. I think your only chance is with cameras in the surrounding areas — red-light cameras, speed cameras."

"What about the congestion charge cameras — all vehicles coming in and out of the city?" suggests Bliss as he pours a couple of coffees from a Thermos.

"Whitechapel is outside the zone."

"I know that," Bliss carries on thoughtfully, offering a biscuit. "But couldn't he have come through there on his way?" But then he shakes his head. "That won't do us any good. Those cameras only take the plate number. We've got to see the whole vehicle to match it against the pickup at the scene."

"Sorry, Dave," says Bryan, tossing his notes onto Bliss's desk. "But this one's down to you. I've already got half a dozen blaggings on my plate thanks to our Muslim mates."

"What's that got to do with the Muslims?" queries Bliss in surprise.

"Nothing directly," admits Bryan before explaining that the six armed robberies of Pakistani convenience stores and Indian curry houses were carried out under cover of running battles between feuding fundamentalists. "By the way," he asks, as he downs his coffee in a couple of gulps. "What did Edwards want yesterday afternoon?"

"He wanted me to lay off this," replies Bliss stabbing at the pickup truck on his computer screen. "Told me to forget it. He even threatened to set his Rottweiler on me."

"And what Rottweiler is that, Chief Inspector?" asks Commander Fox with raised eyebrows as he slinks in without warning.

"Nothing, sir," says Bliss, but Fox isn't paying a social call. He is on a mission.

"Is that the pickup truck you told Mr. Edwards about?" he says as he puts on his reading glasses to peer at the screen.

"Yes, sir," Bliss starts, and is explaining the difficulty he is having in tracing the vehicle when Fox takes off his glasses and holds up his hand.

"Dave," he says. "Cards on the table. I've had Edwards bending my ear on the blower about arrangements for next Friday. I told him about the pickup, and he said there was nothing to it. He reckons he told you to lay off it."

"But I don't work for him, sir. I work for you."

"Precisely, Chief Inspector," says Fox, halfway out of the door. "And this is from me. Lay off it. That's an order."

I guess he threatened to set his Rottweiler on you as well, thinks Bliss as Fox disappears down the corridor, then he turns to Peter Bryan with a serious face. "This is war, Peter. If Edwards wants it dropped that badly, it must be dodgy."

"So, what do you do now?"

"I drop it, of course. You heard the man. It was an order."

Bryan looks askance. "Seriously, Dave. Just like that. You're going to drop it. That's not like you."

"I'm getting too old for this malarkey, Peter," Bliss sighs as he swings an arm around his son-in-law's shoulders and leads him to the door. "I'm tired of carrying people around who haven't got the bottle to stand up for themselves. I've lost it. You, on the other hand, are just a virile young man with a glittering future ahead of you. So you, my dear boy, are going to do it for me."

"Oh, come on, granddad. Don't get me involved," says Bryan, breaking free.

"Stop that granddad stuff and get to work. We've got to find that truck and damn quick."

"You've got mail," sings out the postman, dumping a fistful of letters on the hall table as he makes his morning delivery to St. Michael's Church of England Home for the

Elderly in Westchester. Then he unlocks the residents' mailbox and dumps the outgoing post in his bag.

"Thanks," says Patrick Davenport, looking up momentarily from his desk as he frantically searches the drawers, desperately trying to work out the relevance of certain papers that have disappeared during the night.

"Hello, Patrick?" calls Tony Oswald, with a polite knock on the manager's partially open door, and Davenport's face clouds as he looks up.

"Tony ... sorry ... I should've called you," he says, abandoning his task for a few moments. "Miss Lovelace isn't seeing anyone today."

"Oh ..." begins Oswald in confusion, but Mavis Longbottom steps from behind the giant social worker, grousing, "That's not fair. Mr. Oswald made an appointment especially."

"Sorry," Davenport shrugs before going back to his search. "She absolutely refuses to see anyone. Maybe Sunday or Monday."

"Something funny's going on there. I can feel it in my bones," mutters Mavis as she and Oswald walk back to his car. "Have you seen her recently?"

"Not for a week or so," admits Oswald. "Although she did seem pretty confused when I saw her last. According to the young woman who looks after her, all she does is walk round and round in circles all day."

"That doesn't sound like Daphne. She usually knows exactly where's she's going."

"She was like a little clockwork mouse, according to the girl, although, to be honest, my job was finished when I handed her over."

"So what happens to your patients afterwards?" Mavis questions. "Who's responsible for them?" But she spots the undertaker's van pulling away from the back door and doesn't push for an answer.

Patrick Davenport's face is drawn as he firmly shuts his office door, picks up his phone, and calls Robert Jameson, his lawyer. "Get over here, Bob. We've got a problem," he says succinctly before resuming his search. Upstairs, Hilda Fitzgerald keeps up the pressure on Daphne.

Iris spotted the nocturnal nomad by fluke as Daphne slipped back into her room, and even hailed along the corridor to her. "Are you all right, dear?"

"Cramp," complained Daphne, quickly rubbing a leg. "Didn't want to disturb Esmeralda."

But it was only when Iris was at home in bed, and Hilda phoned and questioned her about the damaged locks on the office desk, that she saw any significance in Daphne's wandering.

"She could've been downstairs, I s'pose," Iris admitted, and since then Hilda has been trying to corner her main suspect. But just as the end of every labyrinth is also the beginning, and the beginning is also the end, Daphne's answers have led Hilda Fitzgerald in circles at least a dozen times already.

"Why were you out of bed?"

"Couldn't sleep."

"Where did you go?"

"Nowhere."

"Why couldn't you sleep?"

"Cramp."

"Why didn't you call the staff?"

"Didn't want to make a fuss."

"Then, why were you out of bed?"

"Couldn't sleep."

Room 27, Daphne's room, looks like a drug dealer's den after a heavy-handed police raid. As soon as Esmeralda, together with her bedside cabinet and her belongings, had been shunted to one of the newly vacated rooms, Fitzgerald and Davenport turned Daphne and her temporary abode upside down, but came up empty-handed.

Now, as Daphne sits amidst the turmoil of upended beds and lifted carpets, she knows that the woman leaning over her wants to ask what happened to the patients' drug records, copies of powers of attorney, and records of their valuables that disappeared from Davenport's desk. But she also knows that Fitzgerald hasn't a scrap of evidence linking her to the crime, so she closes her eyes and plays dead.

"Hey," prods Fitzgerald harshly. "Wake up. I'm talking to you."

Daphne smiles inwardly, but has no intention of answering.

"An unconscious agent won't tell very much," Michael Kent made clear when they got onto the perils of being caught and tortured, and Daphne knows that is the reason why Doctor Williamson hasn't been brought in with his little bag of knockout drops.

"Wake up — wake up," shouts Fitzgerald, shaking Daphne roughly as Davenport and Jameson slip in, black-faced. But Daphne has turned off her senses and spun herself back to Paris, where Michael Kent is playing rough as he tries to inoculate her against the sadistic practices of the Communists.

"Who are you working for?" demands Kent, over and over, as he lashes at her naked buttocks with a leather belt while she hangs by her ankles, her arms pinioned behind her, a canvas bag over her head.

"What's your name? Who are your handlers?" he screams as he hits.

Three days and nights — beaten and harangued; starved and abused; spat at and kicked, until she begged for mercy. Then he started on her mind: offering rewards; proposing compromises; suggesting he will let her go — then switching, menacing her with electrodes and threatening mutilation, but never death.

"Every tortured prisoner prays for death; pleads for death; begs for death," he told her when he finally let up and lovingly bathed her bloodied body and soothed her battered mind. "If you're dead you can't tell them a damn thing," he added, making it very clear that if she was captured and someone stole into her cell in the middle of the night with a knife, it was much more likely to be a friend than a foe.

"Miss Lovelace. Will you please open your eyes. I wish to ask you some questions," demands Robert Jameson in his courtroom voice, but Daphne has played to better interrogators than Jameson will ever encounter — and she has won.

A pall of unease has spread throughout the home — carried from room to room on the morose faces of staff as they go about their morning duties with the knowledge that there is trouble in Room 27 — and Amelia Brimble has hovered outside Daphne's door a few times with the hundred and twenty pounds and a shopping list that includes a one-way train ticket to London burning in her pocket.

"Lovelace. Open your bloody eyes," screeches Hilda Fitzgerald as she finally comes unglued, and the sound of another slap echoes like the crack of a whip along the corridor and sends Amelia scurrying for cover.

Misty Jenkins is laden with the weekend's groceries when she is stopped outside of her neighbour's house by the sight of a middle-aged woman knocking on Daphne's door.

"She ain't there anymore," yells Misty, and the tall stranger leaps at the voice. "She's in a home."

"Oh. You startled me. I was looking for Ophelia ..." starts Isabel Semaurino with an accent that places her in the distant past — the British Raj or Rangoon in the 1930s, perhaps.

"Nah. Wrong house, luv," jumps in Misty. "Her name was Daphne. But she ain't comin' back." Then she puts down a bag, screws a finger into her temple, and laughs. "She's totally round the bloomin' twist. You shoulda seen what she did to my telly."

"That's very strange," says Isabel as she examines a piece of paper. "I was definitely given this address, and the woman I saw the other day said she lived here."

"Sorry, luv," shrugs Misty, picking up her groceries and heading for her own door. "Someone's buggerin' you about. Like I said … she ain't ever comin' back."

"What are you going to do about her, Pat?" questions Robert Jameson as he sits at Davenport's desk while they try to work out where Daphne could have secreted the missing documents.

"I don't bloody know what she's up to. I'm beginning to wonder if she's as daft as she makes out."

"Not her," spits Jameson. "Not the old lady. I meant Hilda — your stupid bloody sister. Christ, you can't have her smacking patients about like that. What if the old bird croaks and someone puts in a word to the Coroner?"

Patrick Davenport slams his hand on the desk. "Bob. Just help find the bloody papers and let me worry about Hilda, all right?"

"But what if it wasn't Lovelace? What if it was an outside job?"

"So what?"

"Well, it won't look good if they show up somewhere and the police start wondering why you didn't report it."

The Metropolitan Police videography department at Scotland Yard constantly buzzes with the hum of computers and the whine of tape decks as a dozen men and women scan the sins of the world through glass eyes.

"What have you got?" questions Bliss excitedly, following a summons from the senior man.

"This what you were looking for?" gloats the technician with a wide grin, and Bliss sits at a console while a familiar pickup truck pulls up to the curb outside the Whitechapel mosque and two recognizable figures begin the process of digging up the pavement. But this time, there is no posse of officers standing at the top of the steps, and Bliss doesn't see himself walk down to talk to the workmen.

"The Monday following the incident," points out Hoskins, the videographer, as he taps the time and date recorded on the bottom of the screen, and as Bliss watches, something wrapped in a blanket is squirreled back into the pickup's cab, the paving slab is replaced, and the vehicle takes off.

"Newton was right," breathes Bliss. "What goes down must come up."

But what is it, and where is it? These are the questions he has now.

"I can't help you with that," says Hoskins, adding smugly, "But you might be interested in this."

"What the hell are you and Bliss up to?" yells Commander Fox as he slams into Peter Bryan's office mid-afternoon with a printout from the brains of the organization, the Police National Computer, showing that Bryan has instituted a search of the vehicle index for the workmen's truck. "I specifically ordered Bliss to drop it."

"Then you'd better talk to him, sir."

"Don't pull that innocent crap with me. You two are in this together. Like father like son-in-law. You did the search. Now, where did you get this number?"

Peter Bryan pulls a blank face, but the visit is not unexpected. The number, spotted by the videographer on the pickup truck as it sped through a junction near the mosque, rang alarms when he phoned for information. The clerk in the vehicle licensing office backed up faster than a politician caught with his pants down in a public loo. "No. Sorry. My mistake. No trace — unregistered," he said only seconds after confirming that he had a match. "It must be a stolen motor or something."

"I think the guy's jerking me around, Dave," Bryan told his father-in-law a few minutes later, so Bliss tried and found himself talking to a different clerk.

"Classified!" Bliss queried in disbelief, but the clerk quickly distanced himself. "But I never told you that."

"Fox on the prowl," warns Peter Bryan by phone the moment the commander leaves his office with Bliss in his sights.

"Meet me at the mosque," says Bliss, and he is out of the building faster than a cockerel out of a coop.

Friday afternoon passes peacefully for Daphne. Three sleeping pills rammed down her throat by Hilda Fitzgerald ensure that she will miss the search.

"Check everywhere," Davenport instructed at a hastily called staff meeting, although he was very circumspect about the object of the hunt. "I seem to have misplaced a few important papers."

However, young Amelia Brimble is not participating. The heart-rending sound of her kindly confidante being abused sent her flying home on her bicycle to vomit, and now she is pacing her bedroom with a handful of money and a shopping list that includes a dress, shoes, a train ticket, and a paperback copy of Paul Brickhill's epic wartime adventure, *The Great Escape*.

"So, why meet here?" questions Peter Bryan as he and Bliss are surrounded by worshippers dawdling to discuss next week's rescheduled royal visit.

"I just had to get away," admits Bliss. "And it was the first place that came into my head. Although I can't help feeling that we've missed something here."

"*You've* missed something," Bryan reminds him forcefully. "I told you — count me out. You've caused me enough ..."

But Bliss tunes him out as he spots the lamp standard across the road and remembers thinking it strange that, on his first visit, he saw two workmen atop a cherry picker painting something that no one would ever see.

"Peter?" he questions, when he figures Bryan has wound down sufficiently. "Was that right that you and Samantha went mountaineering in Wales?"

"Yeah. It was great," admits Bryan cagily. "Why?"

"Just checking," he says as he wonders where he might be able to borrow a cherry picker. "So ... You're okay with heights then, are you?"

chapter twelve

Five high-backed armchairs sit ominously centre stage alongside Samuel Fitzgerald's ersatz altar at St. Michael's Sunday service. But it is the fourth Sunday in August, and the portly Reverend Rollie Rowlands of St. Stephen's-in-the-Vale has taken back the reins from his stand-in for his monthly visit.

"St. Michael the Archangel, defend us in the day of battle," recites Rowlands in a sonorous tone as he puts his hands together and lifts his eyes to the stained ceiling, and then he spurs his elderly flock to war against Satan with a hymn. "Fight the good fight with all thy might …" he begins lustily, in a rumbling bass voice that reverberates around the common room like rolling thunder, but he soon becomes a lone crusader as his aging band of battle-weary warriors run out of breath.

Patrick Davenport and his entourage are not in the congregation this morning. Nearly two days of relentless hunting for the missing documents, coupled with the strain of the situation, have worn the distressed manager to the point of exhaustion. He would happily offer Daphne a deal to recover his missing papers, if only that were possible.

"This past week has been a joyous time for our Dear Lord," carries on Rowlands sanguinely as he puts on a courageous face and points to the empty chairs strategically placed to the right of the altar. "Four of our beloved sisters, and one brave brother, have joined the Almighty in heaven, and for that, we give praise."

"Amen," mutter a scattering of voices as Rowlands begins reading out names.

"Emily Mountjoy, spinster of this parish, whom I am sure we all remember as the moral face of Westchester Library; a brave woman who fought so valiantly for so many years to keep the heretical ramblings of blasphemers and perverts off the shelves."

"Amen," says a lone voice at the back.

"Charles Edward Lacy ..." Rowlands continues, pointing to the next chair as he works his way towards the holy sacrament of bread and wine, symbolizing the body and blood of Christ, which sits on the altar.

Upstairs in Room 27, Daphne's room, there is neither her body nor any trace of the blood that poured from her nose following Hilda Fitzgerald's Friday attack, leaving two Westchester police constables scratching their heads.

"Let's go over this again, ma'am," says P.C. Joan Joveneski as she tries to get Hilda Fitzgerald to look her in the eye. "Because, quite frankly, unless she's Houdini, it doesn't make a lot of sense."

Whilst it may not make sense to Joveneski, the fact is that, sometime between 10:15 Saturday night and 7:00 Sunday morning, when Patrick Davenport arrived to find his elder sister stomping around, swearing, "She can't have gone; the bloody door was locked," Daphne Lovelace vanished from her room.

Hilda Fitzgerald was right. The door to Daphne's room was locked. The manager's sister locked it herself on Friday and pocketed the key, and since that time, for good reason, only she and Davenport have entered.

"You can leave that blasted woman to me," she plainly told each and every staff member with sufficient venom to quell any dissent, although more than one of the care assistants gave her a sideways look. Amelia Brimble even confided her fears to her boyfriend Friday night, when he wondered aloud if her period was due.

"No," protested the young woman, before explaining that her lack of interest was due to her concern over Daphne. "I reckon Hilda's killed the old dear," she whispered morosely as they lay on the grass under the stars in the cathedral's grounds. "You shoulda heard her. The way she wuz carryin' on. Then, *smash*!"

"She smacked her one?"

"Yeah. An' it's not the first time, neither."

"Did you see it? Like, did she smack her in the gob?"

Amelia shook her head. "I dunno. But I heard it aw'right. D'ye reckon I should tell someone?"

"Nah ... Don't worry," said Matt after a few moments' thought, although he didn't have Daphne's interest at heart as he slid his hand up the inside of Amelia's thigh and purred, "I 'spect she'll be okay. She's prob'ly tough as nails."

"She'd have to be a flipping commando," says P.C. Joveneski as she peers at the ground from Daphne's second-floor window and checks out a rusty drainpipe. Then she turns back to the room, rereads her notes, and confronts Hilda Fitzgerald. "Now, ma'am, you said she'd run away, but according to you, she was heavily sedated and locked in her room."

Hilda doesn't have an explanation, and neither does Patrick Davenport. But the worried manager does have a wary eye on his elder sister as she attempts to sweep Daphne into a dark corner.

"We had to sedate her. We couldn't do a thing with her," grumbles Hilda before cataloguing a litany of ungodly afflictions and mental infirmities including senile dementia and devilish possession. "She could've took off on a bloomin' broomstick for all I know," she continues with a black brush, before adding forebodingly, "If you want my opinion, she'll prob'ly reckon we were mistreating her. I wouldn't put it past her to knock herself about and make up all kinda stories. She could do herself a lotta damage."

"And others," agrees Joveneski, explaining, "We're actually well aware of the lady's mental condition, ma'am. She nearly bit the new superintendent's finger off."

"Really ... I didn't know," steps in Davenport.

"Oh. Yes, sir. And she went totally berserk in her next door neighbours' place. Christ, you should have seen the bloody mess ... Oh! Sorry, sir," she says, giving a nod to the crucifix on the wall.

"No problem," says Davenport, cheering a touch.

"We've got a good description, photographs, and fingerprints on file," carries on the constable as her partner examines the door lock. "But we'll need to know what she was wearing and what she might have taken ..."

A cough from the officer's partner gets Joveneski's attention. "Hang on, Joan," says Kevin Scape. "We're talking about a sedated old woman who was locked in. There's no way she could have got out on her own. Someone must have used a key." Then his face darkens as he realizes the implication of his words. "Now, you're absolutely sure you've searched the whole place properly," he asks, nodding to Davenport.

"Absolutely, officer."

"And she couldn't have got hold of a key."

"That's correct."

"Then there can only be one conclusion," he pronounces solemnly. "She must have been abducted."

There is another possibility, and it's one that Patrick Davenport is forced to contemplate as he fiercely eyes his sister and wonders why she so vehemently begged him not to report Daphne's disappearance to the police.

The Reverend Rollie Rowlands has wrapped up his Sunday service and is waiting in Davenport's office for his cheque when Mavis Longbottom shows up with a champion.

"I'll come with you, and I won't take no for an answer," said Angel Robinson, Daphne's mentor, when she spotted Mavis walking the cathedral's labyrinth in search of a shoehorn to slip her past the defences at St. Michael's. "I often wondered what had happened to the old lady. I haven't seen her in weeks."

"Oh dear," says Rowlands gravely when Angel inquires about Daphne. "I think you may have had a wasted journey. I do believe Miss Lovelace has left us."

"Gone!" exclaims Mavis, and the arrival of a glum-faced Davenport in the company of two police officers immediately seals Daphne's fate in her friend's mind. "What have you done with her?" she demands, flying across the room at Davenport. "I knew there was a reason you wouldn't let me see her."

"Madam ..." starts Davenport, but Kevin Scape steps in. "What do you mean, they wouldn't let you see her?"

David Bliss checks the clock on Westchester's Elizabethan Town Hall as he drives along the tree-lined High Street, thronged with Sunday sightseers. It is a little before one o'clock, and he turns into the carriage entrance of the Mitre Hotel, the headquarters of the old school tie and blazer brigade, with lunch in mind.

The quintessentially straitlaced city of Westchester, set amidst the watercress meadows and dairy farms of southern England, is the final pastureland for many of the nation's elite. Knackered warhorses and clapped-out colonials graze leisurely each day in the Mitre and snort disdainfully about Sunday interlopers and "damned foreigners" as they jostle for a table in the packed dining room. Bliss considers a quick bar lunch, but he has time to spare. If he arrives at St. Michael's for three, he tells himself, the residents' afternoon tea bell will save him from Daphne at four, and so he tags onto the lunch line until he spots a familiar figure talking earnestly with the manager. "Ted," he calls, and ex-Superintendent Donaldson spins.

"David. Thank goodness. You got my message, then."

"No ..." he starts, but Donaldson has him by an arm and is hustling him out of the door in a second.

Despite the fact that Superintendent Anne McGregor is still smarting from her encounter with Daphne, she has taken command and is coordinating search efforts from Patrick Davenport's office by the time Bliss and Donaldson arrive.

A forensic team, together with a fingerprint expert and several dog handlers, are on scene and are scouting for scents and leads, while nearly thirty officers from surrounding towns and villages have been bussed in and are strung out across the lawns and grounds as they search for clues. Local officers, armed with hastily photocopied mug shots of the missing woman, are scouring the streets and quizzing passersby throughout the city, while a team of detectives interview staff members.

"Well, if it isn't Ted Donaldson," smiles Anne McGregor as her predecessor walks in. "I might have known you'd soon get wind of this."

"This is Westchester," he reminds her. "The abduction of an eighty-five-year-old from a seniors' home is just about as big as it gets. I'm surprised the BBC haven't shown up."

"They have," she says. "They've just left to get some local reaction."

"There'll be plenty of that," says Donaldson before introducing Bliss as another of Daphne's close friends.

"Oh. A detective chief inspector of the Grand Metropolitan Police Force no less," says McGregor with a touch of cynicism and the hint of a disingenuous curtsy, but Bliss is in no mood for territorial rivalry. He wants information and he wants to help.

"We haven't got much to go on as far as abduction is concerned," admits McGregor, firmly closing the door before explaining that, while she could understand someone smuggling an elderly relative into St. Michael's, it was difficult to see why anybody would want to spirit one away.

"So?" questions Bliss, sensing that there is more.

"I don't know," she begins vaguely, and then lays out a list. "Number one: my nose always twitches when a complainant's lawyer shows up at the scene ahead of me. Two: the staff are jumpier than Michael Flatley and the whole Lord of the Dance shemozzle. Three: Patrick Davenport, the guy in charge, didn't say a dicky-bird to us, but one of the wrinklies let drop that there was a break-in a few nights ago."

"What was taken?"

"I don't know yet," she says as she points to the desk drawers where Daphne used a brass letter opener to wrench out the locks. "But whoever did it knew what they were doing."

"Have you asked Davenport?"

"I'm saving that," she says, then continues. "Four: a friend of the missing woman, Mavis Longbottom, reckons they've been keeping the old turkey under wraps and wouldn't even let her social worker in to visit her."

"That's interesting," admits Bliss, recalling Trina Button's frantic phone call. "That's what she told a friend in Canada last week."

It is barely six o'clock Sunday morning in Vancouver. The buzz of Trina's bedside phone can mean only one thing.

"Oh, no. Not again," grumbles Rick Button as he pulls the duvet over his ears, but it's not the Mounties chasing a semi-naked wrinkly this time. It's David Bliss on a similar mission.

"No. Daphne hasn't called again, why?" asks Trina and he explains, then stands back from the phone as the zany Canadian lets fly.

"I warned you, David. Drugs, I said. Brainwashed, I said. Locked up, I said. But would you listen?"

"Trina —"

"No. Don't 'Trina' me. You lot are as useless as our lot. You couldn't sniff out a skunk in scent shop. I told you … Oh, never mind. I'm coming over."

"No!" It's Rick Button and Bliss together, but Trina hears neither as she slams down the phone and leaps out of bed, yelling, "They've got Daphne. I've gotta go."

"Who's got Daphne?" Now it's only Rick as he wakes to the nightmare scenario of catering for two teenagers and a nutty mother-in-law.

"God's squad," says Trina as she looks up a number for Air Canada. "A bunch of Bible freaks like those idiots up at Beautiful who tried messing with me last year."

"But what about your mother? Who's gonna look after her?"

"Sorry," says Bliss to Anne McGregor as he puts down the phone, knowing that Trina's arrival is likely to add to the young superintendent's woes if Daphne hasn't been found. "But it'll take her a couple of days to get here."

"So, Detective Chief Inspector," queries McGregor. "You obviously knew Miss Lovelace a lot better than I. What do you think could have happened to her? Is there anyone who would want to snatch her?"

Bliss shakes his head. "I doubt it. Although she didn't get the O.B.E. for being a Girl Guide leader."

"That's what I was told," admits the superintendent, although she dismissed most of the superwoman legends as junior officers' inventions intended to make her squirm.

"Just don't underestimate her survival instincts," carries on Bliss, explaining animatedly, "She once broke into, and back out of, a highly secret CIA establishment in Washington State and brought the whole dodgy enterprise down."

"Well," laughs McGregor, "we all do crazy things when we're young."

"Yes, we do," he agrees, then puts on his serious face. "But this was the year before last."

"Really!" exclaims McGregor as Bliss has a thought.

"Talking of young — there was a chatty teenaged girl looking after Daphne when I visited ..."

"Amelia Brimble," McGregor quickly steps in, proving that she has done her homework. "She's on our radar, but it's her day off. Her mother says she's at the beach with her boyfriend, but doesn't know which one."

"Which beach or which boyfriend?" queries Bliss unnecessarily, but a knock at the door interrupts and Anne McGregor sings out, "Come in."

"You might want to have a look, ma'am," says P.C. Scape excitedly. "We've found a ladder thrown behind some bushes by the fence."

Amelia Brimble and her boyfriend also know about the ladder, but they are not at the beach. They are skulking in Mathew's father's Ford van, and like millions of teens worldwide, they watch her parents' house in nervous anticipation, with their eyes set firmly on her snug little bedroom.

"C'mon. Hurry up," sighs Mathew as he drums his fingers on the steering wheel. "You said they'd be gone by two and it's ten past already."

It was only last year that Amelia accompanied her parents to the annual church fête at Moulton-Didsley, albeit with a twisted arm. But her metamorphosis from a fifteen-year-old churchy bookworm to a sixteen-year-old bubbly caregiver (with a car-owning boyfriend) has dropped one-legged egg and spoon races and decorated tea cozies into the same category as the pavement pizza she left on her boyfriend's mother's driveway after forcing down what was described as, "The best jellied eels this side of Margate."

"They gotta go in a minute or they'll miss the cow shit–tossing contest," giggles Amelia as she sits alongside Mathew, stroking his thigh. "But they won't be back till late 'cuz they're going to a cheese and bicky do in the church hall afterwards."

"Did I tell you about the time I saved my life with a packet of chocolate digestives?" calls a muffled voice from under an old carpet in the back of the van.

"Yes, Daffy," chuckles Amelia. "An' you told us the one about the monkey's skeleton you dug up cuz it was a murdered baby."

"It wasn't a joke," insists Daphne, but Amelia gives her boyfriend a sly wink.

"I know," she says. "An' you parachuted into Germany —"

"France," jumps in Daphne. "During the war."

"Right," laughs Amelia. "You parachuted into France and blew up the Germans."

"Not all of them," snaps Daphne, and then she mouths, "Teenagers," with the feeling that the world is moving in reverse and has left her stuck in the future. But when she begins, "When I was your age, young lady ..." Amelia spots her parent's car backing out of their driveway.

"Geddown," she shouts to Mathew, and the young couple shrink in their seats until the car has passed.

"Let's go," says Mathew, turning the ignition, and moments later the youngsters are carrying a loosely rolled Axminster rug into Amelia's bedroom.

"I'm going to get something to eat," Bliss whispers to Ted Donaldson when he realizes that he has nothing constructive to offer at St. Michael's, and five minutes later he is waiting to order a snack alongside a glum-faced woman leaning over an empty gin glass in the Crusader's Bar of the Mitre Hotel.

"Having a bad day?" questions Bliss jokingly, but Isabel Semaurino has had a bad week. Westchester is a long way from her home in Tuscany, and she has had a wasted journey.

"Is that meant to be a pickup line?" questions the sixty-nine-year-old with a wan smile. "If it is, I think that I might be profoundly flattered."

"Sorry," laughs Bliss, shaking his head, but, despite the twenty years between them, he sees a spark of recognition and warns himself to be careful. "I'm already spoken for, but I'll happily buy you a drink," he carries on, guessing that it was nothing more than the fleeting hope of a lonely heart.

"Isabel Semaurino," says the woman, neither accepting nor refusing as she questions soberly, "Do you believe in reincarnation or resurrection or life after death or something like that?"

"You're asking the wrong person," Bliss jokes as he nods to the barman, who is visibly flagging after a hectic lunch rush. "I don't even believe in life before death in many cases." Then he gives her and the empty glass a critical look. "You're not thinking of ..."

"Oh, Good Lord, no," she says and laughs. "It's just that I've waited forever to meet someone and now it looks like I'll have till my next life."

"I know what that's like," claims Bliss. "I've been trying to see my fiancée for the past two ..." He stops at the look on Isabel's face. "Yeah. I know," he says. "Fiancée at my age — I should know better."

"I didn't say that."

"You should've seen your face."

"Sorry," she says, and she thrusts out a hand as the barman finally arrives. "I've got an early flight, so I'd better get packed. Goodbye and good luck."

"And the same to you," he says, shaking the hand, but as he watches her walk away he has the urge to call out, "Don't I know you from somewhere?"

"D'ye wanna order summink or not?" spits the barman, and Bliss turns his back on Isabel and picks up the menu.

"Maybe ... I'm thinking about it."

"What'ya thinking about, Daffy?" questions Amelia as Daphne sits with a tear running down her bruised cheek as she gently strokes Camilla, the young girl's long-haired tabby.

"I used to have a cat," she sniffs. "Missie Rouge. She was ever so pretty."

"Did she die?" questions Amelia gently, but Daphne pauses as if she has to think back a very long way.

"No," she says firmly, once she has wiped her eyes. "She was murdered."

"Oh, Daffy ..."

"The neighbours' dogs got hold of her," she is explaining when Amelia crouches on the bedroom floor in front her, looks her straight in the eye, and demands the truth.

"Daffy — you're not really going loopy, are you?"

"No, dear."

"Then why do you pretend?"

"I didn't at first," replies Daphne, casting her mind back to the time when all she wanted was a little respite from the neighbours' continual hubbub. "But when people think you're crazy, and keep saying you're crazy, then everything you do seems crazy."

"I never thought you wuz crazy."

"I know."

"But when you make up stories about parachuting and escaping and saving your life with biscuits and stuff, people don't know what's right and what isn't."

"Have you ever done anything exciting in your life, Amelia?"

"Not really."

"What about last night?" asks Daphne, mindful of the insistent tapping on her window that finally penetrated her torpid mind, of the heaviness of her limbs as she dragged herself across the room, and of the relief at the sight of Amelia's smiling face atop the ladder with Mathew waiting below.

"Yeah, I know," agrees Amelia. "But my mum'll kill me if she finds out."

Daphne strokes the teenager's face. "When I was your age, well, a couple of years older, I volunteered to go to war, and I thought my mum was going to kill me."

"She didn't."

Daphne shakes her head. "No, of course not. It wouldn't make sense, would it? But I soon learnt that nothing is ever as bad, or as good, as you first think it's going to be."

"Is that true?"

"Usually," she says, then casts her mind back over eight decades in search of contradictions. Michael Kent might have been an exception had he not been captured, tortured, and executed. "I'll love you eternally," he said so many times, and he may have done so had he found his way home. There were others, but the first flush of romance never flourished as promised. "I guess the answer is to never expect too much in the first place."

"Daffy …" starts Amelia diffidently, and Daphne thinks she sees what is coming.

"Don't worry," she says, laying a hand on the young girl's shoulder. "I'll be as quiet as a mouse tonight. I'll sleep under your bed, and tomorrow morning, I promise you, everything will be all right and I'll be able to go home. Your mum will never know."

"No. It's not that," says Amelia, and then she tries again. "It's just that Matt, my boyfriend, well … he wants to do it with me … you know … he wants to go all the way. But God says it's wrong cuz we're not married."

Daphne drops Camilla gently to the floor and strokes the young woman's hair instead. "Have you asked your mum?"

Amelia jumps as if electrified. "I couldn't …"

"All right," soothes Daphne. "But do you want to do it with Matt?"

"I think so."

"Well then. You could always change gods."

"Oh, Daffy." laughs Amelia. "There's only one God."

"Really," says Daphne. "And is that the same one that Mrs. Fitzgerald worships before she hits people around?"

"Yeah. I s'pose so."

"And the same one that all these riots and church burnings are about?"

"I guess so."

"Well. Maybe you should make up your own mind, dear. I'm not sure I'd trust someone who wants his followers to do things like that."

Amelia drops her voice to a whisper and even checks out the ceiling to make sure no one is watching before she asks, "Don't you believe in God, Daffy?"

"Ah. Now that is a very good question," sighs Daphne. "But if he is up there somewhere, I wish he'd hurry up and get down here and stop all the fighting and killing."

"Oh, Daffy. You'll never go to heaven if you say things like that."

Stone angels and archangels ascend heavenwards on the façade of Westchester cathedral, but Bliss takes no notice as he scours the grounds in search of Daphne. The bells are ringing for Evensong, and tardy congregants clasp their Sunday hats to freshly washed hair as they scurry towards the fifteenth-century carved doors.

Mavis Longbottom is there, together with Angel Robinson in her flounciest printed cotton, but not inside the cathedral.

"I bet she'll be walking the labyrinth at the cathedral if she's still alive," Mavis loudly pronounced to Anne McGregor when the search of St. Michael's was winding down without a trace of her missing friend. And the super-intendent gave her a sharp look. "What do you mean, if she is still alive?"

"Don't look at me," said Mavis. "It's this lot you should be looking at. I've said it before and I'll say it again, there's something funny going on here."

Blood on the floor in Room 27 is the best, albeit most alarming, verification of Mavis's claim, notwithstanding Hilda Fitzgerald's efforts to wash it away, but it will take a few days for the Home Office's forensic science laboratory to analyze the samples and several more to match the DNA with Daphne's.

"Chief Inspector?" queries Mavis in surprise, spotting the familiar figure of David Bliss as he stops to wonder at the sight of twenty people walking in circles with their eyes on the ground. "You're Daphne Lovelace's friend, aren't you?"

"Umm ..." hums Bliss as he tries to come up with a name.

"Mavis Longbottom. Christmas at Daphne's a couple of years ago. You'd been shot ... she disappeared ... "

"I remember," says Bliss. Then his face darkens worriedly. "Do you know she's missing again?"

Mavis nods. "It's my fault. She was all right until I brought her here."

"Here?" queries Bliss, then Angel Robinson jumps in. "It's the labyrinth," she explains. "Daphne was having a few problems at home, then she came here and was energized to action."

"Hang on," says Bliss skeptically, watching the slump-shouldered devotees shuffling their way around the meandering paths. "What do you mean, energized?"

"It's all my fault, David," Mavis continues muttering in the background.

Bliss's face screws in confusion, and he focuses on Angel. "I don't know what you're talking about," he says. "How was she energized?"

"The labyrinth is one of the most powerful symbols on earth," lectures the flowery woman. "Examples can be found from ancient Greece to Peru and Scandinavia ..."

But Bliss doesn't want history. He wants facts. And he stops her with a hand. "What do you mean — energized?"

"Well," says Angel. "It's like this powerful bolt of energy that rises up from the core of the labyrinth — it sort of zaps your mind."

"Say that again," says Bliss.

"It rises up out of the ground and zaps your mind?"

chapter thirteen

The sandstone Georgian façade of the Mitre Hotel, complete with its fluted columns, balustraded balconies, and mullioned windows, has changed little in nearly three hundred years, but the lobby has suffered at the hands of several owners.

Isabel Semaurino, with suitcases packed, is wearing a linen suit and a simple pillbox travelling hat as she takes a final wander around the laminate-panelled foyer, idly checking out the magazines in a plastic display rack. The desk clerk is arranging for a cab to take her to the railway station as she leafs through a three-year-old copy of *Horse and Hounds*, when the front door bangs open.

"Papers," sings out the perky pigtailed delivery girl, tossing a bundle of *Gazettes* on the desk and sneaking off with a handful of mints.

"May I?" asks Isabel, dropping the magazine and picking up the top copy of the daily newspaper as the desk clerk comes out of the back office.

"Certainly, madam," says the girl. "And your taxi will be here in five minutes."

The police mug shot of Daphne, front and centre under the one-word headline "Kidnapped?", was snapped when she was still boiling over the iniquity of her treatment compared to the real offenders and could have been culled from the "Britain's most belligerent" edition of *Twentieth-Century Villains*.

"Riddle of eighty-five-year-old dementia patient snatched from seniors' home …" begins the story, and it is a full ten seconds before Isabel reaches the name of "Ophelia Lovelace, better known as Daphne." Then she lets out a startled shriek and rushes back to the desk clerk, saying, "I need to phone the police."

"The officer in charge of the missing woman's case, please," she blurts the moment she's connected.

"Can I ask who's calling, ma'am."

"Yes," she says. "My name is Isabel Semaurino. I am Ophelia Lovelace's daughter."

"Mavis — it's me," whispers Daphne the moment she hears the front door slam behind Amelia and her parents.

"Daphne. Where on earth are you? Everyone's worried to death."

"Shh …" hisses Daphne. "Has the postman been?"

"What's going on? Are you all right?"

"Mavis. Just shut up a minute. Have you got the post?"

"Yes. The blasted man was banging on my flippin' door at seven o'clock this morning, demanding money for a parcel with no stamps. Not blinking likely I said —"

"Oh, no," breaks in Daphne.

"Well it was probably just advertising junk …" Mavis is nattering on as Daphne tunes her out and flops backwards on Amelia's bed. The envelope, full of documents from Davenport's private files, didn't have a stamp. She searched for one for several minutes, but finally gave up and stuffed it in the residents' outgoing mailbox in the early hours of Friday morning assuming Mavis would pay.

"Was it important?" questions Mavis.

"Of course it was."

"Well, I didn't know," shouts Mavis in frustration. "You should've put a stamp on it. I thought it was junk ..."

"All right, don't panic," Daphne is saying, as much to herself as to Mavis, fearing that, without documents to back her claims, any accusations she makes will be labelled by Davenport and his sister as the incoherent ramblings of a confused old lady. "Where is it now?"

"How should I know? The postman just took it back. If you'd put your name on it I would have known."

And so would Davenport, thinks Daphne, if it occurred to him to check the mailbox when he was looking for his lost papers. "All right," she says. "Just run to the post office — tell them it was a mistake and you want it back."

"But where are you?"

Michael Kent springs to mind, warning her never to compromise a partner by giving them information. "It's always easier for them to tell the truth than to lie," he explained, "especially when there's an electrode clamped to their tender bits. So, what they don't know can't hurt them."

"I'll call back in an hour," she says. "Just make sure you get it."

The buzz amongst patients and staff at St. Michael's has the nervous intensity of a lockdown in a maximum-security wing following a breakout.

A dozen newly awakened inmates have been jammed up against the television in the common room since 6:00 a.m., spotting themselves time and again as news cameramen focus on the line of policemen searching the grounds, while a couple of early birds have been hovering by the front door since six-thirty for the morning's papers.

Amelia Brimble slips in through the back gate on her bicycle at eight-forty and slides in the kitchen door with her head down.

"What time d'ye call this, young lady?" grunts Hilda Fitzgerald, slamming a frying pan onto the stove with enough force to shatter an eardrum.

"Sorry, Hilda," replies Amelia, while her twitchy fingers refuse to tie her apron strings. "My alarm didn't go off."

"Heard that before," scoffs Fitzgerald as she dollops porridge into bowls. "Hurry up with that apron."

"I got it," says Amelia as she finally succeeds, but she is still dithery as she picks up a laden tray.

"Be careful," shouts the curmudgeon. "What on earth's the matter with you this morning, girl?"

"Nothing," she sings out as she heads to the common room, but she is well aware of the hullabaloo over Daphne's disappearance and guesses that Patrick Davenport will be lying in wait. And she has been awake since dawn, terrified that Daphne's snores would alert her parents.

"You're gonna be late for work," her mother called at seven-thirty, and Daphne woke and silently urged her to go. But the risk of her elderly guest's discovery held the young girl back, and she stalled in the bathroom until her parents were ready to leave a few minutes after eight, following the local radio news.

"Isn't that the place where you work?" said her father, but she pulled a face and ran back to the bathroom.

"I just feel a bit sicky this morning," she told her mother, not untruthfully, when she reappeared, but she declined the option of a day off, fearing that her absence from St. Michael's would heighten suspicion.

"You missed all the excitement, dear," whispers John Bartlesham as he catches Amelia on her way to the common room and pulls her down to wheelchair level. "Someone's stolen your little clockwork mouse."

"Do you mean Daffy?" questions Amelia with feigned surprise as an inmate sights Anne McGregor arriving and yells, "Put out your reefers, girls, the fuzz are back."

Amelia feels her face draining as she checks the wall clock. It is only 8:45.

"I don't want you to have to tell lies for me," Daphne told her. "But I need you to stall them until at least nine."

It is the middle of Monday morning rush hour in Whitechapel and the habitual snarl-up is being worsened by the presence of a cherry picker parked in the road opposite the new mosque.

"Sorry, guv," the owner/driver said when Bliss approached him about doing the police a favour later in the day. "But I've got a job startin' at nine. It's now or never."

"What can you see?" hollers Bliss to his son-in-law, who is in the swaying bucket fifty feet above him.

"Fox and Edwards at six o'clock," Peter Bryan yells down, and Bliss whips around in time to see the two men standing on the mosque's steps with puzzled expressions.

"Don't say a word," Bliss quietly warns the driver, before putting on a wide smile as Edwards and the commander dodge the slow-moving traffic.

"G'mornin', sirs. You're up early on this beautiful …"

"Cut the crap, Chief Inspector. What's going on?" queries Fox. "You're gumming up the works."

"Looking for the best place to site another camera, guv'nor," Bliss says as he takes a bead on the front of the mosque with his index finger and yells up to Peter Bryan. "What coverage do you get from there, Peter?"

"No one told me about additional cameras," complains Edwards. "Whose idea was that?"

"Just using my initiative," says Bliss, turning to the Home Secretary's man. "We don't want anymore foul-ups, do we, Mr. Edwards, sir?"

"Right," says Fox skeptically as he turns to leave. "Just hurry up and clear the road before Traffic shows up and books you for obstructing the highway."

"Yes, sir."

"And don't waste any more money on that. We're advising the palace to cancel. It's just too much risk with all this unrest. Birmingham got hit again last night."

"Right, sir," says Bliss with a touch of relief, while a voice from above sings out. "Oy, gramps. Are you asleep down there or what?"

"I've got to get some kip," moans Bliss as Bryan returns to earth. "I was up most of the night looking for a damn woman."

"They're twenty quid apiece in Piccadilly," jests Bryan. "All sizes; all colours. And you can have as many as you can handle."

"Very funny, Peter. But I'm worried about Daphne."

"She'll turn up. She always does," laughs Bryan, but he has something behind his back as he questions, "Don't you want to know what I found?"

A miniature satellite dish was strapped to the top of the light unit. "You couldn't see it from down here," explains Bryan as he gives the contraption to his father-in-law. "It was camouflaged to blend with the colour of the lamppost."

"Are you sure it's not part of the light?" questions Bliss, turning the parabolic reflector and its box of circuitry over in his hands.

"Definitely not," says Bryan, struggling out of his overalls and checking his watch. "Although the cheeky beggars had wired it into the system to draw power."

"But what's it for?"

"Your guess is as good as mine," says Bryan as he strides away. "I'm a cop, not a whiz kid. Anyway, I gotta go — we've got an appointment with the gynecologist in an hour."

"Why didn't you say —?" starts Bliss, but the driver cuts in.

"Have you finished, guv?"

"Yeah. Thanks a lot, mate," says Bliss, slipping the man a fifty-pound note. "Much appreciated."

"This is Miss Lovelace's daughter," introduces Anne McGregor as she strides into Patrick Davenport's office just before nine, accompanied by Isabel Semaurino.

"She doesn't have …" starts Davenport as he rises in confusion, then he dries up and starts from a different approach. "We weren't aware she had any …"

"… any family," continues Isabel helpfully as she steps confidently forward, adding, "Don't worry. You're not alone in that belief."

"Any news?" questions Davenport, looking past the strikingly elegant woman to Superintendent McGregor.

"As a matter of fact, we believe we have a break-through," she says as she opens her briefcase and extracts a series of photographs from the security camera above the ATM in the wall of the Midland Bank in Westchester High Street. "Last Friday … using Miss Lovelace's debit card. Do you recognize her?"

The photographs of Amelia Brimble are not particularly flattering, mainly due to her look of panic, but Davenport identifies his young staff member immediately, and seconds later the girl stands in front of them with tears running down her cheeks.

"You don't understand," she sobs. "I didn't steal the money. I got it for Daffy." Then she squirrels into her apron pocket with shaking hands and digs out a crumpled shopping list.

"Clothes, shoes, ticket to London, and a book of

escape methods," reads McGregor aloud as she tosses her head in relief. "Thank goodness for that."

"What do you mean?" steps in Isabel. "What's happened to my mother?"

"Maybe Amelia can tell us," says McGregor, spinning on the snivelling girl. "I assume it was you, young lady, who helped her escape."

"Yes," mumbles Amelia through the tears. "But she's not really loopy at all. She shouldn't've been here."

"So. You're a trained social worker, are you?" sneers McGregor, letting her own opinions about the missing woman through.

"No …" Amelia starts, and then looks up defiantly. "But Hilda shouldn't a' hit her."

"Hilda?" questions McGregor, and Patrick Davenport pales before trying to hustle the squealer out.

"You're fired. Get your things together and I'll deal with you in a minute," he says as he pushes Amelia towards the door, but Isabel grabs the girl as she passes.

"Wait a minute," she demands. "Where is my mother?"

The baritone bell of the cathedral's clock booms the first beat of nine as Daphne slips out of Amelia's house and heads for the labyrinth.

"The post office reckoned they couldn't do anything until the postman gets back from his rounds at twelve," Mavis told her when she phoned her friend back, but with the near certainty that Amelia will break under questioning, Daphne is on the run in a pair of the girl's jogging pants, pink running shoes, and an Adidas sweatshirt chosen because of its hood.

An eighty-five-year-old dressed as a teenager and wearing knockoffs of RayBan mirrored sunglasses wouldn't attract a great deal of attention in Tampa Bay or even Marbella, but Westchester is a very long way from Florida in every respect and, with the story of Daphne's abduction and her photograph in all the papers as well as most television stations, more than one person gives her a double take as she half walks, half jogs through the cathedral grounds.

Mavis Longbottom, on the other hand, is completely in the dark as she stands in the middle of the labyrinth wondering why someone would be silly enough to wear a hood in the heat of the day.

"Why here?" demands Mavis, once Daphne has got her walking around the labyrinth's path.

"No one expects me to be out in the open," explains Daphne, stopping to check around carefully before confiding, "And I wouldn't put it past them to be watching your place."

"Who?"

"St. Michael's mob," whispers Daphne, as if she is afraid of microphones. "They've been keeping me a prisoner."

"Don't be silly ..." starts Mavis, then Daphne takes off her glasses and lifts her hood. "Oh my goodness. Did you fall?"

Daphne puts Amelia's sunglasses back on with the sad realization that, without the documents or an eyewitness, Hilda Fitzgerald will undoubtedly win if it comes down to a judge's decision in the final round.

"We should go to the police ..." begins Mavis, getting her feet going once she has heard about the bruises, but Daphne grabs her arm, pulls her to a stop, and puts her foot down.

"No," she insists adamantly. "I can't trust them. I can't trust anyone until I've got the evidence back from the post office."

"I'm sorry about that —"

"You should be," cuts in Daphne as she picks up the path again and pushes Mavis ahead of her. "And that's another reason we're here. I want you to experience what the labyrinth taught me."

"Why?"

"Because you gave up too easily. When the post office said you had to wait, you should've said, 'Not effin' likely.' And you should've chased that damn postman ..."

"Daphne!" exclaims Mavis, grinding to a halt. "You swore."

"So would you if they'd done this to you," she says, whipping off her glasses and making a stab at her swollen eye.

"Is that why wouldn't they let me see you?"

Daphne puts back her glasses and takes a careful look around before pulling Mavis closer. "They wouldn't let you in," she whispers darkly, "because they were going to kill me."

chapter fourteen

A major storm is brewing as Bliss meanders back to his office, his mind whirling with ideas as he focuses on the miniature apparatus that he carries as delicately as a bomb. It could be a receiver, he surmises as he walks along the riverbank, his eyes tracking the sky as if searching for an orbiting satellite. But the sky is perfectly clear and, despite the persistent haze of pollution, remarkably blue. However, ahead of him, an ominous black cloud is descending over the soaring concrete block of New Scotland Yard.

"Gentlemen," announces the assistant commissioner gravely as he looks around the conference table at his upper echelon. "Her Majesty has refused to cancel Friday's visit."

"Fuck!" swears Commander Fox, and the table erupts in a cacophony of objections as officers and visitors spit out headlines from the past few weeks: British flags aflame throughout the Middle East; chanting mobs; torched embassies; ransacked trade missions; tourists roughed up in Turkey; cartoons of Philip dressed as a suicide bomber in Iran.

"And what about what's going on here?" questions one chief superintendent, mindful of the continuing riots, anti-Semitic graffiti, desecrated graveyards, burned churches, and angry voices within the Church of England demanding that the Reformation be reformed and the Queen dumped in favour of someone less anxious to throw themselves at the feet of Mohammed.

"This isn't getting us anywhere," sighs Michael Edwards in exasperation. "You'd think the Muslims would be pleased."

"You'd think the Christians would be pleased," Commander Fox is responding when one of the American representatives, "Pimple" to David Bliss, quietly assumes the floor.

"The President is now of the opinion that the visit should proceed despite the protests," says the CIA man with calm authority.

"That's flippin' nice of him," mutters Fox, and Pimple colours up and spins.

"It's called democracy, Commander," he explains as if he personally invented it. "Freedom of speech ... freedom to disagree. And the point is, Commander, that we have reached a new understanding of popular dissent."

"Really?"

"Sure," he says flippantly. "We don't give a damn what they think anymore."

"I think it's some sort of radio receiver," suggests Bliss as he hands the device to the technician in the video lab.

"Leave it with me. I'll take a look-see when I've got a minute," says Hoskins with a screwdriver already in his hand. "By the way, did you trace that pickup truck?"

"Not exactly," replies Bliss, unwilling to admit to a civilian that he isn't high enough in the tree to peek through the "Classified" window. "But I've been thinking," he carries on, wondering aloud if it might be possible to find out where the vehicle was going by checking successive surveillance cameras. "After all," he says. "We know which way it was headed when it drove away from the mosque, and we know the exact time it left."

"It's possible," says Hoskins, scratching his ear with the screwdriver. "But it would be a helluva lot of work."

"You find the videos and I'll do the legwork," Bliss offers and gets a nod of agreement.

The crypt of Westchester cathedral has preserved the bodies and memories of its richest and most powerful benefactors for nearly a thousand years, whilst its nave is home to the sarcophagi of kings, knights, and warriors who fought on God's side from the Crusades onwards and whose tattered standards and battle honours glorify their conquests from on high.

Westchester City cemetery, in contrast, has no fan-arched roof from which to fly flags, but at a time in history when death was more commonplace, and burial more fashionable, it was proud of its position in society. However, Georgian and Victorian statues and headstones have been dissolved by more than a century of pollution and rain, and now celebrate generations of nameless, faceless people.

Daphne Lovelace hopes that she is faceless as she wanders amongst the gravestones and monuments with her head down while she waits for Mavis to retrieve her envelope from the post office.

The sight of a straggle of black-hatted mourners heading into the chapel gives her an idea, and she slips in behind them hoping to glimpse the records of the most recent burials.

"Are you family?" questions a gatekeeper, looking her over with a jaundiced eye.

"Not exactly. More a friend," lies Daphne, but the tightly knitted, glum-faced congregants swing as one in her direction, and she backs out.

"Sorry. I must be early … Wrong funeral."

Familiar names make Daphne pause from time to time as she saunters past freshly mounded graves, some still bearing wreaths and cards, and she stops for a few moments where she laid a wreath only a couple of months ago. Phil and Maggie Morgan — "Philip and Margaret — Together Eternally," she reads off the plaque — who bailed out and left her at the mercy of the Jenkinses. And Minnie Dennon, another deserter, whose spectacular demise on the front of an express train caught the attention of the nation and packed the cathedral. How few would have shown up if they knew she jumped, Daphne wonders, recalling the public outcry over her supposed murder, and as she meanders from grave to grave, checking out the ages of her contemporaries, Daphne can't help but notice that she has easily beaten the odds.

Detective Chief Inspector David Bliss is less lucky. With Edwards on his back, Commander Fox has been nosing around for more information about Bliss's imaginary surveillance camera, and he stalks into Bliss's office mid-morning, snarling, "Are you trying to make me look stupid in front of Edwards, Chief Inspector?"

"No, sir," says Bliss as Peter Bryan tries to shrink his head into his father-in-law's coffee percolator.

"Well, how come no one in Surveillance knows a damn thing about another camera for Friday?"

"That's true," confesses Bliss. "We were just checking out the possibilities."

Fox's face is a picture of disbelief as he points a warning finger. "You two better not be up to something," he cautions. "I've got enough problems with Edwards without you."

"Problems?" probes Bliss, but Fox won't bite.

"Just watch it," he says on his way out, but the arrival of Hoskins stops him. "You can take that back," he scowls, stabbing at Bliss's gizmo in the technician's hands. "We're not putting up any more cameras."

"It's not a camera. It's a microwave transceiver," declares the startled video technician as he swivels the miniature dish in demonstration. "It's designed to pick up a concentrated radio signal, give it a boost, and retransmit it."

"I don't care if it's an ejection seat. Mr. Bliss doesn't need it," Fox sneers as he stomps away.

"Where does it send the signal?" questions Bliss, fingering the device speculatively.

"Anywhere you point it. It's entirely directional, like the beam of a flashlight."

"That's interesting," says Bliss, turning to his son-in-law. "Have you ever heard of labyrinths, Peter?"

"Is it a computer game?"

"Not unless Bill Gates was an ancient Greek," laughs Bliss. "No. I'm told they've been around forever. Apparently King Minos had one in Crete where they sacrificed their most beautiful virgins to a monster."

"What a waste," mumbles Bryan facetiously as Bliss continues.

"They're sort of circles on the ground that are supposed to have magical powers. They're all over the world, apparently."

"Magical," echoes Bryan, summoning an imaginary wand. "Hocus-pocus frogs and locusts and that kind of thing?"

"That's what I thought," agrees Bliss. "But I saw one of these labyrinths yesterday, at the cathedral in Westchester, and this airy-fairy kind of woman reckoned that the core gave out a bolt of energy that zapped people's minds, and it got me thinking." Then he picks up the electronic unit. "What if this satellite dish directed a beam that zapped him — you know, when he stopped and looked as though he was having a good clear-out?"

"You're asking the wrong person," says Bryan as he nods to the technician.

"Nah," snorts Hoskins dismissively. "That thing couldn't zap a cockroach at ten paces with the amount of power it gives out."

The buzz of Bliss's cellphone cuts the air as if on cue.

"Okay," says Trina Button without waiting for a greeting as she picks up an Avis car at Heathrow. "We've arrived. Any news? Have they found her?"

"Arrived?" queries Bliss blankly. "Who? Where?"

"I brought my mother," carries on Trina as she firmly straps Winifred in. "She's exactly the same age as Daphne, so she might be able to help track her down."

"That's just what I need — a pair of loonies," mutters Bliss once he has put Trina in the picture. "Although I don't suppose she can do any harm."

Trina flicks off her cellphone and starts the engine as her mother questions, "Where are we, Treenie?"

"England, Mum," shouts Trina as she lifts one of her mother's earphones and catches a blast of U2.

"Great! Are we going to do the El Camino?"

"Yeah. Why not?" says Trina, as she heads off to Westchester.

The cemetery is wearing Daphne down with its irrefutable and particularly pertinent omens. Headstone after headstone remind her that after a lifetime of skirmishes and battles, heartaches and triumphs, lovers and leavers, aches and pains, good times and bad, the only prize for winning is a carved chunk of Carrara marble instead of a lump of polished concrete.

"Not if you believe in heaven," says a seductive voice in Daphne's mind, but it's a voice that she has been ignoring ever since the consecrated bombs of England desecrated Hitler's Teutonic heathens and left her seeking answers in the Bible, the Qu'ran, the Talmud, and even the Bhagavad-gita. But by the time she finished doing the rounds of prophets, messiahs, and evangelists, she had as much respect for John Frum and the Cargo Cult of Vanuatu as she did for any of the mainstreamers.

The cathedral's clock takes hours to strikes eleven, by which time Daphne has visited so many old friends and acquaintances that she is seriously contemplating turning herself in and joining them, but the sound of voices from a blackberry bush stop her. Behind the bush, in an ancient wooden tool shed with a sway-back roof, a couple of gravediggers are making tea on a camping stove.

The earthy smell of dry rot and decayed timber induce memories for Daphne as she pokes her head through the open door — childhood memories of carefree play in the copse surrounding her home; teenage memories of illicit trysts in neglected barns; exhilarating wartime memories of foxholes and shell-shattered hovels.

"The chapel's over there, m'dear," calls Dennis, one of the gravediggers, cutting into her memories and reminding her that she is in a cemetery. Then he sizes her up and scratches his head. "You ain't here for a funeral dressed like that, are you?"

"No," she admits, then explains she was hoping to find out if one of her friends was buried recently.

"The proper records is kept in the office," explains Dennis, while lighting a cigar from the stove. "But they ain't open Mondays."

"Never mind," she says, turning away.

"Hang on," he says moving a copy of the *Gazette* off an old car seat. "Take the weight off … I might be able to help."

"Can you …" she starts, but her mouth drops as she spots a very familiar face on the front page. "Um … thanks," she mumbles, hoping they haven't noticed her surprise, or her likeness to the picture, but a glance at the shiny kettle would have told her not to worry: while the image in print might have mirrored her a few weeks ago, Hilda Fitzgerald's hand has moulded her a new face.

"Have you bin knocking yourself about, luv?" asks Dennis rhetorically before offering her a tea.

"I'd love one," she says, immediately unwinding in their cozy niche with a feeling that the dilapidated hut is a lifeboat in a world of death and that they have come to her rescue. "It's a bit depressing out there," she adds with a shiver.

"Nah, luv," pipes up Dennis's partner, Michael, as he lies back in a wooden rocking chair. "You've got it wrong. You wait. In a minute that lot in the chapel will be out here saying, 'Good old Uncle Fred, Gawd bless his soul, he's gorn to an 'appier place,' and then they'll bawl their bloomin' eyes out with bloomin' joy while they divvy up the old bugger's life savins'."

"So. Do you believe in heaven?"

"Mebbe, luv. But trust me, most of the stiffs that we drop in the hole here just keep on going down an' down an' down."

"Life stinks and then you die, is what I believe," chirps in Dennis mournfully as he hands Daphne a cracked mug. "And then, once you're gorn, you stink a helluva lot more."

"That's not very cheerful."

"That's me, miserable Denny. 'Miserable as sin,' me mother always said. Well, I've had my share of sin and I can tell you … Well, maybe I shouldn't. But if I believed in some sort of beautiful heaven I wouldn't 'a stuck around in this dump for the past forty-odd years, I can tell ya that."

The tea is not Keemun, but after two weeks of avoiding anything but water from the bathroom tap, the sweet milky liquid is honey.

"Now," says Dennis as he carefully washes his hands in a rusty enamel basin. "You wuz asking about recent interments."

"I was wondering about Emily Mountjoy," queries Daphne as Dennis extracts his book of work orders from a plastic cover.

"Names, dates of birth and death, date, and exact place of burial," he explains, and then he sees the inquisitive look on Daphne's face. "I like to keep it neat out of respect."

"Mountjoy," she reminds him as he leafs through the book with as much reverence as he might turn the pages of a Bible.

"Last Wednesday," he declares. "Emily Sophie Mountjoy. Born —"

"That was quick," cuts in Daphne in amazement. "She only died Tuesday night."

"They don't mess around if there ain't no relatives," he explains, then he looks to the shed rafters for inspiration. "If I recall rightly, she only 'ad the vicar — Reverend Rowlands from Dewminster. Mind, she'd come from St. Michael's — the old folks' place."

Meaning? questions Daphne to herself. But she knows the answer; knows that she too would have been stuck in a box and unceremoniously dropped into a hastily dug hole if she had stayed at St. Michael's much longer.

The revelation that Daphne slipped her leash rather than being abducted has turned the earlier excitement at St. Michael's into mild dismay as residents shrink back into their shells. The eighty-five-year-old's daring escape will be the talk of the common room for a few days or even weeks to come but will quickly fall into the realm of folklore as new residents take over. Amelia Brimble will be remembered by the staff more for her juvenile gullibility than her bravery. "If I believed half of what they told me ..." more senior staff members chuckle as they shuffle their elderly charges in and out of soiled beds and search for lost teeth and hidden hearing aids; meanwhile, downstairs, voices are raised behind Patrick Davenport's closed door.

Robert Jameson is on his third handkerchief of the day as he launches into the home's manager. "You specifically said she had no family."

"That's what I was told, Robert," replies Davenport. "It's not my fault."

"But ..." starts Jameson, controlling himself with difficulty. "You should've freakin well checked. We don't need — correction, you don't need —"

"All right. You needn't remind me," says Davenport.

"And what are you going to do about that slap-happy sister of yours?" Jameson is yelling as Trina Button comes knocking.

"Yes," calls Davenport, and the Canadian woman puts her head around the door.

"Sorry to interrupt, but I've left my mother in the car."

Winifred Goodenow is not in the car. She has slipped out and is in the garden starting a relationship with John Bartlesham. "I'm going to do the El Camino," she tells him as she limbers up with a few painful hops. "Do you want to come with me?"

"I wasn't expecting a new resident ..." starts Davenport in confusion, while outside, John is laughing as he points to his wheels. "I don't think I could make it in this."

"Don't worry," says Winifred seriously as she grabs the handles and sets off at a snail's pace. "I'll push you."

"No ... wait," chuckles Bartlesham, but Winifred is hitting her stride.

"I'm not here to discuss new residents," Trina expounds resolutely. "I'm here to investigate the disappearance of my associate, Miss Lovelace."

"Your associate?" echoes Davenport quizzically.

"Yes," says Trina, pulling herself fiercely upright in a tadasana yoga pose. "We are private investigators." Then she hands over a printed card. "Lovelace and Button (International Investigators) Inc.," she says, adding, "Miss Lovelace is my partner and is head of our European division."

Robert Jameson has loosened his tie and is turning puce in the background, while Davenport laughs nervously and scoffs, "Private investigators. Are you pulling my leg? I think you've got the wrong person here."

"I don't think so," says Trina reproachfully. "It says Patrick Davenport on your door."

"No ... I meant Miss Lovelace. She can't possibly be a detective, she's pushing ninety and she's senile."

"Nonsense," says Trina. "I spoke with her just a couple of weeks ago and she was fine."

"All right," says Davenport, dragging Trina to the window overlooking the lawn. "Have a look out there. Do you see a cat?"

"No."

"Miss Lovelace did. 'Here, kitty kitty,' she'd go all day long. Round and round she'd go, hour after hour, calling kitty bloody kitty. It used to get on everyone's nerves."

"Observation," trumpets Trina enigmatically, recalling a chapter from her private investigator's manual, and then she explains, "One of the attributes of a top investigator is that they are able to see things that other people miss."

"Excuse me, ma'am," calls Samuel Fitzgerald as he races into Davenport's office without knocking. "Is that woman with you?"

"Which woman ...?" starts Trina, then she follows Fitzgerald's gaze out of the window just in time to see her mother pushing John Bartlesham out of the gates.

"Mother!" shouts Trina as she tears out of the office and belts down the driveway, and then she turns back to Davenport. "Don't go away. I'll be back."

The disparity between Davenport's image of a crazy old lady and Trina's insistence that Daphne is nothing less than a female Sherlock Holmes is as profound as the difference between the elderly woman's present appearance and the photograph on the front of the *Westchester Gazette*, which explains why Isabel Semaurino walks past her in the High Street without missing a step as she makes her way to the police station to see if there is any news.

The High Street is something of a high wire for Daphne, so she keeps her hood up and concentrates on her feet as she scuttles past familiar stores and a few recognizable figures. But the heat is off. Her red herring, the train ticket to London, has worked, and with the kidnapping put to rest and the local search called off, no one at Westchester police station is particularly concerned about finding her.

Superintendent McGregor is getting down to more serious matters when her phone rings.

"What should I do with the dabs from St. Michael's, ma'am?" asks the fingerprint officer. McGregor is tempted to say, "Chuck them," but she checks herself. What if the remains of a dismembered body turn up in a ditch in five years' time?

"You might as well run them through the mill and stick them on file," she replies, then dumps Daphne's file in her "Out" box, marked, "MissPer — No further action."

"Edwards wants an update at four this afternoon," says Fox as he pops his head into Bliss's office on his way to lunch. "Have you got any ideas at all about protecting her?"

"I might if I knew what that pickup truck was doing outside the mosque."

"I ordered you to leave that alone."

"I know —"

"Look," snaps Fox. "Roughly half the Muslims and half the Christians in the world are threatening to kill her if she shows up, and all you have to worry about is one slightly cranky husband. So just leave everything else to me … understood?"

"Understood, sir."

"This is your last chance, Chief Inspector," Fox warns over his shoulder as Peter Bryan appears in the corridor. "Four o'clock. Don't be late."

"I'll be there," calls Bliss, and then he drags his son-in-law inside and shuts the door.

"It's movie time," he says as he pulls another chair up to his desk.

Bryan raises his eyebrows in mock disapproval and jests, "I hope they're not smutty like the last time. I'm a married man, you know."

"They are … sort of," says Bliss, explaining that the video technician has obtained recordings from all the congestion cameras in a three-mile radius of the mosque. "I had to promise half my pension for these," he says as they begin watching.

With the precise time and known direction of travel it doesn't take long.

"There it is," shouts Bryan time and again as they follow the vehicle's progress from one camera to the next, until …

"Nothing," says Bliss, and they backtrack to the last sighting and put an X on a map.

"Okay," says Bryan, using a pencil as a pointer. "Unless it vaporized into thin air it has to be somewhere in this area, and it was travelling in this direction."

"So what are we waiting for?" asks Bliss.

"What was Fox ranting about when I arrived?"

"Do you know, Peter," says Bliss with a fiercely furrowed brow as he opens the door for his son-in-law, "the biggest problem with getting old and becoming a grandfather is that the memory just goes."

Despite her age, Daphne Lovelace's memory hasn't diminished one iota. She still remembers the velvety life that she enjoyed in the same comfortable house for nearly forty years; the zany scrapes that Trina Button got her into; Missie Rouge, her red-tinged cat; the flowers and vegetables in her garden; the afternoon tea — always Keemun, and always in a pot, never made in the cup.

It's nearing midday, and Mavis's postman will soon be back at the sorting office with the envelope. So, heartened by the fact that the cemetery workers didn't recognize her, Daphne pulls down her hood and slinks through the copse to the cul-de-sac end of her street.

In the eyes of the police and her neighbours, Daphne Lovelace is now just another confused old lady on the loose, so, apart from a few youngsters playing hopscotch and a couple of teens sucking the dregs out of a found cigarette butt, the road is deserted.

Daphne eyes the quiet street carefully and pulls her key out of her purse. It's not far to her front door, but Michael Kent stands in her path.

"Timing is everything," he warned her on so many occasions when she was readying to make a dash for freedom with a defector on her arm or under the back seat of her car, but with Mavis only minutes away from collecting the evidence, she takes a chance.

There's a hole in the kitchen unit where Daphne's fridge used to be, but it's not the loss of the fridge that starts her tears. It's the memory of Missie Rouge, who would sit for hours if necessary, waiting for the fridge door to open and a can of food to appear.

"She must think it's a food factory," Daphne laughed to friends on more than one occasion, and the fridge's removal is the final nail in the cat's coffin.

"I bet they took it for spite," sobs Daphne, immediately

accusing the neighbours, and as she pulls a crack in her curtains to see into their kitchen, she sends the dogs into a frenzy and Misty Jenkins to the phone.

The snarling dogs send Daphne scurrying to the front of the house with her hands over her ears, and she flies up the stairs to her bedroom.

David Bliss, Mavis, and Tony Oswald have all had a hand in trying to protect her belongings, and the sight of several bulging bags and boxes labelled "clothes," "hats," "bedding," and "knick-knacks" stops her as she opens the door, then she breaks down again.

Time warps as Daphne lies on her bed mourning the life that has been taken from her, and she doesn't hear the arrival of Anne McGregor and a car from St. Michael's.

"Miss Lovelace," calls Patrick Davenport through the letterbox, and she wakes in an instant.

"Open the door, please. It's the police," calls Anne McGregor, and Daphne is out of bed and down the stairs in a single move.

"Now where?" she questions and turns to Michael Kent for advice.

"Never hide in a building — the dogs will always find you. Run and you have a chance."

She runs — for the back door and the cornfield beyond, but in her absence Rob Jenkins has ripped down the badly mauled wire fence separating the two gardens, and she is immediately slapped against her coalhouse wall by the snarling pit bulls.

"Get off … get off," she screeches as she tries to push the ferocious creatures away, but the commotion has reached the front of the house, and Anne McGregor's driver throws his shoulder against the door.

"Come along, dear," says the superintendent seconds later, offering a hand from Daphne's kitchen door as Misty Jenkins tries calling the dogs off. "Your daughter's waiting for you."

"Liar," screams Daphne. "You're all liars. Why are you lying?"

"Daphne ..." begins Hilda Fitzgerald, but Daphne would rather take her chances with the dogs.

"They're trying to kill me," she shouts, backing away from Fitzgerald. "They're trying to kill me."

"I'd better call for a doctor ..." starts McGregor, but Davenport has it in hand.

"Dr. Williamson is on his way," he says. "He knows the case personally."

"Good," says McGregor as Misty finally gets the dogs under control.

"Look. They made me sign over everything to a lawyer," Daphne is shouting to anyone who will listen. "Jameson — that was his name. Can't you see what they're doing? They're saying I've got a daughter so they can give her my house and everything."

"Daphne, I'm sure ..." tries McGregor.

"No ... no ... no. You're not listening to me. Please ... please ... please. I'm telling you. Look at his files. See all the drugs they're giving them."

"All our patients need medication," explains Davenport calmingly. "They're all very old people."

"They're killing people to steal their houses. That's how they got Phil and Maggie's place," rants Daphne as the three of them close in. "They made her sign everything over to the lawyer and then they killed her."

"Daphne," asks McGregor condescendingly, "have you got any proof of that at all?"

"The papers ... I had the papers," shouts Daphne.

"Where are they?"

"At the post office. I posted them to Mavis, but she wouldn't pay for them."

"C'mon, luvee," coos Davenport as he makes a grab.

"Get off," screeches Daphne, but Davenport has a firm grip, and his sister snags an arm.

"Come with us, dear," says Hilda Fitzgerald as she and her brother hustle the squirming woman through the house towards the car. Then she turns back to the superintendent. "Don't worry. We'll take good care of her."

"Don't let them take me," screams Daphne. "They're going to kill me."

"Daphne ..." starts McGregor consolingly, but the terrified woman makes a final break, wriggles free of Fitzgerald's grip, and throws herself at the superintendent's legs.

"Please don't let them," she begs as she tightly wraps her arms around the woman. Then Doctor Williamson shows up and sums up the situation at a glance.

"Paranoia can be a very, very frightening thing in the elderly," says Williamson as he carefully removes the hypodermic from Daphne after a few minutes of struggle and drops it into a small disposal unit while Daphne's eyes slowly close.

"Not just in the elderly," says Anne McGregor as she gently unpeels Daphne's arms from her legs and feels her heart thumping against her ribcage. "I've never known someone put up such a struggle."

"The fear of dying is a very potent force," Williamson explains as he helps carry the limp woman to Davenport's car.

chapter fifteen

Westchester's corrugated iron and concrete sorting room is a 1950s canker on the backside of the High Street's historic post office, but despite its leaky roof and draughty walls it is abuzz with robotic sounds of the twenty-first century as computerized hands speed the mail.

The lengthy tables of chatty sorters are long gone. A few po-faced supervisors remain, frustrated from years of attempting to decipher the indecipherable, and one picks up Patrick Davenport's frantic phone call.

"There's been a big mix-up," gushes St. Michael's manager, and then he rattles on about confused staff members, wrong papers, patients' records, silly people, and a major embarrassment, before explaining that the envelope was sent to a resident's friend by mistake.

"Name?" asks the supervisor laconically without taking his eyes off his screen.

"Daphne Lovelace."

"Address?"

"No, sorry," says Davenport realizing he is heading down the wrong road. "You mean, who were the papers sent to, don't you?"

"That would help," groans the supervisor tiredly.

"Her name's Mavis somebody or other, but I don't have the address."

The supervisor stops his screen and swivels his eyes to the ceiling as if trying to visualize the face of an idiot. "Half a million letters a week," he sneers, "and you expect me to find one addressed to Mavis?"

"I've got a phone number…" Davenport says before he realizes that he is talking to himself.

Mavis Longbottom is closer to success as she catches her postman on his way home.

"I weren't gonna lug it around all morning," he explains snottily as he leaps off his bicycle and removes his trouser clips. "You said you didn't want it."

"I do now."

"Too late, luv. I chucked it."

"Where?"

"I dunno — somebody's dustbin I 'spect."

"I'll report you."

"You can tell the bleedin' Pope for all I care."

Rightfully guessing that the Pope might be more attuned to absolution than Daphne, Mavis wears heavy shoes as she trudges back to the cathedral's grounds. However, the absence of Daphne on the labyrinth's pathway cheers her momentarily as she convinces herself that her friend has somehow retrieved the letter and couldn't wait to get home with it.

"Mavis!" hails a distant voice, and Angel Robinson runs up breathlessly. "Where's Daphne? It's in the papers and everything …"

"She's all right," calms Mavis. "She was here earlier, telling me that I could learn something from the labyrinth. But I've been round this thing a dozen times and I just get back to where I started."

"It's a metaphor for life's journey," explains Angel, sweeping an expressive hand across the snaking stone pathway. "It's tortuous and long with many twists and turns, and the ending of one life is the beginning of another."

"But what does it do?"

"*It* does nothing. *It* enables you to find empowerment and spiritual insight. *It* helps you find the right path for your life."

"Well *it* doesn't flipping well work," spits Mavis. "And if I'd bought *it* in Marks and Sparks I would have taken *it* back by now."

"*It* empowered Daphne."

"And look where *it* got her."

"But, where is she?"

Voices echo like whispers in a pitch-black tunnel inside Daphne's mind. People are there, she knows, but she can't seem to reach the light switch.

"Miss Lovelace. Can you hear me?" asks Geoffrey Williamson, with a stethoscope on her chest.

"Daphne ..." calls Isabel Semaurino as she sits by the bedside stroking the lifeless woman's boney hand.

"She didn't even recognize her own daughter," Anne McGregor told Ted Donaldson when she phoned the ex-superintendent to bring him up to speed, and he grunted his surprise.

"Hah! I didn't know she had a daughter," he said, before admitting there was much about Daphne he didn't know.

"So what happens now?" Donaldson asked, but they both knew the answer.

"She *is* eighty-five," stressed McGregor, and he agreed.

It is Prague, summer of 1948, in Daphne's mind. President Klement Gottwald, Stalin's newly appointed puppet, has Czechoslovakia by the throat, and a handful of his thugs in Communist uniforms warm up their fists on a couple of freedom-seeking scientists while she and Michael Kent are forced to listen from the next room. "If they knock you down — stay down," whispers Kent in the darkness of Daphne's mind. "Life can only get worse if you get up."

"Daphne … Mother," calls a voice in the darkness and Daphne knows that she has to stay down as long as possible and hope the cavalry will show up in time.

"Time is the only thing on your side," whispers Michael Kent. "The longer you live, the more chance you have of survival. The moment you give up, you're dead."

"What can I do?" asks Isabel, looking up at the strained face of Geoffrey Williamson as she keeps a grip on Daphne's hand.

"Just talk to her. Judging by the struggle she put up, she could be stronger than we thought. She's lost quite a bit of weight in the last few weeks, but physically she's not bad. It's her mental condition that really bothers me."

"But can she hear me?"

The clear, logical words of Michael Kent override the muffled sounds from outside, so Daphne switches off as Williamson bends to whisper in Isabel's ear on his way out. "Hearing is usually the last faculty to go, so just be careful what you say."

"Okay."

"And try to be cheerful," he cautions. "We don't want her picking up vibes or she'll get hysterical again."

Isabel Semaurino has been an actress all her life and has never had any difficulty finding the right face for any part, but, sitting by Daphne's bedside staring at a complete stranger, she can't help but ask how she is supposed to feel about someone she's never met, someone she never heard of until two weeks ago. What do you say? *I wish I had known you. I wonder what kind of woman you were.*

"I'd like to know something about you before you …" she starts, then stops. "Sorry," she says. "But I've never done this before … well, actually that's not quite true. I have sort of done it once before. Why am I telling you this? You can't hear me, can you? It's just that they didn't really give me enough information. It's like an improv stage show I did in Los Angeles at some downbeat backstreet place. 'Be natural — be yourself,' they said and pushed me on stage — no scenery, no props, nothing. I just froze. I suppose I've always been used to having a script. So what will I say when people ask me about you?"

Isabel stops and tries to get a read on Daphne from her face. The violet bruises are turning black under the parchment skin, like India ink bleeding through airmail paper, and Isabel reaches out with a hand that, too, is showing the scars of age.

"'Was she a good mother?' people will ask," carries on Isabel as she tenderly strokes Daphne's face and tries to connect with the woman inside. "And I won't know what to say."

"Mother," sighs Trina, as Winifred brazenly stuffs the antique brass counter bell from the front desk of the Mitre into her handbag. "Please put it back."

"What, dear?"

"Sorry," says Trina turning to Imelda, the Latvian exchange clerk, after she has quit in a brief tug-of-war with her mother. "You'll have to charge me for it. Just put it on my bill."

"Madam, it is zhe hotel bell," croaks the young girl in astonishment, but Trina sloughs it off.

"It was old. Time you had a new one."

"But, madam ..." Imelda is still calling as Trina drags her mother to the car park and straps her in the back seat of the hire car.

"Are we going to El Camino?" asks Winifred while Trina scans the index of her private investigator's manual for the chapter on missing persons in preparation for her search for Daphne.

"Only if you give the bell back," says the wannabe private eye as she spots the fierce-faced manager pounding in their direction.

"Identify precisely who is missing by compiling a subject profile," Trina reads aloud, once the manager has left, and she begins to reel off a list of requirements: "Description; disabilities; deformities; name; birthdate; sexual orientation; marital status ..." Then she pauses. "This is no good. It'll take forever."

"Are we there yet?" inquiries Winifred from the back seat.

"Won't be long, Mum," replies the young Canadian as she sets off for Daphne's house to see if she can pick up a track from there.

The trail of surveillance tapes has led David Bliss and his son-in-law to a quarter-mile stretch of urbanity where a growing sprawl of industrial units have spread like concrete fungi across a deer park that once backed onto the red brick Victorian terraces.

"I forgot to ask," says Bliss as he and Peter Bryan slowly cruise an area of welding shops and industrial bakers. "Is everything all right, baby-wise?"

"Fine, Dave. No problems at all."

"Problems," muses Bliss to himself, and fiercely focuses on passing factories to avoid listing a catalogue of crises caused by his daughter when she was a baby.

"Although Samantha is beginning to worry that she might not be able to cope," Bryan is saying as Bliss concentrates on overflowing staff car parks and jammed side streets with the growing feeling that, unless God is on their side, they will never find the truck.

"All new parents worry about that," answers Bliss in a reassuring tone, and he smiles inwardly in memory of the fragile young life that lay in his arms only yesterday, and who today is expecting her own baby — his grandchild.

"So ... what's happening with Daisy?" inquires Bryan as they slowly tour row upon row of resting automobiles looking for one that sticks out.

"I've had so much on my plate," says Bliss, conveniently excusing himself for not dropping everything to pursue the woman he calls fiancée. "But I've spoken to her a couple of times."

The conversations have been as torturous as twentieth-century transatlantic telephone calls. "You go." "No, you go." "No, it's your turn," they bickered in between periods of silence, and then they echoed each other. "I'm okay. And you?" "I'm okay." "The weather's good." "It's good here, too." Bliss is still signing off with, "I love you," but whatever has come between them is a festering sore that won't heal, and he would say "Just tell me the truth and get it over with" if he didn't already know how much suffering that would cause him.

"You must understand how hard this is for me," Isabel Semaurino is saying as she talks to herself in Daphne's darkened room. "I wasn't prepared for this. I thought you'd be dead already. They didn't tell me ... I guess they didn't know."

"Is everything all right, miss?" asks Brenda, Amelia Brimble's replacement, as she puts her head around the door. "How is the old duck?"

"Still asleep."

"You can take a break and get some tea if you want," says Brenda as she clatters in with a stand for an intravenous drip. "The nurse is coming to put a tube in to stop her getting dehydrated."

"All right," says Isabel, grateful to be given direction, grateful to be back on the script. *Exit stage left*, she muses internally as she gives Daphne's hand a squeeze and rehearses her lines one more time. "Bye, Mother. I'll come back later."

"Mother," she mouths, recalling the woman who authored and directed her life as she makes her way down the stairs. Do this; Do that; Come here; Go there; Don't do that ... Pushed and shoved into piano and violin, singing and ballet — squeezed into a tutu and crammed into pointes against her will; shouted at and slapped when she outgrew her dancing shoes.

"She's just too tall and gawky to be a ballerina," Mrs. Fairweather, her teacher, finally admitted — something she would have said after the first lesson if she could have afforded to.

"I didn't do it on purpose, Mum," the fifteen-year-old cried, but she was already being thrust in a different direction.

"Never mind, Isabel, dear. There's plenty of tall women in Hollywood."

Stagecraft, elocution, and deportment — years of auditions and humiliations, but she made it to Los Angeles eventually: a few walk-ons; endless propositions; even a couple of lines off-camera to Meryl Streep in the wilds of Africa. At least, Meryl Streep was in Africa — on location on the plains of the Serengeti amongst herds of wildebeest and elephants. Isabel Semaurino, a.k.a. Devonia Dressler, was on a sterile Foley stage in the back lot of an L.A. studio.

Patrick Davenport's door is closed as Isabel slides out to sign back into the Mitre for a few days, and she doesn't hear Hilda Fitzgerald's derisive laughter as her brother attempts to censure her.

"Christ, you're such a drip. What'r'ya gonna do. Fire me?" mocks Hilda. "For God's sake, Pat. Somebody has to wear the f'kin trousers around here."

"This Canadian woman reckons she's some kind of detective."

"So. What can she do? The old baggage fell over and hit her face — big deal. The old crumblies are always on their bums —"

"No," cuts in Davenport, although he lacks conviction as he tries to explain that it is Daphne Lovelace who is supposedly a detective.

"Yeah. And I'm the queen of f'kin Sheba," laughs Fitzgerald as she lets herself out and slams the door.

Daphne's front door still bears the shoulder marks of Anne McGregor's driver when Trina Button arrives with her mother in tow.

"Sorry, luv," says the carpenter brought in by the police. "I don't know nuvving. Maybe the neighbours …"

"They've locked her up again," yells Misty Jenkins above the baying of the pit bulls as soon as Trina inquires. "And not before time. She wuz a damn nuisance."

"You're new here, aren't you?" says Trina, once she has processed the information and decided that she would have visited anyway had she known of her friend's plight.

Misty tosses her head. "So?"

"Nothing," says Trina guilelessly. "I just remember an elderly couple …"

"That's right," Misty steps in quickly. "Dad's brother — Uncle Phil — and Aunt Margaret. He died a month or so ago and they didn't have no kids so dad got the place."

"And gave it to you?"

"Well, we got kicked out of our other place 'cos of the dogs."

"Dangerous Dogs — 24 Hr. Guard," reads the oversize warning sign on the closed gate of an industrial compound, bringing Bliss and Bryan to a halt in their search.

"Eyes," cautions Peter Bryan nodding to several motorized surveillance cameras, perched atop masts, that are swivelling in their direction.

"Well, this isn't another fruitcake factory, that's for sure," says Bliss as he spells out the visible security measures: "Retinal scan entry system; triple-mesh, fifteen-foot fence with razor wire topping; reinforced concrete anti-blast berms; high-intensity halogen spots and floods."

"He doesn't look very friendly," warns Bryan as a uniformed gorilla emerges from the main building and is dragged by his Doberman towards the gates.

The sign over the retinal scanner reads, "Continental and International Imports," and Peter Bryan jots down the telephone number.

"We could pull rank," suggests Bliss, but the approaching primate doesn't look as though he's likely to do more than grunt, so they take off and leave him scratching his dog's ears.

"Leave a message," echoes Bliss once he has called the number, but his cellphone buzzes the moment he's cut the recording off.

"It's nearly four-thirty, Bliss," steams Michael Edwards.

"Shit," mutters Bliss under his breath. "Just on my way, sir. Ten minutes."

"I just want a few minutes with her, that's all," explains Trina to Patrick Davenport, but the manager is holding up the front door post and shows no sign of bending.

"The doctor's examining her. In any case, she wouldn't know you. I'm afraid she's not doing very well."

"What d'you mean?"

"Well," sighs Davenport. "The Good Lord wants to see us all eventually."

"Look here," says Trina as she plants herself on one leg and takes up the vrksasana tree position, "I am a Canadian medical professional and I want to see her right now."

"I thought you said you were a detective."

"I happen to be a nurse as well," she fiercely claims, without admitting that most of her time is spent mopping up vomit and changing colostomy bags for Canadian wrinklies. "So I am perfectly capable of deciding her condition for myself. This isn't a prison, is it?"

"Sorry," says Davenport starting to close the door. "Anyway, her daughter's with her."

"She doesn't have a daughter ..." Trina is saying as the lock clunks firmly into place.

"We could move her to the hospital," explains Geoffrey Williamson to Isabel Semaurino as they talk over Daphne's lifeless form. "But she's probably better off here at the moment. Although, as things progress, we might have to introduce a feeding tube."

"Will that hurt?"

Williamson gives her a straightforward look, saying, "It's good that you're here, Mrs. Semaurino, because we will have to make some very difficult decisions in the next little while."

"I understand," says Isabel, although she feels herself getting off script again and reaches out to trace a finger over Daphne's face. "What happened?" she questions, gently stroking the bruise.

"Easily explained," says Williamson as he lets himself out. "She probably fell when she was running away."

Daphne is still falling — deeper and deeper inside her mind — as she wills herself to stay out of the light. Michael Kent is with her, begging her to let him take the rap. "We both tell them you knew nothing, all right," he whispers through shattered teeth in the darkness. "You were just a passenger — a friend. You knew nothing."

"But they won't let me go."

"Yes, they will," he insists as they huddle together on the stone floor of the old prison. "They'll let you go so they can track you to find out who you report to."

"Mother ... Mother ..." calls a voice from outside, but Daphne shuts down right away, knowing it's a trick. "They might try to trick you," Kent carries on in the blackness. "They'll tell you I pointed the finger at you. They'll mess up your mind. Don't believe them — everything they tell you will be lies."

"Daphne, can you hear me?"

"But what about you?"

"Save yourself. It's too late to worry about me."

"Mother ..." Isabel tries again, squeezing Daphne's hand and chattering into space. "I really would like you to know something about me before you go."

Daphne is still in Prague, trussed together with the man she loves, and she would rather die than live with the torment of his torture.

"I've got two children," Isabel is saying, but Daphne won't hear as she blots out all the pain — past and present — and wills herself to sleep. "They're grown-ups now, of course. Luigi and Maria — they're sort of everyday spaghetti names in Italy — did I tell you that's where I live, in Tuscany? Anyway, that's the problem with having an Italian husband. They have this tradition about naming kids after grandparents. 'Think I'm going to call my kids Annunziata or Pancrazio and you've got another think coming,' I said to

Marco — that's my husband, Marco. He's okay. Well, he was okay. Real machismo kinda guy — tight leather pants, hairy chest, and a way with words." She pauses with sweet memories that sour almost as fast as Marco. "Of course, he's Italian, so it turned out that I wasn't the only one he was talking to ... But we sorted it out eventually."

Daphne's dark tunnel suddenly has a dim light at the end. She sees it coming and quickly turns back.

"Mother. Mother?" calls Isabel earnestly, sensing a slight shift in Daphne's aura, but Daphne has gone again.

"It seems so funny calling you mother considering we've never really met," Isabel carries on once the air has stilled. "Where was I? Oh, Marco. Well he thought he could sing — like I said, he's Italian. He thought he was Mario Lanza until Elvis came along. Of course he's old now. Italian men do that — they're twenty-one from the time that they're ten until they're about fifty-nine, then wallop, they suddenly realize that their hair and teeth are going and they flop into a chair in front of the television, prop themselves up with grappa and pasta, and wait to die."

Anne McGregor is on her way to the front door in civvies as Trina Button steams in demanding to see Ted Donaldson.

"He's gone, madam," explains the duty constable.

That's not good enough for Trina. "Get him back immediately," she demands. "Someone is killing my partner."

"Are you talking murder?" asks McGregor as her shoes squeak to a halt on the polished tile floor.

"Excuse me," says Trina, edging McGregor aside. "I was talking to this nice young man."

"I'm the new superintendent," insists McGregor. "So please talk to me. Now what do you mean — murder?"

Trina's complaint is convoluted by the fact that she continually runs back and forth to the window to make sure Winifred hasn't escaped from the car, and McGregor tires. "Wait a minute," says the superintendent, pulling Trina to a stop. "The only facts that you have offered me are that Mr. Davenport won't let you see Miss Lovelace. Everything else is pure speculation."

"Yes … No … Well, it's a matter of intuition," insists Trina. "It's what differentiates a good detective from a bad one."

"How would you know that?" asks McGregor, beginning to wish that she had kept walking.

Trina senses the skepticism and decides it is time to draw upon her inner strengths, so she twines one leg around the other and her right arm around her left, in the eagle pose, and meditates for a moment.

"What on earth …?"

"The garudasana pose!" exclaims Trina loftily, and then, filled with the confidence of an eagle, she explains, "I am a Canadian law enforcement professional, and Miss Lovelace is my associate."

"What?" scoffs Anne McGregor.

"Excuse me, madam," breaks in the duty constable as he spots Winifred out of the window. "The lady that was in your car seems to be heading towards the cathedral across the park."

"Oh, Mother," sighs Trina, but she keeps her pose — at Winifred's present speed she will arrive just in time for morning communion.

"She does have the O.B.E. you know," says Trina switching back to Anne McGregor.

"Your mother?"

"No. Daphne Lovelace. She solved the Creston murders last year, and then there was the big drug bust at Thraxton Manor —"

"Wait a minute," cuts in McGregor. "I remember the

Creston case. A Scotland Yard man solved that."

"Chief Inspector Bliss," agrees Trina. "But call him and ask who really solved it. He'll tell you. It was me and Daphne Lovelace."

"I haven't got his number —" starts McGregor as an excuse, but Trina has.

"Trina. I'm in a meeting," groans Bliss as Edwards pulls a nasty face.

"David. You've got to help. They're killing Daphne."

"Oh for God's sake, Trina ..." he is complaining as McGregor takes the phone.

"Chief Inspector. It's Anne McGregor," she says, and she waits for an intonation of recognition before asking, "Just put my mind at rest. Did Miss Lovelace solve the Creston murder cases last year?"

Trina folds her arms smugly as the superintendent's face reddens.

"Oh ... Thank you, I had absolutely no idea." McGregor is saying a minute later when she has heard how Daphne nailed the killers after discovering a baby's body in a monkey's grave, while at the other end Michael Edwards is marching up and down in front of Bliss, spitting, "Chief Inspector. Would you please turn that f'kin thing off."

"Sorry, sir," says Bliss, switching back. "You said the Americans had an idea?"

"Finally," says Edwards, rolling his eyes. "Yes, it's a new knockout spray. One puff will drop an attacker in less than two seconds."

"What about side effects?"

"Acceptable."

For whom? Bliss wonders, picturing his head on a block if Prince Philip has a heart attack and falls backwards down a flight of steps.

"Anyway," continues Edwards. "We're meeting his people here at eleven tomorrow and we'll have a demonstration. Try not to be late."

"Is that it?" Bliss says. *You dragged me all the way here just to tell me that?*

"Unless you've something else on your mind, Chief Inspector."

"I'm still concerned about that pickup ..." he starts, just to poke a stick into Edwards' cage.

"I warned you ..." yells the Home Secretary's pit bull, and Bliss backs out, laughing to himself.

"Prairie farmers in Canada reckon they can see their dogs running away for three days," laughs Trina Button to Mavis Longbottom as they stand by the cathedral's labyrinth watching Winifred's slow-motion approach across the park.

"She's like a toddler on the run from kindergarten," agrees Mavis before turning back to the case of the missing documents. "It's lucky I met you. I've been going round in circles worrying what Daphne will say when I tell her."

"Don't worry. I've brought in the police," explains Trina as Winifred finally arrives.

"They wouldn't let me see her," complains Mavis, pointing to Patrick Davenport. "I've said all along that there's something fishy about that place."

"Superintendent McGregor will get to the bottom of it," Trina assures her as her mother takes off again, into the labyrinth. "We have an understanding."

"Is this the El Camino?" calls Winifred over her shoulder as she shuffles into line behind a gaggle of nuns.

"Yes, Mother," calls Trina, and the old lady's eyes light up as she picks up the pace.

"I can't fathom the damn thing out myself," bitches Mavis before explaining that she blames herself and the labyrinth for Daphne's predicament. "She was all right till I brought her here — apart from the neighbours."

With Daphne's accusation over the theft of her neighbours' house still ringing in Anne McGregor's ears, and the terror in the old lady's eyes when she was dragged away, Misty Jenkins is first in line for a visit.

"The old lady probably didn't remember me," explains Misty once she has quieted the dogs. "We used to come an' visit when we wuz kids. Then dad and Uncle Phil had some kinda barney and we never came no more."

"Can you prove this?" P.C. Joveneski questions as Kevin Scape, her partner, eyes the brand new television critically and tries to match it to one that walked out of the back door of Vision-Superstore on Saturday afternoon.

"Sure," snaps Misty, turning her handbag upside down. "Misty Morgan … Misty Morgan …" she says, slapping a birth certificate and a premarital driver's licence on the table. "And if you don't believe me, I'll give you dad's number and you can ask him yer friggin' self."

"Just doing my job …" explains Joveneski as she scrutinizes the documents and jots down the details, while behind her, Scape runs his hands over the fifty-inch monster and says, "This musta cost a packet. Get it locally, did you?"

"Here," says Misty, slamming down a receipt. "Is the old bag accusing us of anything else? Cuz you might as well ask now an' get it over with."

"No. I think that's all," says Joveneski as they retreat.

"I'm not giving up on this," says Bliss as he and Peter Bryan stake out Continental and International Imports with binoculars. But it is nearing midnight, the roads are deserted, and Peter Bryan is getting an itchy backside.

"I don't know what you're hoping to see without a search warrant," he moans for the *n*th time, but they both know that a judge would laugh them out of his chambers.

"That!" exclaims Bliss and they stare in disbelief as a familiar pickup truck emerges from the hangar doors of the building and drives towards the gate.

Bryan whistles. "Talk about synchronicity."

"Get the camera," says Bliss as he turns on the ignition and drops the car into gear. "We can't tail it with roads this dead. We'll have to risk a drive by."

The giant gates are slowly opening as the truck approaches, and Bliss holds back.

"Get ready … Get ready," he repeats with his foot hovering on the pedal.

Security guard Johnny "Tugboat" Wilson, a heavy-fisted, glass-jawed ex-boxer, is at the helm of the truck and is on his way to an all-night gas station a few blocks away, despite the dashboard warning "No Unauthorized Use." He doesn't care; it's only a battered old truck. It's hardly the ambassador's limousine or an embassy staff car.

"I'll take the pickup," he called to Johnson, his supervisor, as he grabbed the keys off the depot's board. "D'ya want anything?"

"Packet of Dunhill and a bag of salt and vinegar, Tug," replied the supervisor without taking his eyes off the surveillance monitors. "And don't be all night, I need a pee."

Wilson hits the gate a few seconds early and has to backpedal, while on the road Bliss starts his run.

"Timing …" breathes Bliss, hoping to pass the gate at the precise moment that the truck is forced to halt.

But Wilson is in no hurry. "Do you want matches?" he calls into his radio as he idles, and Johnson shouts back, "Nope."

"Okay," says Wilson rolling towards the road.

"Here we go," says Bliss, stabbing the throttle.

Then Johnson spots him and yells "Car!" in Wilson's ear.

"Shit!" shouts Wilson, and he stabs the clutch and makes a grab for reverse.

"Gotcha," snaps Bryan as they race by with his camera blazing.

chapter sixteen

Winifred Goodenow is not running this morning. Her race is over, and in her own mind, she has conquered the world.

"I did the El Camino," she trumpets with Olympian pride as Trina wheels her through the Mitre's lobby in a borrowed wheelchair.

Imelda grabs the desk bell. "Zhat is very good, madam," says the Latvian, clasping the antique brass to her chest. "I very please for you."

According to Westchester cathedral's thirteenth-century sundial it is approaching seven-thirty as Trina pushes her mother towards the labyrinth. The path to the cathedral is filled with sinners who religiously attend morning prayers every day in the hope of redemption, but they quickly fall by the wayside when Winifred shouts, "Coming through." As she passes in her wheelchair, the footsore woman acknowledges their subjugation with a wan smile and a regal wave.

Mavis Longbottom is in company with Angel Robinson at the labyrinth this morning. The arrangement was made last evening, just as Winifred Goodenow completed her fourth lap. "I can do the El Camino forever," she triumphantly declared, and then she tripped headlong on one of the flagstones and completely pancaked a bunch of Japanese toddlers.

"Little children shouldn't be playing on the labyrinth," protested Mavis loudly as a dozen parents scrambled to dig out their offspring.

"Don't worry, luv," said a passerby, stepping in to help raise Trina's mother. "They have earthquakes in Japan. They're used to heavy stuff falling on them."

"I'll have to get Angel to show you how it works. It just drives me round in bloomin' circles," said Mavis, after the last of the bawling tots was carried off, when Trina questioned how the ancient pathway could possibly be blamed for Daphne's condition.

"First you need a mantra — perhaps a Rumi poem or a saying by the Dalai Lama," explains the spiritual guide as she introduces the Canadian woman to the mystical path. Then she continues, "Each journey has three parts — the way in, the centre, and the way out. And every step moves you away from the past towards the future."

"But you always end up back where you started," says Trina, already well ahead of the guide.

"Precisely," agrees Angel. "But that's what happens in life. We come into the world with nothing and we leave the same way."

"Hairless, toothless, senseless …"

"Not exactly, but you get the idea," continues Angel before suggesting, "Start with an intention and focus on what you are trying to achieve."

Mavis chimes in with an example. "Daphne wanted to put a boot up her neighbours' backside and get shot of them," she says, but the look on Angel's face suggests that such intent could have been an abuse of the labyrinth's power.

"You can't influence other people's actions or beliefs," she says firmly. "You can only change the way you see them. And Newton's laws are universal — every action has an equal and opposite reaction. So when Daphne pushed against the neighbours, she was the one who went flying off into the abyss."

"But that's not fair," complains Trina.

"It's the law of unintended consequences," replies Angel. "She got exactly what she asked for — some peace and quiet from her neighbours."

"That's the El Camino over there," Winifred Goodenow explains authoritatively to a couple of tourists from Ulaanbaatar, while Angel continues to Trina, "On the way into the centre of the labyrinth you must anticipate the future as you move away from the past."

"But I already know that I'm going to end up back where I started," whinges Trina. "So when I look forward all I see is where I've come from."

"That's what I keep trying to tell her," mutters Mavis, but Angel takes Trina's hand.

"It's the struggle to achieve and the suffering we all endure on the path of life that's important," she explains as she leads Trina into the labyrinth. "It's not getting there that matters. It's how we get there and what we learn along the road. Now just follow me."

The struggle for life goes on much as before for most of the residents at St. Michael's, now that the lost sheep is back in the fold, but Samuel Fitzgerald is already lining up the chairs for next Sunday's service. He only has three so far, but he is definitely expecting a fourth.

Daphne Lovelace has no intention of having her name attached to a chair and is keeping her head down — way down — which perturbs Geoffrey Williamson as he pays a visit on his way to morning surgery.

"It's not a coma," the doctor tells Isabel Semaurino, who has been at Daphne's bedside since dawn. "It could be a psychosomatic reaction to her little escapade yesterday, or it may be that one part of her brain realizes that another part is going haywire, so it's shutting down in sympathy."

"I really should get home. My daughter's baby is due today," Isabel deliberates as she strokes Daphne's hand. "Do you think it would be all right for me to leave Mother for a few days?"

"I don't see why not," says Williamson. "Physically, I think she'll be fine once we get some nourishment into her. Like I said, it's her mental state that's worrying. It could be that she's just lost the will to live."

"There is hope, then?"

"There was when she was still fighting," admits Williamson, unaware that deep down Daphne is not only fighting but, in her own mind, she is winning.

"They will keep you alive as long as they believe you have useful information," Michael Kent is whispering to her in the darkness, and she gambles that Williamson will be told to keep his hands off until Patrick Davenport has his documents back.

"I have to leave now, Mother," says Isabel once the doctor has excused himself, but she cannot tear her hands away from Daphne's serene face, knowing that this may be her only chance to connect. "I'll come back on the weekend," she carries on with a crack in her voice. "I promise." And then she perks up. "Just think — you're going to be a great-grandmother."

The centre of a labyrinth is the mid-point of the journey, and Trina and Mavis pause while their guide explains the next step.

"Here, in the middle, you should spend a few minutes meditating," says Angel, closing her eyes in demonstration, adding, "You should feel cocooned, as if you are the centre of the universe. And then, when you are totally at peace, you can begin the rest of your journey. But, just as in life, you can only get out by following the path."

"Some people take a shortcut," refutes Mavis, recalling Minnie Dennon's suicide and pointing out the fact that there is nothing to prevent someone from simply stepping across the grassy divides and walking away.

"Where's the satisfaction in that?" questions Angel, but Mavis is already looking into the not-too-distant future and weighing her options.

"At least it's quick," she mutters, while at the labyrinth's entrance a small group of befuddled German tourists are getting directions on walking the El Camino from an unofficial guide in a wheelchair.

"Go round four times and make sure you don't trip ..."

Anne McGregor is as confused as the tourists as she makes an early start on Joan Joveneski's report regarding the ownership of the Jenkins house and the seemingly lawful purchase of a television. But the memory of Daphne clinging to her legs won't leg go.

"It's not like Daphne Lovelace to make a mistake," says Ted Donaldson, when she calls her predecessor, ostensibly to let him know that his elderly acquaintance was totally wrong about her neighbours.

"The last thing I want is a war with the local bigwigs," carries on McGregor, revealing the true reason for her inquiry. "But the old cabbage was making some pretty wild allegations — reckoned a Doctor Williamson and a lawyer named Jameson are trying to bump her off to get her estate."

"Well, knowing Daphne the way I do — if I was still in your seat, I would listen to what she has to say."

"Lovelace … C'mon, you f'kin old witch — wake up. I know you can hear me," screeches Hilda Fitzgerald through her teeth as she roughly pokes Daphne in the ribs, but Daphne has been here before.

"Stay down … stay down …" warns Kent in the depths of her mind. "They're just waiting for you to surface."

"Wake up, you —"

"Hilda!" cuts in Patrick Davenport, taking his sister by surprise. "I told you to leave her alone."

"Get stuffed —"

"I've had enough —"

"Give me a break, you snotty little weasel," spits Fitzgerald, turning her finger on her brother. "Can't you see what she's doing? She's caused nothing but trouble ever since she's bin here."

"Look. Just leave her alone, okay."

"Says who? My little brother who used to piss himself every time I shouted at him?"

"That was thirty years ago …" Davenport is saying as his elder sister elbows him aside and storms out.

Patrick Davenport opens the curtains a fraction to the morning sun and waits for the room to still as he takes several deep breaths and utters a silent prayer. Then he pulls a chair up to Daphne's bedside and gently reaches out to her. "Can you hear me, Miss Lovelace?" he begins, his voice dropping until it has the texture of chocolate fudge cake. "I really need to talk to you. Maybe you could squeeze my hand …"

Davenport's mellow tones worm deep into Daphne's mind, and she is tempted to surface, until Michael Kent waves a red flag.

"I want you to know that I'm not doing anything wrong," carries on Davenport without encouragement. "I'm just trying to protect your interests — the interests of all of you — and to continue the Lord's ministry, and I need your help."

The flag flaps furiously, and Michael Kent is very close as he warns of an iron fist inside Davenport's kid glove.

"You'll be safe now, Daphne," continues Davenport, near to tears. "Please believe me. I won't let anything happen to you, but I don't think you understand how important this is. I've got to get the papers back, and I think your friend Mavis must've given me a wrong number 'cos she doesn't answer."

Mavis is not answering her phone now because she and Trina are stalking the postman. "We could always get your mother to fall on top of him until he squeals," jests Mavis as they watch him wheeling his bike from house to house, but Trina has a better idea.

"Fifty bleedin' quid," chortles the man as he pockets the cash, and two minutes later the three of them are staring into an empty dustbin.

"There ain't nothing worth nicking in there," yells the homeowner from his bedroom window. "It were emptied a half-hour ago."

"Thanks," yells Trina, and they leap back into the car and hit the trail again.

David Bliss has also saddled up early this morning and is hoping to catch someone half-asleep at Continental and International Imports.

"Metropolitan Police. Chief Inspector Bliss," he calls into the entryphone, and he immediately feels the eyes of a camera on him.

"What can I do for you, sir?"

She doesn't sound like a gorilla, he thinks as he waffles about investigating a couple of burglaries in the area.

"We've had no problems here at all, sir," continues the chatty guard. "We have our own security."

"I can see that," says Bliss. "That's actually why I'm here. I wonder if I could have a peek at your tapes for the last few nights — see if there were any suspicious vehicles or known villains in the area."

"Sure — no problem," she says as the gate clicks open. "Come straight on up. I've got some coffee on the go."

Interesting accent, muses Bliss, placing the woman somewhere in North America as he tries to pick up clues about the place.

"Texas?" he queries as an opener when she greets him at the door.

"Arizona," admits Cindi Langdon, a petite college girl with a blond ponytail and a disarming smile.

"Really?" he says.

"You sound surprised."

"I was expecting a cockney gorilla with a hyena," admits Bliss as he follows her pert figure into the security office and accepts the offer of coffee.

"We've got a few of those too," she laughs, handing him a cup. "But they're just teddy bears beneath the skin."

"Grizzlies," he mutters under his breath, reflecting on the monster he and Peter Bryan spotted yesterday, then he turns with a quizzical eye on the perimeter surveillance monitors. "Imports and exports," he muses aloud. "You must handle some pretty high-end stuff to warrant this."

"Nah," laughs Cindi. "It's just a garage and workshop for our embassy vehicles. We just don't advertise the fact." Then she drops her tone to a conspiratorial whisper. "We don't know who the good guys are anymore."

That explains the tight security and the classified licence plate, he tells himself, scanning the rows of parked vehicles inside the hangar until he spots the pickup. But it doesn't explain why an official American vehicle was being used by a couple of pavement artists.

"So, what exactly were you searching for?" inquires Cindi with her hands on the controls.

Mavis and Trina's search for the missing envelope has led them to the municipal dump, but they've run into a road-block. "You're joking," laughs the gatekeeper as truck after truck rumbles past on the dusty approach road. "I've had ten loads from the Council already this morning. Anyway, it's more than my job's worth to let you in."

On the other side of the city, Anne McGregor and Joan Joveneski have no problems getting in the front door of St. Michael's, but they run into a gatekeeper at the front office.

"Sorry," says Davenport. "She's just not up to having visitors."

"We're not visitors," insists McGregor. "We're police officers, and we want to talk to her about allegations she made regarding her neighbours."

Davenport stands firm. "Sorry," he repeats. "She won't be able to help you at present."

"Now look here …" starts Joveneski, but the superintendent pulls her back, saying, "In that case we'll talk to her daughter. Is Mrs. Semaurino here?"

"No. She's gone."

When is she coming back? Address? Telephone number? Full name? are all questions that leave St. Michael's manager dancing with a red face.

"Hold on," says McGregor with a wary eye. "Are you trying to tell us that you have absolutely no information about Miss Lovelace's next of kin?"

"Well …"

"What about in her file? I assume you keep patients' records."

"File …" he echoes vaguely, not daring to open his

desk drawers, and then the front door flies open and Amelia Brimble walks in with her mother.

"I wanna word with you," snorts Betty Brimble, going for Davenport's jugular, and his legs give way.

"Hi, Daffy. It's me, Amelia," the young girl tries a few minutes later while the others stand over the inert figure seeking signs of life.

The youngster's cheerful voice breaks through the protective layers and touches Daphne, but this is another of Davenport's tricks that she has been expecting ever since her so-called daughter showed up, and she refuses to be drawn.

"Daphne … Miss Lovelace …" tries Anne McGregor gently, moving in for a closer look. Then she turns to Davenport. "How did she get the bruises on her face?"

"She fell," insists the manager, finding his feet and stepping in quickly, but Amelia is right behind him.

"Hilda smacked her in the gob," says the girl defiantly, and then she spins accusingly on Davenport. "An' he chucked me out when I tried telling you yesterday."

It is no great surprise to David Bliss to find that the CIA's Lefty and Pimple are at the centre of things when he arrives for Edwards' eleven o'clock meeting.

"This is Mr. Smith and Mr. Jones from Homeland Security," says Edwards by way of introduction, and Bliss barely controls himself.

"Something funny, Chief Inspector?" questions the ex-superintendent, and then he turns the tables. "I hope you don't mind, but I told them that you would be happy to help demonstrate —"

"I certainly will …" cuts in Bliss, but he hits the floor before he can say "not."

"Right," says Edwards, casually stepping over Bliss's slumped body to address Fox and the other commanders. "The full effect lasts from ten to fifteen minutes depending on the amount of agent administered, as well as the age, weight, and general physical condition of the victim."

"S'cuse me, sir," pipes up Pimple as he puts the lid on the aerosol can. "But we prefer the term 'Temporarily disabled person' or simply 'TDP' rather than 'victim.'"

"Sorry," apologizes Edwards. "I suppose it's like calling a freedom fighter an enemy combatant. It just depends whose side you're on." And then he is barraged by a dozen questions about the gas and its after-effects.

"Gentlemen," he says, holding up his hands. "By the time we've had coffee and a bite to eat, Chief Inspector Bliss, our TDP of the day, should be in a position to answer for himself."

"So, precisely what is the CIA's role in all this?" Bliss demands of Edwards, once he's shaken off the grogginess and the meeting has broken up.

"That's highly classified information, Chief Inspector," says Edwards. "I'm quite surprised that you would even ask."

"Classified?" says Bliss, then he tosses a firecracker. "Do you mean 'Classified' as in the licence plates on a certain American embassy pickup truck?"

"How the hell d'ya know that?" demands Edwards in a single word.

"I didn't," lies Bliss with a deadpan face. "But now I do."

"Leave it alone, Bliss. And I'm not gonna warn you again."

"I'm warning you," says Trina Button to Patrick Davenport, as she stands at St. Michael's front door with

Mavis and Angel as backup. "Either let us in to see her or I'll call the police and tell them you're keeping her prisoner."

"Look, she's just very tired. Her daughter was here —"

"What do you mean, her daughter?"

"Miss Lovelace's daughter, Isabel ..." starts Davenport, although the look on Trina's face tells him that he is horribly off track, and he grinds to a halt.

"I don't know what you're playing at, young man," steps in Mavis. "But I've known her since we were at school together, and I know for certain that she doesn't have a daughter. So you'd better let us in this instant or I'm going to the police."

"The police are already aware," says Davenport, on firmer ground, but, as for Daphne's daughter, he is quickly coming to the realization that he may be on quicksand. "You'd have to ask Mrs. Semaurino about that yourself," he says, with an uneasy feeling that he too should be asking questions about the missing woman.

"So where is she?" demands Trina, but she draws a blank from the confused man as he stands firm and turns them away.

The identity and whereabouts of Isabel Semaurino are also high on the agenda for Superintendent Anne McGregor as she calls a detective inspector and half a dozen officers into a huddle for a late-morning briefing.

"I think someone's trying to pull a fast one," admits the senior officer once she has recounted the highlights of Daphne's dash for freedom. "She was yelling that they were going to kill her and give her house to her daughter. So what happens when I turn up and want to speak to the daughter? She's vanished and they have no record of her. And this is the interesting bit: everyone, apart from the high priest in charge of the place, tells me there is no daughter.

I've even checked with D.C.I. Bliss at the Yard, and he's known the old lady for years."

"I've known her for years too," chips in one of the detectives. "And I never knew she had a daughter."

"David," Trina yells into her cellphone as soon as Bliss answers. "You've got to get down here right away."

"Trina …"

"They won't let me and Mavis see Daphne, and they're lying about her having a daughter."

"I just heard that from the local police," admits Bliss. "But I don't know what you expect me to do."

"Arrest them or get a court order or something …" she starts, but he stops her.

"You don't need a policeman, Trina. You need a lawyer."

The sudden and seemingly mysterious disappearance of Isabel Semaurino has Davenport frenziedly quizzing patients and staff for any details that may help him find her. And then his phone rings.

"I am the lawyer representing Miss Daphne Lovelace," says Samantha Bliss, once she has been briefed by Trina, and Davenport is momentarily off balance.

"Oh … no … no …" he starts, but he quickly recovers. "Actually, she already has a lawyer. Robert Jameson of Jameson and Fidditch." And then he overstretches. "In any case, I assume her daughter will be dealing with her affairs from now on."

"What daughter? She doesn't have a daughter."

chapter seventeen

"St. Michael the Archangel, be our safeguard against the wickedness and snares of the Devil," Patrick Davenport prays in a sing-song voice as he clasps his hands in supplication and kneels on the floor of his office with the door firmly closed, and then he risks the ire of his Almighty by asking for a personal favour. "I pray that you always have guided me wisely in the past," he carries on. "But now I need to be certain that I have made the right decision. Please give me the strength to do what is right and just, irrespective of the consequences."

"Brenda said you wanted to see me," grumbles Hilda Fitzgerald, storming in without knocking as she dries her hands on a tea towel. "I'm trying to get lunch finished up."

Davenport rises slowly and eyes his sister carefully before saying, "Daphne Lovelace doesn't have a daughter."

Hilda shrugs. "It weren't me who said she did."

"Hilda …" starts Davenport warily, hoping not to trigger an explosion. "I just want to be absolutely certain that you aren't involved." He stops as momentary anger flares in her eyes, but he doesn't back off. "'Have faith in me,' you said. 'Trust me,' you said, and I did."

"And that's what I'm sayin' now. It's nothing to do with me."

"But you also promised not to hit anyone again."

Fitzgerald shrugs. "She drove me to it. The old bat was just winding me up. Now, unless you want burnt tapioca pudding …"

Davenport's face suggests that he is prepared to accept a culinary catastrophe as he pushes one more time. "Give me your word, Hilda. Just to put my mind at rest."

"Look, Pat. I ain't telling you again. Isabel whatsername is nothing to do with me. I dunno who she is or what she's up to. I thought she really was her bloomin' daughter."

"Well, she's not," he says. "She definitely doesn't have a daughter."

"So what's her game?"

"What's *their* game?" Davenport muses aloud, reminding himself that it was the police superintendent who first introduced Isabel Semaurino as Daphne's daughter, and he picks up the phone as Hilda marches out.

"I'm with a client, Patrick," snaps Robert Jameson after Davenport has hustled the lawyer's receptionist. "What's the panic?"

"I think the police have put in a plant …" the anxious manager is saying when Jameson stops him with a deliberate cough.

"Not on the phone. Meet me in the lounge at the Mitre in half an hour."

Anne McGregor is also hustling now that she realizes that she may have taken the wrong bus, and she brainstorms with Matt Roberts, the station's detective chief inspector, once she has expressed her fears.

"Get a statement from the young girl who was taking care of her," she says, starting a checklist. "She reckoned that they were knocking her about."

"I'll arrange for photographs of the injuries and get forensics to look for possible weapons," adds Roberts.

"You'd better get the police surgeon to take a good look at her. She was fighting fit when she clung on to me. God knows what happened to her once they got her back there."

"Done," says Roberts, nodding. "And I'll put a small team together to interview the rest of the inmates — see if there's a pattern."

"I'll have a word with Social Services about shifting her to another home, and we need a handle on the so-called daughter," continues McGregor. "Who is she? What's her game? Has she got previous?"

"I'll do some digging with the Fraud Squad on that. And I'll see if the owners or staff have got any form as well."

"And get hold of the old duck's friends, her neighbours, and that nutty Canadian woman and her mother who've shown up. See what they know."

"Will do, ma'am. Anything else?"

"Oh, yes. I just remembered. She was ranting on about some sort of proof she mailed to her friend. See if you can track that down."

"What about putting someone on her door?"

"We could …" begins McGregor, then she shakes her head. "No. I think they got the message from our visit. They won't touch her now."

"It was definitely a gypsy's warning," David Bliss moans to Peter Bryan over a grilled sirloin sandwich in a corner of the Blue Lamp pub. "Edwards set me up and those smug bastards stepped in and zapped me."

"But what are they up to?"

"We're talking CIA, Peter," Bliss reminds him with raised eyebrows, and then he heads a list of illegal stunts pulled by the American secret service with the abduction of Manuel Noriega, the Bay of Pigs, the Gulf of Tonkin, and Saddam Hussein's nightmarish, but entirely non-existent, stockpile of weapons. "They've been kidnapping, torturing, and murdering inconvenient people for years." Bliss continues ranting. "And don't forget, they tried warning me off with machine guns when Daphne and Trina rumbled their organ transplant scam in Seattle a couple of years ago."

"I'd forgotten ..." starts Bryan, but Bliss is in full flight.

"What gets me is that they're so bloody self-righteous. They actually believe that God is on their side. They think he's given them permission to rule the bloody world."

"Keep your hair on, granddad," laughs Bryan, and he gives his father-in-law a few seconds to cool down before asking, "Where do you go from here?"

"*We*, Peter. It's where *we* go from here. *We* take the fight to the enemy's door. You've always been interested in American automobiles, haven't you?"

"No."

"Well, you are now. So let's just hope that Miss Arizona is on duty again tomorrow morning. Right now I'm going back to the videographer to try to get a better close-up of the pickaxe squad."

"The Mahabharata is about the way that really religious people, called Brahmans, kill each other in India," says Trina Button, standing on her head in the salamba sirsasana pose in front of a totally bemused Kevin Scape, trying to explain the Bhagavad-Gita as she waits for a meeting with Anne McGregor.

"Krishna, the eighth avatar of the god Vishnu, teaches that yoga protects you when you go into battle," claims

Trina, but Scape is just saying that he would prefer to rely on his truncheon and bulletproof vest when the superintendent arrives.

"Ms. Button," calls Anne McGregor, as if the sight of a woman on her head in the foyer of Westchester Police Station is commonplace.

"They're keeping her a prisoner," yells Trina without losing her pose. "I told you, but you wouldn't listen."

"Ms. Button —"

"No one ever listens to me."

"Ms. Button —"

"Sometimes I think I'm invisible."

"Oh, for goodness' sake, Ms. Button. Will you please stand up and talk to me."

"Good," says Trina springing to her feet. "I thought that might work. Now perhaps you'll listen."

"Daphne, love," coos Trina, once Anne McGregor has opened the door for her. "It's Trina. I'm here with Mavis. Can you hear me?"

Daphne hears the words, and even recognizes the voice, but the labyrinth she has been following for the past few days has become a maze of dark tunnels — no matter which way she runs she isn't able to find her way to the surface. The spirit of Michael Kent is still with her, but his handsome image is turning ghoulish as she reruns the past while searching for the future.

"I've brought a policewoman to talk to you," carries on Trina, but deep in Daphne's mind it's 1946, and a barrel-chested sadist presses a knife into the flesh of Kent's little finger, demanding, "Who are you working for?"

The English agent isn't expected to answer — the rubber gag biting into his mouth makes certain of that. Daphne is the one in the hot seat, pinioned to the chair by a foul-smelling guard with iron fingers.

"I ask you a question, Miss Masterson," spits the leering torturer as a trace of blood oozes from Kent's hand. "Who do you work for?"

"No one. I don't know what you mean," cries Daphne. "Please don't …"

"So again, I ask," he says as he calmly drops the severed finger into a bucket and readies the bloodied knife on the next joint.

"No … No … Please don't …"

"Then you must tell me."

"But I don't … No … No … Please don't … Oh, no!"

"Miss Masterson. You don't understand. First his fingers, then his toes, then … well, let us hope that your memory has returned before then. So, ready again," he says as the knife goes to a third finger.

Sweat pours off Daphne's face, and Trina grabs a Kleenex and looks to Mavis. "Get a cold flannel," says the homecare nurse as Daphne's body begins to heat up. "She's got a fever."

"Daphne, dear. Can you hear me?" asks Trina as she gently mops the old lady's brow, but the cold flannel is a blade of steel in the tormented woman's mind, and she sees it gouging into Michael Kent's left eye and lets out a strangled scream.

"Oh my God," says Davenport as he races off to phone for an ambulance, while inside Daphne's head blood-gushing parts of Michael Kent's body are chasing her down blind alleys.

"Daphne," calls Trina, but the anguished woman is deaf to the outside world as the torture continues.

"Who are you working for?" yells the interrogator as he fiercely grasps one of her lover's ears. "Tell me now or …"

"Daphne … Daphne …" voices are desperately calling as she writhes and thrashes in the bed.

"Tell me! Tell me!" shrieks the maniacal sadist as he slices through cartilage and flesh, then sticks the dismembered ear into her face.

"Miss Lovelace ... Daphne ..." tries Brenda.

"Look at it, Miss Masterson," demands the guard, wrenching back her head until her neck cracks. "Look at it and tell us who you are working for."

"Go and get a doctor," shouts Anne McGregor to Brenda while Daphne's body is jerking in spasms of agony, and the terrified woman is yelling, "No ... No ... No ..." as she watches Michael Kent's nose, lips, and tongue drop into the blood-spattered bucket.

"Daphne. Wake up. Wake up. It's me, Mavis," calls her friend, and the lights finally go on in Daphne's mind.

"Mavis?" she questions as she opens her eyes to the searing light for the first time in two days. "Curtains," she says, holding a hand over her face, and Trina rushes to close them.

"I've called for an ambulance and the doctor," says Davenport, returning, but Daphne is already pulling herself up in bed.

"Well, you certainly gave us a scare," says Geoffrey Williamson, once he has checked her over and sent the ambulance away, but Patrick Davenport's pallid expression suggests that, for him, the scare is not yet over.

"The Jenkinses stole Phil and Maggie's house," proclaims Daphne, aware that she now has an attentive audience, but Trina shakes her head.

"No, they didn't, Daphne."

"Don't you remember Misty Morgan?" steps in Mavis. "It's Phil's brother's little girl."

"No, I don't."

"Oh, dear. Perhaps you are losing your marbles," suggests Mavis a touch acerbically, and Daphne stomps on her.

"No, I am not, Mavis. I'm well aware of who you mean. But I haven't seen Phil's brother for donkey's years." However, despite a minute's concentration, she can't place a daughter and ends up confessing, "I suppose my memory really is going."

"That's what happens when you get older," agrees Mavis, and then Anne McGregor steps into view. "Remember me?" she says, holding up her index finger.

Daphne flushes pink around the edges of the bruise. "Sorry about that," she says. "I was just so cross that no one would listen to me, and they were driving me round the bend."

"Never mind. That's all in the past. I'm more interested in your daughter, Isabel, right now."

"But I thought I told you. I don't have —"

"Think carefully, Daphne," says McGregor, while Patrick Davenport's knees are beginning to buckle in the background.

"What's she talking about, Mavis?" asks Daphne.

"Someone was here," says Mavis, not linking Isabel Semaurino with the woman she saw at Daphne's house. "And she reckoned she was your daughter …"

"She certainly told me she was your daughter," chimes in Williamson, and all eyes turn on him. But the doctor has little to offer other than the apparent sincerity of the mysterious woman. However, the news that Daphne is about to become a great-grandmother certainly adds to the mystique — especially in the elderly spinster's mind.

"Now I really am worried that I'm going cuckoo," she laughs — the first time she has laughed in weeks.

"Isabel Semaurino. The name rings a bell," admits Bliss to Trina when she phones to give him an update on Daphne's condition, but he has too much on his mind to recall the woman he met in the bar of the Mitre. It's already Tuesday evening. Only two clear days before Friday's rescheduled mission to the mosque — the first public appearance of the royal couple since the ill-fated visit — and the video recording of the men and their pickup truck has disappeared.

"It's been wiped," Hoskins the videographer explained when Bliss went back for a closer look. "Commander Fox told me to ..." then the technician paused, "... actually, he ordered me to get rid of everything I had from the mosque."

"When?" asked Bliss and wasn't surprised that it occurred while he was out cold.

The transceiver is the best physical evidence remaining from the day that Prince Philip went berserk. At least it would be the best evidence if it was still in Bliss's possession.

"Somebody smashed the lock off my bloody cupboard," he complains angrily to his son-in-law as they meet for a strategy session in the back bar of Peter Bryans local pub, the Pheasant.

"Who the hell?" asks Bryan as he cues up for a game of snooker.

"Fox ... I bet Edwards has got the black on him."

"Edwards has got the black on most people, Dave. But what's his game?"

"What's the Yanks' game? They're the ones who bother me most."

"I guess we might find out in the morning," says Peter Bryan as he slams a red ball into a pocket.

"One for you," says Bliss as he keeps score, and then he questions, "How's your interest in American cars coming along?"

"Hi Cindi. It's me again, Chief Inspector Bliss," he says as he and Bryan stand at the gates of the security compound on Wednesday morning. "I've brought a colleague to go over those tapes."

The momentary silence from the bubbly young American indicates a problem. "I'm sorry," she says once she drums up the courage. "But I got shit for letting you in yesterday."

"But I'm a senior police officer."

"I'm real sorry," says Cindi. "The cameras are linked to the Embassy, and I guess someone saw you."

"Lefty and bloody Pimple," Bliss mutters under his breath. "I bloody knew it."

"You'll have to get clearance from the Embassy to come in again. Sorry."

"What now, Dave?"

"At least they didn't come after me with machine guns this time," says Bliss as they walk back to their car under the nose of one of the tower-cameras.

"So, Michael," says Lefty, stabbing at Bliss on the screen of a laptop in front of Edwards. "I thought you said you had a leash on him."

"Maybe he should have a little accident," says Pimple, pumping his right fist into his left palm. "Just enough to keep him out of the way on Friday. The President sure ain't gonna be happy if there's another screw-up."

"Leave him to me," says Edwards. "You just concentrate on what you have to do."

Superintendent Anne McGregor starts the daily service with a prayer of thanksgiving for the blessed news that no prisoners died overnight in custody, no murders or riots were reported, and the only complaint against an officer was made by a certifiable lunatic.

"So. What's on the agenda?" she asks, and Matt Roberts brings up Daphne Lovelace.

"From what we've got so far," the detective chief inspector explains as he flicks through his officer's reports, "she sounds as though she's our second loony of the day."

"Really?" says McGregor, brightening at the thought that she may have been right about Daphne all along.

"Nothing the old faggot claims holds water," carries on Roberts, and then he summarizes. "Rob and Misty Jenkins are the lawful occupiers of her uncle's place. Recent deaths at the home … nothing suspicious and, considering the heat, not out of line with what you would expect. No complaints from other residents — apart from the food." Roberts stops to look up and laugh. "Apparently the woman who usually does the cooking — a Hilda Fitzgerald — is a bit of a butcher in the kitchen."

"What about the bruising on her face?" asks McGregor, and Roberts goes back to the reports.

"There's no eyewitnesses. They say she fell. She says she didn't. But I know who a court would believe."

"What about the Brimble girl?"

"She didn't actually see anything," he says, digging out Amelia's statement. "According to her, the first time it happened the old lady admitted she fell out of bed in the night, and the next time the only person in the room was this Hilda Fitzgerald woman because she sent Brimble off to give another patient a bath."

"Who is this Hilda woman?" asks McGregor. "Is she the cook or what?"

"General factotum — like her husband, as far as I can gather. They live on the premises and pretty well run it," says Roberts, before continuing with his roundup and detailing the various searches and inquiries that have been made with negative results.

"Patrick Davenport has had a few speeding tickets and got a couple of endorsements on his licence," he concludes. "Otherwise the place is squeaky clean."

"So that only leaves us with the papers that she reckoned were proof they were trying to kill her."

"I've spoken to her about that," says Roberts with a tone that says he is not convinced. "She admits breaking into Davenport's desk, stealing them, and mailing them to a friend. But somehow they've ended up on the dump. I've got half a dozen men out there now having a look, but I don't have a lot of hope."

"What are they supposed to prove —" starts McGregor as a sergeant, with triumph all over his face, knocks and then rushes in with an envelope addressed to Mavis Longbottom. "Wow. That was good timing."

The medical records of St. Michael's residents could be used as a practitioner's training guide for professionals entering the field of gerontology. Alzheimer's, osteoporosis, emphysema, diabetes, and a host of cancer-related complaints top the list, and the numerous treatments and medications all appear to be meticulously recorded. But it means nothing to the officers.

"I wouldn't know an Aspirin from Viagra myself," admits Roberts as they scan the documents.

"I'll steer clear of you when you've got a headache then," jokes McGregor, before handing the records over to the sergeant, saying, "Get these to the Police Surgeon and ask him to give me an analysis, stat."

"Yes, ma'am," he replies as McGregor and Roberts take a closer look at the remainder of the paperwork.

"Power of attorney," says Roberts skimming a dozen similar documents. "Now this is more interesting," he adds, as he flicks through them. "Yes. She's right about that. They all name a lawyer called Robert Jameson."

"And look at this," says McGregor, finding a signed affidavit giving Jameson withdrawal privileges on their bank accounts attached to the back of each document. "I think someone should have a few words with our lawyer friend."

"I wanna word with you," snorts Fox mid-afternoon as he catches Bliss out in the open. "I've been looking for you all bloody day. Where have you been?"

"Out and about," says Bliss cheerily as he willingly accompanies the commander to his top-floor office.

The walk to the gallows is the longest walk on earth, but Bliss takes it with a bounce in his stride. He has been practising for this moment ever since his attempt to get into the American embassy garage backfired.

"Fox is gunning for you," he has been warned by cellphone time and again, as the commander slunk around the Yard trying to sniff him out. But he went to ground in the legal aisles of the British Library and kept his head down until he was in possession of all the ammunition he needed.

"Now," starts Fox as he slams the door behind his detective chief inspector and plonks himself behind his desk. "What's this I hear —"

"Hang on a minute, sir," says Bliss, holding the commander up with the palm of his hand. "I'd just like you to read this before you go any further."

Fifteen minutes later David Bliss is standing on London Bridge, staring down at the sludgy water, trying to see into his future again.

Well, you've done it now, haven't you, he tells himself, but he is still smiling in memory of the look on Fox's face when he smoothed out his crumpled resignation letter and slammed it on the commander's desk.

"Dave. You really don't have to go that far," Fox tried remonstrating, but Bliss wasn't listening.

"Actually, I do," he said. "To be honest, I've had enough of all the conniving politics and underhanded crap. When I joined I thought I'd spend my life fighting villains, I didn't expect to be working for them."

"Now that's uncalled-for."

"Is it?" said Bliss. "I don't think so. I've spent the past five years being jerked around by that scum Edwards, until someone managed to put the skids under him, and then the poisonous little bastard weaseled his way back in the Home Secretary's pocket."

"I will not have you saying …" Fox was shouting when Bliss walked out. And then the commander's words, "All right. Resignation accepted. You are finished, Bliss," followed him down the corridor.

"Not for another four weeks," Bliss shouted back, although he has already tallied his outstanding leave and knows he has only two days of actual duty to work before he will be free.

"Finally free … after twenty-eight years," he muses aloud as he stares down at the Thames. "Free — with a good pension and a clean record."

Now what are you going to do?

Maybe I'll write another book like Samantha suggested.

Are you crazy? The last one nearly killed you. Why not do something easy like brain surgery or climbing Everest?

Anyway, first I have to do something about Daisy.

You could go this weekend. There's nothing stopping you now. You could go and never come back.

But there is something stopping him and he knows it. And it's not just her "cousin," whoever the man may be. It's the same problem he's faced for the past two years since the start of their relationship.

"Where were the fireworks?" he has questioned a thousand times, recalling the three months that he tangoed around her before he finally took her home after the last dance. But just as the kindling took a long time to catch, so the smouldering embers are taking forever to die.

It's like someone dying a slow and peaceful death, he thinks, and is reminded of Daphne Lovelace as he imagines her deciding when she might finally turn in her passport. "Not today — I might wait till the weather worsens or I might even wait till Christmas."

And then he ponders just how many old people have said to themselves, "I'll just hang on to see one last Christmas," and have ruined subsequent Christmases for the rest of the family for years to come.

Now or never, he tells himself as he stands midway on the bridge and phones. *I guess my Christmas is over — time to start a new year.*

"Daavid. I want you to come to see me after zhe Queen," says Daisy, before he has a chance to gather his words. "Is zhat possible? I have somezhing very important to tell you."

It's a long way to travel just to be told to pack his bags, but he can't help feeling that he might need an excuse to get out of the country in a hurry on Friday, so he agrees.

"I'm into my fifties now," Bliss claims as his reason for resigning when he makes the next call to his son-in-law. "Whereas you are just a young whippersnapper with family responsibilities."

"Cut the crap, grandpa," says Bryan. "What are you planning?"

"Hey. Enough of the grandpa stuff. But you're right. I do have a little surprise in mind."

"So, why quit?"

"Because, my son, as I'm sure you are aware, they can't fire me if I've already put my ticket in."

"Dave. Whatever it is, don't go it alone. Count me in."

"In that case — Edwards has called a meeting at nine-thirty tomorrow morning at his office, and I think we should be there."

"I wasn't invited."

"Neither was I," admits Bliss, before adding sternly, "Just one thing, Peter. If the wheel comes off, I'm taking the rap. You had no idea what I was planning."

"I don't know what you're planning."

"That's precisely what I just said."

chapter eighteen

The clock in the tower of Big Ben is winding itself up to strike nine as hundreds of lesser civil servants make a frantic dash from bus stops and tube stations to the front doors of the Home Office, a few blocks east of the tower at St. Anne's Gate.

It is the start of just another day for the bureaucrats responsible for the internal security of the nation — blue-suited men and women whose daily contact with the police takes them deep into the murky underworld, without them ever having to risk the inconvenience of a bullet in the head or a knife in the back.

Her Majesty's Chief Inspectors of Constabulary and Prisons, the loftiest guardians of law and order, will arrive at the front door in chauffeured limousines, but not until their desks have been cleaned and their cappuccinos made. Middle rankers, together with invited guests, will park their Audis and Volvos in the car park at the rear of the building under the noses of Bill and Fred (Tweedle-Dum and Tweedle-Dee behind their backs), a couple of jovial pensioners dressed up as security guards.

"M'ning, Bill … M'ning, Fred … Nice day … How's the lumbago?" calls driver after driver as regulars sweep by without needing to be checked by the two old-timers.

Michael Edwards, in his BMW, stops to hand over a list of visitors due for his meeting. "See if you can find them a decent spot, please," he requests and gets an affirmative nod. "They're mainly people from the palace," he adds, hoping to lend weight to his own credence rather than his visitors'.

"Right'o, sir," says Bill.

Lefty and Pimple are hot on Edwards' tail and pull up at the gatehouse just a minute later.

"We have a meeting with Mr. Edwards," says Lefty, handing over their American Embassy ID passes, and Fred ticks them off Edwards' list.

"Just one moment, sir," says Fred as he disappears into the backroom of the gatehouse, where he seemingly morphs into a couple of uniformed police constables and two detective chief inspectors.

"Would you gentlemen please step out of the car," requests David Bliss, emerging with the Americans' IDs in hand, while Peter Bryan and one of the constables make their way around the car to the passenger's door.

"What is this, Bliss?" sneers Lefty as he tries to snatch the passes back, but Bliss grabs his arm and spits, "I said, step out of the car."

"And you as well," says Bryan to Pimple, wrenching open the passenger's door.

Time stops as Lefty's arm tenses under Bliss's grip, and his eyes burn into his captor's brain as he weighs the odds. The moment of decision for a cornered man whose entire future turns on this moment. Make the right move and he can be free. But what is the right move — fight or flight?

"What the hell's going on?" demands Edwards, breaking the spell as he spots the commotion and races across the car park in their direction.

"I am arresting you for administering a noxious substance under Section 24 of the Offences Against the Person Act 1861," cautions Bliss as he hauls Lefty from the car. "You do not have to say anything —"

"On what evidence?" cuts in Lefty as he struggles to free himself from Bliss's grip. "You ain't got no witnesses."

"Mr. Edwards here saw it happen. Didn't you, sir?"

"Now look here, Bliss …"

"Unless he would prefer to be arrested as an accomplice."

"Now you're going too far."

"I haven't even begun," says Bliss as Pimple is pulled from the passenger's seat and rubbed down by Peter Bryan.

"Oh," says Bryan as he draws a loaded Smith and Wesson from the CIA man's shoulder holster. "That's very naughty."

"I am authorized to carry …"

"In America, maybe. But this is dear old Blighty," says Bryan as he drops the magazine out of the pistol and hands it to the constable. "We get very touchy about people having guns. In fact, all handguns are illegal here — didn't anyone warn you?"

"Bliss, Bryan. You two are finished," snarls Edwards from the sidelines as he pulls out his cellphone. "The U.S. Ambassador will have them out in no time. You have no idea what you're dealing with."

"That may well be true, sir," says Bliss while the two struggling Americans are being handcuffed and Peter Bryan is reading them their rights. "But in the meantime, as long as they are in my custody, I have the right to search them and anything in their possession for evidence."

"That's American Embassy property," shouts Pimple, squirming to free himself from the handcuffs as

Bliss begins a search of the car. "Touch that and you're dead."

"Threatening to kill a police officer. Now that is a very serious offence under Section 16 of the same Act," says Bliss delightedly as he sticks his nose into the American's face. "So now you're under arrest for another crime, but we shouldn't overlook a further offence under the Firearms Act of committing a crime whilst in possession of a loaded weapon."

Michael Edwards eventually attempts conciliation. "Look, Dave," he tries warmly. "This is ridiculous. Just save yourself a lot of grief and let these men go."

"I can't do that, sir. You know that," says Bliss with a deliberately smarmy smile. "They've committed serious crimes. What would the Home Secretary say if he knew we were letting foreign terrorists rule our streets?"

"They're not terrorists ..." explodes Edwards as Bliss opens the trunk of the car and lets out a low whistle. The transceiver taken from his office cupboard still has his signed evidence tag attached when he lifts it out and holds it aloft.

"Oh. Look what I found," he says gleefully. "I do believe this is stolen property."

"It ain't stolen, it's ours ..." starts Lefty, but Pimple kicks his shin.

"Shuddup. We ain't ever seen it before. He's trying to stitch us up."

"Yeah. I'd agree with that," says Edwards, and Bliss spins on the ex–chief superintendent and jabs a finger into his chest.

"You're not attempting to pervert the course of justice are you, sir?" he says with deadpan sincerity. "'Cuz I ought to remind you that such an offence at common law carries a maximum punishment of life imprisonment." And then he digs deeper into the car's trunk.

"I wonder what this is — gentlemen?" he says, unwrapping a very familiar blanket and drawing out a steel box the size of a large biscuit tin.

"That's U.S. government property," warns Pimple in a voice that suggests it should be considered sacrosanct.

"Really," says Bliss. "Then I'd better take very good care of it until you both get out of jail in a few years."

"Look here, Chief Inspector," says Edwards, bootlicking. "I'm really not trying to interfere, but you have to understand that sometimes the end justifies the means."

"Absolutely, sir. My feelings exactly," says Bliss, before helping bundle the detainees into a car and instructing the constables to drive them to the nearest police station by the longest possible route. "And don't take them anywhere near Scotland Yard," he whispers to the driver, knowing that Fox will have them out of the front door as soon as they are in the back. And then he turns to Bryan as he switches off his cellphone. "Get back to the office, Peter, and stall Fox for at least an hour."

Lawyer Robert Jameson has a clean handkerchief in his pocket, a fresh rose in his buttonhole, and a swagger to his step when he walks in the front door of Westchester Police Station at precisely nine-thirty and doffs his Panama hat to the desk clerk.

"Detective Chief Inspector Roberts is expecting me," he says, announcing himself as if arriving to defend a local miscreant rather than himself.

"You'll find all the paperwork's in order," he claims to Roberts as he blusters in to the chief inspector's office and hands his Panama hat to the senior detective as he would hand it to a coat check girl. And then he pulls sheaves from an enormous document case and carefully piles them on the D.C.I.'s desk.

"I'm sure it is," replies Roberts handing back the hat, knowing that it would take a sharp-eyed forensic account-ant to spot a deliberate slip of the pen in most lawyers' ledgers. Which is why the detective chief inspector is more interested in Jameson's answers to awkward questions, such as, "Why would so many residents at St. Michael's choose you to administer their power of attorney?"

"Who else can they trust when they have no living relatives?" replies Jameson with an open face.

"But you must appreciate that it could look a little suspicious."

"I warned Mr. Davenport about the optics," agrees Jameson. "But I can assure you every penny can be accounted for. It's all in here," he adds, tapping the paperwork. "Keep them as long as you like."

"So where has the money gone?"

"You'll find that much of it went to worthy causes."

"Really," says Roberts. "And that wouldn't by any chance include the lining of Mr. Davenport's pockets would it?"

"Good grief, no. Is that what you think?"

"Well he does have a large, expensive house."

"More like a mansion," agrees Jameson with a jealous edge. "But that's all his own money. He never received a penny from St. Michael's he wasn't entitled to in wages and expenses. He was most particular about that."

"So if I said we'd received a tip about certain irregularities …?"

"I would say you have been grossly misinformed, Chief Inspector," Jameson says, putting his hat on. "I can assure you, St. Michael's affairs are entirely free of sin."

"So where has the residents' money gone?" asks Roberts as the lawyer terminates the interview by picking up his case and turning to the door.

"Most of it has gone to God," he says with his hand on the door handle. "But you'll find all the details in the files."

Hoskins, the videographer, is on his way out and locking his door when Bliss grabs him.

"I need you to take a look at this," he says, turning the technician around and closing the office door behind them.

Hoskins shakes his head at the large metal container that Bliss has unwrapped onto his desk, together with the transceiver. "I suppose it could be some kind of anti-personnel mine," he suggests, backing away.

"I never thought of that," confesses Bliss, retreating a couple of steps. "Maybe we should get it outside."

But Hoskins steps back in for a closer inspection and puts two and two together. "Look," he says, pointing out the similarity of the materials used in the construction of the transceiver and the box — especially the stub aerials that protrude from both. "These two go together, whatever they are."

"Meaning?"

"I think the transceiver is the control unit. It receives a signal from a distant transmitter, maybe even from a satellite in orbit, and redirects it to the box."

"But what does the box do?"

"Well. If it's a mine it will detonate," he says fatalistically as he opens a toolkit and selects a screwdriver.

The box's innards are a jumbled maze of components that leave Hoskins with a furrowed brow. "At least it's not a bomb," he says, once he's picked at the circuit boards, batteries, and miscellaneous elements.

"But what is it?"

"There's one way to find out," he says as he plugs the satellite transceiver into a power bar and plays with a couple of wires.

"Absolutely nothing ..." starts Bliss in relief. And then his brain explodes.

Excruciating pains and incredible pleasures jerk him rigid, while fireworks rocket around inside his mind with brilliant flashes of colour and a deafening cacophony of sound that coalesces into a maelstrom of sensations, kicking his nervous system into overdrive.

"Off!" he yells, fighting to escape the nightmare, but Hoskins is under attack as well and stands in spasm.

"Turn it off!" Bliss tries again, but the technician is locked into place by an invisible hand.

"I can't!" shouts Hoskins as demons chase through his head and threaten his sanity.

"Help!" Bliss is screeching when the machine cuts out by itself.

"What the hell?" Hoskins says as he pulls out the plug, but his mind is still in turmoil, and he has to sit.

"Oh my God," says Bliss, slumping to the floor.

"Did you say you got this from the CIA?" asks Hoskins once the room has stopped spinning.

Bliss nods. "A couple of our so-called friends from the evil empire. Why?"

"Have you ever heard of Mk-Ultra?"

"No ..." starts Bliss, then he thinks back. "Yes," he says. "I remember someone mentioned it," he adds, although he doesn't attribute it to Edwards. "What is it?"

"It's not what it *is*. It is what it was supposed to be. Mk-Ultra was a secret CIA program in the sixties. They experimented on people with all kinds of drugs and electromagnetic devices to win the Cold War by scrambling the brains of people who didn't agree with their philosophies."

"That gave them a pretty wide target. So what happened?"

"The whole thing was a fiasco. They tried to nobble Fidel Castro with drugs, and they killed God knows how many people, including one of the top researchers — a Canadian professor, if I remember rightly. And there was a huge stink in Congress when it was discovered that they used prisoners and psychiatric patients for deadly experiments without anyone's permission."

"And you think this could be connected?"

"They were supposed to have shut it down when they were caught," says Hoskins, but he deliberately leaves his answer open. "If you go online you'll find plenty of information."

"So what do you think happened?" asks Bliss, with his mind on the day of the royal visit.

"If I still had the pictures of the Duke —" Hoskins starts, but Bliss jumps in and takes off for his office, saying, "I do. You made me a copy, remember?"

"What have you got on Jameson?" Anne McGregor questions as she wanders into Matt Roberts's office and peers over his shoulder.

"Do you mean Saint Jameson?" says Roberts. "I'm beginning to think our dearly beloved Miss Lovelace was in the right place — talk about befuddled. If these records are straight, Jameson and Davenport could knock Mother Theresa off the Nobel podium for philanthropy."

"Oh, dear," says McGregor. "I've just had the police doctor on the phone. He reckons the medications seem perfectly above-board to him."

"That's it then," says Roberts, bundling Jameson's files and dropping them into a box. "I've got some real crimes to deal with."

"Chief Inspector," shouts Fox, catching Bliss in the open again as he makes a run for his office to collect the DVD. "Found you at last."

"I didn't know I was lost, sir."

"Don't give me that innocent crap, Bliss. I know what you've done," carries on Fox as junior officers scatter, while civilian clerks slink by with their heads in their paperwork.

"Done, sir?" says Bliss, with no intention of helping the commander tie a noose.

"The American Ambassador has been on the phone to the Home Secretary," Fox continues, before saying that the

CIA are demanding the return of their property, and their men, with a full apology.

"CIA?" Bliss says blankly. "Are you trying to tell me that those two men who attacked me with nerve gas —"

"They didn't attack you."

"That's a matter for a judge and jury," says Bliss as he starts to walk away. "And they were certainly in possession of an illegal weapon and stolen property."

"Cut this nonsense right now, Bliss," Fox calls after him. "I've ordered them to be released and I'm dropping all charges. Now where the fuck is their stuff?"

"He'll never find it," Bliss laughs to Peter Bryan as they slink into a dimly lit booth of a backstreet joint and order a couple of beers in celebration. "It's labelled 'Sonic Generator — A/V department use only,' and Hoskins already had his screwdriver out when I left."

"So. Show me," says Bryan, sliding closer as Bliss opens his laptop.

"Keep your eyes on the rest of the entourage," Bliss whispers as they focus on the screen with the eagerness of teenagers watching porn. "And see what happens when the old boy makes his way to the pavement."

"Wow!" exclaims Bryan; the protection officers and footmen all seem to freeze for just a second at precisely the same moment as Prince Philip.

"I thought they were just reacting to him," explains Bliss as he reruns the clip several times. "But they obviously felt it as well."

"Yes. But they were just on the fringe. He obviously took the full brunt of it."

"Hi," drawls a husky-voiced female with a dolled-up fifteen-year-old Korean girl in tow. "Would you two hunks like to buy me and my friend a drink?"

"Police," says Bryan, flicking open his warrant.

"Sorry. We don't do freebies for the law, luv," sneers the hooker.

"I don't want a freebie," says Bryan. "I want you to piss off before I'm forced to arrest you for impersonating a woman."

"And fuck you, too," she mutters as they strut off to the next booth.

"So, where was it activated from?" asks Bryan, but Bliss can only speculate. According to Hoskins, the transceiver's dish on top of the lamppost could have picked up a satellite signal from just about anywhere.

"Either the U.S. Embassy or direct from Washington is my bet," he says, although he has to admit that anyone watching the event on television anywhere in the world could have triggered the signal.

"So," summarizes Bryan. "Someone pushes a button and *zap*, the gizmo under the pavement gives Phil a very nasty shock."

"That's it," concurs Bliss. "And if it was anything like the shock I got, the poor old devil could've been so screwed up that he thought it was Armageddon."

"So he attacked his missus?" questions Bryan skeptically.

"No," says Bliss as he reruns the clip and points to the confused man struggling with his sword before lunging for the reception line. "First he went for the holy rollers. Then the Queen started in on him and he was so far gone he just turned on her."

"That's pretty far-fetched," suggests Bryan, but Bliss shakes his head.

"Here," he says, as he goes online and Googles Mk-Ultra. "Have a gander at this and then tell me it's off the wall."

"You're friggin' crazy," laughs Misty Jenkins as she leans on her broken front gate and watches Trina Button supervise the delivery of a new fridge to Daphne's house. "She ain't ever coming out."

"Misty," Trina starts, dying to tell the woman that Daphne is actually in hospital for a check-up and is well on her way to coming home, but then she pauses to reflect on Angel's admonition at the labyrinth. "You can't influence other people's actions or beliefs," the free-spirited woman told her. "You can only change the way you see them."

"You could be right," Trina concedes to Daphne's neighbour. "But I just thought I'd get the place spruced up anyway."

"Well, you're wasting your friggin' money."

"Mebbe," says Trina, and then she turns to the delivery driver. "Straight into the kitchen and would you please plug it in. Thanks."

But the refrigerator is only the beginning. A painter's van is scheduled to arrive at three, and a gardener has promised to get digging on Friday morning — weather permitting — which only leaves the inside of the house. Mavis would help, but she has her hands full with Trina's mother.

"I want to do the El Camino again," said Winifred as they were having breakfast with Mavis in the rose garden of the Mitre Hotel, and the Englishwoman quickly volunteered to take her.

"Maybe if I go round the thing enough bloomin' times I'll figure it out in the end," she said, without admitting that by taking Winifred to the labyrinth she was, in some way, trying to atone for her neglect of Daphne.

"I don't suppose you …" starts Trina to Misty, but the Canadian homecare nurse lets the idea go. "No. Don't bother. It's okay."

"What? Don't suppose what?" asks Misty, and ten minutes later she is pulling on a pair of latex gloves, saying, "I want cash, mind. No friggin' cheques. I don't want the Social docking it off my welfare."

"I told you, Misty, ten pounds an hour straight cash," says Trina as they begin work on cleaning Daphne's kitchen walls, adding, "And maybe I'll teach you some yoga if we have time."

All three of David Bliss's voicemail boxes — home, work, and cell — and his email inbox are overflowing as the chief inspector treats his daughter and son-in-law to dinner in a secluded corner of La Côte d'Or on Thursday evening. Transatlantic phone lines may be melting and the lights still burning on the top floors of New Scotland Yard, the Home Office, and the American Embassy, but Bliss only has his retirement in mind as he orders champagne.

"I'm flying down to Cannes as soon as I've handed in my boots tomorrow," he tells the young couple. "I think Daisy wants to come clean."

"Your champagne, monsieur," says Greasy in his faux French, spinning Bliss back a few weeks to his fiftieth birthday and his delight at the sight of his fiancée amongst the surprise guests.

Is it all over? he wonders as Samantha proposes a toast to mark the end of his career. *Twenty-eight years — for what? A certificate of service and a long service medal. But did I really make a difference? Would the world be a better place if I had been a dustman or a bus driver?*

"Dad," Samantha cuts in to his musings, "I was asking — are you sure you're right about Daisy? She seemed so much in love with you when she came to the party."

"Is it all over?" he questions aloud, speaking of Daisy, the force, and life in general. "I guess I'll find out tomorrow."

"I reckon they'll have your boots off you the moment you walk in the door in the morning," chuckles his son-in-law, knowing that a posse of senior officers spent the afternoon trying to round Bliss up after he wound Fox up with a warning and disappeared with the CIA's mind-bending machine.

"I just wonder what the press will make of all this," Bliss mused aloud when Fox ordered him to hand over the equipment or face the consequences.

"You wouldn't …" dared Fox, but the look on Bliss's face said that he would.

"Look, Dave. This isn't necessary," tried Fox, knowing that with Bliss's resignation already accepted he had no leverage, and Bliss laid into him.

"In my books, the end never justifies the means," he said through clenched teeth. "So tell Edwards and his Yankee mates to get stuffed. They won't get any help from me, whatever they're trying to achieve."

"What was their motive?" Samantha wants to know as they wait for their main course. "What were they after?"

"Oil, probably. Isn't it always?" proposes Bliss, although he's guessing when he suggests that someone wants to start all-out inter-religious war as a cover for a major resource grab.

"I just don't buy that," says Peter Bryan. "How did they know he would attack the imams? It's not as though they had any control over its effects."

"Lobsters, Dad?" says Samantha in surprise as the waiter delivers the platters.

"Make the most of it. After tomorrow I'll be a pensioner."

"And soon to be a grandfather," slips in Bryan, and Bliss smiles with the realization that he hasn't reached the end of the road after all — just a fork.

chapter nineteen

It is 5:30 a.m. and the rumblings of an underground train shake the quiet London dawn around the mosque, while six uniformed men struggle up the steps under the weight of a piece of equipment the size and shape of a coffin. Commander Fox, in the lead, calls to the security guard at the top of the steps. "Give us a hand, mate. It's heavy."

"What the hell is it?" queries the puzzled guard, a man who looks distinctly like Edwards dressed as a mullah.

"X-ray machine. The same as the ones at the airport."

"No one told me ..."

"That's security for you," moans Lefty as he carries the rear corner. "Always the last to be told anything."

"I oughta check ..."

"Just open the poxin' door first, will you? We're breaking our backs here," says Fox, and David Bliss, watching through a surveillance camera, panics.

"It's a bomb. It's a bomb," he tries yelling, but no one is listening. "Help! Help! It's a bomb," he shouts into microphones — dozens of microphones, but everyone is dead, even Daisy is dead — it is her name on the coffin, and the air is suddenly filled with the shrill scream of sirens and alarms.

"It's a bomb," Bliss is still shouting as he jerks up in bed and desperately tries to get his bearings in the darkness. "What the hell?" he says as the alarms continue, and then he grabs the phone.

"Dave. They've called it off," Peter Bryan is trying to tell him as the cacophony continues.

"Wait a minute." Bliss yawns as he fumbles for the light and turns off the radio and his bedside alarm clock.

"I've just got a call from the Yard," explains Bryan. "They're standing everyone down."

The six o'clock newsreader gives Bliss the full story once he has made coffee and showered himself awake.

"A flare-up of bombings across the Middle East in protest at today's visit has destroyed dozens of mosques and left many dead … Her Majesty has indefinitely postponed … The price of oil on the world market has jumped by another five dollars …"

"I bet Lefty and bloody Pimple had a hand in that," Bliss says when he calls his son-in-law back, but he is wrong.

The two CIA men, with passports in the names of Andrews and Blake, have just arrived at an American air base in Virginia and are being escorted to a debriefing at their headquarters in Langley by their unhappy controller.

"There is some serious shit flying at the Big House," grumbles the straight-faced woman as they sit in the back of a chauffeured limousine with a soundproof panel separating them from the driver.

"We tried ... everyone tried," says Lefty. "Their Home Secretary tried, even their Prime Minister tried, but she wouldn't listen. She was determined to go through with it."

"There was always that chance," the handler agrees. "But what's really pissed the deputy is that you two amateurs were taken down by a regular cop, and he even got the scrambler. For Jesus' sake, do you realize how stupid that makes us look to the Brits? And you know how sensitive that thing is."

"You authorized us to use it."

"To use it, not to lose it. And you were supposed to give her a headache, not turn her husband into a raving lunatic. 'We'll just give her a headache and she'll jump back in the car and hightail it back to her palace,' you said. So what went wrong?"

"I dunno — Edwards was pulling the shots and missed the timing I suppose."

"And whose stupid idea was it for his lordship to wear his toy soldier outfit?"

"That was Edwards. He said that if the old guy showed up in uniform someone would stop them going in."

"Or, just maybe, try to skewer his wife," says the handler, adding, "I'm beginning to have serious doubts about our man Edwards."

Michael Edwards has no doubts about himself. He never has doubted himself or his ability to swing even the most unfavourable situations in his direction. Not that his present situation is unfavourable. He may have suffered financial disasters through bad investments in the past — one major loss he lays at David Bliss's door — but now, with his gold-plated chief superintendent's pension, a substantial retainer from the CIA, and a handout from the Home Office, he is well on his way to Shangri-La. And as he sits with his feet up in front of his computer enjoying another champagne breakfast, he watches his oil stocks pumping money into his offshore accounts faster than he can count it. However, there is a fly in his glass of bubbly: D.C.I. David Anthony Bliss.

"Keep your friends close, but your enemies closer," has always been Edwards' motto, and with that in mind he chose Bliss to work under his thumb. But now that Bliss has his hands on the Mk-Ultra machine, he may be just too close for comfort.

"It's me, Roger," says Edwards, phoning Commander Fox as soon it is late enough not to appear desperate. "We need to talk."

New Scotland Yard is in so much turmoil over the last-minute cancellation that no one seems to take any notice of David Bliss as he slides in one of the back entrances to begin clearing out his desk at eight-thirty. But someone has beaten him to it, and a few minutes later he stares at a couple of handfuls of his personal knick-knacks that have been pointedly piled on the floor of his otherwise empty office. Then the heavies show up — Commander Fox, Michael Edwards, and two superintendents from the Internal Investigations Department.

"The game's over, Bliss. Where is it?" demands Fox, and, in a preplanned attack, one of the superintendents steps in to remind Bliss that he is still a serving officer and that failure to obey a lawful order will cause him all kinds of hardships.

Bliss is tempted to play the superintendents along to see if they know what they are dealing with, but he doesn't bother.

"So what are your paymasters up to?" he asks, turning on Edwards in a bid to get at least one matter cleared up.

"I'm paid to protect Her Majesty," starts Edwards, while deliberately invading Bliss's territory by picking up a photograph of Daisy from the heap of personal effects and snorting his disapproval.

Bliss grabs the picture and sneers, "The only thing you've ever protected is your own backside. Anyway, I'm not talking about the Home Office, I'm talking about …"

Edwards' fist comes from nowhere and lands cleanly on Bliss's nose.

"Oh, shit," mutters Fox as Bliss crumples, then the commander spins on Edwards. "You'd better leave, Michael."

"Wait a minute," says Bliss from the floor as he tries to stem blood. "I want him arrested and charged."

"For what?" spits Fox. "I didn't see a thing. You must've fallen."

Bliss looks to the superintendents for support, but they have apparently spotted something of great interest out of the window, and he realizes that he is on his own.

"I guess I will have to consult my lawyer about talking to the press, after all," he says defiantly as he gets up, pockets a few of his valuables, snatches up the picture of Daisy, and makes his way to the door.

"Bliss …" starts Fox, but Edwards grabs the commander. "Leave him, Roger. He wouldn't dare go public."

"Well, Detective Chief Inspector, thank you very much for your twenty-eight years of loyal service to Her Majesty and the good citizens of London," Bliss apes into a washroom mirror as he stems the flow of blood from his nose, then he checks to make sure that all the cubicles are unoccupied before calling Peter Bryan on his cellphone.

"Get someone in fingerprints to go over the thing," Bliss says, without going into detail. "Lefty and Pimple's prints are bound to be on it unless they wore gloves, and you'll need elims from me and from the videographer."

"Will do," says Bryan. "But what will it prove?"

"That a certain Judas is in the pocket of god almighty."

"Edwards?" queries Bryan.

"Yes," says Bliss, taking a close look at the photograph of Daisy that Edwards plucked off the floor. "And my lovely Daisy has his fingerprints all over her."

Elims — elimination prints — enable the fingerprint examiner to distinguish the loops, whorls, and bifurcations on a suspect's fingertips from the multitude of impressions left on surfaces by innocent people. Although, as Superintendent Anne McGregor is well aware, often the only difference between the guilty and the innocent is that the latter has yet to be caught.

"Excuse me, ma'am," says Pete Reagan, the civilian dactylographer at Westchester Police Station, catching the superintendent as soon as she reaches her office. "Do you remember those elimination prints that I took at St. Michael's — the seniors' home?"

"Yes," replies McGregor, without taking her eyes off the night's incident log. "You can get shot of them now. The case is closed. The place is clean."

"Really," says Reagan, and something in the smugness of his tone makes her look up.

"What is it?" she asks, and he presents her with a file labelled, "Hilda Anne Fitzgerald, nee Davenport, a.k.a Hilda Anne Williams," saying, "Does the name ring a bell, ma'am?"

"Yes. She's the manager's sister."

"No, ma'am," he says, gloating over the fact that he has an ace up his sleeve. "Try again. Hilda Williams. Ten years ago — Liverpool?"

"Don't worry. He's bluffing about going public," Edwards assures his American contact as soon as he has explained that the mind machine is still missing. "Anyway, the dumb bastard hasn't got the brains to figure out what it is."

"Michael," says the New Yorker patiently, "that's not an acceptable risk. You assured us that it would be returned."

"Well. What d'ya expect me to do — use thumbscrews?"

"We expected you to get back our property," says the voice coldly. "But I guess we'll have to do it ourselves, and you will have to pay."

"Wait a minute ..." begins Edwards, but he's talking to himself.

It's Friday and it's Bliss's final poet's day as he walks out of Scotland Yard a couple of hours after he walked in.

Piss off early, tomorrow is the first day of the rest of your life, he tells himself, and after his treatment at the hands of Fox he sees no reason to prolong his old life a moment longer. He has said his farewells and is booked on the five o'clock flight to Nice, but the idea of hanging around London with both Edwards and Fox on the prowl doesn't appeal, so, as he takes the tube home to pack for a few days in Provence, he makes plans for lunch in Westchester with a very old friend.

Daphne Lovelace is still in hospital, although she has the okay to go home. Trina is to collect her after lunch, but now the veteran has a visitor. Social worker Tony Oswald hasn't caught on to fact that his client's apparent psychosis was her ticket to St. Michael's and is explaining the arrangements he has made for a homecare nurse to call in on her a few days each week.

"I really don't need anyone. I'm quite capable of taking care of myself, thank you very much," remonstrates Daphne, but her convincing portrayal of a demented old lady will haunt Oswald for some time to come.

"And I've had a word with the animal control people at the Council," he continues, changing the subject before she can object further. "They're going to serve a notice on Mr. Jenkins to stop his dogs annoying you or he'll have to get rid of them."

The dogs, and especially the garden fence between Daphne's property and her neighbours', are also matters of concern to Trina as she and Misty work on the preparations for Daphne's homecoming party.

"I don't mind paying for the materials to fix it," explains Trina, while Misty rolls the pastry for banana cream pies.

"Okay," says Misty as she dusts flour off her hands, and then she opens the back door and yells at her sons, who are helping the gardener straighten some of the plants damaged by the dogs. "Tell your dad to get his lazy backside over here."

"Right, Mum."

"And tell 'im to turn that friggin' stereo down. It's givin' me a friggin' headache."

"That will be Mother and Mavis," says Trina as she hears the front doorbell.

"We've got eleven adults and fourteen children," says Mavis proudly as she wheels Winifred into the kitchen. "And that doesn't include us and the Jenkinses."

"I want to come as well," pipes up Trina's mother from her chair, although she's not entirely sure what she is volunteering for. Her feet have recovered, and in truth, she can hobble around perfectly well. But she has grown attached to the wheelchair and the attention it brings, and she delights in recounting far-fetched tales of the trials and torments of her great pilgrimage, insisting, "The El Camino ruined my feet."

"The house is looking wonderful, Trina," says Mavis as she sneaks a freshly made chocolate cookie. "Daphne will be so happy."

"Thanks to Misty and her boys," says Trina as she throws her arm around the young neighbour's shoulder, but much of the credit is due to the painters and the professional tradesmen Trina hired to smarten up the property.

Professional burglars are in many ways similar to the tradesmen who spruced up Daphne's house. Most work quickly and efficiently and leave the premises as neat and tidy as when they started. However, the team who turned David Bliss's house upside down in search of the mind machine made sure their visit wasn't overlooked.

"They've totally wrecked the place," Bliss whinges to his son-in-law by phone as he gets a glimpse of daily life in Kandahar and Kirkik. "The bastards smashed the lock off the door and trashed the place."

"Vandals?" queries Bryan, but he knows better.

"No. The Americans. Lefty and bloody Pimple," Bliss fumes as he picks through the wreckage in his front hallway. Then an unopened envelope catches his eye amongst the debris.

"Or Edwards," suggests Bryan, revealing that his friend in the fingerprint department has matched Edwards' prints on Daisy's photograph to some he found on the transceiver.

"I expected that," says Bliss. "I bet Fox nicked the thing from my cupboard and dropped it on Edwards' desk, and he gave it back to the dynamic duo."

"What do we do now?" asks Bryan, and Bliss makes him wait a few moments while he rips open the envelope.

"You'd better dump the damn thing on Fox's doorstep," Bliss replies eventually, but his mind is in turmoil as he reads and rereads the note, and he is barely able to keep his voice straight. "They won't quit till they get it back."

"You're giving up?" Bryan says in amazement, but his father-in-law is uncharacteristically blasé, explaining that his twenty-eight years of fighting criminals and idiots on both sides of the thin blue line officially ends in just six hours and he can't be bothered to pursue the matter for another moment.

"D'ye know, Peter," says Bliss resignedly, "I've been trying to pin something on Edwards for years, and each time I was sure I'd nailed him he pulled a dodge and I ended up back where I started. Everyone knows he's a sack of you-know-what, but when he looks in the mirror he sees a rose, and I'll just have to accept that."

"Are you sure that you are all right, Dave?"

"Yes, Peter. I know it's difficult to believe," says Bliss. Then he nonchalantly adds, "In any case, I've just sold my first book."

"What?"

"We believe that your historical narrative, *The Truth Behind the Mask*, has bestseller potential," Bliss reads at speed, before saying that the publisher wants a meeting to discuss terms as soon as possible.

"Bestseller! That's brilliant, Dave."

"I know. I can't believe it myself," admits Bliss as he continually rereads the note. Then he has an idea. "Why don't you borrow Hoskins's screwdriver, take the thing apart, and lose one or two pieces before you give it back."

"That's sneaky," laughs Bryan, but he agrees, guessing that it might give Fox and Edwards a headache once they've returned it to the CIA.

"That'll make up for the headache they gave Phil and me," says Bliss as he puts down the phone to take another look at the publisher's letter.

"Bestseller potential," he muses, and he is still rolling the title of his book off his tongue ten minutes later when he has waded through the wreckage to find enough clothes for his trip.

"*The Truth Behind the Mask*, by David Anthony Bliss," he recites again and again as he drives half a dozen hefty screws into the frame of his front door, then, with a hastily packed bag and a broad grin, he takes off to Westchester en route to an entirely new world.

The report of the recovery of the Mk-Ultra equipment reaches Lefty and Pimple in Langley, Virginia, just as Bliss pulls into the entrance of Westchester General, and their euphoria will last until someone switches it on.

"I just made a few alterations," Bryan tells Bliss when he calls his son-in-law to find out what happened, explaining that no one could accuse him of stealing if he merely rejigged some of the wiring. "I had a few bits and pieces left over from when I tried fixing my computer, so I thought, why waste them?"

"David," calls Daphne, taking off her broad-rimmed sun hat and gaily waving to him from a chair in the hospital garden as he gets out of his car.

"You soon got your memory back," he says, hugging her warmly. "You're just a big fraud."

"I know," she says as she buries her nose in the bouquet of roses he presents to her. "But I was so sure they were up to no good at that St. Michael's place."

"You should have told me."

"I did," she reminds him reproachfully. "I tried telling everyone, and no one would listen."

"Sorry. I had a lot on my mind," he says. "But Samantha tells me that nothing was going on at the home after all."

"This was," replies Daphne, pointing to the fading bruise on her face. But she has already been advised by P.C. Joveneski that, because of the lack of corroborative evidence, they won't be taking any further action.

"Amelia heard that woman knocking me about," continues the elderly patient bitterly, suggesting that she doesn't agree with the verdict, but Bliss can only commiserate, knowing that the defence would have a field day with the young girl in the witness box, accusing her of sour grapes because she was fired.

"It's very annoying," he says in sympathy, guessing that his nose will soon be the colour of his elderly friend's cheek and he will be equally robbed of legal recourse.

"At least I managed to get out of there alive," she carries on with a note of triumph, knowing that she succeeded where so many others have failed.

"I'm not surprised," chuckles Bliss. "If I recall rightly, you once saved your neck with a packet of chocolate digestives."

"You remembered," she laughs, and then she has a quizzical look in her eye as she says, "You seem very chirpy today. Did you win the lottery or something?"

"In a way —" starts Bliss, with both his retirement and his book deal on the tip of his tongue, but Amelia Brimble interrupts.

"Hi, Daffy," calls the young girl excitedly as she rushes across the lawn. "I brought a visitor to cheer you up."

Camilla, Amelia's tabby, leaps from her arms straight into Daphne's lap and begins washing.

"Oh. She loves you, Daffy," burbles the teenager as she simultaneously strokes Daphne and her cat, and then, as if entirely unplanned, she says, "Why don't you keep her for a while, Daffy?"

"Oh. I couldn't …"

"Just until Missie Rouge comes home."

"I'm not sure …"

"I could visit …" she chatters on, and Bliss stands back and smiles at the happy tableau. Then Trina Button shows up and digs him in the ribs.

"Look at Daphne's face. See what they did to her. You wouldn't listen to me. I told you they were keeping her prisoner and drugging her. Nobody ever listens … Oh! What happened to your nose?"

"I fell over," Bliss is trying to say as Trina ditches him in favour of Amelia's cat.

"Oh, what a pretty pussy," she coos.

"Daffy's gonna look after her, aren't you?" says Amelia proudly, and Bliss feels himself fading from the picture as three generations of women come together over the purring young tabby.

"I suppose I'd better be off," he says. "I've got to be at Heathrow in an hour. I just wanted to tell you …"

"Ooh, look at her little tiny white feet," mews Daphne as the others sigh in unison, and Bliss comes to the realization that being an author can't compare with having whiskers and a fluffy tail, so he slips away to catch his flight.

"Time to get you home," says Trina, once Daphne has been given her freedom, and she puts out an arm for the old warhorse.

"I can manage on my own, thank you," says Daphne, levering herself out of the chair. "She didn't break my legs."

"Okay," says Trina, leading the way to her car. "Amelia and Camilla in the back and you can drive."

"I can't …" starts Daphne, then she laughs. "Very funny, Trina."

"I don't even wanna look at that place," says Amelia as they approach St. Michael's on their way home from the hospital, and Daphne is in agreement.

"I still can't understand it," she mutters aloud. "I'm not usually wrong about people."

"How could I have been so wrong?" Anne McGregor asks herself for the *n*th time since Hilda Fitzgerald's file hit her desk at breakfast time, and then she smartens herself up at the sound of a knock on her office door.

"Detective Chief Superintendent Malloy from Liverpool, ma'am," says Joan Joveneski as Malloy and four of his most senior detectives enter.

Malloy is young for his rank, barely forty, and he bristles with enthusiasm as he shuns the offer of coffee and scans the fingerprints and photographs that McGregor lays out for him.

"Well, well, well," he muses contentedly as he passes the evidence to his juniors and turns to McGregor. "So what's the plan, Superintendent?"

In the six hours since Hilda Fitzgerald set off the alarm on the Police National Computer, a team of social workers have been assembled and briefed, twenty off-duty officers have cursed the invention of cellphones and pagers, and a dozen detectives have wandered up and down the streets surrounding St. Michael's looking like lost tourists.

It's exactly 3:00 p.m. when Daphne arrives home. Her celebrity as the pensioner who was kidnapped from St. Michael's has not been tarnished by the suggestion that she engineered her own escape, and more than half of the street's residents have turned up for the victory party.

"Welcome Home, Daphne," reads the banner outside her freshly painted home, while young couples who previously took little notice of the dapper lady with a hat for every occasion now conjure up fond memories as they stand with their children beside tables laden with cakes, sandwiches, and banana cream pies and applaud her arrival.

"I never realized she had the O.B.E. till I saw it in the paper," admits one, while others recall the way that she would always stop to smell their roses or say hello to the children.

As a beaming Daphne steps out of Trina's car in Westchester, David Bliss plonks his bag on the check-in scales at Heathrow Airport, while in the same terminal Isabel Semaurino, arriving from Florence, is collecting her bag from a carousel. And at St. Michael's Church of

England Home for the Elderly, a cavalcade of police and social services cars draw up to the front door.

"Mr. Davenport. Do you know a woman by the name of Hilda Williams?" asks D.C.S. Malloy, head of the Merseyside Police, Criminal Investigation Department, once the home's manager has been cornered in his office.

Davenport's chair develops spikes, and he asks, "Why?"

"I'm asking the questions, sir," says the Chief Superintendent, and he looks to Davenport for an answer.

"My sister's first husband was a Williams — Trevor Williams," admits Davenport, although his face says that he would rather be having a lobotomy without anaesthetic.

"So, at that time — say, ten years ago," carries on Malloy, knowing from the fingerprints found in Daphne's room that he owns the situation, "— your sister would have been known as Mrs. Hilda Williams?"

"I suppose so."

"You suppose so?" Malloy questions, piling on the pressure.

"Yes. All right. That was her name."

"And where do you suppose she was living at that time, Mr. Davenport?"

"All right. I know what this is about," Davenport concedes to relieve the pain. "But it was nothing to do with Hilda. It was him — her husband. He did it."

The question "What did he do?" is redundant, but Malloy asks anyway.

The answer sticks in Davenport's throat, so Malloy leans in to the squirming man, saying, "Mr. Davenport. Were you aware that your sister was wanted for questioning regarding the suspected murders of at least twenty-five senior citizens — possibly many more — in the home that she and her husband were operating at the time?"

chapter twenty

Life is a labyrinth — a long, winding pathway full of experiences and challenges that eventually doubles back on itself to end at the place where it all began. And as Isabel Semaurino finally reaches the end of one circuit in her life and is about to begin anew, she steps out of a taxi and walks into the midst of Daphne's homecoming celebration.

Balloons, streamers, and flags festoon the street outside Daphne's house. An island of tables, dragged from outhouses and carried from dining rooms into the centre of the cul-de-sac, is decorated with flowers and topped with cakes, pies, sandwiches and pots of Daphne's favourite tea — Keemun.

Daphne herself is as vibrant and colourful as the decorations. Wearing a flowery printed cotton dress flounced with ribbons, a floppy straw hat with a taffeta bow, and a giant smile, she is fending off a dozen uninhibited urchins as they tug at her for attention. "I saw you in the paper ...

Mum says you're famous ... I bet you know the Queen."
And then one grabs a paper napkin off the table and starts
an avalanche as they all push for autographs.

At the table, Misty Jenkins, wearing her best jeans, cuts
Mavis Longbottom a slice of her banana cream pie, saying,
"... and I told him straight. Either those friggin' dogs go or
I will," while her teenage sons — caught between childhood
and whatever passes for maturity in their world — try to
appear cool as they wash down pink-iced fairy cakes and
raspberry marshmallows with cans of beer.

Trina Button is lying face-down on the pavement,
demonstrating the one-armed vasisthasana pose to Angel
Robinson and a group of women neighbours, saying, "This
one hurts like hell ... it's great ... you'll love it," while her
wheelchair-bound mother strokes Camilla the cat as she
mourns the ruination of her feet to anyone who will listen.
And then, as if someone pulled the plug, the world stops
and everyone's eyes go to the woman with Italian chic who
is advancing on Daphne.

Sixty-nine-year-old grandmother Isabel Semaurino,
wearing a slinky red dress and a broad-rimmed silk hat, has
tears in her eyes as she cheerily calls, "Hello. Do you
remember me?"

"You came back then," steps in Mavis, restarting the
world, then she turns to Daphne. "This was the lady I was
telling you about. The one who was asking about you."

"I don't remember ..." Daphne is saying vaguely as the
urchins sense a problem and fade away, while Trina, Misty,
Amelia, and several neighbours nose in on the situation
and collectively hold their breath.

With the weight of a dozen pairs of eyes on her, Isabel
is under pressure and searches for a way out. "Maybe I
shouldn't have come till later ..." she starts, but Daphne
steps forward.

"Well, you're here now, dear. So what do you want?"
Daphne's phone rings and breaks the tension.

"I'll get it," yells Trina, and Isabel's walk into the future is momentarily postponed until the Canadian races back, gushing, "It's the police for you, Daphne. They've arrested Hilda Fitzgerald."

"For beating me up?"

"No," says Trina in shocked tones. "For murdering twenty-five old dears."

"What!" exclaims Daphne, but her concern for John Bartlesham and the rest of St. Michael's residents is quickly assuaged as she takes the phone and learns that the deaths occurred in Liverpool ten years ago.

"I was just at St. Michael's," explains Isabel, realizing that she is still in the hot seat as Daphne gets details from P.C. Joveneski. "The police wouldn't let me in, so I came here."

"I said that woman was evil," trumpets Daphne, once she has relayed the information that Fitzgerald and her ex-husband not only swindled dozens of seniors in their care but hastened the old-timers into the next world to ensure a speedy collection of the spoils. "They thought she drowned with her husband when their yacht sank," she continues, "until they found her fingerprints on my bedside table."

"So you were right all along," trills Trina jubilantly, and then she uses her hands to write a headline in the sky. "Daphne Lovelace, of Lovelace and Button (International Investigators) Inc., cracks mass murder case."

"Well, the police cracked it really ..." Daphne is trying to say, but Trina won't hear of it.

"Crap!" she snorts. "Most of them couldn't crack an egg."

The news of Fitzgerald's arrest has taken the spotlight off the gatecrasher for a few minutes, but Isabel Semaurino has been winding herself up for this moment for several months, and she finally snaps.

"Could we talk ... inside ... just us?" she asks, taking Daphne firmly by the arm, and the small crowd's exuberance deflates as Daphne walks up the front path of her house like a woman being led to the gallows.

"I don't want to spoil your day," starts Isabel as soon as they are seated in Daphne's parlour. "But when Mum died a few months ago I went through her papers and found this."

The sepia-edged letter, now stained with Isabel's tears, is sixty-nine years old. There is no question of that. The date is clearly written in the top right-hand corner, underneath an address that is immediately recognized by Daphne.

"That's where we used to live," she says, still not comprehending that the letter is signed by her parents, Alfred and Alice.

"It was hidden in a secret drawer inside my mother's wooden writing case," explains Isabel, but Daphne is still in the dark as she begins to read.

"We want to thank you for taking Ophelia's baby …"

Daphne stops and pushes the letter away. "What is this?" she demands. "Some kind of trick. What are you playing at?"

"Ophelia Lovelace. That is you, isn't it?" says Isabel as she reaches out to the woman. "Did you have a baby when you were young?"

Daphne is watchful as she tries to fit the woman into the same mould as Hilda Fitzgerald by skimming through a catalogue of potential scams in her mind. "Who are you?" she wants to know, and Isabel points to the letter and tells her.

"If that was your address, and those were your parents, then I must be your daughter."

But Daphne shoots straight back. "I don't have a daughter. My baby died. It was stillborn. We put it in a box and buried it in the woods." The words come out. The same words she has used over the years to comfort herself whenever called upon to coo over someone else's baby. Yet, deep down, she always knew there was no baby in the box. She heard her baby cry as it was whisked from her bedroom inside a blanket. Subconsciously, she even suspected that the young couple who appeared in her parents' life, and just as quickly disappeared, had arranged some kind of deal. But it was her parents' deal, not hers. She would have kept the baby, had it lived. But it died. Her mother told her so.

"Never mind, Ophelia," Alice Lovelace said as she wept alongside her sixteen-year-old at the graveside of a heavy old firebrick. "It's probably for the best. And you're very young. You'll have plenty of opportunity for more."

The ruse worked. The family closed ranks over Ophelia Lovelace's little indiscretion, and the world kept turning. But there was never another baby. The onset of war intervened in the natural rhythm of her young life, and she quickly sloughed off the childlike naïveté of her Shakespearean namesake to take her middle name, Daphne, and become the heroine that Hamlet's Ophelia never would.

"Your baby didn't die," says Isabel plainly and firmly, as she invites the confused old lady to look into her eyes. "And when I saw you lying in that bed I knew straight away that you were my mother."

"This isn't possible …"

"My parents never told me I was adopted," continues Isabel, sensing that she must keep up the pressure. "They just registered me as their baby. I was a Whittaker before I married Marco and moved to Florence. I never knew — would never have known — if I hadn't found the letter."

Outside in the street the children are partying on, but clouds are building, a storm is brewing and, with the birthday girl absent, the adults are growing anxious.

"Do you think she's all right?" asks Trina, and Mavis is eventually pushed in.

"Did you want some tea?" she questions nervously as she taps lightly and sticks her head around the parlour door.

"I think I need a large brandy," says Daphne, and she hurriedly turns the letter over while she comes to grips with the past and looks for a way into the future.

David Bliss is firmly on another lap of his life's labyrinth as he heads into the future as an author and grandfather, although as he drove from Westchester to Heathrow he couldn't help but take a look over his shoulder at the fiasco of the Queen's visit.

"It's a classic Orwellian plot, Peter," he says excitedly, calling his son-in-law while waiting for his flight to Nice. "Straight out of 1984: Big Brother, mind control, constant East/West wars, everybody lying."

"Why?"

"Power ... money ... greed. Isn't it always the same?"

"But why stop the Queen?"

"Think about it, Peter," says Bliss, having worked out the scenario in his own mind, concluding that religious harmony, however unlikely after more than two thousand years of constant war, could be catastrophic for Western defence industries and oil companies. "If the Queen got them all singing from the same hymn sheet, who would the Americans fight?"

"Do they have to fight?"

"Peter, history — the Nazis did the same. The best way to control the populace, make them obedient to government, and prevent civil uprising is to keep them terrified, keep warning them they are under attack. And if anyone says otherwise or complains about loss of freedom or civil liberties, label them unpatriotic and tell them they're putting their countrymen in danger."

"And you think the American government is doing this?"

"Sure. They've been doing it for the last sixty years or more," says Bliss, starting a long list beginning with the Cold War, Korea, Vietnam, and Cambodia. "And when there was no real enemy, they had drug wars or wars on terrorism, or they attacked their neighbours like Grenada and Panama."

"I don't know …" starts Bryan, unconvinced, then he tries to throw a wrench. "Okay. Let's say I buy that. Why did they drop their objections the second time around?"

"Because," says Bliss. "By that time they'd realized it caused less trouble for everyone if she went than if she didn't."

"Paris on our starboard side," sings out the captain on the P.A. as Bliss heads to Provence with a clear plan in mind. "Daisy," he will say, "as much as I love you, it is time that we both moved on."

The logo for the BBC's six o'clock news appears on Bliss's seat-back screen, and he is fully expecting another round of burning mosques and torched churches when the name *Westchester* takes him by surprise.

"After ten years on the run, Hilda Fitzgerald, wanted for questioning over the deaths of …"

"Well, I'm damned," muses Bliss as he slots the arrested woman into place in his mind.

"It is believed that as many as forty senior citizens may have been murdered by the couple," says the national news reporter as she stands outside Westchester Police Station, before explaining that, while apparently unconnected to the original crimes, Patrick Davenport and Robert Jameson are being interviewed in connection with possession of money from the victims' estates. Then, as the camera zooms in for a close-up, she concludes by saying, "Superintendent Anne McGregor of Westchester Police earlier confirmed that the arrest had come about due to their inquiries into a complaint of abuse at the home."

"Well, well, well," laughs Bliss to himself. "Daphne Lovelace strikes again. Will she ever give up?"

It is roughly two hours since Daphne was felled by her daughter's arrival, and with her mind already overburdened by the traumatic events of the past few weeks, she has been struggling to come to terms with the situation. Perhaps it's a trick, a dream — or even death.

"Two grandchildren?" she questions Isabel for the fifth time.

"Luigi and Maria," says Isabel, nodding. "But they are both grown up and married now, Mother."

Daphne's eyes begin watering again, and Isabel hands her a tissue, saying, "Is it all right if I call you 'Mother'? Only I always called my other mother 'Mum.'"

"Mother?" Daphne muses. Now this must be a dream. But it's a dream come true. How many times in her life has she heard a child call "Mother" and never once reacted. And how many times in her life has she wished that she could. Now she can.

Isabel is still waiting for an answer, but as much as Daphne wants to say, "Yes, please call me Mother," she can't, not yet. Then she has an idea and turns to Isabel.

"Would you mind if we took a walk to the cathedral?"

"Of course — if you want to," says Isabel, although there is a note of reticence in the reply, and Daphne's daughter colours slightly as she adds, "I hope you won't be disappointed in me, but I don't believe in God."

Daphne leans in as if she is concerned that she might be overheard, but she doesn't whisper as she says, "Neither do I. In fact, I never have. I used to look around in church and think I must be the Devil because I couldn't see God like everyone else. I used to squeeze my eyes shut till I saw stars and force my palms together so hard my hands shook, but it didn't make any difference. I couldn't see Him. And I really wanted to, because all my friends kept saying how wonderful he was."

"Oh, Mother," laughs Isabel

Daphne smiles — the first time in two hours — and asks, "Can I touch you? Would you mind?"

Red-eyed Daisy LeBlanc is holding firmly onto the crush barrier in the arrivals hall as Bliss arrives in Nice. He has flowers — a parting gift: thanks for standing by me; thanks for loving me; sorry it had to end.

"Daisy …" he starts, but his heart is beating so hard he hears the blood pumping through his temples and he daren't touch her. They stand in silence, staring longingly at each other for ten seconds that stretch to a week. He knows the rest of the speech — he's been practising it since Paris — but his mouth won't take him in the direction he wants to go.

"We should sit over zhere," says Daisy, pointing to a few empty chairs, when she eventually breaks the silence. "I have somezhing to say to you."

Now Bliss walks to the gallows. He knows what's happening and has been preparing for it ever since Daisy pronounced sentence on their relationship a few weeks ago. But now, facing death, he wants life.

"I can't marry you, Daavid," she says as she hands back the ring. "I am very sorry."

"I know," he replies. "I won't ask his name."

"*Non!*" exclaims Daisy as if she has been stung. "It is not what you are zhinking."

"Zhen what is it?"

"You should not laugh at me, Daavid. Zhis is very difficult for me."

"Well, it's not easy for me either. What the hell is going on?"

"Okay. I will tell. I cannot marry you because my mozher — she is totally crazy."

"So?"

"But, you would not want a wife who has a crazy mozher."

"Is that it?" he questions in disbelief. "Three weeks driving me nuts — thinking there was another man — and all the time it was just your mother?"

"But, I did not know how to tell you. I hide when you came."

"So you don't have a cousin?"

"*Non.*"

"But I knew your mother was nuts the first time I met her."

"And still, you did not care?"

"Daisy — everyone is crazy in some ways. Although sometimes I think that the ones who seem craziest are often the most sensible. Prince Philip wasn't crazy, but he looked it when he stabbed the Queen, and I was sure Daphne was going senile when she said that she was being kept prisoner and they were going to kill her."

Daphne Lovelace would bristle at such a suggestion as she and Isabel begin to walk the cathedral's labyrinth. "They were evil people," she says. "I knew it straight away. Anyone who has to pray for forgiveness twice a day must have an awful lot of sins to repent — deadly sins, as it turned out."

"So you planned the whole thing just to find out what they were up to?" asks Isabel in admiration.

"I didn't plan on getting bashed around."

"Or becoming a great-grandmother."

The concept of matriarchy for someone who, in her own mind, was childless is too much to accept at short notice, but the journey to the centre of a labyrinth is a time for letting go of the past and preparing for the future. So as the two pensioners slowly navigate the winding path, holding hands, they walk through the sixty-nine missing years, swapping tales of family, friends, places, adventures, and experiences.

"It was only when I saw your picture in the paper and read your real name that I knew it was you," explains Isabel as they near the end of the first leg of their walk together.

"I didn't like Ophelia very much," admits Daphne, scrunching up her nose. "She was a very silly girl. She even managed to get pregnant on a church bicycle ride."

"Really?" says Isabel, and Daphne laughs in memory of the summer's day and of the fresh-faced choirboy who wasn't quite as naïve as he pretended to be.

"I got a puncture, and he reckoned he had just the right thing to pump me up."

"Mother!" cries Isabel in mock disbelief, and as they laugh they hug, and as they hug they unite — mother and daughter — and step together into the heart of the labyrinth.

"This is the middle," says Daphne as they stop to admire the intricately patterned floor. "Angel calls it the core. And she says that we should concentrate very hard on what we want before we set off back. Because it's on the way out that we get to choose the way forward into the future."

Isabel wants a mother and says so, but Daphne has a word of caution.

"Angel says that you can't influence other people's actions or beliefs. You can only change the way you see them."

David Bliss is singing a similar song as he assures Daisy that her mother's mental infirmity is of no consequence.

"But I cannot live in England," insists Daisy. "I must stay here and take care for her."

"Of course you must."

"But for us zhat is not good."

"Then I must move here."

"But your job. It is *impossible, n'est-ce pas?*"

"*Non. C'est possible*," he explains with a broad grin. "Because I am no longer a policeman. I am now the author of a soon-to-be bestselling historical novel."

In Westchester, the heat wave has finally broken, the drought is over, and a sharp cloudburst sends mother and daughter scurrying into the cathedral's doorway.

"What on earth will your friend Mavis think when you tell her?" asks Isabel as they hold each other tightly.

"She can think what she bloomin' well wants," says Daphne defiantly. "I shall tell her straight, 'This is my daughter, Isabel, and I've two grandchildren and a great-granddaughter.'"

"And you're going to Florence to visit them next week."

Daphne stops dead as reality finally catches up to her. "Oh my God," she cries. "I have a whole family of Italians waiting to meet me and the only Italian I can remember is *arrivederci*."

The previous installment of the popular Inspector Bliss series:

The seventh David Bliss novel is another action-packed mystery filled with nail-biting adventures. When an RCMP officer is murdered in Vancouver, suspicion falls upon Janet Thurgood, a woman in her sixties who appears to everyone, apart from Trina Button, to be completely mad. Trina is quick to embroil Daphne Lovelace in her efforts to discover the truth about Janet. Dave Bliss, meanwhile, tries to stay out of the way in the south of France, where he encounters problems of his own when, to his utter amazement, he rediscovers his one true love. Can he finally pull the trigger and make a commitment?

Praise for *Crazy Lady*:

"This is the seventh in the excellent series featuring Chief Inspector David Bliss and it's one of the best of the bunch. Hawkins is a deft writer and, as a former police commander in the U.K. and a private investigator, he's good at the details of police work. He also has a penchant for thinking globally, so we have a plot that ranges from a murdered policeman in Vancouver to the international trade in cocoa. … This novel is great fun, in addition to being a solidly plotted mystery. Hawkins is definitely on the right track here."
– Margaret Cannon, *Globe and Mail*

"Written to hold your interest, this multi-mystery will keep you reading. Recommended as a well told tale you will enjoy. I did."
– Anne K. Edwards, *New Mystery Reader*

Missing: Presumed Dead
Detective Inspector David Bliss has been transferred from London, England, to Hampshire in what appears a move down the career ladder. His first day on the job begins with a murder: Jonathan Dauntsey willingly confesses to murdering his father. It's an open-and-shut case, until the police can't find the body. Bliss follows a trail of clues that lead him back to the question: who did Jonathan Dauntsey murder, if anyone at all? As the mystery of the murder begins to resolve itself, so does the mystery of Bliss's transfer from the big city to a small town.

The Fish Kisser
When a megalomaniac becomes determined to exact revenge on the Western world through a devious plot of global cyber-warfare, he tracks down and kidnaps the experts that can help him accomplish the unthinkable. When his hired henchmen target Roger LeClarc, an English computer expert with a dark secret of his own, the hunters become the hunted. English detective David Bliss teams up with Dutch detective Yolanda Pieters to solve this improbable affair. Together they chase a trail of blood, intrigue, and romance across Europe to Iraq in a desperate search for the kidnapped specialists.

No Cherubs for Melanie
Melanie Gordonstone, a cherubic six-year-old, was Daddy's favourite in every way. So Margaret, her jealous twelve-year-old sister, drowned her. Inexperience led young Detective Bliss to attribute the girl's death to accident, but Melanie's mother drives herself mad believing her husband to be the killer. Margaret taunts her deranged mother for ten years before putting her out of her misery, hanging her from a chandelier in a faked suicide. Now, frightened for his safety, Margaret's father sends her to live in a remote

Canadian community where he believes she can do no further damage — big mistake!

A Year Less a Day
David Bliss teams up with Daphne Lovelace to trace the father of a Canadian woman whose husband is dying of cancer. While Ruth Jackson believes that she was sired by a Beatle, Bliss and Daphne have other ideas. In Vancouver, Ruth's world falls apart when her dying husband suddenly disappears and she is arrested on suspicion of murder. His substantial life insurance policy and the blood-stained knife in her kitchen don't help her case. Detective Sergeant Phillips of the Mounties takes up the case, and Trina Button, a zany homecare nurse, stirs up trouble for everyone in this intriguing international story.

The Dave Bliss Quintet
Inspector David Bliss goes undercover once again, and heads to St-Juan-sur-Mer on the Côte d'Azur. His mission is so secret that even Bliss doesn't know why he is there: he only knows that he is tracking down a man the force wants in custody for an unstated reason. But the winds of the Mediterranean provide clues that take Bliss off course and lead him to unravel two of the world's best known unsolved mysteries: the identity of the Man in the Iron Mask and the location of the stolen Nazi gold.

Lovelace and Button (International Investigators) Inc.
A bizarre series of suicides by elderly women in England raises the eyebrow of newly promoted Chief Inspector David Bliss, who discovers that all the women had recently sent large sums of money to a Western Union account in Vancouver. As Bliss uncovers the truth behind the deaths, old friends Daphne Lovelace and Trina Button are on a road trip through North America, raising funds to help

those in need of kidney transplants. But when their fabulous Kidneymobile is found unoccupied, a perplexed Bliss searches frantically for his friends — and the astonishing secret that links their disappearance with the suicides.